NOCTURNE
DARK AWAKENINGS

Welcome to the dark, seductive world of Nocturne.

Let *New York Times* bestselling author Sharon Sala and fan-favourites Janis Reams Hudson, Debra Cowan, Michele Hauf and Vivi Anna take you on five spine-tingling, heart-stopping romantic journeys.

Can't get enough dark desires and supernatural seductions?

NOCTURNE MIDNIGHT CRAVINGS, another fresh collection of six powerful paranormal short stories, is out now.

For more information on the new paranormal romances available from Mills & Boon visit www.millsandboon.co.uk

NOCTURNE
DARK AWAKENINGS

SHARON SALA
JANIS REAMS HUDSON
DEBRA COWAN
MICHELE HAUF
VIVI ANNA

All the characters in this book have no existence outside the imagination of
the author, and have no relation whatsoever to anyone bearing the same name
or names. They are not even distantly inspired by any individual known or
unknown to the author, and all the incidents are pure invention.

M&B™ and M&B™ with the Rose Device
are trademarks of the publisher.
Harlequin Mills & Boon Limited, Eton House,
18-24 Paradise Road, Richmond, Surrey TW9 1SR

First published in Great Britain 2010
Harlequin Mills & Boon Limited,
Eton House, 18-24 Paradise Road, Richmond, Surrey TW9 1SR

NOCTURNE DARK AWAKENINGS © Harlequin Books S.A. 2010

The publisher acknowledges the copyright holders of the
individual works as follows:

Penance © Sharon Sala 2008
After the Lightning © Janis Reams Hudson 2008
Seeing Red © Debra Cowan 2008
A Kiss of Frost © Michele Hauf 2008
Ice Bound © Tawny Stokes 2008

ISBN: 978 0 263 87056 5

009-0210

Printed and bound in Spain
by Litografia Rosés S.A., Barcelona

CONTENTS

PENANCE

SHARON SALA

Dear Reader,

Even at the worst of times there is a positive to be found. We just have to look for it. When we've lost loved ones we can't bear to live without, there will be a friend who will come shining through. During the most frightening of storms, we are given a rainbow. Through any kind of tragedy or loss, there will be one positive thing, even if it is just, "I have survived."

Such was the case for the heroine in my story, "Penance". Shot and left to die, she survived. Embarrassed by her surgery scars and her troubles with memory and mobility, she can't seem to see the positive in being alive, and focuses on what she's lost.

But then something begins to happen that she doesn't understand. What she first views as her penance for surviving becomes the most powerful gift she could be given.

I hope when you read my story you take a moment to look into your own life and look past what you've lost to see what you've gained. Be thankful for all that you have and remember – there are people all over the world who would trade places with you in a heartbeat.

So, as I give you my story to read, I hope you enjoy the journey.

Sharon Sala

Sharon Sala is a child of the country. As a farmer's daughter she found her vivid imagination made her solitude a thing to cherish. During her adult life, she learned to survive by taking things one day at a time. An inveterate dreamer, she yearned to share stories her imagination created. Sharon's dreams have come true, and she claims one of her greatest joys is when her stories become tools of healing.

Life isn't fair. It's one of first lessons we learn. But life is precious, regardless of what we endure to live it.

I believe that the people who come and go throughout our lifetime are meant to do so for a purpose.

Some teach us a lesson.

Some give us joy.

And some appear for the sole reason of showing us the way life should be lived.

I call those people our angels.

I have had many angels in my life, and each and every one has been an influence as to the woman I've become.

I want to dedicate this book to my newest angel.

To Erin McClune.

Live every day with joy.

Chapter 1

Nicole Masters was sitting cross-legged on her sofa while a cold, autumn rain peppered against the windows of her fourth-floor apartment. She was poking at the ice cream in her bowl and trying not to be in a mood. The past few weeks had been life-changing in a very negative way, which was making it difficult for her to stay upbeat.

Six weeks ago, a simple trip to her neighborhood pharmacy had turned into a nightmare. She'd walked into the middle of a robbery. She never even saw the man who shot her in the head and left her for dead. She'd survived, but some of her senses had not. She was dealing with short-term memory loss and a tendency to stagger. Even though she'd been told the problems were most likely temporary, she waged a daily battle with depression.

Her parents had been killed in a car wreck when she was twenty-one. They'd owned the apartment building in which she had grown up, so finances were never going to be a problem. But she was alone. There were no aunts. No cousins. No grandparents. Except for a few friends—and most recently her boyfriend, Dominic Tucci, who lived in the apartment right above hers—she was alone. Her doctor kept reminding her that she should be grateful to be alive, and on one level, she knew he was right. But he wasn't living in her shoes.

If she'd been anywhere else but at that pharmacy when the robbery happened, then she wouldn't have died twice on the way to the hospital. She wouldn't be mistaking salt for sugar. She wouldn't be missing a head of hair and staggering like a drunk when she stood up. Instead of being grateful that she'd survived, she couldn't quit thinking of what she'd lost.

But that wasn't the end of her troubles. On top of everything else, something strange was happening inside her head. She'd begun to hear odd things. Sounds, not voices—at least, she didn't think it was voices. It sounded more like the distant sound of rapids—a rush of wind and water inside her head that, when it came, blocked out everything around her. It didn't happen often, but when it did, it was frightening, and it was driving her crazy.

The blank moments, as she called them, even had a rhythm. First came that sound, then a cold sweat, then panic with no reason. Part of her feared it was the beginning of an emotional breakdown. And part of her feared it wasn't—that it was going to turn out to be a permanent souvenir of her resurrection.

She was twenty-six years old and living the life of a senior citizen with dementia, and tonight was living proof. Here she was, alone in her apartment on a Saturday night, eating ice cream and watching the news like some old maid. All she needed was a cat.

Frustrated with herself and the situation as it stood, she stabbed her spoon into the mound of mocha fudge and then scooped up another bite, letting it melt on her tongue while she upped the sound on the TV and watched Pat Sajak bantering with Vanna White. A few moments later, an announcer broke into "Wheel of Fortune" with a special bulletin.

"This just in. Police are on the scene of a kidnapping that occurred only hours ago at The Dakota. Molly Dane, the five-year-old daughter of one of Hollywood's blockbuster stars, Lyla Dane, was taken by force from the family apartment. At this time, they have yet to receive a ransom demand. The housekeeper was seriously injured during the abduction and is, at the present time, in surgery. Police are hoping to be able to talk to her once she regains consciousness. In the meantime, we are going now to a press conference with Lyla Dane."

Horrified, Nicole stilled as the cameras went live to where the actress was speaking before a bank of microphones.

"I thought I had problems," she muttered, instantly ashamed of herself and her attitude.

When the woman began to speak, Nicole leaned forward, absently resting the bowl of ice cream in her lap. The shock and terror in Lyla Dane's voice were physically painful to watch, but even though Nicole kept upping the volume, the sound continued to fade.

Just when she was beginning to think something was wrong with her set, the broadcast suddenly switched from the Dane press conference to what appeared to be footage of the kidnapping.

The clip began inside the apartment. When the front door suddenly flew back against the wall and four men rushed in, Nicole gasped. Horrified, she quickly realized that this must have been caught on the Danes' security camera inside.

As Nicole continued to watch, a small Asian woman, who she guessed was the housekeeper, rushed forward in an effort to keep them out. When one of the men hit her in the face with his gun, Nicole moaned. The violence was too reminiscent of what she'd lived through to ignore. Sick to her stomach, she fisted her hands against her belly, wishing it was over, but unable to tear her gaze away.

When the maid dropped to the carpet, the same man followed with a vicious kick to her midsection that lifted her off the floor.

"Oh, my God," Nicole said. When blood began to pool beneath the maid's head, she started to cry.

As the clip played on, the four men split up in different directions. The camera caught one running down a long marble hallway, then disappearing into a room. Moments later, he reappeared, carrying a little girl, who Nicole assumed was Molly Dane. The child was wearing a pair of red pants and a white turtleneck sweater, and her hair was partially blocking her abductor's face as he carried her down the hall. She was kicking and screaming in his arms, and when he slapped her, it elicited an agonized screech that brought the other three running. Nicole watched in horror as one of them ran up and put his hand over Molly's face. Seconds later, she went limp.

One moment they were in the foyer, then they were gone.

Nicole jumped to her feet, then staggered drunkenly. The bowl of ice cream that had been in her lap fell at her feet, splattering glass and melting ice cream everywhere.

The picture on the screen abruptly switched from the kidnapping to what Nicole assumed was a rerun of Lyla Dane's plea for her daughter's safe return, but she was too numb to really pay attention.

Before she could think what to do next, the doorbell rang. Startled by the unexpected sound, she shakily swiped at her tears and took a step forward. She didn't feel the glass shards piercing her feet until she took the second step. At that point, sharp pains shot through her foot. She gasped, then looked down in confusion. Her ice-cream-spattered legs looked as if she'd been running through mud, and she was standing in broken glass and melting mocha fudge, while a thin ribbon of blood seeped out from beneath her toes.

"Oh, no," she mumbled, then stifled a second moan of pain.

The doorbell rang again. She shivered, then clutched her head in confusion.

"Just a minute!" she yelled, trying to sidestep the rest of the debris as she limped to the door.

When she looked through the peephole, she didn't know whether to be relieved or regretful.

It was Dominic, and, as usual, she was a mess.

Dominic Tucci was a six-foot-three-inch, third-generation Italian American, and the first member of his family to have a job outside the food industry. He'd been a member of the NYPD for ten years, and a homicide detective for the last three. He loved his job—and his downstairs neighbor.

He'd been on the scene only minutes after she'd arrived in the E.R., and had prayed like he'd never prayed before for her to survive. She had, and with what he was determined to view as only temporary complications.

He knew she was struggling with depression, but he also knew that nothing was going to change his love for her. He would take her any way he could get her—warts and all.

And loving her was only one of the reasons why he was at her door tonight. The other was the large, thick-crust pizza he was carrying—one half pepperoni, the other half cheese. Just the way they liked it.

He shifted the pizza box to his other hand and rang the doorbell. Moments later, he heard what sounded like breaking glass. Well aware of her tendency to stagger upon standing, he quickly rang the doorbell again. Just as he was on the verge of ringing a third time, the door opened.

"Hey, Nikki, I thought—"

His gaze went from the strained expression on her face to something brown running down her legs and the blood beneath her feet.

"Oh, honey…what have you done?"

"It fell," she said.

She hadn't mentioned what had fallen, but he knew this wasn't the time to press for details. As the door slammed shut behind him, he set the pizza box on the hall table and scooped her up in his arms. He carried her into the kitchen, leaving droplets of blood behind them as they went. When he set her on the island in the middle of the room, then squatted down to look at the bottom of her foot, he cursed beneath his breath. She'd really done it this time.

"Oh, baby…there's glass in your foot. Do you have some tweezers?"

"Top drawer on the night… I mean top drawer on the right…in the bathroom," Nicole said. "Alcohol and those…uh…those sticky strips…are in the cabinet on the middle shelf."

Dominic ignored her momentary word confusion to steal a kiss.

"I'm so sorry you're hurt. Hang on a sec. I'll be right back," he said, and hurried from the room.

Nicole sighed. Either the man was a saint or a sucker for trouble, because that was all she seemed able to produce.

He came back with his hands full of first-aid supplies and a look of concern on his face.

"Are you in much pain?"

"Some. It actually burns more than it hurts."

Dominic dumped the stuff he'd been carrying onto the counter beside her, then reached for the tweezers.

"Now then, let's see about getting you all fixed up."

Nicole sniffled. She hated herself for being such a loser, and hated herself even more for whining. But she had to admit she was glad he'd shown up.

"How did it happen, honey? Did you get dizzy again?"

Nicole frowned. "I guess…but mostly it was because I wasn't paying attention. I'd been watching the news when they broke in with a bulletin about a kidnapping. Lyla Dane's little girl." She winced as Dominic pulled a sliver of glass from between her toes. "Ouch," she muttered, then sighed. "I should be ashamed. Compared to Lyla Dane, I have nothing to complain about."

Dominic paused, then glanced up. "Look at me!"

When she did, he continued. "I don't want to hear anything negative come out of your mouth again."

Nicole shifted her gaze, silently admiring the perfect arch of Dominic's brows, as well as the warm, caramel color of his eyes.

"Nikki…"

"What? What? I'm looking, I'm looking."

He grinned. "But you're not listening."

"It's all your fault," she said.

His grin slipped sideways. "Why is that?"

"If you weren't so pretty, I wouldn't be distracted."

He laughed out loud. "Talk like that is liable to get you laid."

"Promises, promises," she said, and then bit her bottom lip as he removed two more pieces of glass. A few minutes passed before he had removed all the slivers. After that, he grabbed a handful of wet paper towels and cleaned the ice cream from her feet and legs before swabbing the cuts with antiseptic.

"What do you think?" she asked.

"About your foot? I think you could use some stitches in a couple of places."

"No, not my foot," Nicole said. "About the kidnapping."

"Oh. Nasty business. Sometimes being famous isn't all it's cracked up to be."

"I guess," she said. "And you can forget the stitches. I've been to the doctor too many times as it is."

"You're the boss," he said, and began opening some gauze pads to bandage up her foot.

His tenderness didn't go unnoticed. As he bent to the task, Nicole reached out and combed her fingers through his hair. It was black and thick, and straight as string. She loved the feel of it against her palm.

"You're a good man," she said softly.

Dominic paused, then looked up. The new growth of baby fuzz on her head gave her an innocent, child-like look, but he knew there wasn't anything childish about her. Before the shooting, she had been a vibrant, sexy woman. That woman was still in there, healing along with the rest of her.

"Thank you, baby," he said softly.

Nicole smiled a little self-consciously.

Dominic started to say something else, then hesitated. Now was not the time to broach the subject of their relationship. It was all she could do to get through a day. She didn't have the mental fortitude to deal with anything else. Instead of talking about their future, he returned to tending to her foot.

Nicole watched silently as he finished the bandages. Once he was done, she started to get down, but he stopped her with a look.

"Stay there until I get the rest of the broken glass cleaned up," he said.

Nicole's shoulders slumped. "Oh…yes, I forgot. I'm sorry to be such a bother."

He frowned. "Hey, don't talk about my woman like that."

She rode the surge of delight his words brought.

"So, I'm still your woman?"

"You better believe it," Dominic said. "Now, don't move. I'm still on the job."

Nicole laughed as he headed into the living room with a broom, a wastebasket and a pan of warm water. From where she was sitting, she could still see the television. They were playing clips marking Lyla Dane's rise to fame.

She frowned. Poor woman. Poor little girl.

"Hey, Dominic."

"Yeah?"

"Have they identified any of the four men, yet?"

He dropped the last of the debris into the wastebasket, wiped up the sticky spots and started back into the kitchen.

"What four men, honey?"

She pointed toward the television. "You know… the ones who were on the security tape."

Dominic frowned. "There wasn't any security tape."

Nicole rubbed the fuzz on her head in frustration.

"I know I'm not the sharpest tack in the wall these days, but there's nothing wrong with my eyes. There was footage. They were showing it right before you arrived."

Dominic frowned. He was Homicide, not Crimes, but he was pretty sure about his facts.

"Honey, I'm almost positive there was no security footage."

Nicole pointed.

"Damn it, Dominic. I sat right there on the sofa and watched four men kick in the floor…. I mean…door to the apartment. A small Asian woman, who must have been the maid, ran toward them. I guess she was trying to close the door. One of the men hit her in the face with a handgun, and when she fell, he kicked her so hard in the stomach that it lifted her off the floor. Then the four men cut up…no. Crap." She hit the side of her leg with her fist in frustration. "Not cut. Not cut. They split up."

Dominic laid a hand on her knee. "Slow down, honey. You're going too fast."

She took a deep breath, then sighed. "Anyway…it showed one of them running down a hallway and into another room. He came out carrying the little girl. She was wearing red pants and a white turtleneck sweater. She was kicking and screaming, and then he hit her. At that point, the other three came back. One of them put his hand over her face and she went lump…. No, damn it…that's not the word." Nicole took another slow breath, then started again. "She went…uh, limp…then they ran out of the apartment. After that, they switched back to a rerun of Lyla Dane's press conference."

Dominic was staring at Nicole as if he'd never seen her before. The detail in what she was saying was oddly specific, but he couldn't believe that the cops had all that info and he didn't know about it.

"Hang on a minute, honey. I'm going to make a couple of calls."

"Um…Dom?"

"What, honey?"

"Is that pizza I smell?"

He grinned. "You know it is."

Nicole arched an eyebrow. "So…why don't you bring it in here before you make your calls?"

"You got it, baby," he said, then retrieved the pizza, which she dug in to with relish, before pulling his cell phone out of his pocket.

"Don't bother waiting on me," he said, as she started demolishing her first slice.

Nicole looked up. There was a tiny smear of tomato sauce at the corner of her mouth.

"Okay," she said, and took another bite.

Dominic grinned as he wiped away the pizza sauce with the tip of his finger, then stuck it in his mouth.

"Um, tasty."

She smiled.

It took him a minute to remember what he'd been going to do.

"Right. Phone calls," he said.

"So go make them. Thanks to you, I'm fine."

Dominic was too distracted by the shape of her lower lip to do more than nod. He was already dialing the precinct as she downed her last bite and reached for another slice.

* * *

Detective Andy Sanders had spent the last four hours
at the Dane apartment and was just getting back to the
station. With four kids of his own, he was sick at heart
over what had happened to the little girl, but he couldn't
let his emotions get in the way of doing his job.

They'd set up a phone line at the apartment for the
expected ransom call, and several officers were waiting
on site with Lyla Dane and her family.

His partner, Tomas Garcia, was at the hospital with
the maid's family, waiting to see if she survived the
surgery. If so, they would be requesting permission to
question her. So far, she was their only witness to what
had happened.

With all that whirling in his head, when his cell
phone rang, he was expecting it to be Garcia. When
he saw Dominic Tucci's name instead, he frowned as
he answered.

"Hey, Tucci, what's up?"

Dominic heard the frustration in his friend's voice and
could only imagine how busy they were, but he needed
to make sure of his facts before he spoke to Nikki again.

"I'm just checking on a couple of things regarding
the Dane kidnapping," he said.

Sanders frowned. "Since when does Homicide
have anything to do with kidnapping? Oh. Shit. Did
the maid die?"

"No, no, nothing like that. At least, I haven't heard
anything about her."

"Then what's up?"

Dominic took a deep breath. There was no easy way to ask this and not appear to be interfering.

"I heard a rumor that you guys have a security tape showing four men and the kidnapping going down. Any truth to that?"

Sanders cursed softly. "Hell no. We couldn't be that lucky," he said, then picked up a pen and began doodling on a piece of paper. "So who's spreading that crap? Hollywood?"

"No, not Hollywood."

Sanders frowned. "Then who told you that?"

"The maid…is she Asian?" Dominic asked.

"Yeah," Sanders said. "So what?"

"Did she suffer a blow to the head and then a kick in the belly?"

Sanders dropped the pen and sat up. "Damn it, Tucci, what gives?"

Dominic persisted, even though he was unsure of what this meant to Nicole's state of mind.

"Was the little girl wearing red pants and a white turtleneck sweater?"

Sanders's voice turned into a low, husky growl. "No one fucking knows this except the family. I want to know where you came by this information and who you're getting it from, and I want to know now."

Dominic glanced over his shoulder, making sure that Nicole couldn't overhear him before he answered.

"I came by to check on my girlfriend…. She got

shot in the head during a drugstore robbery and nearly died, remember?"

"Yeah, I remember you telling me about that. So...she's doing okay, right?"

"I'm not so sure," Dominic said.

"Come on, Tucci. You know I'm swamped. I'm sorry as hell about your girlfriend, but enough about her. Who told you that stuff about the kidnapping?"

"She did."

Sanders froze. "She who? Your girl?"

"Yeah."

"When did she tell you this?" Sanders asked.

"About fifteen minutes ago."

"Where is she now?"

"In her apartment."

"Are you with her?"

"Yeah, but—"

"Stay right there," Sanders said. "Garcia and I will be over within the hour."

"She doesn't have anything to do with the kidnapping," Dominic said. "She's still suffering from the gunshot wound to her head. Hell, half the time she can't tell the difference between her right foot and her left."

"I don't care if she can't spell her name anymore," Sanders snapped. "She knows about stuff we haven't released to the press, and I want to know how."

"Just don't come over here and scare her," Dominic warned. "She's been through too damned much as it is."

The line went dead in his ear.

"Great," Dominic muttered.

"Who's going to scare me?"

Dominic frowned. He hadn't known she was there, but apparently she had heard every bit of his last sentence.

"A couple of detectives working the Dane kidnapping are coming to talk to you."

Nicole frowned. "Me? Whatever for?"

"They want to hear about that security tape you said you saw."

Nicole's frown deepened. "What do you mean? I did see it…. On TV, just like everyone else."

Dominic reached for her, but she pulled back.

"Don't touch me. I need truth, not coddling."

"There was no security tape."

Nicole's heart started pounding. The rush of sound was back, pushing inside her head so fast that she could barely hear Dominic's voice.

"But I saw it—all of it—right there on the TV."

"I'm not saying you didn't see something. What I'm saying is, you didn't see it on TV."

The sound was so loud now that it was like a roar inside her brain.

"Stop it…stop it now," she mumbled, and put her hands over her ears.

"Stop what, baby?" Dominic asked.

"The noise…in my head. Make it stop," Nicole muttered, and then her eyes rolled back in her head.

Dominic caught her before she fell. He was shaking so hard all the way to her bedroom that he was afraid he would drop her. He laid her down on her bed, then ran to the bathroom to get a wet cloth.

He was wiping it across her forehead when she came to.

"Dominic?"

"I'm here, baby," he said softly.

"I fainted."

"Yeah, I know, but you're okay. You just got a little bit upset."

"I always get upset when someone thinks I'm lying."

Dominic frowned. "I never said you lied."

"Oh, yes… I remember. It was more along the lines of 'I think you're, uh…lazy.' No. Shit. *Crazy*, that's the word. You think I'm crazy, or at least you should. I certainly sound like a nut job. I can't even form a proper sentence."

Dominic's frown deepened. "Damn it, Nicole. I never said anything like *that*, either. I'm going to get you something cold to drink. The detectives will be here soon, and the last thing you want to be is hysterical."

"Why?" she muttered. "Don't you know that crazy women can be hysterical all they want?"

"I'm not listening to this," he said, then shoved the wet washcloth into her hands and walked out of her bedroom.

Nicole got up from the bed, put the washcloth back

in the bathroom and then changed into a clean shirt. If she was going to have company, it might be best if she wasn't wearing the ice cream she'd been eating earlier.

By the time she got changed into a pair of sweat pants and a T-shirt, and headed for the living room sofa, Dominic met her with a bottle of wine and two wine-glasses.

"You're not still taking pain meds, are you?"

"No," she said, and eased herself down on the cushions.

He sat down beside her. "Good. You might not need this, but I do," he said, and poured the wine into the glasses, then handed her one, while he took the other. "To us," he said.

Nicole hesitated. "Why do you do this?"

He frowned. "Do what?"

"Still put up with me."

Dominic sighed, then leaned forward, cupped the back of her neck and pulled her close enough to kiss. Her lips were soft and warm, and she smelled faintly of mocha chocolate ice cream. He groaned beneath his breath as he finally pulled away.

"Because I'll never get enough of that," he whispered.

Nicole's vision blurred as she clutched the stem of her wineglass.

"To us," she echoed.

The perfect clink of crystal marked the toast. Within the space of two sips, the doorbell rang.

Nicole jumped, sending the wine dangerously close to sloshing over the edge of the glass.

"Easy, they're just cops like me," Dominic said, as he steadied her glass, then went to the door.

Detectives Sanders and Garcia nodded when they saw him, but they weren't smiling. His stomach knotted.

"Detectives," he said, as they entered. He gestured toward Nicole, who was still seated on the sofa. "This is my girlfriend, Nicole Masters. Nikki, Detective Sanders and Detective Garcia."

Both men were slightly taken aback by the dark circles under her eyes, as well as the lack of hair highlighting a fierce scar on her scalp. Then there was the matter of the fresh bandage on her foot. She looked like anything but an accomplice to a kidnapping.

"Detectives, excuse my lack of manners in not standing, but as you can see, I'm still an accident in progress. Please have a seat."

They sat; then Sanders spoke first.

"I'll get right to the point. We've been told you have some information regarding the kidnapping of Molly Dane."

"I was watching the broadcast of the kidnapping, and then I saw…" She paused, looked at Dominic, then started again. "I saw what appeared to be a tape of the kidnapping from inside the Dane apartment. I'm told I was mistaken."

Sanders nodded as Garcia took out a notebook.

"So, Miss Masters…"

"Please, call me Nicole."

"Nicole it is," Sanders said. "We'd like to ask you some questions about this…uh…what you saw. I understand you said you saw four men."

"Yes. They kicked in the floor…." Her cheeks reddened. "Crap. I think I mean door…. They kicked in the door to the apartment…. At least I think they kicked it. It flew back so suddenly. Then I saw the maid running toward them. One of the men hit her in the face with a handgun, then, after she fell, he kicked her in the stomach. She was bleeding badly when they all broke…no, uh…you know, they…" She looked to Dominic for help.

"Do you mean they split up, honey?"

She sighed, then nodded. "Yes, they split up. One of the men came out with the little girl. She was fighting him, so he hit her. Then the other men came back, and one of them put a hand over her face, and after that she didn't fight anymore. Then they left. End of story."

Garcia was silent as he wrote quickly, intent on getting down everything she said.

Sanders was frowning. They had one witness who could corroborate the four men theory, but it hadn't been released to the press. The maid was Asian, and had injuries to her head and her midsection, the details of which also had not been released.

"You say you saw what the little girl was wearing?"

"Um…yes, she had on red pants and a white turtle-neck sweater."

"Mother of God," Garcia muttered, and made the sign of the cross.

Nicole stared at him for a few moments, and suddenly the room faded away and instead she saw an older woman standing in a hallway, crying. Then everything shifted again, and she was once more inside her apartment. Without understanding why, she pointed to his phone.

"Your mother has been trying to get in touch with you all day. You need to call her."

Dominic was too startled to hide his shock. Before he could speak, Sanders attacked.

"What's that supposed to be? A…demonstration of your psychic abilities?"

Nicole was near tears again, but she was determined that these men not see her cry. She fisted her hands in her lap and stared the detective down. Her voice was shaking, but her gaze was firm.

"I don't have…abilities. Most of what I once knew is lost somewhere inside my head. I can't explain what I saw. I'm sorry I saw it. It wasn't pleasant to watch. I just want my life back the way it used to be…before someone put a bullet in my head. I just want to be normal again."

Sanders frowned. Part of him felt sorry for her, but he was certain she was either part of the kidnapping or trying to run some kind of scam.

"Lady, just for the record, there was no security tape, and you should not know the things you've just told me…unless you had something to do with the crime."

Dominic stood up. "Listen, both of you! Nicole is not a criminal. She's a victim. I don't know how she knows what she just told you, but I can guarantee she's telling the truth. If she says she saw this, then she saw it…somehow."

"So you *are* claiming that you've become psychic?" Sanders asked.

Nicole wanted to scream. Instead, she took a deep breath and made herself stay calm. "I'm not claiming anything. I just know what I saw, not how I saw it."

"Have you ever 'seen' anything like this before?" Sanders asked.

"No," she said.

Sanders chose to ignore Dominic and rubbed his bald head in frustration.

"So. In this so-called tape you claim to have seen, by any chance did you get a good look at the men's faces?"

"Only two of them," Nicole said.

Sanders perked up. "Do you think you could identify them if you saw them again?"

"Yes, especially the one who had the girl."

"Would you come down to the precinct and work with a sketch artist?"

Nicole's hands instantly went to her head. The lack of hair was still embarrassing to her, and going out in public looking this way seemed daunting.

"I, uh…I don't have any hair."

The tremble in her voice finally got to Sanders. He

wasn't a woman, but he could imagine how devastating something like this could be to one.

"I don't either, ma'am, but it hasn't stopped me yet."

Nicole almost smiled. "Yes, well, I haven't been out since I came home from the hospital," she added.

"I'll get her there," Dominic said.

"But, Dom, my hair…" she said, and self-consciously rubbed her hand across the top of her head.

Sanders had the grace to look away.

"You're beautiful any way you look," Dominic said, then added, "I'll stay with you, honey. It will be okay."

She nodded. It seemed stupid to worry about going out in public with no hair when a child's life was in danger.

"Okay, I'll do it—if you'll do me a favor first."

Dominic touched the side of her face. "Anything."

"I need a hat…or a scarf…. Something I can wear over my head."

"Done," Dominic said.

Nicole nodded, then glanced up. As she did, she began to lose focus on Detective Garcia's face, then on her surroundings.

"No, no, not again," she mumbled, and put her head between her knees to keep from passing out.

Dominic reached for her as the other two men stood abruptly. She was moaning beneath her breath when Dominic put his hand on the middle of her back.

The moment he touched her, she sat up. Her eyes were wide open, but without focus, and she seemed to be staring at a spot above Garcia's head.

"There aren't any windows and she's afraid of the dark. She's been crying for so long that her eyes are almost swollen shut. There's a bruise on her cheek. A door is opening. Someone's coming. She's afraid—so afraid. She crawls up onto the bed to get away from the man who's coming in. She can see his silhouette and the red shirt he's wearing. It's got words on it. Minsky's Gym. It says Minsky's Gym."

Nicole shuddered, then blinked.

Sanders didn't know whether to believe her or not, but it was definitely weird. He looked at his partner.

"Did you get all that?"

Garcia was still writing when his cell phone rang. He glanced at Caller ID.

"Excuse me," he said, and walked into the kitchen. A few moments later he came back, pale and shaken. He stared at Nicole, and then turned to his partner. "That was my wife. She said my mother has been trying to reach me all day, but she got the numbers mixed up. She said my father has been in an accident and they need me to come to Boston."

Sanders wouldn't look at Dominic and couldn't bring himself to look at Nicole.

"Get going, then," he said to his partner, then looked at Dominic at last. "We're done here for now, anyway," he said.

"I'll bring her by in the morning," Dominic promised, as he walked the two detectives to the door.

Sanders made himself turn and look at Nicole

Masters. She was sitting quietly, watching their every move. He glanced once at the baby fuzz just coming through her scalp and wondered what she'd been like before she'd been shot, then shook off the thought.

"Thank you for your time," he said. "We'll be in touch."

As soon as they were gone, Nicole began to breathe easier. "I think that went well, don't you?"

Her sarcasm was obvious. Dominic shrugged.

"They've got a lot on their plates, and it's hard for them to understand what's happening to you."

"I don't understand what's happening to me, either. I think I'm losing my mind."

He walked back to the sofa, pulled her to her feet, then lowered his head.

Their lips met.

The kiss proceeded.

Slowly.

Thoroughly.

"I think you're beautiful and you're exhausted, and that you need to rest, that's what I think," he said, and then picked her up and carried her to her bed. He stepped back after he tucked her in. "I'll check on you later, honey. For now, just sleep."

As the sound of Dominic's footsteps receded, Nicole closed her eyes. She heard the front door open, then close, and shut her eyes.

Chapter 2

After everything that had happened, sleeping was impossible.

Nicole spent most of the night on the sofa, staring at the ceiling. Every time she closed her eyes, she saw one disjointed image after another—of faces she'd never seen before and people she didn't know. It was as if seeing what had happened to Molly Dane had opened a floodgate. She still didn't know what to call what was happening to her, but she was firmly convinced that it had to do with her head injury.

Either she was going crazy, or she had been given some kind of "sight" into people's lives. In which case, even if she wasn't crazy yet, this could send her over the edge.

As time moved toward daybreak, she knew when Dominic got up to go to work, because she could hear him walking around on the floor above. Just thinking about him made her weak with longing. They'd just been getting serious when she'd been shot. After that, he'd been the perfect boyfriend. Solicitous, sympathetic—always ready to help with whatever she needed. But there was a part of her that feared he'd stayed around only because it was the proper thing to do. She couldn't imagine a single, good-looking man willing to wait it out to see if she quit dribbling her food and falling over.

When she heard him getting out of the shower, she gave him a call. If she was going to have to go down to the precinct today, she needed to know details.

The phone rang twice before he picked up, and when he did, she could hear him chewing.

"What's for breakfast?" she asked.

"If I was down there instead of up here, it would be you."

She smiled. Their sex life had pretty much come to a halt after she'd been shot, but at least he still thought about it. That in itself was encouraging.

"Sounds interesting," she said, then shifted the subject before he felt obligated to make good on his threats. "Are we still on for the police sketch artist?"

"Absolutely," he said. "Just let me get to work and see what's happening before I block out some time."

"I can always take a cab," she said.

"I know, but I want to take you. I don't want you going through any of this alone."

Nicole was silent for a few moments, but there was something she had to know.

"Dominic, do you think I'm crazy?"

"Lord, no, baby...but I'm crazy about you. Does that count?"

"Dom, I'm serious."

She heard him sigh.

"I know, Nikki. I just don't know what to tell you."

Her voice shook. She hated showing weakness, but there was nothing she could do to change what was.

"But what do you think...really?"

His hesitation was brief, but his answer was firm. She could tell he'd been giving it some thought.

"I think something is happening that's scary to you. But if your injury has triggered some kind of psychic ability, I would look on it as a blessing, not something to fear."

"That's because it's not happening to you," she muttered.

"If it hurts you, it hurts me, too."

She sighed. "Okay, I get it. So I should wait for your call, right?"

"Right."

She disconnected, thought about trying to sleep, then changed her mind and got up. She had showered and dressed, and was downing some toast and jelly, when her doorbell rang. Surprised, she wiped her mouth, then slid off the kitchen bar stool and steadied herself before hobbling to the door. After a quick glance through the peephole, she let in the unexpected visitor.

"Detective Sanders, I thought I was supposed to go down to the precinct. Was I wrong?"

Sanders fidgeted without looking her directly in the face. "No, no. That's still on. I wanted to come by and show you something first."

"Oh, sure. Please, come in. How's your partner?"

He hesitated, then answered. "He's on his way to Boston."

"I hope his father will be all right," Nicole said.

Sanders eyed her curiously. She had yet to push it in his face that she'd predicted the call.

"Yeah, me too."

"Have a seat," she said.

Instead of sitting, Sanders reached in his pocket and pulled out a stuffed toy—a green Beanie Baby dinosaur—and thrust it into Nicole's hands.

The moment she touched it, she staggered. She didn't feel Sanders steady her or see the concern on his face. All she could see was a fleeting image of a three-story brownstone, then Molly Dane, standing in front of a mirror. As the child's focus shifted, so did Nicole's view of her location.

The room was no longer in darkness. What she could see of the furniture in the room was old and shabby. The floor was hardwood and in need of refinishing, and there was a blue-and-green spread on the bed. Then, between one breath and the next, the vision was gone.

She shuddered, then looked down at the stuffed toy and handed it back to Sanders.

"What just happened?" he asked.

"I saw her standing in front of a mirror. They're holding her inside a three-story brownstone, but I didn't see an address. All I do know is that she doesn't have any new bruises. They haven't hurt her again." Then she told him what the room looked like inside.

Sanders made notes as she talked, including the description of the room in which she said Molly Dane was being kept, then put the toy back in his pocket. He still didn't know what to think, but he did believe that Nicole Masters was serious. She believed she was seeing something, even if it was nothing but her imagination. Unfortunately, fantasy wasn't going to help them find the little girl.

"Well, it was worth a try," he said. "I may not be at the precinct when you arrive, but you won't need me. Frankie McAnally, the police sketch artist, is good at what he does. Hopefully we'll get something from the rendering."

"I'll do my best," Nicole said.

Sanders paused, then put a hand on her shoulder. "I know you will, and that's all anyone can do."

Nicole shuddered as a rush of wind blew through her mind, then looked straight into Andy Sanders's eyes.

"It's benign."

Sanders grunted as if he'd been punched. There was a knot in his gut that was making him suddenly sick, and his voice shook as he asked, "What did you just say?"

Nicole blinked slowly, as if she'd just awakened from a long sleep.

"The biopsy they did on your wife's breast…it's benign."

The color faded from Sanders's face. He turned on his heel and let himself out of the apartment without looking at her again. The minute he got down to his car, he called his wife. When she answered, she was crying. His heart sank.

"Nora?"

"I was just about to call you," she said. "The doctor just called. Oh, honey…it's benign. It's benign."

Tears blurred his vision. All he could think was that she'd been right. Damn it all to hell, she'd been right.

It was just after eleven-thirty when Dominic arrived carrying a yellow box with a large white bow. Nicole was finishing a tuna salad sandwich, and when she let him in, he blew her a kiss, then pointed to the tuna salad that was left in the bowl.

"Are you eating that?" he asked.

She grinned. "It's yours. There's thread in the thread box." Then she rolled her eyes. "Crap. Bread. Thread. You know what I mean." She pointed at the package. "Is that for me?"

He nodded as he spooned the tuna salad onto a slice of bread, then topped it with a second slice.

"Umm, good. Did you make this yourself?"

"Yep," Nicole said. "And nothing got mixed up this time."

He laughed, remembering when she'd salted her cereal instead of sugaring it. He gave her a wink and then took a big bite. As long as she could laugh at her situation, they were fine.

Nicole tore the ribbon from the box, then lifted the lid and pushed the layers of yellow tissue paper aside. She saw a flash of red, and then sighed.

"Oh, Dom," she whispered, as she pulled out a red crocheted hat made of the softest cashmere. It had a small ruffled brim and a perky little pompon on the crown. "It's perfect."

Gently, he cupped her head with his hand, dodging the scars and feeling the soft fuzz of regrowth.

"Is it soft enough? I didn't want anything that would be uncomfortable for you."

Nicole quickly pulled it down on her head, then hobbled to the mirror over the sofa. The fact that it made her look even younger was immaterial. Because what it also did was make her feel almost normal again.

"I love it," she said. "And yes, it's soft enough."

Dominic downed the last of the sandwich, helped himself to a can of Coke and drank it quickly. He'd promised to have her at the precinct by one. Traffic was worse than usual today, so they didn't have much time.

"Can you leave now?" he asked.

She nodded. "Just let me put on some lipstick and change my shoes."

He looked down at the bandaged foot and frowned. "Can you get a shoe over that?"

"I have a pair of Indians…" She laughed. "I mean moccasins, that I wear as slippers. I'll wear those."

"It's pretty cold outside."

"I'll wear socks, too," she said, and walked carefully out of the room, still wearing the flirty little hat.

When she came back, Dominic realized that she'd changed in honor of her hat. She was wearing black slacks, and a red-and-black sweater. The little hat on her head was like the cherry on a hot fudge sundae.

"Looking good, woman," he said softly, then wrapped his arms around her and kissed her until her cheeks were as red as her hat.

"When we're through at the station, if you're not too tired, how would you feel about having an early dinner with me?"

Nicole's instincts for survival kicked in again. She touched her head, felt the red hat and sighed. She couldn't hide inside forever.

"If you're not ashamed to be seen with me, then I think I can manage."

Dominic frowned. "Don't, Nikki. You're alive. When are you going to realize that's all that freaking matters to me?"

"Then, okay, I would love to. My coat and purse are in the living room. I'm ready when you are."

A few minutes later, they were on their way downtown.

It was almost 5:00 p.m. when the sketch artist leaned back in his chair. Nicole breathed a slow sigh of relief. They had spent hours recreating the faces of two of the men she'd "seen" kidnap Molly Dane.

"What do you think?" McAnally asked, showing her the sketch of the second man. "Is the nose better now, or do you still want it a bit wider at the nostrils?"

Nicole stared at the face, then shivered. "It's him."

McAnally nodded. "I'll print these out and give them to Detective Sanders. He'll run them through the system. Maybe we'll get lucky."

Nicole's head was pounding, and she felt sick to her stomach as she watched him walk away. She reached for the can of Coke they'd given her hours earlier, then realized it was empty.

"Here you go, baby. This one is good and cold."

Nicole looked up to see Dominic pop the top of a fresh can, then hand it to her. The slight fizz and the condensation on the outside were a promise of what was inside. She took a small sip, then swallowed slowly, savoring the cold liquid and the slight bite as it went down.

"Umm, good. Thank you so much," she said, then

dug in her purse for some of the painkillers she hadn't
needed recently but definitely required today.

Dominic had seen the pain in her eyes and knew
she was exhausted. He pulled up a chair beside her,
then sat down.

"Are you all right?"

Nicole nodded. "Just a little headache."

"You did great," he said.

She sighed. "I hope it helps."

He slid a hand along her shoulder to the back of her
neck, then rubbed gently, massaging the knot he felt
beneath his fingers.

"Do you want to go home?"

She frowned. "You promised me dinner, remember?"

He smiled. "I remember. Do you like Italian?"

She grinned. "I love Italians."

He laughed out loud. "You *are* getting better."

The sketch artist came back into the room. "Detective Sanders said to thank you for your help and that
he'd be in touch."

"Does that mean I'm dismissed?" Nicole asked.

"You got it," Dominic said. "Do you want to freshen
up before we leave?"

"Please."

After a quick trip to the bathroom, she came out to
find Dominic in deep discussion with one of the detectives.

"Is something wrong?" she asked.

"No. Quite the contrary. One of the guys thinks the man from the first sketch looks a little like a perp named Raul Gomez. He's checking some details right now. In the meantime, we're going to dinner. I hope you're hungry."

"I'm starved," she said, and was surprised to realize she meant it.

A half hour later, Dominic pulled up in front of a busy Italian restaurant. A parking valet headed toward them, then opened the door for Nicole.

"You're going to love the food here," Dominic said, as he pocketed the claim ticket the valet gave him. Just before he opened the restaurant door, he bent down and kissed the side of her cheek.

"Hey," she said.

"Couldn't resist. It's that hat. You look like a pixie."

She grinned. "Pixie, huh? Just so you know, I'm too hungry to eat like one."

Dominic eyed the dark circles under her eyes and made a mental note not to linger over their food. She looked like she needed to be in bed, but he wasn't going to put a damper on her first journey back into normalcy.

"That's good to hear. My Uncle Dom owns the place, and he loves a healthy appetite. Since I was named for him, I'm his favorite nephew."

Nicole's hand automatically went to her head. The little red hat was firmly in place. Still, of all times to meet part of Dominic's family, she had to look like this.

Dominic read her mind. "They already know what happened to you. Like me, they're just grateful that you survived. Besides, I've been getting flak for not bringing you around before."

"Then why didn't you?" she asked.

He cupped her cheek, gently rubbing his thumb along her chin.

"Timing messed that up," he said. "If you hadn't been shot, this would have already happened. Then, afterward, I didn't want to scare you off until I was sure that I'd swept you firmly back off your feet."

"You lie," she said softly, "but that's okay. You just wanted to make sure I wasn't still drooling."

His eyes narrowed almost angrily. "No. I wasn't sure you could handle the truth, but since you've challenged me, lady, then you're going to have to hear the rest of it. I'm in love with you, Nicole. I've known it for a while. I just wanted to make sure that you remembered me…us. I didn't want to push you into something you weren't ready for."

Her jaw dropped; then her eyes filled with tears.

"Oh, Dom. You love me?"

"That's what I just said. No response is necessary. Can we go eat now?"

Too distracted to do more than nod, she let herself be led inside.

The scent of freshly baking bread and mouth-watering tomato sauces hit her like a lover's kiss.

"Umm, everything smells good," she said.

Dominic sighed. He'd said more than he'd meant to and was relieved that she hadn't balked. Maybe his uncle's chef could put her in a safer frame of mind.

"It tastes even better," he promised, then squeezed her elbow. "Hang on to that cute little hat, because here comes Uncle Dom."

Nicole barely had time to look up before they were engulfed.

"Dominic! Welcome, welcome. "

Nicole grinned. She'd never seen Dominic bow to another man's authority before, but his body language said he was definitely catering to his uncle.

Once his nephew had been welcomed properly, Uncle Dom turned his attention to Nicole.

"You must be our Nikki," he said, and then lifted her hand to his lips and kissed it in an old-world gesture that would have charmed her completely, had he not already done so by claiming her as their own. "Welcome. I hope you brought your appetite."

She smiled, then touched her head briefly, as if making sure the little red hat was still in place.

"I'm starving," she said. "Will that do?"

He smiled, then bent his head and kissed her on both cheeks before offering her his arm.

"Come, come…I will seat you at our best table."

Dominic followed along behind, smiling as they went. Nicole had fallen under his uncle's spell, which was good.

They were soon sipping a bottle of the house's best

wine while they decided what to eat. Nicole kept reading and rereading the menu, but the words had begun to run together. She was tired, and it was starting to show.

"Dom…"

"What, baby?"

"All the words are running together," she said. "Would you order for me?"

Dominic frowned. "I'm so sorry, Nikki. Are you sure you're up for this? We can always do it another time."

She nodded. "Yes, I'm sure. Order me something with marinara rather than Alfredo sauce. Maybe some eggplant Parmesan or shrimp prima vera. I love either one."

Dominic cupped the side of her face. "How about we order both and share?"

She beamed. "Perfect."

Dominic gave the waiter their order and was pouring some more wine in her glass when his uncle reappeared.

"For you, *bella* Nikki," he said, and slid a basket of warm bread sticks and some marinara sauce on the table. "Eat. Eat. You make me happy if you eat."

Nicole's smile widened. "That will make *me* happy, too. Thank you."

Dom's uncle winked at her. "You make Dominic bring you to Sunday dinner. You will meet all the family."

"Easy, Uncle Dom. I don't want to scare her off."

"Hey. I'm not that easy to scare, remember?" Nicole said.

Dominic's gaze slid from her shadowed eyes to the red hat and he tried not to think of how scared he'd been, sitting at her bedside in the hospital and waiting for her to wake up from the head wound—waiting to see if the woman he loved was still there.

"Yeah, you're a real tough one," he said, then nodded at his uncle. "Thanks again, Uncle Dom."

His uncle beamed, then moved away.

"He's really sweet," Nicole said, as she dipped a bread stick in marinara sauce, then took a big bite. "Mmm, so good."

The meal progressed and she found herself forgetting about her clumsiness and lack of hair. It wasn't until Dominic's cell phone rang that everything changed.

"Excuse me," he said. "I meant to turn off the ringer."

He was reaching into his pocket as she felt the noise in the room fade away.

"The maid died," she said.

Dominic froze. "What did you say?" he asked.

The phone rang again, but Nicole already knew what the message would be.

"Lyla Dane's housekeeper…she died."

A muscle jerked near the corner of Dominic's jaw. It was the only sign of what he was feeling. He looked down at the Caller ID, frowned, then answered.

"Tucci."

It was his lieutenant. "I know this is your night off, but considering the day you spent with your girlfriend,

I thought you would want to know that the Danes' maid died. Or…maybe you already knew it, since she's psychic and all."

"As a matter of fact, she mentioned it," Dominic snapped, furious at the sarcasm in his boss's voice.

There was a long moment of silence; then the lieutenant cleared his throat and continued as if Dominic hadn't spoken. "This has ramped up the pressure big-time. Now we've got a homicide to go with the kidnapping, and the mayor is breathing down our throats."

"Who's got the case?" Dominic asked.

"Miller and Betts. So if your so-called psychic comes up with another vision or two, you might want to share the news."

Dominic took a deep breath to keep from saying something he would regret later.

"If Nicole keys in on anything else, we'll be sure to let you know."

Dominic disconnected, then dropped the phone back in his pocket.

Nicole was watching him, waiting for him to look at her. When he did, she knew she'd been right.

"God," she muttered, and rubbed her hands over her face. "Why is this happening?"

Dominic glanced down at their plates. "Do you want dessert?"

Her chin trembled. "I just want to go home, please."

He dropped a handful of bills onto the table and stood abruptly. He waved at his uncle from across the room, then motioned that they had to leave. Before anyone could stop them, he had Nicole out the door. The valet brought up the car, and they were soon driving away.

Nicole shivered. "I'm sorry for ruining the mood."

Dominic glanced at her briefly, then gave her knee a squeeze. "Honey, you haven't ruined a thing. We had a great meal and a good time, and now we're going home. The end."

She sighed, then leaned back and closed her eyes. Before long they were back at their apartment building. Dominic parked in the garage across the street, then helped her out of the car.

She stumbled.

He cursed softly, then picked her up and carried her across the street. Once inside, he put her down. They rode the elevator up to Nicole's apartment. When they reached the door, he followed her inside.

They paused in the foyer, staring intently into each other's eyes.

Nicole sighed, then took off her coat and hat, and hung them on the hall tree.

He waited. The tension between them was growing.

She looked up. "Dominic... I—"

"I want to make love with you."

She flinched. Without thinking, her hands went to her head.

"I'm not in love with your hair."

He sounded angry.

Her vision blurred.

"If you're too tired," he said, "then I—"

Nicole put her fingers on his lips, silencing the rest of what he'd been about to say.

"I want to make love with you, too," she whispered.

Dominic swallowed past the knot in his throat.

"Thank God," he muttered, and picked her up in his arms and carried her into her bedroom.

Lit by the faint glow coming from the living room lamps, they undressed in silence.

He finished first, then turned to help her. She had her shoes and slacks off, and was trying to pull her sweater over her head, when he took over. Within seconds, she was naked and flat on her back in the bed.

"Oh, Dom… I didn't think this would ever happen again."

Dominic hated the fear in her voice. He stretched out beside her, then took her in his arms. His voice was rough and shaky.

"Back when you were in the hospital, there were a few days when I didn't think it would, either."

Nicole swallowed a sob as she put her arms around his neck and pulled him down to her. His mouth settled on her lips for the slowest, sweetest kiss she'd ever had. His tenderness was unmistakable. She could tell he was afraid he would hurt her.

"I won't break," she said. "Just love me, Dom…like you used to."

He groaned.

The second kiss was overwhelming, sweeping through her last defenses as he took her in his arms. Heat spread through her body like a blast of hot wind. There had been so many days when she'd felt like she would have been better off dead. But this moment was a reminder of why she'd been wrong.

When Dominic levered himself above her, she clutched his shoulders, urging him closer. Then he paused.

"What?" she asked.

His arms were shaking. He wanted her so much, but this was scary. "I'm so damned afraid I'll hurt you."

Nicole sighed. Everything that had been wrong with her now seemed inconsequential. Nothing mattered but him—and her.

"Only if you stop."

He gritted his teeth, then slid into her.

Nicole moaned. "Oh, Dom…so good, so good."

It was all he needed to hear.

And so the dance began.

Body to body.

Heart to heart.

They moved to the internal rhythm that only lovers can hear. For the first time since before she'd walked into that pharmacy, she was living again. Dominic gave her pleasure upon pleasure, rocking her senses until she was weak and breathless. At the point of being unbearable, it changed, breaking through her last defense and shattering her consciousness.

Dominic felt her climax and let go of the last of his control, following her up, then following her down. As she'd said…good, so good.

He groaned, then rolled, taking her with him until she was stretched out on top of his body.

"Are you okay?" he asked.

"Mmm."

He grinned as he tightened his hold. "So what you mean is…it was so good I've left you speechless."

She would have punched him, but there was no denying the truth.

"Mmm."

He laughed. Their world was back on track.

Chapter 3

The ransom call came at four in the morning, giving Lyla Dane until twelve noon to come up with twenty million dollars. At noon there would be a second call, at which time she would be given a numbered account where the money was to be transferred. They would have fifteen minutes to make the transfer or Molly Dane would die. Once the transfer was made, they would get a third call telling them where to find the child. Before anyone could object or ask to speak to Molly, the caller, wise to the presence of the authorities, disconnected.

Because the ransom call had taken so long to come in, Lyla had proactively offered a million-dollar reward for information leading to the arrest of the kidnappers. That had set off a barrage of tips that were driving the NYPD crazy. Despite the fact that most of the calls coming in were bogus, the cops couldn't ignore the possibility of a lead. And now the eight-hour deadline was looming. As for Nicole's sketches, most of the cops were convinced they were chasing ghosts.

But there was one lead that Detectives Sanders and Garcia—who was back from Boston, his father's injuries having turned out to be minor—were following up on. Early on, one of the homicide cops had mentioned that the first sketch resembled a man named Raul Gomez, a perp he'd arrested when he'd been working vice.

Hours before the ransom call had come in, they'd pulled Gomez's rap sheet, and made the rounds of his known hangouts and friends. According to the sheet, he went by the street name of Romeo and ran with an old cell mate from Attica named Ed Wolchek. Raul had fancied himself something of a boxer, and one of his hangouts had been Minsky's Gym. Sanders remembered Nicole saying that the man in her second vision had been wearing a T-shirt with the name Minsky's Gym on it. It could be a coincidence, but if so, it was an odd one, for sure.

The second sketch didn't fit Wolchek's description, but both Nicole and their one eyewitness had claimed four men were involved, so he could be one of the others.

The last known address they had on Gomez didn't turn up anything useful, other than the fact that he'd moved about a month ago and left no forwarding address, but they'd located his mother and were knocking on her door before daybreak.

Maria Gomez had come to the door in her robe and nightgown, taken one look at the badges that the detectives were flashing and burst into tears. They'd spent fifteen minutes calming her down and reassuring her that no one had died. Then they'd gotten down to business.

Maria Gomez was staring at the sketch in Detective Garcia's hand.

"*Sí, sí,* it looks like my son, Raul. Why do you have this? What has he done?"

Detective Sanders glanced at Garcia, then gave him a nod. They were betting on Maria opening up better to a man of her own culture.

Garcia leaned forward and set down a photo of Molly Dane. "You know this little girl?"

Maria frowned. "No…wait…is that the child of the movie star? The girl who was kidnapped?"

Garcia nodded. "Yes, ma'am. Her name is Molly. She's only five years old."

Maria clasped her hands to her cheeks. "Aiyee…the same age as my grandson, Manuel. Poor baby. Poor little girl." Then she must have made the connection between the pictures in her mind, because she asked suspiciously, "Why do you show me this picture?"

"The sketch we showed you, the one you identified as your son, is, according to an eyewitness, one of the kidnappers."

Maria Gomez sat up, then clasped her hands in her lap and shut down.

Sanders felt her withdrawal.

"I don't think that looks so much like my son after all."

Garcia shoved the little girl's picture closer, and the tone of his voice turned harsh.

"That baby is crying for her mama. Can you hear her? Strangers took her out of her room and into the cold. She's afraid of the dark. She wants to go home. Do you want that guilt on your conscience? What if that was your baby? What if it was Manuelito crying for his mama?"

Tears filled the old woman's eyes, but Sanders knew there was an unwritten law in her world that family loyalty trumped all. She didn't have it in her to give up her son.

"It doesn't matter whether it's Raul or it's not Raul. I don't know where he is. I haven't seen him in weeks."

Sanders frowned. That wasn't the information they'd gotten at his last address. According to neighbors, Gomez's mother had been a regular visitor to the place. He didn't figure Gomez as the kind to suddenly cut her off. Even the worst perps often maintained civil—even loving—relationships with family members. He figured Gomez for one of those.

"But you know how to contact him, don't you?"

Maria's chin jutted mutinously.

"Maybe I do. Maybe I don't."

Garcia picked up Molly Dane's picture. "If she dies and you did nothing to help, her blood will be on your hands."

Maria gasped and then crossed herself. "If I hear from my son, I will ask him about this thing."

Sanders sighed, then handed her his card.

"Time is running out for that little girl. Try hard... for Molly Dane, will you?"

They left without having accomplished much.

Two-plus hours gone. Five-plus left and counting. The pressure was on.

Nicole woke up to the sound of ringing. Thinking it was the alarm, she took a swing at it without opening her eyes. When the sound didn't stop, she rose up on one elbow, blinking in confusion. It took her a few seconds to realize she was hearing a phone. And that the phone wasn't hers but belonged to Dom. It took her another second to reconcile the sound of running water with the probability that he was in her bathroom, taking a shower.

With a muffled groan, she grabbed the phone and crawled out of bed. The cuts on the bottom of her foot were sore and healing slowly, which meant Dominic had probably been right about needing stitches. Still, she managed to hobble into the bathroom, carrying the ringing phone.

He heard the sound just as the shower curtain slid back behind him. Surprised, he turned around in time to grab the phone Nicole put in his hand.

"Alarm," she said, then frowned. "That didn't sound right."

He grinned as he turned off the shower. "It's a phone, baby, and thank you," he said.

She gave his wet, naked body an appreciative look as he grabbed a towel and exited the bathroom, leaving it all to her. By the time she came out, Dominic was dressed and in the kitchen making coffee, if her nose was telling her the truth. She pulled on a pair of sweats and an old sweater, then stepped into some backless slippers and followed the scent of brewing coffee.

Dominic felt her presence before he saw her. Last night had been magic and he didn't want it to end. Unfortunately, the phone call had changed whatever plans he'd been thinking of making.

"There's news," he said, as he poured her some coffee.

"Good news?" she asked, as she added a dollop of cream.

"Depends on how you look at it," he said. "The ransom call finally came. They want twenty million transferred to a numbered account by noon today."

She frowned. "Transferred?"

"Yeah, it will make it a lot more difficult to catch them, and even after it's delivered, there's still no guarantee they'll give the girl back."

"Oh, Dom. I can't quit thinking about her. She's scared...so scared."

"I know, Nikki. We're doing all we can, but technology is making it easier for criminals to get away with things. However, Ms. Dane is also offering a reward of her own—a million dollars for information leading to the arrest and conviction of the people responsible. You might find yourself with a lapful of money, honey."

Nicole's frown deepened. "No way. I have all the money I'll ever need. I'll never need to work, though I love working part-time at the bookstore. Of course, that's over unless I can remember how to talk again without making a fool of myself."

Dominic brushed his finger down the side of her face. There was little to be said about her problems that hadn't already been said. Still, he could only imagine what she was going through.

Nikki leaned into his touch, but she was firm in her conviction about not wanting money.

"You don't understand," she said. "It took me years not to think of my parents' investments and life insurance as blood money. You couldn't make me take anything like that again. If these visions, or whatever you want to call them, keep happening, I don't intend to turn them into a damned business."

Dominic nodded. "I get it, baby, and I didn't mean to upset you. Consider the subject dropped."

She lifted her face for a good-morning kiss, which he gladly provided. Her senses quickened, but she let them settle. Dominic was already in work mode, and there was no time for messing around.

A couple of pieces of toast and jelly and two cups of coffee later, he was getting ready to leave. He was on his way out the door when she looked at him from the other side of the room.

"Call me," she said.

He paused, then turned around, took his cell phone out of his pocket and punched in some numbers. As soon as he finished, her phone began to ring. A bit surprised by the coincidence, she quickly answered.

"Hello."

"It's me."

She looked up. Dominic was grinning. For goodness sakes, he'd called her. She smiled back and asked, "What?"

"You told me to call," he said.

She laughed out loud, and he had to stifle the urge to close the door and take her back to bed.

"You're crazy…maybe crazier than me," she said, still smiling.

"I'm crazy all right…crazy about you, just like I said before. And just so you know, I lost something last night. You can be looking for it while I'm gone."

Her smile slipped. "Oh no. What was it?"

"My heart. It's here somewhere. When you find it, take really good care of it, because I've been trying to give it to you for weeks."

Nicole's eyes widened, then her voice softened.

"Oh, Dom, that might be the sweetest thing anyone has ever said to me."

"I mean it, baby. You're everything I've ever wanted in a woman. I love you, Nicole."

She sighed. "I love you, too."

He nodded. "Then keep that thought. We have bigger things to talk about tonight, okay?"

Her heart thumped crazily. "Are you talking about the birds and the bees?"

He grinned. "We've already covered that subject. I'm talking about weddings."

She rolled her eyes, then ran her hand over the fuzz on her head. "That's what I said…almost."

"So…tonight?"

She swallowed past the lump in her throat, then nodded.

"Absolutely…tonight it is."

Moments later, he was gone.

At ten minutes to six in the morning, Raul Gomez's cell phone began to ring. He rolled off the sofa on which he'd been sleeping and reached for his phone. The only people who should be calling him were in the room. When he saw the Caller ID, he frowned.

"Hello, Mama. What's wrong? Are you ill?"

Maria Gomez was furious. She had a horrible feeling that everything the police had suggested was true. She loved her son, but not what he'd become. And there was the child. He had not been raised to be cruel like that.

"No, I am not ill. I am upset. The police were just here, looking for you. They think you had something to do with the kidnapping of that little girl who belongs to the actress. *Madre de Dios*, tell me you did not. Tell me that the sketch they have is not you."

"Sketch? What sketch?" he asked.

He hadn't denied being involved, she thought. His first comment had been about the sketch. Maria began to wail, claiming he was going to hell for his sins if the police didn't kill him first.

Raul groaned. Shit.

"Mama, Mama, stop crying. You don't know what you're saying. Of course I didn't do it. How could you think that of me?"

She screamed into the phone. "Shut up, Raul. If you can't tell the truth, don't talk to me at all. You never could lie to me, and you know it. You are lying now. I hear it in your voice."

Raul cursed. "Fine. Then I won't be surprising you if I hang up."

He disconnected, then, ignoring the three other men sleeping on various pieces of furniture, he turned on the television and flipped to CNN.

It would seem that things were definitely not going as planned. He would have sworn they hadn't been spotted, yet sketches of two suspects were being aired. Accurate sketches. One was clearly of him, and the other was Benny Jarvis.

The other three men woke up when the TV came

on, and when Benny saw his own face on the screen, he leapt out of the recliner, cursing and waving his hands.

"Shit! Shit! How has this happened? No one saw us. You said so yourself. It's over. We're dead. We're dead."

Benny ran to the window. There were no cops lining the streets. He ran into the room where the kid was still sleeping, then back to Raul and the others.

"This is bogus. It's over. They know who we are. We gotta get out of here now!"

Raul grabbed his arm, then slapped him. Benny staggered, then fell onto the sofa with a thump.

"What did you do that for?" he mumbled, holding his jaw.

"You freaked. They don't know anything. Those are just sketches. They didn't give names. You didn't hear any names, did you?"

Benny shuddered, then shook his head.

"So calm the hell down. Everything is still fine. We just need to…readjust a few things."

"Like what?" Benny asked.

Before Wolchek had turned to a life of crime, he'd been a dockworker. He knew all about readjustments. Now he pushed between Benny and Raul, and took control of the conversation.

"The maid is dead. She can't identify us. The kid is next. We get the money, and we leave no witnesses."

Benny stared at the bald, muscle-bound psycho and freaked again. "No one was supposed to get hurt! You said so, Romeo, remember?" he said frantically, turning to Raul. "*Remember*? No one gets hurt. You said so."

Raul didn't comment. It was Wolchek who answered. "Shut the fuck up. Things change."

"I won't have any part of it," Benny said.

"I'll do her," Wolchek said.

Raul felt sick to his stomach. This felt wrong, but they were too far in to pull back.

"Fine," he said. "But not until the money is in the bank."

"No," Benny said. "I don't agree."

Raul leaned down until he was only inches away from Benny's face.

"You agree, or you die with her."

Benny paled, then dropped his head in his hands and began to weep.

Wolchek slapped the back of Benny's head.

"Suck it up."

Benny shuddered but wisely shut up. He knew them well enough to know they would make good on their threats.

Wolchek and Gomez turned to look at Jeff Whitson, who was Benny's cousin and the fourth man. He was also the computer geek. They couldn't kill him. They needed him to make sure the first transfer went as planned, then he would take it from there.

Jeff looked at the pair and then held up his hands in surrender.

"As long as I don't have to watch, do what you want."

Raul nodded. *"Bueno."*

They stood, watching the news anchor talking about Lyla Dane and her career, and when the broadcast flashed to a press conference that was just starting, Wolchek upped the volume.

The Danes' attorney was verifying that Lyla Dane was offering a million-dollar reward for information leading to the arrest and conviction of the people responsible for the crime. Suddenly Raul panicked. His mother was so pissed, he wouldn't put it past her to give him up for the money herself. And thanks to Wolchek, there was also a murder charge hanging over their heads.

Raul glanced at Wolchek. He knew the man had done a lot of bad things in his life, but volunteering to kill a kid was a new low. Still, five million dollars apiece was a lot of dough for four boys from the projects, and he believed their plan was solid.

As soon as Jeff could verify the transfer, they were heading to Canada in Wolchek's van. The ransom money would initially be sent to an account in the Cayman Islands. But they planned a twist on the game that the cops wouldn't be expecting. As soon as the first transfer was made, Jeff would transfer the funds again while they were en route to Canada. The second transfer would be to another account, this time in the Bahamas. And while the authorities were playing catch-up, the twenty mil would be transferred one last time, to a bank in Canada. They would have the money in hand and be gone before the cops ever realized what was happening.

Raul considered the plan genius, but they needed Jeff to make it happen. By this time tomorrow, they would be in Canada—twenty millions dollars to the good. The next few hours were crucial, though. He couldn't afford to have someone balk.

He glanced at the door on the other side of the room, listening for sounds to indicate that the kid was moving around, but he heard nothing. Despite his mother's panic, he was confident that everything was in place. She didn't know where he was, and the apartment belonged to Jeff Whitson, so even if she gave him up, they wouldn't know where to look. Still, just to be sure, he moved to the window, checking the street in front of the old brownstone.

The area was a beehive of illegal activities. The possibility of seeing NYPD black-and-whites was high at any time. He just needed to make sure they weren't here for them.

When he didn't see anything out of the ordinary, he walked away. This time tomorrow, they would be in Canada. The money would have hopped continents, and the apartment was paid up to the end of the month. When Jeff didn't pay next month, the landlord would just rent it out to someone else. No one would ever know they'd been here. They would dump the kid's body in the woods somewhere upstate on their way to the border.

What could go wrong?

* * *

All morning, Nicole had been aware of the clock. Knowing that everything was going down at noon was frightening. What if something went wrong? What if they didn't turn Molly Dane loose? She had tried, without success, to force another vision and finally given up, knowing that whatever was happening was out of her control.

It was just after eleven and she was in the kitchen, opening a can of soup for her lunch, when the air around her suddenly shimmered. The music playing on the stereo in the other room began to fade, and she felt the skin of her face tightening.

It was happening again.

She took a deep breath and leaned against the cabinet, waiting for the rush of wind.

It came, and with it came another vision. One moment she was pouring soup into a pan, and the next she was watching a short, stocky man walking toward her.

Thinking she was about to be attacked, it took her a few moments to realize that the man wasn't coming toward her. In fact, he wasn't even in her apartment. He was in the same room she'd seen before, and he was approaching Molly Dane. Somehow she was seeing through Molly's eyes—seeing everything Molly was seeing.

Then the man spoke.

"Here, kid…you gotta eat. I brought you a Happy Meal. It's got a toy in it and everything."

Nicole felt Molly's despair as the man shoved the food in her hands.

"Eat it!" he demanded.

In what Nicole could only call an out-of-body experience, she and Molly took the food to a table. She saw the little girl's hands trembling as she opened the small box and took out the plastic-wrapped toy. Without looking up, she set it aside.

Someone in the other room called out, "Benny, come here!"

Nicole saw Molly look up. The man, who Nicole now realized was one of the two men she'd seen at the kidnapping, glanced at Molly, then walked into the other room. As soon as he was gone, Molly ran to a window. It was boarded up, but she thrust her little fingers into a crack and pulled, trying to loosen the boards.

Nicole winced as she saw the child lose her grip. When she pulled back, her fingers came away with splinters. Molly grimaced with pain but had the foresight not to cry out. Instead, she clenched her fists, then glanced over her shoulder to make sure she was still alone before peeking through the crack. Nicole felt Molly's helplessness and despair.

Nicole's heart skipped a beat as Molly's gaze went from the graffiti-sprayed wall of the building across the way to the street signs at the corner.

"Oh, God…oh, God…look at them, baby. Look at the signs," Nicole whispered.

And Molly did. Her gaze went straight to the corner as if she'd heard Nicole's long-distance plea.

East 149th Street and Morris Avenue.

Nicole read the names twice, locking them firmly in her mind as Molly suddenly spun and headed for the table. She was tearing into the paper around her hamburger when Benny came back into the room. Benny was staring at Molly for what seemed like a very long time. Then suddenly he shook his head and looked away. At that point Nicole panicked. The thought ran through her mind that they weren't going to let Molly Dane go. Once the money was transferred, they were going to kill her. She had to tell Dominic and the detectives.

And just like that, the vision was gone. She glanced at the clock. It was less than an hour before the transfer had to be made. If they didn't find Molly before noon, it would be too late.

Andy Sanders and Tomas Garcia were on their way to the Dakota to wait for everything to go down. There would be the transfer, then a brief wait for the call that would give them a pickup location for the girl.

"What do you think?" Garcia asked, as Sanders stopped for a red light.

"I think we're screwed," Sanders muttered.

"We didn't get anything out of Gomez's mother."

Sanders shook his head. "No, and it's too late now to worry about it. Even if she knew something, she wasn't telling. "

"You'd think a million dollars would bring someone forward," Garcia said.

The light changed. Sanders accelerated through the intersection.

"We just didn't have enough time to make it work," he said.

His cell phone rang. He glanced at the Caller ID, then cursed beneath his breath. It was Nicole Masters.

"This better be good," he said, and answered the call. "Sanders."

"There's white and red and black gang graffiti on the wall of an abandoned building across the street from the three-story brownstone. From the window, Molly can read the street signs. East 149th Street and Morris Avenue. You have to hurry. When they get the money, they're going to kill her."

Sanders swerved, then tightened his grip on the steering wheel as he swung the car sharply to the curb.

"Say it again!" he yelled, as he put the cell on speaker.

Nicole repeated everything while Garcia wrote furiously.

"Hurry," she begged. "You have to find her before the transfer goes through or she's dead. Oh God… you have to believe me. Help her. She's so little and so scared."

"I hear you," he said, and disconnected. For a split second he and Garcia stared at each other.

"I know that area," Garcia said. "That's the Mott

Haven section of the Bronx. I grew up there. What do you think we should do?"

Sanders shrugged. "What the hell. It's only my pension if she's wrong."

Garcia grabbed the radio and began calling it in as Sanders pulled out into traffic. He turned on the lights and siren, and stomped on the gas.

Dominic signed off on the report he'd just finished and was on his way to turn it in when his cell phone rang. He paused to dig it out of his pocket, then saw that the call was from Nicole and answered with a smile.

"Hey, baby."

Her voice was shaking, and it was all she could do not to scream. The urgency she was feeling was overwhelming. They all had to believe her. They had to understand.

"Dominic...I saw where she is. I saw the address. Molly was looking through a crack in the boarded-up window, and it was as if I was seeing through her eyes. She's at East 149th Street and Morris Avenue. It's a three-story brownstone that sits across the street from an abandoned building covered in white and red and black gang graffiti. I've already called Detective Sanders. I'm going to catch a cab and go there, too. If something happens, maybe I can still help."

Dominic flipped the report toward his lieutenant's in-basket and started toward the door.

"No, Nicole, no. There might be gunfire. You do not leave the apartment. Do you hear me?"

His answer was a dial tone.

As he sprinted for his car, the only thing going through his head was the call he'd gotten after the robbery, when Nicole had been caught in the line of fire.

"Please, not again," he prayed.

Chapter 4

Nicole wrote down the intersection that she'd seen in her vision, then grabbed her red hat, her coat and purse, and headed out of her apartment on the run—or as much of a run as she could manage with her sore foot. Her heart was pounding as she waited in the hall for the elevator. When the doors opened, she almost leapt into the car. As the car started to move, she automatically reached for her head, felt the soft red wool and thought of Dominic. There was so much riding on the vision she'd had. She wished he was with her. Maybe then she wouldn't feel so anxious.

When she got out to the curb to hail a cab, it dawned on her how cold it had become. She buttoned her coat all the way to the collar while wishing she'd brought her scarf. A single drop of rain fell on her face just as she realized she was only wearing one shoe. There was nothing on her injured foot but the bandages and a heavy sock.

Not only was she without a shoe, but she was also without an umbrella. She glanced at her watch, then discarded the notion of going back upstairs. In the grand scheme of what was about to happen, the possibility of getting drenched was definitely unimportant, so she turned her attention to hailing a cab.

The driver of the first empty cab to come down the street flew past without even noticing her. When she saw the second coming, she began waving and yelling as loudly as she could, but that driver, too, somehow missed her. When she saw the third one coming and realized it was empty, she jumped off the curb and ran into the street.

The driver hit the brakes, fishtailing slightly and leaving two streaks of rubber on the street as he came to a stop only inches from where she was standing. He was still cursing at the top of his lungs as she dived into the backseat.

"Drive!" she screamed and, not trusting herself to give the proper address, reached toward the bullet-proof partition between them and shoved the written address through the payment opening, so it fell onto the seat beside him. "There's the address. Take me there, and hurry. It's a matter of life and death."

The cabby was still angry as he glanced at the address. "Right, lady. I've heard that before."

Nicole leaned forward, stared at the back of his head for a minute and said, "You've been taking money from the church offering for the past six weeks instead of putting it in. Father Patrick knows you're doing it and is waiting for your confession."

The cabbie paled, his eyes widening in disbelief as he stared at her in the rearview mirror.

"How did you know that?"

"The same way I know that this ride is a matter of life and death. Now drive—and hurry!"

He took off, leaving a second set of marks on the street as Nicole grabbed for her seat belt.

She didn't know if it was going to matter whether she was at the scene or not, but instinct told her that the closer she was to what was happening, the better off they would all be.

Dominic was in a panic. He was running hot, with lights and sirens, and still afraid he wouldn't be in time. This thing that was happening with Nicole had him up against the wall. He didn't understand how she was doing it, but he was convinced it was real. And if he didn't get to her in time, it could very easily get her killed.

Suddenly he hit the brakes and swerved just in time to miss two black-and-whites flying through the intersection from the south. As he drove farther, it appeared they might all be going in the same direction, which meant Sanders had taken Nicole's warning seriously and put the word out. He had no way of proving it, but he knew in his gut that when they got there, they would find Molly Dane. Whether she was still alive or not would be their responsibility, not Nikki's.

Two minutes passed, then three, then five, and he was still at least five minutes away when he saw an ambulance turn off a side street and fall in behind him. He gripped the steering wheel a little tighter and stomped the accelerator harder.

The cab driver was performing what Nicole could only call miracles, getting through traffic, moving past construction areas by taking side streets and alleys, and all without giving her a backward glance. It was as if the immediacy of her panic had seeped into him, as well.

Nicole felt sick. She couldn't "see" anything else that was going on inside the brownstone, but she could feel it. Molly Dane's life force was dimming, as if the veil between life and death was thinner than it had been mere hours ago.

But she had hope. She'd seen a number of police cars going in the same direction they were. All she could think was, please, God, let them get there in time.

Suddenly the cab driver slammed on the brakes. Her seat belt popped loose, and she went flying forward, hitting the bullet-proof partition between them with her forehead.

"Oh, my God," she groaned, and clutched her head with both hands as the cab came to a stop. Another head wound? Could this get any worse?

"I'm sorry," the cabbie said, eyeing the swiftly rising lump and trickling blood on her forehead. "Are you all right?"

"What happened?" she asked, and wondered if it was really beginning to rain in earnest, or if she was just seeing spots.

"See for yourself," he said, pointing forward.

She squinted past the pain, only to realize that the streets had been blocked, and that there were black-and-whites everywhere. They must be close.

"They've blocked off the streets, lady. I can't take you any farther. You want to go somewhere else?"

She scrambled for her purse, pulled out a handful of bills and thrust them through the pass-through.

"No. I have to be here. Thank you for the ride."

He pocketed the money, then frowned. "Are you sure? I don't think this neighborhood is what you're used to."

Nicole looked out the windows. "You're right. I'm not used to it, but it's definitely where I have to be."

She jumped out of the cab before he could argue, pulled her little red hat down tighter on her head and started walking. Almost immediately, she realized that the single shoe on her right foot was going to be of no use in keeping the sock and bandages dry on her left.

"I should have gone back for my other shoe," she

muttered, then felt moisture on her forehead. To her horror, it wasn't rain, it was blood. There was a knot the size of an egg above her left eyebrow and blood on her hands.

Gritting her teeth against the pain, she started walking. She'd gone about a half block when it began to rain for real. She didn't look up, and she didn't look back. The farther she walked, the more certain she was that she was going in the right direction, because the sound of Molly's heartbeat was like thunder in her ears.

Her jaunty red hat was now soaked, and water was dripping down her neck. The bottom of the sock on her bandaged foot was stained a pale, watery red from the wounds that had come open, but she could see the police perimeter less than three blocks away. With her goal in sight, she lengthened her stride.

Then someone yelled at her.

"Hey, lady! You can't go down there!"

She paused to look behind her. A uniformed policeman was coming toward her at a fast clip. She couldn't stop. Not now. She started to run in an awkward, hopping gait that made her foot bleed harder. Cold rain peppered her face, but she kept going, terrified that if she didn't get there, it would be a disaster.

Suddenly the cop's hands were on her shoulders, yanking her to a stop. She immediately began struggling against his grip.

"Let me go! You don't understand. She's going to die if I don't get there in time!"

The cop, who clearly thought he had hold of a crazy woman, was pulling out handcuffs when a car came to a screeching halt in the street beside them. The cop was already reaching for his gun when he saw the driver fly out of the car, holding up his badge as he ran.

"She's with me!" Dominic yelled, as he raced toward her through the rain.

Nicole went limp. Dominic. She should have known he would come.

He swung her up into his arms and made a run for his car. In seconds he had her in the passenger seat and was headed for the driver's side.

The rain sounded louder from inside the car. Nicole began to shiver. The warm draft of air from the heater was blowing directly onto her feet. She sighed as the warmth began to seep in.

Dominic slid into the seat beside her, then frowned at the bleeding wound on her head and the obvious blood on her sock. The fact that she'd come out in this weather without proper clothing was crazy.

"Nikki...Nikki...what am I going to do with you?"

She grabbed his arm. "Take me down there, Dom. Please. Just get me there."

"Hang on," he said, and stomped the accelerator.

Nicole's panic began to recede. Dominic was here. It was going to be all right after all.

The rhythm of the windshield wipers was almost hypnotic. Dominic drove swiftly, passing a pair of black-and-whites parked at opposite alleys.

Nicole's hands were clenched in her lap as she looked up at the sky.

"Duck. It just had to rain. All we need now is for the rain to turn to snow."

Dominic began braking as he neared the perimeter; he parked near a pair of ambulances before he spoke.

"Duck? Why did you say *duck*?" he asked.

Nicole frowned, then rolled her eyes when she realized what she'd said. "That's not a curse word, is it?"

Dominic grinned. "Close."

She sighed. "It had all the earmarks of one until it came out of my mouth."

Dominic noticed her shivering, as well as the blue tinge to her lips. Without comment, he took the soaked hat from her head and laid it on the dash.

"My hat!" she said, and reached up to cover her head.

"...is wet," Dominic added. "You're wet clear through, your head is bleeding, and so is your damned foot." This his voice softened, as did the look in his eyes. "Nikki...baby...what am I going to do with you?" he asked again.

"Understand me," she said, and grabbed his hand. "I need you to understand me."

It didn't take a genius to figure out the answer.

"Consider it done," he said, and lifted her hand to his lips, kissing the white-edged knuckles, before rubbing them with his hands to get her warm.

Nicole peered through the windshield. They were parked at an angle to the brownstone. She couldn't see the front door, but, through the rain, she saw a boarded-up window on the third floor. The white, red and black gang graffiti on the opposite building confirmed for her that it was the same one she'd seen in her vision.

"She's in that room," she said. "The one with the boarded-up window."

His eyes widened; then he grabbed his cell phone and punched in a call.

"Sanders, it's Tucci. We're on scene. Nicole says the girl is in the third-floor room with the boarded-up window."

Detective Sanders was standing beside a SWAT van when he spun on his heel, quickly scanning the area for Tucci's car. When he saw the woman in the passenger seat beside him, he signaled the SWAT commander, who was about to send in a team. With a few quick words, they readjusted their plan of action.

Nicole held her breath. The building was surrounded by New York's finest, while more officers were going inside. She'd done all she could do. The rest was up to them. She just prayed the kidnappers hadn't done something irrevocable when they noticed the huge police presence on the street.

Benny came running into the apartment. He'd been loading their gear into Wolchek's van when he'd seen all the black-and-whites arriving. There was a brief moment when he'd seriously considered making a run for it on his own and leaving the others to fend for themselves. Then he thought of his cousin, Jeff, and bolted back up the stairs and into the apartment.

"There's cops out there! They found us! I told you we should've made a run for it. I told you. I told all of you."

Wolchek was the closest to the front door. He grabbed Benny and punched him in the mouth without saying a word. Before anyone else could react, he headed for the room where they'd been keeping the girl.

Raul was in shock. How had the cops found them? It must have been his mother. Maybe they'd traced her call. He couldn't believe she would give him up—not even for the million-dollar reward. Then he realized where Wolchek was going.

"Wolchek, leave her be. We've gotta get out of here. I know how to get out of the building without anyone seeing us."

"Not without the girl!" Wolchek yelled, and hit the door with the flat of his hand. It ricocheted against the inside wall with a thud.

Jeff was helping Benny up off the floor as Raul ran for Wolchek, who already had Molly Dane by the arm. She was begging and crying, and there was already a new red mark on her face where Wolchek had obviously struck her. At that moment, Raul had a revelation. He could hear his mother's voice, reminding him of how he'd been raised. He snapped and pulled a knife. The switchblade opened with a small but distinct click, revealing a long, thin blade.

"I said…leave her. She's not worth anything to us anymore, and we're not killing anyone else."

Wolchek took one look at the switchblade and slung Molly against the wall. She slammed into it hard, then fell to the floor.

Raul cursed. "You're a psycho, a damn psycho!"

Wolchek lunged, wrapping his hands around Raul's neck as Raul shoved the switchblade into his old cellmate's belly. Then, for good measure, he pushed, shoving it upward, shoving it deeper.

Wolchek's eyes widened as his grip began to loosen.

"Damn you," he mumbled, then grabbed his belly as his knees gave way and he slumped lifelessly to the floor.

Raul moved past the body without giving it or Molly Dane a second look. Benny and Jeff were waiting for someone to make a decision, so he took control.

"Follow me," he said, running toward the kitchen.

The door to the old dumbwaiter was still there, even though it was no longer in operation. But it was a way into the basement. From there, Raul knew how to get into the sewer system without leaving the building. There was no guarantee they would get away, but they would have a better chance if the cops were occupied with rescuing the kid.

He wouldn't let himself dwell on the fortune they'd

just lost, but it was clear that Molly Dane was of no use to them anymore, and there was sure as hell no point in killing her. If the cops already knew where to find them, that meant they knew who they were, which meant the kid being able to identify them no longer mattered.

As all hell was breaking loose inside, Dominic had Nicole sitting on a gurney in the back of an ambulance. A paramedic named Julio had applied a butterfly bandage to the cut on her head, then taken the wet sock off her foot and begun to swab the cuts with antiseptic.

"You needed stitches," he said, as he cleaned up the mess she'd made of her foot.

She refused to look at Dominic. "So I've been told."

Then, as he began to apply new gauze pads, the sounds around her began to fade. When she heard the sound of rushing wind, she knew it wasn't from the storm.

Suddenly she was inside the building with Molly again.

Molly was hurt.

Nicole could feel her pain, but she didn't know where it was coming from.

"She's been hurt again," she said. "It feels like her back...or maybe her shoulder."

Dominic had been watching the paramedic, but when he realized Nicole was swaying where she sat, he thought she was passing out. It took a few seconds for him to realize that she was "seeing" Molly Dane, instead. Then, when she began to speak, he jumped up beside her to make sure he got everything she was saying.

"Molly's watching them from the doorway. One of them is on the floor. The others are climbing into a small door in the wall. She wants to run, but she's afraid they'll see her. Oh! Wait! They're gone now. She's running for the door. Now she's out in the hallway. She doesn't know which way to go. She hears people coming up the stairs. She can hear their footsteps. She's afraid. She's afraid the men are coming back."

Dominic was on the phone, relaying everything Nicole was saying to Sanders, who had the SWAT commander with him, passing everything on to his men.

When the officers realized she was probably hearing their SWAT team coming up the stairs, and that the perps they were after were on the run, most likely heading for the basement, they rushed up the stairs.

Suddenly, through Molly's eyes, Nicole saw a team of armed men swarming through the door at the end of the hall. One of them was already calling out that they were the police. She felt Molly falter, then run toward them. Only after the first SWAT member had the girl in his arms did Nicole lose contact.

"She's safe," she said, and collapsed.

The minute the paramedic finished bandaging Nikki's foot, Dom quickly got her out of the way.

"They'll be coming out with the child any minute," he said, then carried Nicole back to the car.

The emergency personnel began to shuffle, preparing for the unexpected.

Police were swarming the basement. Within minutes, they found an opening into the sewers and a second SWAT team went in.

In the car, Dominic's phone began to ring.

It was Sanders. "They've got the girl. She's alert and asking for her mother. One of the perps was dead when we found him. We caught the others in the sewers."

"Good work," Dominic said. "Thanks for the call."

Sanders hesitated, then added in a lower tone of voice, "Yeah, well, tell your lady friend that we appreciate the help."

"I'll do that," Dominic said, and then dropped the phone in his pocket before turning to Nicole. "It's over, Nikki, and Sanders says thanks."

Nicole was weak with relief. "Thank you, God."

"Come on, baby…it's time you went home."

Nicole leaned against the seat and closed her eyes.

The rain stopped a few minutes before they reached the apartment. The sharp blast of wind cut through her wet clothes as Dominic helped her out of the car. By the time they got to the elevator, she was shivering again.

"God. You're going to be sick," Dominic said, as he pulled her close.

"No, I'm not," she said.

He didn't bother to argue. The proof would be in how she felt after he got her into a hot bath and then to bed.

Once inside the apartment, he put her bandaged foot into a plastic bag, then taped it around her leg before lowering her into a tub of hot water.

"Prop your foot on the side of the tub, Nikki. I'll be in the other room. Call me when you're through, and I'll help you get out."

She was too cold and tired to argue. With a sigh, she sank into the depths of the claw-foot tub and didn't stop until the water was at the edge of her ear-lobes. With no hair to get wet, she let herself relax.

"There's something to be said for bald heads after all," she muttered, as the water lapped at the back of her neck.

Dominic started the coffeepot, then went back to her bedroom. He stood in the doorway, staring blindly at her things, noting the slightly obsessive way she had of matching her clothes as they hung in the closet, and sorting shoes by color rather than by use. There was a pair of white tennis shoes sitting right next to a pair of white summer sandals and a pair of white fuzzy house shoes.

He looked at them for a few moments, then felt his knees give way. He dropped to the side of her bed with a thump and started to shake. Her phone call had scared him, but not as much as the sight of her on that street, standing in her own blood and struggling with a cop who was trying to handcuff her.

He swiped his hands across his face, then looked toward the bathroom door. The woman he loved more than life was behind it. She was still a little bit hurt and very fragile. This thing that had happened to her was unsettling, but he wasn't horrified by it as much as he was in awe. There was no doubt that she'd been on target with the kidnapping from day one. He didn't know if this gift would stay with her after she was healed, but he did know that it didn't change a thing. Not for him.

He reached into his pocket for the small velvet box he'd been carrying around all day. He'd meant to take her out to dinner tonight and make an occasion out of his proposal of marriage. But now, all he could do was be grateful she would be going to bed in one piece.

Minutes passed. He sat without moving, waiting for her to call. Finally her sweet but weary voice broke the silence.

"Dominic…honey…can you come help me out now?"

His hands were steady as he stood. The box with the engagement ring was hidden beneath her pillow.

He had her out, dressed and sitting on the edge of the bed within minutes. As she slid between the covers, then laid her head on the pillow, Dominic realized he was holding his breath.

Nicole looked up at him. Such a beautiful man. Shoulders so wide. Eyes so dark. Then she looked—really looked—into his eyes, and her heart skipped a beat.

He had a secret.

She sat back up.

"What do you know that I don't?" she asked.

She looked so young, with her hair gone and her face completely devoid of makeup. But there was passion in her. So much passion. He wanted it. He wanted *her*.

"You're not much of a psychic or you wouldn't be asking me that," he said.

"Dominic...don't play with—" Her eyes widened; then she rolled over and thrust her hand beneath the pillow. The look on her face was priceless when she pulled out the box.

To his credit, Dominic showed none of the shock he was feeling. God in heaven...she was the real deal.

"Oh, Dom..."

He took the box from her hand, then opened it and took out the ring.

"This was supposed to have happened over steak and champagne."

Nicole's vision blurred. "Oh, Dom."

He grinned. "You already said that."

She stifled a sob and held out her hand.

"Wait," he said. "I need to do this right."

He got down on his knees. "This isn't meant to appear as if I'm begging or anything, but I love you so much. I can't even see my life without you in it. Please...say that you'll marry me."

She swung her legs over the side of the bed and hugged him fiercely.

"Yes, yes, a thousand times, yes."

He slipped the ring onto her finger.

"Here's to forever," he said softly, then leaned forward and sealed the deal with a kiss.

Epilogue

One year later

Searchlights were sweeping the dark, choppy waters of the Hudson River as the Port Authority police cruised around the floating debris from the commuter jet that had crashed into the water less than an hour ago. With the plane completely submerged except for the tip of one wing and most of the tail portion, they were frantically scanning the surface for possible survivors. So far, the only bodies to come out of the Hudson had been lifeless.

A slim woman with dark, curly hair stood near the edge of one pier, staring blindly into the darkness. The man beside her was on the phone, repeating the short, staccato sentences coming out of the woman's mouth.

"She says there's a survivor. He's in the tail section of the plane and treading water. He tried twice to find his way out and nearly drowned both times. You have to hurry. Hypothermia is setting in."

Within seconds, they watched as men in wet suits went over the side of one of the search boats and slipped beneath the dark water.

Motionless, Nicole felt the trapped survivor's fear, but had no way to assure him that help was on the way, even though she was in his head, sharing the darkness with him. It wasn't until the man saw the divers' search-lights begin cutting through the water around him that she felt his relief and thanksgiving.

She went limp.

Dominic had been waiting for it. It was the sign that told him it was over. He slid an arm across her shoulders to remind her that he was there if she needed him. When she leaned against him, he gave her arm a squeeze.

"They found him. It's over," she said.

"Is it safe to go home now?"

She nodded. Concern was in Dom's voice—compassion in his eyes. But it was his confidence in her that mattered most.

"Yes. We can go home now."

He took her by the hand, and together they walked toward the car, moving past all the dozens of police and emergency vehicles.

As they got inside, Nicole reached for her seat belt, then paused, watching as her husband slid behind the wheel. His dark hair was windblown, his eyes red-rimmed, and he was as weary looking as she felt. But then their gazes met. When he winked and smiled, she smiled back.

"If you're a real good girl, I've got a surprise waiting for you at home."

Nicole laughed out loud. "I'm always good."

He grinned. "No. You're outstanding. However, I am not talking about sex."

"But I was."

"Good," Dominic said. "Then you won't be disappointed by the surprise."

She closed her eyes as he drove away from the scene. The farther away he drove, the lighter her heart became. Distancing herself from despair was part of the separation she needed to gain control of her own thoughts.

Her life was strange now, but as Dominic reminded her on a daily basis, it didn't matter. If they had to interrupt their lives now and then to help someone in danger, then so be it.

It was a quarter to three in the morning when they got back to the apartment. Dominic unlocked the door, then surprised Nicole by picking her up and carrying her inside.

She leaned her head against his chest as he carried her into the bedroom, then sat her down on the side of the bed.

"Ooh, it feels good to be home," she said, as she began to kick off her shoes.

When she looked up, Dominic was at the bureau. As he turned around, she saw something in his hand.

"What's that?" she asked, as he sat down beside her.

He was holding a long silver chain.

"Tomorrow is our anniversary, but I thought, considering everything that was going on…"

She held out her hand as he dropped the silver chain into her palm and she saw the charm on the necklace. When she realized what it was, her vision blurred.

"Oh, Dominic, it's perfect."

She looked up at him, smiling through tears.

He smiled, pleased that he'd actually surprised her.

"The way I figured it, every little witch needs a crystal ball."

"So I'm a witch, am I?"

"Yes. But you're my witch," he added.

Suddenly she stood up and began stripping off her clothes until she was standing naked before him. She gave him a slow, sultry glance, handed him the necklace, then turned her back.

"Would you please put it on me?"

Dominic's concentration had shattered when she'd begun taking off her clothes. Now she wanted him to maneuver something this delicate when his damn fingers all felt like thumbs?

The small silver-and-crystal charm was cold

between her breasts as she turned around and pretended to stare into the tiny crystal ball.

"I foresee a long session of passionate sex," she said.

"Thanks for the warning. Now I know what to expect," he said, as he laid her in the bed, then began taking off his clothes.

Nicole rose up on her elbow to watch, the small crystal ball dangling between her breasts.

"You're wrong, my love," Nicole said softly. "You have no idea of what's coming."

Dominic laughed out loud as he fell into bed beside her, then in one swoop, covered her body with his own.

"That's okay, my little witch. I always did like surprises."

* * * * *

AFTER THE LIGHTNING

JANIS REAMS HUDSON

Dear Reader,

Did you ever get stuck in a rut for so long that it became comfortable? You know, that same ol' route to work, while you nag about the bad road, when another road will take you there, a better road. It's just not your road, so you forget about it?

Or perhaps the same meals each successive week. My mother did that. Monday night was tacos. The only kind we had in town that year were the frozen kind. Hmm. Yum. Sunday was roast beef. That was good. Thankfully I've forgotten the rest. Not that they weren't good, but the same ones for each night of the week, over and over for ten years...

I'm not griping about my mother, though. She worked two jobs to put that food on the table. Not all people have a good mother or an available alternate route. Some of us just have to stand and face the winds of life on our own and drive that same old route while we look for something better. Eat that taco Monday. But along the way, if life pushes you into the path of someone special, slow down. Reach out and offer a hand if they need help, or ask for help if *you* do.

In my story, lifelong bonds are formed when people stop to help each other – a girl struck by lightning, an investigator on the trail of a bad guy, plus a missing child whose mother is in a coma. Well, her body is. But since lightning has turned our heroine into a receptor of sorts, things get interesting. Hope you enjoy my story. And if you do, please tell two friends.

Happy reading,

Janis Reams Hudson

Janis Reams Hudson is a prolific author of more than thirty-five novels, both contemporary and historical romances. Her titles have appeared on the bestseller lists of Waldenbooks, B Dalton and BookRak, and have earned numerous awards, including a Reviewer's Choice award from *Romantic Times BOOKreviews* and National Reader's Choice Award. She's a three-time finalist for the Romance Writers of America's coveted RITA® Award, and is a past president of that ten-thousand-member organisation.

Dedicated to Sharon, for nursing me through this story.
And Deb, the third sister in this deal.

Chapter 1

One minute she was jogging along, two blocks from home, enjoying the outdoors, the sunshine, the strong wind. Then suddenly, every hair on her body stood on end and the air exploded around her. The smell of sulphur nearly knocked her over, and a giant fist struck her in the chest and lifted her off the ground.

After that, Hailey Cameron didn't know anything until she found herself lying flat on her back staring up at fluorescent lighting while two nurses and a doctor poked and prodded her. This time it was the smell of antiseptic that stung her eyes and nose.

"Honey, you must be the luckiest girl on earth."

"Wha...?" She tried to ask what had happened,

where she was, how had she gotten here, why her skin was tingling, could she have a drink of water, *what day is it?* But her voice wouldn't work. Her fingers and toes seemed to move okay, but she couldn't decide if what she felt overall was a dull ache or numbness or out-and-out pain. She felt vaguely as if she'd been run over by a truck. Twice.

"You just rest now, and lie still," the nurse ordered. "You're in Baton Rouge Hospital. Can you tell me your name?"

"Why?" Hailey managed.

"You got struck by lightning."

"What?" Hailey struggled against the hands that held her down.

"Easy, now. Stop that. Can you tell me your name?" the nurse repeated.

"Hailey." She paused and licked her lips. "Hailey Cameron." She chose that moment to glance down. "Yikes! Why am I naked?"

"Relax, relax. Here." The nurse covered Hailey with a sheet. "That's better. We had to cut off what was left of your clothes to check you for injuries."

"Cut them?" Hailey's voice was coming back, and her brain was clearing rapidly. "You cut up my clothes? Am I supposed to go home naked?"

"You're not supposed to go home at all," the nurse announced. "Not until tomorrow. We don't get all that many lightning strike victims. The doctor wants to keep you overnight for observation. And no, we won't send you home naked. There wasn't enough left of your clothes, anyway. The lightning shredded them."

Hailey was so out of it that it took her a minute to grasp everything that had happened, especially that the doctor and nurses meant for her to spend the night in the hospital. She tried to gather enough strength to protest but found she'd used all her energy already. The few words she'd managed had drained her. She gave up the effort and dozed.

They woke her sometime later to tell her to lie still for a CT scan of her brain.

Then there were the X rays, blood tests, ECG and heaven knew what else.

She woke again in the middle of being transferred from gurney to bed in a semiprivate room. Room 312, they told her. Was she supposed to care about the room number?

The nurses tried repeatedly to get her oxygen to work, but no matter what they did, nothing came from the connection in the wall above her bed. No stream of oxygen, not even a puff.

"Stupid thing," one nurse muttered. "Terry," she said to the orderly, "see if there's a concentrator in the supply closet down the hall. Not to worry." She smiled at Hailey. "We'll get you all fixed up in no time."

Hailey could still feel a slight tingle along her skin. It might have been pleasant, but it was lasting way too long. To take her mind off it, she glanced around the room. Plain white walls, one window with white miniblinds, a white curtain ready to pull between her bed and the next one.

"Who's that?" she asked, nodding toward the woman in the other bed. "What's wrong with her?"

"That's LaShonda Martin. Bless her heart, she was in that apartment building that was hit by the tornado last night."

"Ouch," Hailey said in sympathy. "Sorry to hear about your troubles," she said, louder, so her roommate could hear her. "I'm Hailey."

"Talk all you want, *cher*." The nurse hung the IV from the bag holder beside Hailey's bed. "She can't answer. We've got her in a drug-induced coma until some of her injuries heal and she's over the worst of the pain. Ah, here we go."

The orderly wheeled in a machine that stood about as tall as Hailey's bed and was about eighteen inches wide. He and the nurse fiddled with filters that looked like thin sponges, a humidifier for distilled water and a clear hose that connected to the tube running into Hailey's nose.

"Oxygen?" she asked.

"Yes, ma'am. When we turn it on it will suck in air from the room. It will filter out all the nitrogen and impurities until all that's left for you to breathe is pure oxygen."

The nurse pushed the on switch, but nothing happened. She and the orderly fussed over the power cord.

Hailey swallowed and tuned out their voices. Her gaze trailed over to her roommate. If that tornado had touched down a mile sooner, that could be her in a coma in that bed by the window. "Is she in pain?"

"If she is," the nurse said, "she doesn't know it, so I guess she's not."

In the next bed, LaShonda Joy Martin tried to scream in frustration, but all she managed was a pitiful whimper she knew no one could hear.

Something was wrong. A lot of things were wrong, the biggest being that her son was missing. How could she find him if she was trapped in this ever-lovin' coma? Yet, if she was in a coma, why could she hear and see everything around her? With her eyes closed. Why did she feel like she was floating in and out of her body, like gravity was letting go of her? If a good stiff wind blew through the room, she would be swept away from her body and right on out the door.

She wondered what they were talking about over there at the other bed. Could one of them find her baby boy?

She tried to raise her head, but it wobbled, then flopped down. *Come on, dammit.* She tried again with all her might, until finally she managed to sit up far enough that she could see the foot of her bed. She turned her head and saw the nurse, the orderly and her new roommate. And from the corner of her eye, she saw herself, lying on the bed.

Her heart leapt into her throat. How could she be

lying down and sitting up at the same time? From her head to her toes, she started to shake. She shook hard enough to vibrate the bed. But the bed did not move. Not even the sheets moved.

From that odd machine the orderly had wheeled in a few minutes earlier came a long, loud beep. The air began to stir. The wind tugged on her. She grabbed the sheet to hold on, but when she closed her fist, there was no sheet in it. What was happening?

No matter how hard she tried to stay put, she was no match for the air current sweeping the room. She was being pulled inexplicably toward that noisy machine. But her body remained motionless on the bed.

A sudden swirl of air literally sucked her away. She screamed. No one heard her.

Like a heat-seeking missile, she shot headfirst into the air intake valve of the oxygen concentrator. She waited for the pain, waited to feel her flesh being peeled from her bones. But her body still lay on the bed behind her. She felt no pain at all. Only sheer terror as she was sucked through one filter after another, then up through a series of clear plastic tubes and…up her roommate's *nose*?

Oh, my God.

The voice echoed inside Hailey's head, sounding utterly miserable.

"How can she talk if she's in a coma?" Hailey asked.

"Who?" the nurse asked, distracted, as she straightened a tube.

"Her," Hailey said. "LaShonda."

The nurse double checked the IV in Hailey's hand. "She can't talk, remember? She's in a coma. She must have moaned."

Hailey eyed the nurse warily. "So how come I hear her voice?"

Slowly, the nurse asked, "You're hearing voices?"

"Only one. Hers, I think."

A tearful voice rang inside Hailey's head. *You think? You* think? *Who else's voice could it be but mine? I'm LaShonda Joy Martin. I'm right here in your head, and I'm not going anywhere 'til you help me find my baby.*

Hailey stared at the nurse. "You're telling me you didn't hear that?"

"Hear what?"

"Oh, brother," Hailey muttered. "Am I losing my mind?"

"I doubt it," the nurse said easily. "I'll talk to your doctor, but it's probably just some temporary leftover electrical mix-up in your brain from the lightning."

The nurse patted her on the arm, then left the room, leaving Hailey alone. Sort of.

You gotta help me, the voice said.

"Says who? You're an electrical impulse in my brain," Hailey said firmly. "I don't have to help an electrical impulse."

I'm not any ol' impulse. I'm LaShonda Martin.

"LaShonda Martin is in a coma. I'm staring at her right now."

Yeah. Somebody oughta comb my hair for me. Damn. The latter came out in a deep-South two-syllable way, as day-*yum.*

"Your lips aren't moving," Hailey accused. "If I can hear your voice, why don't I see your lips move?"

Because I'm in a coma.

"I rest my case," Hailey said. "If you're in a coma, you can't be talking."

A loud sigh echoed in Hailey's brain. *Look. My body is—*

A dark arm—too dark for a simple tan—pointed toward LaShonda's bed, and Hailey screamed, because both of her own arms—her own tanned but definitely Caucasian arms—were still lying at her sides.

Day-yum, white girl, hold it down, will ya? You nearly scared me to death.

"Me? Scare you? I've suddenly sprouted a third arm. What the hell is going on? How did you get in my head?"

Don't you yell at me. It isn't my fault I'm stuck in here like a sardine in a can. I was just lying there minding my own business, trying to stay in my body, but I kept floating up and out, ya know?

"No, I don't know. You mean you died?"

No, I didn't die. Look at those machines, all beeping just like they're supposed to. I'm alive. But while my body's in a coma, I guess the rest of me isn't. When they turned on your oxygen machine I got sucked in, right through the filter and that skinny little tube, and

*straight up your dainty white nose. You ain't lived 'til
you've been up inside somebody else's nose, let me tell
you. It's not something I ever wanna do again, that's
for sure.*

"Well, then, get out," Hailey demanded.

The voice was silent for several long moments.

"Hey." Hailey felt stupid and self-conscious talking
to someone who wasn't there. "LaShonda? Did you
leave?"

You told me to.

"Yes, but did you?"

There was a distinct sniff, then, *I don't know how.*

"What do you mean, you don't know how?"

I mean, I don't know how to leave, LaShonda said,
sounding very much as if she thought she was talking
to an idiot.

"Why don't I blow my nose?" Hailey asked tersely.
"Maybe you'll end up in my tissue."

Oooh, gross. LaShonda made a gagging noise.

Out in the hallway, Aaron Trent, a special investigator for the District Attorney, folded his arms and
leaned against the wall, waiting for the woman in
Room 312 to finish her phone conversation. From the
sound of things, she and whomever she was talking to
were not getting along.

After nearly ten minutes, he was getting antsy.
Somebody was going to call security on him for loi-
tering if he had to hang around out there much longer.

Finally he approached the open door and leaned in…only to find, to his surprise, that the woman he'd been listening to all this time was not on the phone. She couldn't even reach the phone from where she lay. She was talking to herself.

That fact took him so much by surprise that he must have made a sound, and he failed to duck back out of sight before she spotted him.

His brothers and sisters would give him holy hell for hanging around and waiting on a woman who spoke to herself. His grandmother would thoroughly enjoy the idea.

Not that he planned to tell any of them. He would never live it down. He took a deep breath, walked in and gripped the foot of the bedframe.

"Hi," he offered with a smile.

She frowned. "Don't tell me you're another doctor."

"Okay, I won't tell you." She looked a little ragged, but not nearly as ragged as he'd imagined someone recently struck by lightning might look.

"Who are you?" she asked.

"Aaron Trent. I'm a special investigator with the district attorney's office." He flashed his badge, then tucked it away. "You're Hailey Cameron, the woman who was struck by lightning this afternoon, right?"

"Unless there's someone else around here with singed hair and shredded clothes."

He narrowed his eyes with interest. *Shredded clothes? So does that mean you're—*

She stared right back at him. "Don't be ordinary, Mr. Trent."

Aaron straightened in surprise. He knew he hadn't spoken aloud. Had she read his mind? Regardless, he'd learned long ago from the women in his family that if a man was in doubt, the best course was to apologize. It didn't matter if he'd done anything wrong or not; he just needed to apologize. He gave Hailey a short bow. "My apologies."

Her gaze sharpened. "For what?"

"For being ordinary?"

"Nice save. What do you want with the woman who got hit by lightning?"

"I'm actually looking for the woman who lives in the white house on the corner of the street you were on when the lightning struck you. I understand you run the same route past that house nearly every day. Maybe you've seen her lately? She's elderly, stooped shoulders, white hair."

"You seem to know a lot about her...and me."

"That's my job, finding out information. Do you know the woman I'm talking about?"

"Mrs. Shelton?"

Aaron felt the tension between his shoulder blades ease. "So you know her."

"I do. I've missed her lately, though. Haven't seen her around. Is she all right?"

Damn. He'd been hoping... "I'd know more about that if I could find her. How well do you know her?"

"She likes to interrupt my jogging by standing on her porch with a glass of iced tea or lemonade for me, with enough sweat dripping off the glass to make me beg. Gets me every time. I can't imagine she's done something to warrant the D.A. sending out a special investigator."

"Ah, no. I just have a few questions for her. I'm trying to find her nephew. I was hoping she could help me."

She shrugged, then twitched, as if she'd been slapped, or maybe poked. "Maybe you could help a, uh, friend of mine. Help us find her little boy."

That was just about the last question he'd expected her to ask. He was no expert on finding missing children, but wasn't it the same as finding the bad guys who took them? He could find bad guys. He was good at that. He'd done it as a cop, and he was still doing it. He was after one right now.

"What happened to the kid?" Aaron asked Hailey.

She had a way of tilting her head before speaking, as if thinking over her words before opening her mouth. Or perhaps listening to some inner voice before she spoke. It was an odd habit, but her smile was so distracting that he might not have noticed the way her gaze turned inward if he weren't a trained observer. And if he didn't have Claudia Jean Trent for his grandmother.

"The tornado," Hailey said.

"The tornado took him? Somebody must have found him by now," Aaron stated. "When was he reported missing?"

"Not the tornado, *after* the tornado. He never got reported missing until now because I—" She stopped and swallowed. "Because his mother has been in a coma since they brought her to the hospital." She waved her arm toward the other bed.

"She's the boy's mother?"

"That's right. LaShonda Joy. Martin. LaShonda Joy Martin."

"She and the boy—"

"Keenan. Keenan Martin. Four years old. And beautiful." Emotion made her voice wobble.

"They lived in that apartment complex that got hit last night?"

"Yes. But they came through the tornado fine," she said in a rush. "There was plenty of damage to their unit, but they rode it out in the bathtub with a mattress on top of them." She paused again.

"And…?" he prodded.

"And…a man came and pulled the rubble off of them. He took Keenan and said he would get him out of there before anything else fell down on them, and then he'd come back for LaShonda. He was only going to the street, so she thought it was okay."

"Did the guy come back for her?"

"We assume he did."

"Assume?"

She nodded. "Someone beat the daylights out of her. I'm told it took the surgeons all night to put her face and skull back together. They're keeping her in a drug-induced coma for now to help her heal better. When she wakes up, the first thing she's going to ask for is her son. I have to find him, but I have no idea what to do, other than go to the police."

"That's exactly what you *should* do. It's been, what, around eighteen hours since the kid went missing? That's an eternity in cases like this. When will you be able to get out of here?"

She made a face. "Tomorrow."

Aaron didn't recall making a conscious decision; the words came out of his mouth all on their own. "I'll take care of getting the police started today."

It was a no-brainer, really, on more than one level. There was the personal man-woman level that would have had him licking her boots if she'd asked. On the cop level, there was a scary similarity to the case he was currently working on, which involved children stolen from their families and sold into slavery, mostly overseas.

How convenient was it that he'd come here seeking information about that child-stealing creep Charlie Howard and run into a woman whose child was missing?

Aaron didn't believe in coincidence, not when it came to chasing after bad guys. Even if the missing child in this case had nothing to do with Charlie, there was a reason why he'd been brought to this room, to this woman. At some point that reason would become clear. Meanwhile, he wanted to help find the boy. He could get the investigation started today.

"Can you? Really? Oh, thank you, Aaron."

The way her smile lit her eyes made him want to lap her up, one long stroke of his tongue at a time.

"LaShonda," Hailey continued, "will be so grateful."

Aaron wanted to ask if *she* would be grateful, too, but he swallowed the words. It was definitely too soon to make an ass of himself. Especially when she was holding something back.

"What aren't you telling me?" he asked her.

Her brow wrinkled. "What do you mean?"

"I mean," he said in his lead-'em-where-you-want-'em-to-go voice, "the man took the boy away, and then she was in the hospital having her face put back together. Why did she only assume the man came back?"

"Why?"

"Yes, why?" he asked.

She made a low growling sound somewhere deep in her throat. "Why? Why…because…because she… When she came to for a few minutes in the hospital, the last thing she remembered, she was uninjured and the man was taking Keenan away. She had no memory of getting the crap beaten out of her, yet when rescue workers found her, she had two broken arms, a broken leg, and Lord knows how many head injuries. We hope when they bring her out of the coma that she'll be able to describe what the man looked like, because he seems like a logical suspect, don't you think?"

Aaron nodded and mulled over everything Hailey

had told him. On the surface, it sounded credible. Why, then, did he still feel as if she were leaving something out? Something important.

Chapter 2

The next morning, Hailey woke with a groan. She heard a deep, loud groan inside her head, along with a soft *day-yum*.

Oh, hell. "LaShonda." Hailey blinked her eyes open. "You're still here."

Where else you think I'd be, girlfriend?

Hailey stared grimly at the woman in the next bed. LaShonda's lips did *not* move when she spoke. "Back in your own body. Would that be too much to ask?"

You think I like being stuck inside a white girl? Not on your life, sister. But I'm here, so you're all I've got to help me find Keenan. You still gonna help me?

"I talked to Aaron about it yesterday, didn't I?"

Ah yes, Aaron. He looked like a keeper to me, LaShonda said. *You think he'll really help you?*

"Us. I think he'll help *us.* But either way, when I leave here today, I'm going straight to the police to report Keenan being kidnapped."

LaShonda gasped. *I've tried not to think that word, but he was, wasn't he? Kidnapped.*

"If that man took him like you said he did, then yeah, I'd say *kidnapped* is the word," Hailey said. "We need to figure out how to get you back into your body."

Good luck with that. You think I haven't been trying all night? It seems like the harder I try to move, the more frozen in place I become.

Hailey would have asked a dozen questions, made a hundred suggestions and at least one demand—get out of my head—but just then a cheerful teenager in a candy-striper smock brought in a breakfast tray. Before the girl made it back out the door, a nurse arrived with a sickeningly cheerful "Good morning," singing it out as though it were her own personal morning anthem as she took Hailey's blood pressure, pulse and temperature.

Hailey was relieved to find out that her vital signs were normal. She felt a little stiff and achy—okay, maybe a lot stiff and achy—but otherwise fine. Her mind was certainly clearer than it had been yesterday.

It was nearly noon before things fell together. She was eager to go home, dressed in the borrowed scrubs the nurses provided, and ready for the required wheelchair to carry her to the front door of the hospital. She reached for the phone beside her bed to call for a taxi, but Aaron Trent walked in before she could finish dialing.

She hung up and greeted him.

"What are you doing here again?" she asked, smiling at him, amazed at the way her pulse spiked when he smiled back.

"Thought I'd offer you a ride home."

"You don't have to do that."

"No, but on the drive to your place I can tell you about the file I got them to open for the kid, Keenan."

"Oh, Aaron, thank you." Inside her head, LaShonda practically wept with joy.

The door swung open, and the doctor entered with a large X ray in one hand. He glanced at the wheelchair, then at Hailey. "Oh, no, don't think you get to leave us this soon."

"I thought you said I was fine," Hailey protested.

"I said you *seem* fine, but there was a shadow on that last head X ray we took this morning, so we need to get a new shot to make sure."

"A shadow?" Hailey's mouth turned to cotton. "On my X ray?"

"Yes, ma'am."

She realized with a frown that he had yet to look her in the eye. She could have blood gushing from her head and he wouldn't have noticed. "Doctor?"

"Mmm?" he replied, still distracted.

Hailey glanced at Aaron, who was also frowning at the doctor.

"Humph," he said. "If I didn't know any better, I'd swear that we double-exposed your film—which, now that we're digital, just doesn't happen—or you had a friend in there with you."

Jeeze Louise, Hailey thought. Had some out-of-body form of LaShonda shown up in the X ray?

"LaShonda Joy," Hailey chided the unconscious woman in the next bed, "have you been playing around in my X rays?"

The doctor, who looked as if he might have started shaving sometime during the past six months, laughed. "I guess it did sound a little crazy. Come on, Ms. Cameron, let's get a new picture of your head.

The orderly turned Hailey's wheelchair toward the door and pushed her forward.

Hailey looked back at Aaron. "Do you have time to wait? I'd really like to talk to you."

"I'm in no hurry," he said. "I'll wait here while you get your picture taken. Smile and say *lightning*."

While Hailey got her follow-up head X ray, she tried to think of a legitimate reason to send Aaron on his way and call for a cab to take her home.

So why was she searching for an excuse to turn down his offer of a ride home, when she wanted very much to accept it? Since she had asked him to wait for her, to help her find Keenan.

She wanted to tell herself that she had only asked because she needed his help. But she knew better. Above and beyond that perfectly legitimate reason, she just flat-out wanted to spend time with him. Wanted it so badly that it tugged hard and deep inside her, taking her by surprise with its strength.

Must be a leftover side effect of the lightning, she thought. That bolt of electricity had left her off balance. That was her story, and she was sticking to it.

The new X rays—they took two, just in case—came out clear, so Hailey and Aaron were soon on their way. Halfway to her apartment Hailey thought to ask, "How do you know where I live?"

"Hey, I'm a detective, remember?"

"Oh. Yeah."

LaShonda laughed inside Hailey's head. *He's gotcha there, white girl.*

"Shut up," Hailey muttered.

"Pardon?" Aaron asked with a frown.

"Sorry. I was talking to myself."

"You seem to do that a lot."

"I do?"

"You remind me of my grandmother."

Feigning outrage, Hailey slapped him on the shoulder with the paperwork the hospital had given her when she checked out. "Are you saying I look like—" She realized that she hadn't looked in a mirror since she'd left her house the day before to go jogging.

Considering that she felt as if she'd been run over by a semi, she probably looked as if she had been, too. "Never mind."

Aaron chuckled. "I didn't mean you look like my grandmother, I meant you act like her. She talks to herself, too. At least, that's what it looks like, but she swears she's talking to ghosts, that she can see them, hear them."

Hailey glanced at him from the corner of her eye. "Ghosts?"

"The dearly departed. Earthbound spirits. Whatever you want to call dead people who hang around instead of going off to their great reward or whatever."

"And you let her walk around on her own? When did she have her breakdown?" Hailey was nearer and nearer her own breakdown by the minute.

Aaron laughed. "Wait 'til you meet her. She's sharp as a tack and saner than most people you'll ever know."

Block by block, they drew closer to Hailey's apartment. When they arrived, he parked on the street in front of her building. The 1840s redbrick structure was split into eight apartments, four upstairs, four down. Fortunately the plumbing and electricity were much newer than the building itself.

"Nice place," Aaron told her.

"I like it. The owners live downstairs, so they spend the time and money to keep things in good condition, especially on the outside, but they're pretty good with indoor repairs, too." *Listen to me, rattling on like an* idiot, she thought. Maybe I really am losing it. "Thanks for the ride home."

"You're welcome."

Hailey placed her hand on the door handle and looked over at him. LaShonda had been right—he looked like a keeper, with his dark brown hair and eyes, that sharp jawline, those taut cheekbones. Not to mention lips that looked designed for kissing.

She swallowed and looked away. "I'd invite you up for a drink or a snack, but truth be told, I'm still pretty much out of it."

"Of course you are," he said.

"Tell your grandmother hello for me," she added.

"I'll be glad to. But it's my grand*father*," he said, as he exited the car, "who used to say that a gentleman always walks a lady to her door."

Hailey got out and stood on the sidewalk while he walked around the car to join her. "He did?" she asked.

"He did. Always," he said. "Every time. No excuses."

Hailey bit back a smile. "Am I to assume that you learned this lesson?"

"Since we're halfway to your door, that would probably be a safe assumption."

It had been a long time since a man had walked Hailey to her door. A long time since she had allowed one to. A long time since the possibility had even arisen. The series of losers she'd dated during the past couple of years had all but ground her interest in the opposite sex into dust.

But at the moment she didn't feel like saying no to this particular man.

She didn't know whether to be thrilled at the idea or run screaming in the opposite direction.

He walked beside her up the sidewalk and stood back while she unlocked the front door.

She turned to thank him and say goodbye but never got the chance.

"After you," he said. "Which unit is yours?" At her enquiring look he added, "*This* is not your door."

"Two-A." She led the way up the wide staircase to the second floor. With every aching step, she wished she'd taken the elevator. So much for trying to look fit.

At her front corner apartment, she once again unlocked the door and stepped inside, then turned again to thank Aaron but stopped abruptly.

At the hospital, she'd known she probably looked like death warmed over, so she hadn't dared to look in a mirror. The scrubs, for which she was admittedly grateful, were a singularly unflattering shade of baby-puke green.

Her recovery time, she'd told herself, would be that much faster if she didn't see firsthand how washed-out she looked. Ignorance, they said, was bliss.

Until it came back and slapped you in the face, which was what it felt like when she accidently caught a glimpse of her reflection in the wall mirror next to the door. The sight that greeted her stopped her heart, then drew a scream from her throat. That was *not* her face in the mirror.

Well, it *was* her face, but it was also LaShonda Martin's face, like a transparent mask laid over Hailey's own.

Both faces, and both voices, screamed.

Aaron's training and instincts shot into action. He jumped in front of Hailey and placed himself between her and whatever danger had terrified her into screaming. In less than a second he had his gun out and aimed at…the mirror? The wall?

"What the hell's going on?" he demanded. He could see every square inch of the entry from where he stood. There was no one there but Hailey and himself. Two steps gave him a complete view of the kitchen, dinette, and living room to his left. Three steps to his right he found a bathroom, then a bedroom. He finished by checking the closets and under the bed. There was not another soul in the place.

"Hailey?" he asked, his heart still thundering.

"I'm sorry." She pressed a hand to her chest. "I was just surprised."

"By what? You sounded like you'd been surprised by your friendly neighborhood axe murderer."

"Oh, come on." She reached deep inside herself for control. "The way I look right now, I'm surprised you and everyone else haven't screamed on sight of me."

He narrowed his gaze and studied her. He looked at her so long that she found herself shifting beneath his stare.

"Was that the first time you've looked in a mirror?"

"Since I got fried? Yes. I'm a mess."

Aaron holstered his weapon, then propped his fists on his hips. "I don't think so."

"I beg your pardon?"

"No matter how good you're used to looking, the way you look right now isn't near bad enough to make you scream like you've just seen a giant wart on the end of your nose. Besides, I don't see you as being vain enough to care that much about your looks. So I ask again, what on earth scared you half to death?"

Hailey took a slow, deep breath.

LaShonda snickered. *Yeah, and don't think I'm not insulted that you'd take one look at me and scream.*

"Shut up," Hailey muttered.

Aaron threw both hands in the air. "Fine. I'll be back in an hour—"

"No," she told him. "I'm sorry. I wasn't talking to you."

"You weren't telling me to shut up?"

"No. As for the screaming, the fact is, I *am* that vain."

"If you weren't telling me to shut up, who were you talking to?"

To a woman who's in a coma back in the hospital, she answered silently. Like he would believe that. *She* didn't believe it, and it was happening to her.

Tell him, LaShonda dared her. *Tell him the truth and see what he's made of. Go on, I dare you.*

"I was talking to this stupid voice I keep hearing in my head," Hailey said.

"Yeah? That's the second time you've told that little voice, the one only you can hear, to shut up since we left the hospital."

"That's because that little voice in my head talks too much."

Hey, white girl, I resent that.

"At the risk of sounding like a broken record," Hailey muttered, "shut up."

"There you go again," Aaron said.

"I'm going to take a shower."

"I'll be back in about an hour to take you to the police station."

"Fine. I assume that's to find a missing child and not to have me arrested for talking to myself."

"I don't think that's against the law."

Before he could blink, Aaron found himself outside her closed door. He tried to recall if he'd ever been put out of a woman's home so gently yet firmly, but, no, he decided this was a first for him. Hailey Cameron was a first for him.

Not the voices she heard. Women who heard voices of people who weren't there were nothing new to him. But a woman who had him volunteering to haul her around town without even hinting she might enjoy the ride, a woman who didn't seem to care one way or the other if she ever saw him again, and still he volunteered? Very definitely something new.

Chapter 3

"We have an errand to run before we go to the police station," Hailey told him when he returned to pick her up and they were back in his car, pulling away from the curb.

"We do?" Aaron asked.

"Yes. We need to go by LaShonda's apartment and find a picture of Keenan for the cops."

Aaron scowled at her.

"What's wrong?" she asked.

"Nothing." He huffed out a breath of disgust. "I should have thought of that myself."

Most of the tornado damage at the two-story Willow Crossing apartment complex—where LaShonda and one hundred and twenty-seven of her nearest neighbors resided—was confined, structurally speaking, to the upper floor.

Streets in the neighborhood were still blocked off due to downed trees, limbs and other debris. Aaron had to park three blocks away, and then they were forced to walk, giving them a chance to admire the lovely blue tarps and sheet after sheet of plywood covering gaping holes in roofs up and down the street.

With LaShonda giving directions inside Hailey's head, the party of three—two?—proceeded to LaShonda's building, halfway along the front side of the complex, facing the communal courtyard.

The courtyard boasted a small patch of thick grass, a couple of picnic tables and a swimming pool that had surely once been pristine but now was littered with mud, leaves, patio furniture, trash—you name it.

Inside the apartment, the bedroom windows provided a scenic view of the parking lot, currently littered with piles of debris from the storm. Random furniture, crushed and overturned cars, broken trees and limbs of all sizes. What trees were left had had the bark stripped off by the tornado. The parking lot looked like a war zone.

The apartment itself was pretty much a disaster, with half the roof gone, followed by wind and rain damage, and the occasional tree limb or two that had blown in. The hole in the roof was covered with a bright blue tarp to keep out whatever it could until real repairs could be made.

Inside the apartment, so many small things had oddly remained in place: a ceramic set of red-breasted bluebirds on the sill over the sink; a shelf of books and children's CDs on the far wall.

Oh, God, LaShonda wailed in Hailey's head.

Hailey wanted to wail with her, but she swallowed her words of sorrow and sympathy. She couldn't explain herself to Aaron, and the words wouldn't help get things done.

"Okay." Hailey rubbed her hands together. "If I were a picture of Keenan…"

LaShonda sniffed. *You'd be in that photo album next to the CDs. Please, God, let it have survived.* Her tear-filled whisper echoed through Hailey's brain.

Hailey reached for the photo album and found it in perfect condition. Thumbing through the book, she found dozens of pictures of Keenan and LaShonda, and other family members and friends.

"They've got quite a family going here," Hailey said to Aaron.

"Can't be as big as mine," he told her. "What about you? Big family?"

She shook her head. "Just me." She sounded so pitiful, even to her own ears, that she forced herself to focus on the album. Most of the photos it held were of Keenan. "What an adorable kid."

"He's a winner, all right," Aaron said.

They thumbed through the album until they found a recent five-by-seven they thought would be a good one for the cops and the media, including the Internet, to use.

"We'll make copies," Aaron muttered, glancing around the room. "Does your friend have insurance to take care of this mess?"

Startled, Hailey held her breath. "Insurance? LaShonda? I…"

Yes! LaShonda cried. *Oh, thank God. I hadn't thought of that.*

"Yes," Hailey said. "Yes, she has insurance. As soon as I'm finished at the police station, I'll get in touch with the insurance company and see what they can do to help."

The voice in Hailey's head, the sniffing and soft crying, stopped. Her mind and LaShonda were quiet.

"I hope Ms. Martin knows what a good friend you are."

"It's not that big a deal," Hailey protested.

Ms. Martin's learnin' fast, LaShonda said. *You're the best, white girl.*

For one irrevocable moment, Hailey forgot to watch her words around Aaron and spoke directly to LaShonda. "Just out of curiosity, since you feel free to call me White Girl all the time, I'm guessing you won't mind if I call you Black Girl?"

All sound seemed to be sucked out of the room. For a long moment, not even their breathing broke the silence.

Finally Aaron spoke. "This time you have to tell me what's going on."

Thinking of trying to play dumb one more time, Hailey opened her mouth to deny knowing what he was talking about.

He beat her to the punch. "And don't bother telling me you don't know what I'm talking about. Who are you talking to? Trust me, I've heard it all, so you won't surprise me."

"You say that now," Hailey muttered.

What're you going to do? LaShonda asked her.

Hailey shook her head. "Maybe I'll surprise you after all," she told Aaron. "I'm talking to LaShonda Martin."

"The kid's mother?"

"Yes."

"The woman in the other bed in your hospital room?"

"One and the same."

"But she's not dead. Is she?" he asked, his brow furrowed with obvious concern.

"No, she's not dead. She's in a coma."

"She's in a coma," Aaron repeated. "In the hospital."

"That's right," Hailey assured him.

"She's in a coma, in the hospital," Aaron repeated, and started ticking items off on his fingers. "And you're here, several miles away, and you're talking to her. You can hear her, and I can't. Can you see her?"

"It's complicated," Hailey said.

It's a cop-out, LaShonda said. *You're a wimp, white girl.*

"Will you shut up?" Hailey demanded. "I'm telling him, aren't I?"

Aaron rubbed his hands together like a pirate getting ready to count his booty. "Oh, this is going to be good, I can tell."

"You enjoy watching someone have a breakdown right before your eyes?" Hailey said. Her hands were shaking.

"A breakdown?"

"That's what they call it when a person starts hearing voices, isn't it?" she asked.

"Or maybe that's what they call it when you try to change the subject and avoid answering the question."

"I'm not trying to change the subject." Hailey took a deep breath to calm her nerves. "It's just that nothing like this has ever happened to me before. It's a little unsettling."

"Nothing like what? Like hearing voices?"

"Yes. But it's really only one voice." She decided to ignore the moment back in the hospital when she'd known quite clearly that he was thinking about her naked.

"LaShonda Joy Martin."

"That's right. My hospital roomie."

"She's in a coma, but she can talk to you? How does that work?" Aaron asked.

He was way too accepting of the idea of her hearing voices. He should be skeptical, at the least, rather than looking her up and down, making her spine tingle. Why wasn't he laughing at her, or scoffing, or shaking his head and walking away? Just because his grandmother claimed to talk to ghosts? He didn't really believe *her*, did he?

"Talk to me, Hailey. Tell me what's going on."

"It happened at the hospital," she said. Once she started, the words wouldn't stop. She told him all she and LaShonda knew, or guessed, about how the other woman's spirit had ended up inside her head.

"How long have you known each other?"

"Now you're talking like a cop, trying to put words in my mouth. LaShonda and I have never met. I mean, we never even heard of each other until they hooked me up to that oxygen machine. I inhaled, and there she was, talking from inside my head."

"So she's not a ghost."

"That's right."

"Okay," he said. "Let's get to the police station so you can file a report about the boy."

Keenan. His name is Keenan, LaShonda said.

"LaShonda says his name is Keenan."

"Right. Sorry. We'll stop on the way to the station and make copies of Keenan's photo so we can put the original back."

"That's all you have to say? I tell you I have conversations with a coma patient, and you say we'll stop and make copies?"

"Hmm. You're right." He grabbed her gently by the shoulders and kissed her hard and quick. He gave her a grin. "This is where I'm supposed to ask if you're crazy. Are you having a breakdown? Going schizo on me?"

Hailey sputtered. He'd kissed her, and now he was all but laughing at her. Hailey stiffened her shoulders and turned toward the door. She might not be going schizo, but any moment she was going to start drooling. " Let's get to the police station before I start to drool."

He laughed as he followed her out the door and down the stairs.

They made color copies of Keenan's photo, then drove to the police station. Aaron was treated by everyone there as one of their own.

Hailey didn't know what to think of this man who rolled so easily with whatever punches came his way. Punches such as a complete stranger who talked to herself. He acted as if she was normal, the day was normal, and everything was right with the world.

He led her into a large open room filled with desks and what sounded like two million ringing telephones. They stopped beside a desk near the back corner, and Aaron introduced her to Officer Mike Fontain, who had already started the paperwork for Keenan based on Aaron's input earlier. Now, with Hailey's information, especially Keenan's photo, they could move ahead.

Hailey gave Officer Fontain all the information she had and, with LaShonda's help, answered all his questions. They worked for a time with a sketch artist until they had a vague picture of the suspect. It wasn't much, because LaShonda couldn't remember the man's face.

"All right." Fontain pushed back his chair and stood. "Hope Howard's not in on this. We'll get this photo out, and we'll add it to the Amber Alert right away."

"You've already put out an Amber Alert?" Hailey asked.

"As soon as Aaron came in yesterday afternoon," Fontain told her.

Inside Hailey's head, LaShonda gushed her thanks at the officer and begged Hailey to kiss the man and worship at his feet, if he would only find her baby boy.

Hailey smiled but otherwise ignored her.

Once they were all back in Aaron's car, he offered to buy lunch. Because she was hungry, Hailey accepted. She told herself it had nothing to do with not being ready to leave his company.

Hailey was usually comfortable being alone. She considered herself an independent woman, more than capable of taking care of herself. Most of the time she preferred her own company to anyone else's. She saw plenty of people at work, and that was enough socializing for her. Especially since she'd caught her boyfriend of two years ago, dear ol' Randy, cheating on her with one of her best friends, dear ol' Donna. Hailey hadn't been the most open or trusting person since then.

Yet today she didn't want to be alone. She found Aaron interesting, wanted to trust him. *Did* trust him.

When would she ever learn?

Maybe it was because she had come close to dying, or realizing how lucky she was compared to LaShonda. Or maybe it was simply the magnetic pull of the man behind the wheel.

"Where were you thinking of eating?" she asked.

"I'm not sure. Let me check something." He placed a call on his cell phone. "Hey, beautiful, what's on the menu today?" He lowered the phone and looked at Hailey. "How's your cholesterol?"

"My cholesterol's normal to low. How's yours?"

"Mine's fine and dandy. You up for the world's greatest pork chops, breaded and fried, with fried okra, mashed potatoes and the equally sinful works?"

"It sounds delicious."

"We're on our way," he said into the phone. "Two for lunch. I'm not going to be seeing my brothers or sisters, am I? Great. Thanks. Be there in twenty." He disconnected and clipped the phone back to his belt.

"No brothers or sisters? Where are we going?" Hailey asked, her heart speeding at their teasing banter.

"How freaked out are you going to be when I tell you I'm taking you to my grandmother's for lunch?"

Even LaShonda fell silent at that.

Claudia Jean Trent lived in a beautiful old two-story Victorian in the quiet countryside beyond the Baton Rouge city limits. Tall, glossy-green magnolia trees decorated the huge yard, with rows and pools of flowers—reds, yellows, whites, purples—and shrubs ranging from dark to light green in various beds around the house, up and down the front yard, following every curve, every bend, every sidewalk.

There was enough work here, Hailey thought, to keep a full-time gardener busy on the flowers alone. She sincerely hoped Aaron's grandmother had regular help.

Aaron barreled up the circular gravel drive and parked near the front door. By the time he exited the car, rounded the hood and opened the passenger door for her, the cloud of gravel dust raised by the car had wafted away in the warm southern breeze.

He opened the front door without knocking, just stepped inside and took Hailey with him.

Sudden nervousness seized her. He had brought her home to meet his grandmother. What did it mean? This couldn't be the same as a guy taking her home to meet his mother, surely. They hadn't known each other that long, or in that way.

So what *was* this all about?

"Aaron, why are we here?" she asked quietly in the doorway before anyone saw them.

Oh, sister, why do you want to rock that boat? LaShonda cried.

"What do you mean?" Aaron asked. "We're here for lunch."

LaShonda gave out a hoot.

"Come on," Hailey told him. "We could have eaten

lunch anywhere, but you bring me to your grand-mother's. I figure you must have a reason for bringing me here other than her pork chops."

He placed his hands lightly on her shoulders and looked at her for a long moment. Long enough to make Hailey want to squirm.

"All right," he said. "I wanted you to meet Gran. When you do, I think you'll see why."

"Why don't you just tell me?"

"You know that voice you hear in your head?"

"LaShonda," Hailey said, defiant, daring him to argue that she was making it all up.

"Gran is going to understand what you're experienc-ing."

As if hearing her cue, Claudia Jean Trent stepped into the entry hall. "There you are, Aaron, dear." She reached out to hug her grandson.

"Gran." He returned the hug.

Hailey smiled and looked on. At a guess, Aaron was around thirty-five, so his grandmother must be about seventy-five. She looked more like sixty, with salt-and-pepper hair, smiling blue eyes and enough wrinkles around her face to give the impression of a life well-lived, filled with her share of both pain and laughter.

"Who have you brought with you, dear?" She turned toward Hailey, and her smile froze in place. "Oh, my heavens. Pardon me for asking, but do you know you're not, uh, not alone?"

"You can see her?" Hailey asked, her heart racing.

You can see me? LaShonda asked at the same moment, with a quiver in her voice.

"I can see both of you, which I'm sure is why my number-three grandson brought you to me, isn't that right, Aaron, dear? Why don't you run off to the kitchen and get us each a tall glass of sweet tea, while this lovely lady—both lovely ladies—come with me to the parlor, so we can get to know each other." She turned and threaded her arm through Hailey's. "I'm just dying to hear how you ended up this way."

Hailey felt as if a whirlwind had swept through the house and rearranged things to suit Mrs. Trent's wishes. Before Hailey could blink or LaShonda could comment, they found themselves in what must have been the parlor in question. The room looked out over the front yard. Drapes, walls and furniture all gleamed in white and gold, with turquoise accents. Definitely a woman's room. A lady's room. Dainty and spotless.

"My goodness, where are my manners? I didn't even give poor Aaron a chance to introduce us. I'm Claudia Jean Trent. You can call me Claudia Jean. And you are?"

"I'm Hailey Cameron."

I'm LaShonda Joy Martin. Can you really see me? Can you hear me, too?

"Yes, I can." Claudia smiled. "How did you end up in there? Are you dead, sweetheart?"

"No," Hailey responded.

No, LaShonda said. *I'm in a coma, at the hospital.*

Hailey smiled. A small sense of relief filled her, the first since realizing she was no longer alone in her own head. "And you can speak for yourself."

How about that? I can.

It took only a few minutes for Hailey and LaShonda to explain their situation to Claudia. Halfway through the telling, Aaron brought in a round of tall glasses of sweet iced tea, and a tray of carrot sticks, stuffed celery, cauliflower and broccoli and joined the women.

"What can they do, Gran?" he asked when the tale was told.

"Seems to me they're doing it already. They've both received medical attention, they've accepted that they are, shall we say, psychically joined. They've got you and the police looking for the child, and you've started securing LaShonda's belongings."

"But we can't seem to separate," Hailey pointed out.

"Ah, yes, there is that," Claudia said. "Why do you think you can't return to your own body, LaShonda?"

Hailey could practically feel LaShonda blushing beneath Claudia's steady gaze.

Well, if I knew that, LaShonda griped, *don't you think I'd do it?*

"Would you?" Claudia asked.

Hailey gnawed on the inside of her jaw to keep from butting in and blaming LaShonda for staying in her body to force her into searching for Keenan. As if Hailey could have turned away from such a plea from a woman who, at present, had no way to help herself.

Of course I would. On the other hand, if I go back to my body and get stuck in the hospital, who's going to remind white girl here to keep looking for my son?

"I see." Claudia took a sip of tea and sat back in her seat. "I can understand that."

"Is she giving you a line about needing to make sure Hailey keeps looking for her kid?" Aaron asked.

A small chuckle of laughter slipped from Hailey's mouth. "I forgot. This time you're the only one in the room who's different. Now everybody can hear La-Shonda except you."

He rolled his eyes. "That's nothing new around here, believe me."

"I beg your pardon?" she asked.

"Ladies," Claudia called. "Come out and meet our guests."

"Wha—" But that was as far as Hailey got before two figures shimmered into view, as if generated by the wave of a moviemaker's magic special effects wand. First a faint outline, then it started to fill in, fading and glowing, fading and glowing, until each figure settled into a steady visual image standing on either side of Claudia's chair.

Suddenly they were no longer glimmering images. As if Scotty had beamed them up, they were women, solid flesh-and-blood bodies. Hailey could see their chests rise and fall beneath their period costumes. One woman wore a soft gingham dress trimmed in white ruffles, while the other dressed in dire black, with her dark hair pulled back sharply from her face into a tight bun at her nape.

"So," Claudia said to Hailey, "you can see them."

Hailey swallowed. "Wh-who?"

I see them, LaShonda stated. *Who are they?*

The woman in black sighed. "More people to talk about us as if we're not here, Claudia? How tedious."

Oh, we see you, all righty, LaShonda shot back, *so you can just wipe that attitude off your face.*

"Hush up," Hailey warned. If she could have, she would have jerked on LaShonda's arm. She had the feeling that Aaron thought his grandmother might be able to help them in some way. She didn't want to make her mad by having LaShonda's mouth running off at her...friends.

The woman in black stiffened, perhaps in offense.

Claudia chuckled. "It's all right, Hailey. I can't recall the last time anyone but me could see or hear Marva or Mrs. Porterman."

"I don't understand," Hailey said, her nerves clacking.

"I imagine it is a tad confusing," Claudia said.

"Ah, Gran, the master of understatement." On their own, Aaron's words might have stung. They were, however, said with a smile and followed by a wink.

None of which did anything to help Hailey understand what was going on.

"You didn't tell her," Claudia said.

He reached over and touched the back of his grandmother's hand. The smile in his eyes softened. "Not everything. It's yours to tell, Gran, not mine."

"Smart boy," Claudia told Aaron. "You bring me this lovely young woman, and she brings me her friend. Both of them can see and hear my friends. You might want to keep this one."

"Gran," Aaron warned, "let's get back to the subject. Both of you can see things other people can't. Hailey's ability started when she was struck by lightning the other day."

"And LaShonda's alive but in a coma," Claudia said thoughtfully. "That's a new one on me. Maybe it's because of the drugs they're using to keep you unconscious?"

If I'm new to you, LaShonda said, *that means they're...dead?*

"Yes," Claudia said.

"But...how can that be?" Hailey asked.

I'd say, when you're dead, you're gone, LaShonda said. *But then, here I am, hanging out inside a white girl, so what do I know?*

"Sometimes," Claudia said, "the spirit of a dead person simply isn't ready, or willing, to leave, to go...wherever it's supposed go. Sometimes it needs help, or needs to offer help. That's what people like you and I are for," she said to Hailey.

"To help them?" Hailey asked, not sure she was ready or willing to accept such a responsibility.

Like, to help me find my Keenan, LaShonda said.

"That's right," Claudia agreed.

"While we're doing that," Aaron said, "maybe one of your ghosts will help me find Charlie Howard."

"Who is he?" Hailey asked.

"He's that guy I told you I'm looking for. His aunt is the woman you jog past every day. The one we talked about."

From there the conversation traveled from the fancy parlor to the comfortable eat-in kitchen, where Claudia served the salad. While they ate, she checked the pork chops in the oven and the vegetables on the stove.

She agreed with Hailey that LaShonda needed to return to her own body. Marva and Mrs. Porterman recalled the days shortly after their own passings—the only things they could compare to her coma. They remembered how weak they had been, how disoriented. It had been weeks, months, before they'd felt in control of themselves and learned how to navigate through the new dimension in which they found themselves. How to live with the frustration of not being seen or heard by anyone but Claudia Jean and an old hound that lived in the barn.

"LaShonda doesn't have weeks or months," Hailey said. "In a day or two they're going to pull her out of her coma and someone needs to be in there." She tapped a finger to the side of her head.

"From what Marva and Mrs. Porterman went through," Claudia Jean said, "the best thing to me would be relaxing. Both of you. That might help LaShonda ease back into her own body."

The two ghosts agreed.

Relaxing sounded easier said than done, when so much counted on it, but Hailey and LaShonda agreed to give it their best that afternoon.

After the meal, everyone helped clean up, then Hailey, LaShonda and Aaron headed back to town.

"What do you think?" They were a mile from his grandmother's house before Aaron spoke.

"I think your Gran truly loves you, to allow you to show up with our kind of trouble," Hailey said.

"But did it help?" He couldn't believe how much her answer mattered. How much he wanted to be able to help her. "Can you use anything she and her pals had to say?"

Hailey chuckled. "Her pals? Oh, God, they would love that."

"You're not angry with me for butting in on your and LaShonda's problem?"

"Never." She reached out and covered the back of his hand with hers, where he gripped the gearshift. "I'm grateful," she said, giving his hand a slight squeeze. "I know what to do now. And I know I'm not losing my mind. That I'm not the only person who hears voices. That LaShonda's not the only invisible person floating around."

Without thinking, Aaron turned his hand and threaded his fingers through hers. "You're not losing your mind, and you're not going through this alone."

"I'm not?"

"You're not."

"Thank you." She squeezed his hand again. "When you drop me off at my car, I'm going straight to the hospital and give LaShonda a chance to relax."

Chapter 4

Except for the hum and beep of life-affirming machines, dusk was quiet in LaShonda's hospital room.

In the morning the doctor was going to bring LaShonda slowly out of her coma.

Hailey could feel LaShonda's spirit relaxing. The visit to Aaron's grandmother had given the other woman the confidence she needed to let go of Hailey and return to her own body. Thank God for that, Hailey thought. Thank God for Aaron and his family.

Somehow, throughout lunch, Hailey had managed to learn more than a little about the Trent family. First, it was large. She wasn't even certain how many brothers and sisters Aaron had, but there were several.

Then came the aunts and uncles and cousins, at least half of whom had children of their own.

Hailey had been an only child of older parents, each one also an only child. They'd died before she reached her teens. Foster care had bounced her around until she had aged out of the system.

She'd never had a roommate—except at a foster home.

She'd never had a best friend.

She'd never had a brother or sister, never gotten close enough to any of her foster siblings to think of them that way.

She once developed a crush on one of her older so-called foster brothers and learned quickly enough not to trust boys.

She had learned that she was her own best friend, and she liked it that way.

Maybe those things helped explain why she had taken to LaShonda as well as she had. They'd been together less than two days, but it felt much more per-manent to Hailey than anything she'd known as a child. Yes, she looked forward to recovering her privacy, but having someone to talk to whenever she wanted was a heady thing. Sort of like a best friend and sister rolled into one.

Maybe she had been lonely after all.

Not that she thought LaShonda necessarily returned the sentiment. The woman had her own family and, un-doubtedly, friends. In fact, tomorrow should see the

arrival of an aunt from New Orleans, who would look
after LaShonda while she mended and help her get her
home and life back together as the police searched for
Keenan.

Thoughts of Keenan brought thoughts of Aaron. To
Hailey's shame, Aaron quickly crowded the young boy
from her mind. Tomorrow she would start seeing what
she could do to help search for Keenan, but she had to
go back to work at the restaurant tomorrow evening.

For now, she would let herself think of large, loving
families who produced intriguing men such as Aaron
Trent. If she let herself, she could still feel the taut skin
across the back of his hand where it rested on the
gearshift knob. His warmth had surprised her. She'd
been even more surprised when he had turned his hand
and threaded his fingers through hers. The mere
memory weakened her joints.

You're thinking of him, aren't you?

Hailey gave a start. "LaShonda? You sound different. Are you all right?"

*Good way to change the subject, girlfriend, but I'm
back where I belong, if that's what you mean.*

It took a moment for Hailey to realize what
LaShonda meant, and then…

Hailey had expected that once she had her body
back to herself once more, that feeling of loneliness
she never let herself acknowledge would seep back in
again. If she were honest, she had to admit it was one
reason why she stood at the entrance to a popular

restaurant and greeted the diners every evening. Faux family.

Looking at things now, she could see that it was the reason she jogged three miles every other day—to outrun the emptiness.

That it was the reason she stopped and visited with an elderly lady over a glass of lemonade mid-run—to relieve someone else's loneliness as well as her own.

But for the past couple of days she had felt the need for neither the diners nor the jogging. She'd had Aaron to share herself with. And she'd had LaShonda. Temporary, both of them, to be sure, but she'd had them. It was surprising how good that felt.

Not so surprising was the burning in her eyes and the closing of her throat when relief for LaShonda swamped her. The fear had been larger than Hailey had realized that LaShonda would not be able to return to her own body. Ever.

Fear of losing Aaron still weighed like a ball of ice in her gut, but the fear of sharing her mind with LaShonda forever was gone. In the odd mixture of remaining fear and sheer relief, Hailey's composure crumbled.

It was late when Aaron finally made it to the hospital to check on Hailey. He hadn't meant—hadn't wanted—to leave her there alone with LaShonda so long, but he'd wasted two hours trying to connect with a particular informant who might have a line on Charlie. He'd also tried again to reach the elderly lady Hailey jogged past every day. No luck there, either.

The air-conditioned interior of the hospital revived him from the heat of the day. He pushed open the door to LaShonda's room and nearly fell to his knees.

The light was low, and all he heard over the quiet beeping and whooshing of the machines that carried LaShonda through her coma was the soft weeping of a woman.

Without question, he knew it was Hailey.

When his eyes adjusted to the dim light, he saw her, slumped in her chair, shoulders shaking, face and fists buried in the bedding at LaShonda's hip.

Thinking the worst had happened, his heart filled with dread.

"Hailey!" He rushed to her side and slipped his arms around her. "Hailey, honey, what's wrong? Did we lose her? Talk to me. Is she gone?"

"Gone? No, no. She's good. She's fine. She's back."

He was too busy nuzzling his nose into the warmth of her neck to realize what she was saying at first, and then it hit him.

"What?"

"She's back."

"You mean…back? As in, back in her own body?"

"Ye-yes."

Aaron's heart rate settled slightly at the news. Still, her tears touched something inside him that he'd thought never to feel. He hadn't known he even had that soft spot deep inside. "Then why are you crying?"

"Relief. I was afraid she wouldn't be able to get back to herself in time."

"In time?"

"The doctor's coming in the morning to start pulling her out of the coma."

"Doesn't sound like fun. Are you going to be here for that?" he asked.

She started to pull away and sit up, but he tucked her head into the crook of his neck and held her closer, as if they sat this way every day.

She shifted around, then finally settled. "Yes. Seven a.m. Shirley, her aunt, is coming up from New Orleans to be here for her."

"You sound exhausted," he said. She felt more frail than he'd realized, too.

"I wasn't tired until LaShonda said she'd made it back. Then I just…went limp, I guess."

"No wonder," he told her. "With the way you've been going these past couple of days. Why don't I take you home so you can get some rest?"

"I haven't done anything but sit around," she protested.

"Yeah, with another person hanging out in your head. That, plus getting struck by lightning, plus spending the night in a strange place, where nurses wake you up at regular intervals to make sure you're asleep. Then you go through a tornado-damaged building. Then you have lunch with ghosts. And that was only half your day."

"Okay." She laughed. "I think I'm too tired to argue."

"There. You admitted it," he said. "You're tired. LaShonda, I'm taking her out of here for a while. We'll be back in the morning, when they turn off your juice and bring you out of hiding. I've never had injuries as severe as yours, but I've had my share, so trust me, you're going to want to ask for more drugs. Lots of drugs."

Against his shoulder, Hailey shuddered. "You never said why you're not a cop anymore. Did you end up with a drug habit from your hospital stay?"

He pulled her to her feet and walked her toward the door. "No, no drug habit, from the hospital or elsewhere. I took one to the shoulder. Tore up my rotator cuff and cost me too much range of motion to pass the annual physical."

"Took one? You mean…you were shot?"

"Yeah. It happens now and then in my line of work."

"I'm sorry. It must have been hard to accept the loss of your job."

"Yeah, it's been hard. But it might not be permanent," he said. "If I can find the right therapy to get my range of motion back, I might be able to pass the physical again."

"Really?" She raised her head from his shoulder and looked up at him.

Aaron met her gaze with wonder. Her eyes glowed like a small child's at Christmas, having been told that Santa was on the roof.

"Why do you care so much?" he asked.

She ducked her head and looked away. "It's in your eyes, how much you think of yourself as a cop."

With one finger to her chin, Aaron turned her head and peered down into her bright blue eyes. "You're pretty observant."

"It's what I do, observe people."

"You do? Why is it that the only thing I seem to know about you is that you work at Chez Gigi?"

"You know that much? I don't know why you don't know more. We've been best friends for, what, less than thirty-six hours?"

Outside, the parking lot was well lit. He walked her to the passenger door of his car and opened it with a flourish that would have been grand if he'd worn a cape. "Your chariot awaits. Hop in and I'll take you home."

"My car's over there." She nodded toward her small car, parked another ten yards away.

"I'll take you home and bring you back in the morning," he offered.

"Thank you, but that's too much trouble for you, plus it leaves me stranded at home if I decide I want to go out tonight."

He leaned one arm on the open door of his car. "If you're too tired to drive…"

"I'm fine, really," she offered.

"If you say so," he said as he walked her to her car. "I'll just follow you home to make sure."

"I wonder what that says about you, that you would go to the trouble," she said. "I wonder what it says about me, that I don't seem to mind. If anybody but you said they were going to follow me home, I'd accuse them of stalking."

"It says that you have excellent sense."

Hailey chuckled. "Says you."

Aaron's cell phone rang. He pulled it from the case on his belt loop and read the text message on the screen. "I guess my stalking days are over, at least for now," he told Hailey.

She reached for him. He stepped into her embrace and hugged her.

"You have to work?" she asked.

"An informant has some information on Charlie Howard."

"Your bail-jumping child stealer?"

"That's the one. You'll be here in the morning for LaShonda?" he asked. He ran his hand up and down her arm.

"At seven, yes. You?" She wanted to curl up against him and let whatever happened happen.

"I'll be here," he said. "I won't be able to stay long, but I'll be here in case she wakes up with perfect memory of the man who took Keenan."

"I won't be able to stay long, either," she admitted. "I have to go back to work tomorrow at four. Before that, I want to see if there's anything I can do to help look for Keenan. And I'm going to start jogging again."

"Do yourself a favor and check the weather first, please."

"Don't remind me. I'm trying not to think about lightning, or I might be too scared to run."

"Think about this instead." He turned her in his arms until they were aligned chest to chest. Their mouths met, tasted, toyed with each other. Then they parted and said good-night.

The first thing Hailey did when she made it home was sleep. She dreamed of kissing Aaron. When she woke it was the middle of the night, and she felt slightly disoriented. She had her life back. She knew she had to go to work that evening, even looked forward to it. But for now, she was alone with her thoughts.

Her thoughts turned to LaShonda. She was looking forward to being there for the next step in LaShonda's recovery.

She wondered what it said about her that she was looking forward even more to seeing Aaron again.

7:00 a.m. came at its usual time, and Hailey was at the hospital a few minutes early. She turned the last corner before LaShonda's room, and there stood Aaron. At the sight of him, her heart jolted.

"Hey," she said in greeting. It was so good to see him.

"Morning." He stood back and allowed her to enter the room before him.

She paused in the doorway, her shoulder brushing his chest. She could feel his gaze on her and couldn't help but look up at him. When their gazes met, she felt the remnants of lightning dancing down her spine.

A sound from near LaShonda's bed drew their attention. They tore their gazes apart and stepped through the doorway.

The room was already so crowded, Hailey was afraid someone would throw them out. She saw one doctor, three nurses and a woman who had to be LaShonda's Aunt Shirley, whom Hailey had met by phone the day before. Add Hailey and Aaron, and LaShonda herself, and the head count peaked at eight. That was a lot for such a small room. Thankfully the second bed was still empty.

Hailey probably should have hugged the wall to keep from getting in anyone's way, but she needed to let LaShonda know she was there. So she made a place for herself at the bedside opposite the doctor and touched LaShonda's free hand.

"I'm here, girlfriend, just like I promised. Aaron's with me, and Aunt Shirley's here to take care of you. Now it's your turn to do your thing and wake up when the doctor says, okay?"

She squeezed LaShonda's hand again, then stepped back toward the wall. Instead of a cool, solid wall at her back, she felt a warm, sculpted chest. Two strong arms wrapped around her and pulled her close. Her heart stumbled.

For fear Aaron would let go of her if she so much as breathed, she stood still and stared as the doctor fiddled with the IV in LaShonda's arm.

In a short time, LaShonda groaned. Her eyes blinked open. They were the color of dark coffee, and filled with pain and tears. Her lips, nostrils, eyes and ears were swollen and the only things not covered by white bandages. She looked straight at Hailey, and her eyes slowly blinked again. Her lips moved.

Hailey leaned forward and touched LaShonda's hand again. Aaron moved, too, staying pressed against Hailey's back.

"LaShonda, it's me, Hailey."

"White girl," Hailey managed to say through cracked lips.

Relief flooded Hailey. LaShonda remembered the time she'd spent out of her body. How miraculous, Hailey thought.

She repeated to LaShonda what she'd said mere moments ago, letting her know specifically that Aunt Shirley was there for her. "You made it, girlfriend."

"Day-yum."

Hailey laughed. "That's right. Day-yum."

And then LaShonda closed her eyes and fell sound asleep.

As they left the hospital room together sometime later, Hailey wanted badly to think of a reason not to part company with Aaron, but she couldn't think of one. The independent woman in her insisted she was glad they weren't going to be together for the rest of the day. She didn't need a man in her life. She was more than capable of taking care of herself. She earned enough at her job to support herself in a comfortable style. She was more than content with her own company. She even liked to travel alone.

Her happiness did not depend on anyone other than herself.

A man was handy now and then for sex and for moving heavy furniture.

If only she could believe herself.

Chapter 5

Hailey and Aaron parted company in the hospital parking lot. He had to check in with the district attorney's office. Hailey had to do…something.

Jog. She wanted to jog. She felt the need to stretch her muscles and exercise her lungs. To run away from these conflicting feelings of needing to stand on her own and wanting to lean on—and lap up—Aaron Trent.

She threw on a pair of running shorts and shoes, and an oversize New Orleans Saints T-shirt. She clipped a bottle of water and her cell phone and keys onto her belt loops, and trotted out the door.

Outside, the morning sun burned the bare skin of her

forearms. She made a U-turn and slathered on plenty of sunscreen, then hit the sidewalk again.

The sky was a clear summer blue. Not a bolt of lightning in sight.

She stretched out her legs and hit her stride in less than a block. She started out on her usual route, with plans to cut it in half and jog only one and a half miles this first time out after a couple of days off.

A few blocks later she neared Mrs. Shelton's house, hoping the woman was home and offering her usual lemonade.

She was one house away when she was hit by disappointment at finding the front porch empty. No sweet gray-haired lady, no sweaty pitcher of lemonade beside two gleaming glasses. Not plastic cups, but crystal glasses. Mrs. Shelton's motto was Only the Best.

Hailey forced herself to maintain her pace as she jogged past the house.

A loud crash from inside stopped her cold. Two voices, a man's and a woman's, rose in anger. Another crash.

Hailey started up the sidewalk. At the front door, she rang the bell and pounded on the door.

"Mrs. Shelton? It's Hailey, Mrs. Shelton. Are you all right?"

No answer.

"If I don't get an answer, Mrs. Shelton, I'm calling 911."

The response was barely audible. "I'm fine."

Hailey called 911 anyway and explained the situation, adding that Aaron Trent with the district attorney's office was looking for the woman who lived there. Then she pounded on the door again and tried the doorknob, which turned beneath her hand, so she let herself in.

The door slammed back at her, and hit her hard in the head and shoulder. Hailey stumbled and cried out.

"Interfering bitch," a man snarled.

Hailey put to use all the various self-defense classes she'd taken over the years, kicking out sideways and taking him hard in the thigh.

Damn. A few inches short of her mark.

Across the room, Mrs. Shelton struggled to get to her feet. A trickle of blood streamed down one temple.

Outraged on behalf of the woman, Hailey whirled on the assailant. "You bastard." This time she aimed her fists at his head. "Who do you think you are?" She hit him again with a jab to his shoulder.

He hit back with a punch to her face that knocked her into the end table beside the sofa. When she straightened, he was swinging at Mrs. Shelton with a knife.

The older woman screamed, "Charlie, no!"

"Shut up, Auntie, and gimme my damn key." He lunged and sliced her arm open from shoulder to elbow.

Oh, God, Hailey thought. This was the nephew Aaron was after. The bail jumper. The child stealer.

She threw herself at his back and pulled with all her

strength to get him away from his aunt. She managed to knock the knife from his hand. He dove for it, but she held on to him, making him fall short of his goal by bare inches.

They rolled across the floor, trading punches, crashing into furniture. Sheer terror kept Hailey from giving in to the pain of his blows.

Charlie got his hands on his knife again and lunged toward his aunt, with Hailey wrapped around his legs.

"No!" Hailey cried. She managed to pull him back just barely enough to keep him from stabbing his aunt.

He kicked out with one boot and caught her in the chest, knocking the breath out of her.

There was a loud crash and a scramble of voices. Hailey knew she was losing it, because one of the voices sounded like Aaron. She gasped harder to bring air into her tortured lungs. Please, God, just...one... breath.

"Easy, baby."

A familiar hand reached for her arm.

"Just breathe. In and out, real slow. Don't panic. Just breathe. It'll happen, baby, don't be afraid."

If strength of will could make a difference, she would breathe again. She would do whatever it took to keep feeling that hand on her arm. Her gasping breath wheezed in and out of her throat so loudly that she could barely hear him, but Aaron's voice soothed her enough to allow her airways to relax in small stages. They had to relax, because if she couldn't breathe again, she would die. And if she died, she would never feel Aaron's touch or hear his voice again.

"That's it, baby," he told her. "Stay with me and just breathe. That's it."

Finally, slowly, Hailey managed to drag enough air into her lungs to make her think she perhaps wasn't going to die after all.

When Aaron realized she was breathing, he lowered his forehead to her shoulder and started shaking. Damn, he'd nearly lost her. He barely knew her, but he knew enough about her to want to know more. Time and time again she put herself out for the sake of others. LaShonda, Keenan, Mrs. Shelton.

When was the last time someone put her first? When was the last time she allowed such a thing? He wanted, he realized as her breathing settled to normal, to be the person she let get close to her.

"Aaron."

"Thank God," he said fiercely.

"You came." She struggled to sit up.

He shifted her until she sat and leaned against him, then held on as tightly as he could without hurting her. Around them, the room was in chaos, with police and EMTs everywhere. Charlie Howard, being handcuffed and dragged out the door, was cussing a blue streak. His aunt, Wynona Shelton, five feet from where Hailey and Aaron sat, moaned quietly while the EMTs stanched the bleeding from the long cut on her arm, and the several cuts on her hands and face.

Hailey looked worried. "Is she going to be all right?"

"Looks like it," Aaron said. "I'll check when they've had a few more minutes with her."

"Hailey?" the older woman called weakly.

"Mrs. Shelton? I'm over here. Are you all right?"

"Am I all right, young man?" she asked the EMT.

"You're going to be right as rain, ma'am. Just a few cuts that will probably pain you some for a bit. And we need to take you in for some X rays and to check for any internal injuries, or maybe a mild concussion."

"My. Did you hear all of that, Hailey?" Mrs. Shelton asked faintly.

"I did. I'll come by the hospital and check on you, so you do what they tell you, all right?"

"Yes, dear."

After a few minutes the EMTs lifted Mrs. Shelton onto a gurney and wheeled her out of the house.

"Oh, thank God." Hailey went limp in Aaron's arms as she watched Mrs. Shelton being carried away and let relief wash through her veins. The steely warmth of Aaron's arms around her gave her the security she needed—security she hadn't realized she lacked or longed for—to release the tight rein she usually held on her emotions and let her tears free.

"I hardly ever cry," she managed to say between sobs.

"You go ahead and cry all you want," he told her, rubbing his hand up and down her back. "Just keep breathing."

"It's like all I ever do is cry around you."

Aaron held her close and let her cry. Her tears opened a yawning hole deep inside and pulled him in.

Dear God, he'd almost lost her before he'd even realized how important she was to him.

"Not true, not true. You're no crybaby. Today you were Wonder Woman."

The next few hours went by in a fog for Hailey. EMTs poked and prodded her. Aaron encouraged them, over her objections, to take her to the hospital.

She lost that argument. She barely even remembered it a few minutes later.

Sometime after that, there were nurses, a doctor, and more poking and prodding. A bandage here and there. A prescription for painkillers. Swallow this antibiotic. A call to her boss to say she wouldn't be in that night.

She remembered spending an eternity in the waiting area for word on Mrs. Shelton, with occasional forays to see LaShonda, who was still sleeping, this time thanks to painkillers and plain old exhaustion. Aaron was with Hailey every step of the way.

"Why don't I take you home?" he offered when they came back from LaShonda's room. "You're exhausted. Let me drive you home." He looked at her quizzically. "Why are you smiling?"

"I don't get babied often," she said. "It's kind of fun."

He brushed a finger across her cheek and smiled. "I'm glad to be of service."

"Why don't you be of further service and find out how much longer it'll be before we can see Mrs. Shelton?"

"Now you're taking advantage of my willingness to please."

"And you're pointing this out because…?"

"Thought you'd want to know—I like being taken advantage of." He left her in her hard plastic chair and crossed to the information desk just down the hall.

He was back in no time, shaking his head as he took the seat next to her. "Nothing yet. She said it should-n't be much longer."

"Isn't that what they said more than an hour ago?"

"Yeah," he said. "I wanted to ask, I mean, I've been curious."

"About what?"

"About what you see and hear now that you don't have LaShonda in your head."

"So far everything's normal. No ghosts or other spirits. I wonder if I went back to your grandmother's, would I still see her friends?"

"All we have to do is drive out there and find out," he offered. "What are you going to do if you start seeing ghosts of your own?"

"I don't know," she said. "I'll just have to take them as they come. Does the idea bother you?"

"That you might have ghosts hanging around you? Not a bit. Neither will it bother me if you never see another one. Makes no difference to me."

Before long Aaron went again to find out about Mrs. Shelton.

He made three more trips like that throughout the evening before they, along with the police, were allowed to see Mrs. Shelton.

Hailey ignored the cops and their questions, and held Mrs. Shelton's hand to offer the woman, and herself, whatever comfort could be found.

"Mrs. Shelton," Aaron said softly from behind Hailey's shoulder, "what set Charlie off? Why was he so mad today?"

"I lost his key," the woman said.

Hailey leaned forward, knowing this was important. "What key?" she asked.

"That spare key he gave me, the one to the shed."

Chapter 6

One of the cops stepped forward immediately and asked, "What shed?"

Unfortunately, Mrs. Shelton didn't know the answer to that question, and she didn't remember where the key was, either, since Charlie had given it to her five years ago, so they couldn't use it to figure out the location, which Aaron suspected with a sinking feeling was where Charlie kept the kids he stole before he sold them.

With nothing more to be gained from talking to Mrs. Shelton, they heeded the doctor's suggestion that they let her get some rest. The cops went off to lean even harder on Charlie, and Hailey and Aaron went to check on LaShonda one last time for the night.

She was alone in her room, no new roommate yet, and Aunt Shirley was gone for the night—and she was awake.

"I have to ask, LaShonda," Aaron said, as soon as he could break into the two women's greetings. "Have you remembered anything about the man who took Keenan?"

She rocked her head back and forth on her pillow, then winced at the pain it caused. "No. I knew when he came to the apartment, I'd seen him before, but I can't remember where."

"Okay, that's fine. I'm going to come back tomorrow with a picture for you to—"

"Oh, my God," LaShonda cried, cutting him off. "Look! It's you two, on the news!" She pushed a button in her bed frame and turned up the audio on the TV.

Hailey gasped. "It is."

The 10:00 p.m. newscast was airing a story about Charlie's arrest. Right there on the screen were pictures of Mrs. Shelton, Aaron and Hailey, followed by a shot of Charlie Howard, with a short rundown of his rap sheet.

"That's him!" LaShonda shrieked. "He's the one who took Keenan. Oh, my God! He's the guy from the self-storage place."

"Whoa, back up," Aaron said, his heart going into overdrive. "Where did you say you saw him?"

"The self-storage place. I came out of my unit to get back in the car with Keenan, and he was there. He and

Keenan were waving at each other. He was four or five units away."

"What day was this?" Aaron asked.

"It was the day of the tornado. We drove home from there, and the storm hit about an hour later."

"That has to be the shed Mrs. Shelton was talking about," Hailey said to Aaron.

"What are you talking about?" LaShonda demanded. "Do you know where my Keenan is?"

"Not yet," Aaron told her. "Where's this self-storage place?"

The minute she told them, they were out the door. Aaron was on the phone to the cops before they even got to the car.

Because it was after hours when Aaron and Hailey pulled up, the gate was locked, and the place was tightly surrounded in eight-foot-tall chain-link fence, which itself was topped with razor wire.

"Sheesh," Hailey said. "I guess they really don't want anyone to get inside."

"No problem." Aaron drove around the perimeter to the security shack, where he got out of the car to speak with the guard.

Hailey couldn't hear what they said, though she saw Aaron show what she assumed was his D.A.'s office ID, but the guard soon began checking a list and shaking his head.

She got out and joined them. "What's wrong?"

"No listing of Charlie or Charles Howard," Aaron said in disgust. "I knew it was too easy to be true."

"But why would LaShonda have seen him here if he doesn't have a unit here?" Hailey asked.

Aaron shook his head. "She wouldn't. But, hell, the shed doesn't have to be in his name. In fact, if it was, we would have found it months ago."

"What if it's in his aunt's name?" she asked.

Aaron stared at her for a moment, then grasped her head in his hands and planted a hard kiss on her mouth.

"Shelton," he told the guard. "Wynona Shelton."

"Got her," the guard said.

"Take us there," Aaron demanded.

The guard let them in and took them on his security-company golf cart to the unit in question.

"This is it," he told them.

"Okay, open it up," Aaron said.

"Only the renter of each unit has the key," The guard said. "They have to provide their own locks."

Aaron pinched the bridge of his nose. "Look at it this way. I'm an officer of the court, and I'm sure I heard a sound from inside this unit. Since the man I have reason to believe frequents this unit happens to be awaiting trial for kidnapping and selling children, I don't think I want to wait until we can wake up a judge to get a search warrant. I'm sure I hear someone crying inside this unit. This is what we call exigent circumstances."

Hailey heard the sounds of approaching sirens just as

the guard pulled a pair of bolt cutters from beneath his seat.

"Let's use my master key," the guard said.

In less than a minute, they were inside the unit and had the light on.

Hailey leaned around the edge of the door to find three sets of terrified young eyes peeking back from behind a row of boxes. "Oh, my God," she breathed, seeing the three boys cowering in fear.

Aaron stepped inside and spoke quietly. "Hello, boys. You're safe now. I'm Aaron, and this is Hailey. We've come to take you back to your parents."

One of the boys sniffed. "They don't want us anymore."

Aaron squatted down in front of them. "Who told you that?"

"The man."

"The man who brought you here?"

"We're not supposed to talk to strangers," another boy said.

"That's good advice. But it's okay if you talk to me, because I work with the police. And you know what? I think I hear them coming now. Why don't you talk to Hailey while I go meet them?"

While he did that, Hailey stepped inside. There he was. LaShonda's baby.

"You're Keenan," she said softly, hunkering down right in front of him.

His eyes widened. "How did you know that?"

"Because your mother told me." She decided to prepare the boy for what was coming so he wouldn't be shocked or scared when he saw his mother. "She would have come for you herself, but the man who brought you here hurt her, and she's in the hospital. She asked us to find you and bring you to her."

The four-year-old used his fists to rub his eyes. "You mean she didn't give me away?"

"Oh, honey, no. Your mama loves you very much and can't wait to see you again. Will you introduce me to your friends, so we can find their families?"

The next hours were total chaos, with cops and EMTs and reporters overrunning the self-storage grounds.

It was only a few hours until sunrise when Hailey leaned close to LaShonda's bed and woke her. "Hey, girlfriend, wake up, I've got a surprise for you."

LaShonda groaned. "Your name better be Ed McMahon."

Hailey chuckled. "Nope. Come on, wake up. This is better than that. We brought you a visitor."

"Mama?"

"Oh! Keenan? Baby?"

Hailey stepped back out of the way and helped Keenan scoot up onto the bed at his mother's side.

Hailey knew that eventually LaShonda would have dozens of questions, but for now she needed only to hold her son and reassure herself that he was alive and safe.

She backed out of the room and straight into Aaron's arms. He pressed himself against her back and held her close while they peered through the open door at the mother-and-son reunion.

After a few minutes, she turned into his arms and pressed her face against the warmth of his neck.

"Are you crying?" he asked.

She sniffed. "Only a little, the good kind of crying."

"It's okay to feel good. We did a really good thing tonight."

She sniffed and smiled. "I know. You were great tonight."

"So were you."

"We were a good pair, huh?"

"Are," he said. "We *are* a good pair."

Hailey smiled. "You'll get no argument from me."

Chapter 7

"It'll be a miracle if I can stay awake for the ride home," Hailey said when they got to his car.

In the end, she didn't make it. She couldn't remember when she fell asleep, but when she woke, they were parked in front of her building.

She rolled her head against the headrest until she could look him in the eye. "I want, very much, to be brave and bold and sexy and invite you to come up with me."

"Why do I hear a *but* coming next?"

"But I'm about to fall asleep, and you'll be insulted. Besides, I'm still a little shaky from tonight. The only knives I'm used to seeing are of the dinner, steak and butter varieties. And then finding those kids…"

Aaron reached for her hand and held it. "How about if I hold you until you fall asleep?"

Hailey nearly collapsed, she was so grateful for his offer. "You would do that?"

"In a heartbeat. As long as you won't get mad if I fall asleep next to you. I'm still a little shaky myself, after walking into that house and seeing you fighting the sleazeball I've been after for weeks, blood everywhere. I could have lost you today. I could use a little recovery time myself."

If she hadn't have been strapped into her seat, Hailey would have thrown herself into his arms. Getting unstrapped was simple enough. But she saved throwing herself at him for later. Instead, she got slowly out of the car and led him up to her apartment, where she closed the door, sealing them in, shutting the world out.

"I don't mean to sound trite," she told him, "but I don't usually do this sort of thing."

"You mean sleep with a man?"

It was all she could do to keep from stuttering. "What?"

"That's all we're talking about, Hailey. Sleeping. Right?"

She had to clear her throat before she could speak. "Right." She was more nervous now than when she had stared down the creep with the knife. "Right. Maybe this wasn't such a good idea."

Aaron felt her slipping away from him. He didn't

want her to slip away. He wanted to hold her, to prove to himself that she was safe and would stay safe at least for tonight.

"Come on," he said. "Let's get you into your bed. Or do you want something to eat first? We should have stopped and had an early breakfast on the way."

"You're hungry?" she asked, relief in her eyes.

Damn, she really was nervous, if mention of food could make her look as if her execution had been postponed.

"I've got frozen pizza," she offered.

"That sounds better than breakfast."

While the pizza heated, Hailey took a shower and changed clothes, since her others had been torn and bloody.

They shared their pizza on the sofa, watching television and catching sight of themselves again on the morning news, which this time also reported on the rescue of the three boys. By the end of the sportscast, Hailey was curled up at one end of the couch, sound asleep.

Aaron smiled softly. She had worn herself out. Trying to act nonchalant about his being there had done her in. He should leave, but he couldn't bring himself to. If she woke up screaming, or even merely scared, he didn't want her to find herself alone.

He knew she would argue with him, but he felt responsible for her nearly getting killed yesterday. He and the police and the bail bondsman and the court should have had Charlie Howard behind bars. If they had, Mrs. Shelton would be home and uninjured. And those three boys would never have gone missing.

He couldn't leave her alone now with her fear.

Gently, he scooped her up in his arms and carried her to bed. She never woke when he took off her shoes. He left the rest of her clothes on, as well as her bedside lamp.

She looked so damn sweet. The scrapes and bruises she'd suffered earlier made her look vulnerable, but he knew she wasn't. She'd dealt with lightning, ghosts and LaShonda in her head. But not until she'd had to literally fight for her life against an armed man had she shown any fear, and even then, only after the fact.

No, he couldn't leave her. Instead, he slid onto the bed, curled up at her back and wrapped his arms around her.

It was a small, quiet snore that woke Hailey. The way her love life had been going lately, the only sound in her bedroom should have been the alarm clock. Yet she didn't even have time to stiffen before she recognized the heat that snuggled against her back.

The snore was Aaron's.

She smiled. He'd promised to stay until she fell asleep. Apparently he'd been as tired as she had and *had* fallen asleep as he'd suggested he might.

"You're smiling."

"You fell asleep," she said, twisting around until she faced him.

"I did not."

"You snored."

He traced his thumb up and down her arm. "I did not."

"How would you know?" she protested, laughing, shivering from his touch. "You were asleep."

"I see your point."

She followed his suggestive gaze to find her nipples hard and pointing. Heat stung her cheeks. The sweater she'd put on after her shower was thin, and even with her bra covering her beneath it, there was still no mistaking her protruding nipple.

"What are you thinking of?" he asked.

"Lightning."

Her voice was soft and breathy. Aaron was drawn to her the way he had never been drawn to a woman before. He leaned forward and brushed his lips across hers.

"Now," he said, dragging his mouth to a sweet, sweet spot beneath her ear, "is the time for you to tell me to leave."

She arched her neck to give him better access. "Why?"

"Because I'm not going to be able to stop on my own."

She swallowed. "Why would you want to stop?"

Aaron pulled his head away until he could see her eyes. "We're not talking about sleeping this time. We're talking about sex. About making love."

"Oh, I hope so." She slid her arms around his chest and took his mouth with hers. She didn't know where such forwardness came from, she was only grateful she'd found it. She wanted him. She poured herself into the kiss.

A moment later they backed away from each other long enough for her clothes and his to fall away and land on the floor as if by magic. Then they were together again, bare torso to bare torso, breaths comingling, hearts pounding.

For a woman who prided herself on her independence, Hailey gave herself fast to his heat and his strength. After donning a condom from his wallet, he settled himself between her thighs, and she instinctively knew he would give her pleasure the way no other man before him had. He tested and found her ready, then began to enter her.

"Oh, yes," she breathed.

Aaron couldn't speak. She was everything he'd ever wanted in a woman. He might never get enough of her. Then he was there, fully seated. Easing in, then out, back, then forth. Slowly, then slower. Then slow was not enough to feed the hunger inside him. Fire stoked where their bodies were joined and every place she touched him with her soft, delicate hands.

She was with him. He could feel her quivering beneath his weight. Then suddenly she threw her head back and arched her back. A tiny, heart-wrenching scream escaped her throat.

Someone might have said he growled. He couldn't remember one way or the other. All he remembered was flying off the edge of the earth with Hailey in his arms.

He felt as if they'd both been struck by lightning.

Hailey didn't know how long it took her to regain her breath, but when she realized she was finally breathing normally, she felt…reborn. Each breath she took tasted sweeter than any before, regardless of Aaron's weight, which, since he was lying completely atop her, should have been crushing her but instead made her feel safe and cared for. And aroused. Again.

If she felt what she thought she felt against her leg, she wasn't the only one who was already aroused again. She smiled.

Aaron pushed himself up on his forearms. "You look pretty pleased with yourself."

"I'm pretty pleased with you, me and the whole wide world right now."

He nudged his nose against hers and trailed his lips across her cheeks. "Sounds like a sentiment I can endorse."

"I was hoping you'd say that." She reached over and pulled open the drawer of her nightstand. She pulled out a box of condoms and placed it next to the lamp.

The next hours proved to be unlike any Hailey could have imagined. They made love in the bed twice, and then in the shower. They might have gone another round, but then they realized that would mean another shower, which would mean showering together. Since he had to go to the office, they were going to have to stop making love.

"For now," they both agreed.

"Remind me when I go see Mrs. Shelton again to thank her. If it wasn't for her I might never have seen this, um, side of you."

"Oh, yes, you would have." He sidled up to her until his towel pressed against hers. He slipped his arms around her and pulled her to his damp chest. "I like to think that we would have found each other one way or another, you and I."

"I'm glad you feel that way." She flattened her hand against his chest. "I need to be completely honest with you before anything between us goes any further."

"This sounds serious." Aaron pressed a fingertip to the pulse at the base of her throat. "Your heart's pounding."

She nodded. "I guess it is, but…what I'm going to say doesn't have to be a big deal unless you want it to be. I'm just telling you so you'll know before we spend any more time together. Sometime between your grandmother's pork chops and the snore that woke me up a little while ago, I managed to go and fall in love with you."

"Oh, yeah?" He draped his arms over her shoulders.

"I don't expect you to say anything about it," she said. "I just wanted you to know, that's all."

"You lay yourself open like that and don't expect me to say anything? What if I want to say something?"

She shook her head. "We barely know each other. It's too soon. I'm out of my mind. I shouldn't have said anything."

"So you're taking it back?"

"Are you trying to make me crazy?" she asked. "No, I'm not taking back anything."

"So you still love me?"

"Of course I do."

"So it's not too soon for you to love me, but it is too soon for me to return the feeling?"

"No, that's not what I meant."

"Good." He leaned down and kissed her, softly at first, then deeper. "Because I do." He kissed her again. "Return the feeling."

He pressed his lips gently to hers again. "I love you, too. How could I not?"

* * * * *

SEEING RED

DEBRA COWAN

Dear Reader,

While reading stories written by people who had nearly died, I wondered if there were others who had experienced full death and then come back. People who suffered no visible ill effects after too many minutes of being without a pulse and oxygen to the brain. People who regained their ability to function normally...except for one thing.

Firefighter Cass Hollister finds out what happens next after surviving what should've been a fatal fire. She begins to experience bizarre, startling episodes in which she sees full-blown images of fires that haven't happened yet. Fires that could be the work of the vengeful, ex-con brother she sent to prison for arson.

Fires she must report to Ben Wyrick, the sexy fire investigator she walked away from months ago.

Now, to catch a deadly arsonist, Cass and Ben will have to trust each other and believe in the visions neither of them can explain.

Dying could be the worst thing that's ever happened to Cass. Or the best. I hope you enjoy finding out.

Warmly,

Debra Cowan

Like many writers, **Debra Cowan** made up stories in her head as a child. Her BA in English was obtained with the intention of following family tradition and becoming a teacher, but after she wrote her first novel, there was no looking back. After years of working another job in addition to writing, she now devotes herself full-time to penning both historical and contemporary romances. An avid history buff, Debra enjoys travelling. She has visited places as diverse as Europe and Honduras, where she and her husband served as part of a medical-mission team.

Debra invites her readers to contact her at PO Box 30123, Coffee Creek Station, Edmond, Oklahoma 73003-0003, USA, or via e-mail at her website at www.debracowan.net.

To Sharon Sala, for inviting me to join this anthology.
Thanks for your friendship and constant
support through the years
(and the massage therapist you've
been known to share on occasion).

Chapter 1

Cass Hollister's problems began the day she died.

One minute she was pinned beneath a burning beam, flames tearing at her flesh like teeth. The next, she lay on a gurney in the emergency room of a nearby hospital.

Eyes wide, she stared through a gloomy fog at the white acoustical tile ceiling. She tried to blink or respond in some way as a sea of medical personnel flew around her in controlled chaos.

A gray-haired nurse leaned over Cass, checking the IV line already inserted and adjusting the bag of fluids. "CPR isn't working! No pulse, Doctor!"

A young black man worked frantically over her. "Give me one milligram epi!"

Epinephrine? Why? Her heart didn't need to be restarted. She tried to tell them she wasn't dead, but they couldn't hear her.

She felt herself being sucked into a chilling blackness that slowly squeezed the life out of her. Her entire body went flat like a piece of cardboard, no energy, no pain—nothing.

A wave of electricity ripped through her. The lights began to strobe. Suddenly she felt herself being snapped back and forth through a tight blistering space.

She was back at the fire. Moving through the flames, trying to help a fellow firefighter in trouble. Just as she reached him, a gust of searing air whooshed past her. A scalding solid weight hit her in the back, slamming her face-first into the floor.

Pinned across her back and legs by a beam, she couldn't move as sparks rained down on her, gnawing at exposed flesh.

Her teeth snapped together as she was jerked through another narrow space, then into a dense lifeless sphere.

She was trapped! Why didn't someone help her?

Cass heard someone say, "You have to call it, Dr. Hill."

She was back in the E.R., staring into the physician's dark determined features. He shook his head, filled a syringe and plunged it into her chest.

Crushing pressure bore down on her, and she felt as if a piece of her was breaking off. There was no pain, just a gaping hole.

"She's gone, Doctor. You've done all you can."

I'm not gone! I can hear you! The words wouldn't come.

Cass was dragged down into a spinning vortex of frenzied energy and dropped next to her father, who lay in his casket wearing his dress uniform.

A shrill buzzing sounded in her ears, followed by absolute quiet. Tentacles of smoke wrapped around her, cutting off her air. Suffocating, she tried to fight.

Suddenly a sharp biting acid boiled up her throat. She choked, struggling to claw her way out of the writhing smoke, fighting for oxygen. Finally clean air flowed in. She coughed sharply. Her esophagus felt lacerated.

Someone adjusted the air mask over her nose and mouth, urging her to keep breathing. She blinked up into several disbelieving faces.

"Let's put her on a mechanical ventilator," the young doctor said quietly. "Did someone notify her emergency contact? Decisions will need to be made about the extent of her care."

"I can make them." Cass's voice was muffled behind the oxygen mask.

The people above her started violently, giving a collective gasp.

"Land's sake," breathed a nurse close to Cass.

Looking stunned, the doctor lifted the air mask. "Do you know your name?"

"Cass Hollister." Her throat was raw; her lungs

burned. She was suffering from smoke inhalation. Not unusual after fighting a fire, so why were they looking at her so strangely?

The doctor lifted her eyelids and shone his penlight into her eyes. "Today's date?"

She told him.

"Do you remember what happened?"

"We were fighting a fire. A beam fell on me."

"This is incredible," he murmured. "Unheard of."

Things registered for Cass in random order. She smelled like smoke. His name tag read Dr. Hill. Her wrists were burned. "I've been treated for smoke inhalation before, Doc."

"This isn't only smoke inhalation." The man's expression went from shock to amazement. "You had no heartbeat for eleven minutes, Miss Hollister. And no oxygen to your brain."

"Eleven—" Cass's mind whirled. "That's…"

"You flatlined," the doctor said gently. "By every measure we have, you were dead."

Cass gave a choked laugh. "That's impossible."

Dr. Hill shook his head. "I would agree—except that we witnessed it."

Her throat, already sore from smoke, went tight. "Dead as in *dead?*"

Panic and inexplicable dread unfurled inside her. She fought to remain calm. She was probably pumped full of some drug, and it was playing with her mind.

He nodded, watching her as if he expected her to pass

out any minute. "You came in with severe hypoxia. No oxygen to the brain. That caused an elevated heart rate, but your heart couldn't keep that up, so it stopped pumping."

She heard him, but the words seemed to come from far away.

Her head throbbed sharply. Smoke headache, not uncommon after fighting a fire. Although she hadn't felt this strange sense of floating after fighting other fires.

The doctor was talking about running tests for brain damage, but all Cass could think was *dead*. She'd been dead.

Maybe that explained the weird sense of being yanked through space. Had she had a near-death experience? Did people really have those?

The pain in her throat should have been excruciating, but it wasn't. Another strange thing. A sense of euphoria swelled inside her, followed by a hollowed-out feeling of sadness.

When Dr. Hill said he would update her captain, she nodded absently.

Dead. Was that why she'd seen her father? Mike Hollister had been gone six years. Six long years in which she'd followed in his footsteps as an Oklahoma City firefighter and tried to make him proud. Six years in which her twin brother, Lee, had landed himself in prison for arson.

He hated their father. He hated Cass.

Dr. Hill removed the air mask and asked her to

breathe. When she did, his jaw dropped. "You shouldn't be breathing on your own yet. Of course, you shouldn't be doing any of this."

Her heart had stopped. She'd died. Overwhelmed by emotion, she grabbed his hand. "Thank you."

He squeezed her hand in return, smiling. "There are some questions I want to ask, but a fire department investigator has been waiting to talk to you. If you're not up to it, I'll tell him to come back later."

"I'm up to it."

"That's good," a man said in a quiet baritone from the doorway.

Sensation broke through her hard shell of numbness. A shiver stroked up her spine. Only one voice had ever melted her from the inside out.

The brawny black-haired man stepped into view, and Cass's heart took a tumble. Ben Wyrick.

Maybe she really *was* dead, and this was hell.

She'd nearly died. In fact, according to everything the nurse had told him, she *had* died. He didn't want to admit how hard the news had hit him.

It had been eight months since that night at his house when Cass had told him they were over. The sight of her, the memory of her silky skin, made his pulse hitch, but it was her pale, soot-streaked face and the emotion swimming in her eyes that shook something loose inside him. Being this close to her brought on a tide of emotions, ranging from anger to relief.

It wouldn't matter if eight months passed or eight decades. Ben didn't think he would ever be able to look at her without wanting to touch her. It was more than the way she looked. There was a sweetness about her, a warmth.

Her thick shoulder-length hair, the color of spiced tea, was in its usual neatly twisted braid. French braid, she'd told him once.

She wore a pale blue hospital gown, her breasts full and loose beneath the fabric. Her boots and navy pants sat neatly under the gurney.

The raw burns on her wrists looked tender and sent anger sweeping through him. Right now, she was staring at him with those dusky green eyes, and they shut off his brain for just a moment, just as they had the first time he'd met her. Thumping himself mentally, he rubbed his nape. "How're you feeling?"

"Like I swallowed fire," she said hoarsely.

The deep dimple to the left of her mouth flashed, then was gone, but it was enough to make his body go tight.

For the fiftieth time, he wished he didn't have to see her, but thanks to training classes, vacations and illness, the other fire investigators were unavailable. And he'd cussed about that the whole way to the hospital. Admittedly, part of him had wanted to reassure himself that she was okay. She was and he had, but he couldn't leave.

"Is it okay to talk now? How's your throat?"

"It's a little uncomfortable, but nothing like what I've felt before." She gave a wan smile, brushing her bangs away from her eyes.

The gesture reminded him of the first time he'd seen her hair down. It had also been the first time they'd slept together. Images of the thick ginger-colored silk against his belly, sliding through his hands, flooded his mind.

Her appeal wasn't only physical. She had more integrity than almost anyone he knew, and it had cost her dearly when she'd testified against her brother for arson.

Hell. He needed to do his job and get out. "Can you walk me through what happened?"

She recapped the sequence of events after her arrival at the downtown hotel, which was in the midst of being renovated. Despite having eaten a massive quantity of smoke, her voice hardly sounded hoarse.

"Captain Tenney ordered us out. I was in the rear of the hotel and headed for the nearest exit when I saw another firefighter in one of the offices. His radio wasn't working."

She paused, and Ben looked up from his notes to find her waiting expectantly. He had questions, but he wanted to hear her version of events uninterrupted first. "Go on."

"I went over to lead him out, and the next thing I knew, the beam knocked me flat."

And caused her death. He still couldn't believe it. "Who was it? The other firefighter."

"I don't know. His helmet was pulled down so low, I could barely see his eyes."

"Didn't he have a name on his turnout coat?" The smells of antiseptic and smoke drifted around Ben.

"No, not that I saw, and I didn't see a station number on the side of his helmet, either."

"So you have no idea who it was?"

She shook her head. "Someone else on the crew might."

"I'll be talking to them later. Probably figure it out then."

"You'll let me know what you find out?"

"Sure." He needed to talk to the other firefighters, her captain and the incident commander and get a better picture, but Ben already had a kink in his gut.

It was curious but not impossible that Cass hadn't recognized the firefighter, but he might have been from one of the other station houses that had responded to the alarm. That wasn't what got Ben's attention. What did was the fact that the man had worn no identification, neither station number nor name.

The woman in front of him still brought out his primitive instinct to protect. He wanted to touch her so he could feel for himself that she was okay. But he didn't need to do that. And he sure as hell *shouldn't* do it.

She wasn't interested in a relationship. That was what she'd told him. The thought that she was probably already seeing someone else had his jaw clamping tight enough to shatter his teeth.

He wasn't going to ask. It had nothing to do with the case, but his next question did. He had no evidence to support his suspicion, but he couldn't dismiss the possibility that a too-familiar arsonist might be involved.

"I heard Lee was out."

Guilt and sadness crossed her face. "I heard that, too."

"Has he contacted you?"

"C'mon, Ben. You know he hates my guts."

"I thought he might've gotten in touch with you just to rub it in that he's free."

Three years ago, Cass had caught her twin in the act of arson and provided the testimony that sent him to prison. She'd become something of a legend after that.

From Ben's short time with her, he knew she had tried to keep in touch with her brother, but after being rejected constantly when she visited him in prison, she'd finally let it go.

"His parole officer contacted me the second day Lee was out, saying he hadn't checked in. I doubt he has since—or will."

"I imagine you're right. I'm going to ask around, see if I can get a lead on where he might be. Just to rule him out."

"Good idea." Fatigue shadowed her eyes. "If I hear anything, I'll pass it on."

"Okay." He had enough from her for now, so he should get out of here. The longer he stayed, the closer the walls seemed to get. She didn't exactly look comfortable with his presence, either. "If I have more questions, I'll be in touch."

Something flashed in her eyes—longing?—then disappeared. "Okay."

He turned to go. "I'm glad you're all right."

"Thanks."

He nodded, wishing he didn't feel the need to escape, especially since he didn't have the option of keeping his distance from her, at least not until he figured out what had started the blaze at the hotel.

Why had Cass been the only one hurt? From her description of what had happened, and the pictures he'd taken, that beam shouldn't have been loosened by the part of the roof that had collapsed.

Looking at her pale face made Ben furious that this had happened to her. And it made him feel, he had to admit, furious at *her*. He'd been kidding himself to think he could see her and not feel anger. Or the heavy throb of desire. He wanted her. He would probably always want her. But he wasn't going to do anything about it.

Thinking about how she'd walked away should've cooled his blood, but it didn't. He'd finally gotten her out of his head. And seeing her just now had put her right back in.

Despite trying not to, Cass was still thinking about Ben hours later as she lay in the darkness, listening to the softly humming monitors hooked up to her head and chest. Moonlight lapped like water against the floor each time the air from the vent fluttered the thin curtains.

After Ben left, the doctor had moved her to a permanent room, saying she had to stay at least overnight for observation.

Seeing Ben had filled her with regret. She still believed she'd made the right decision to end their relationship, but she'd handled it poorly. He was better off without her.

His presence had caused a swell of longing inside her. It had also set off the awareness that skimmed the surface of her skin whenever he was near. He was a big man. Shoulders as wide as a door, strong neck, brawny chest covered with hair as black as that on his head. He was a wall of hard striated muscle.

His deep blue eyes were intense, perfect for the unpolished bluntness of his features. Her dad would've said Ben's face had character. His nose was slightly crooked. Deep laugh lines bracketed his mouth, and the dark shadow of a beard was always there on his sunweathered skin. His hands were big, too, callused, with long fingers. And incredibly gentle.

His appearance might've been too bold for some, but not for her. She'd been drawn to everything about him. After not seeing him for so long, that realization had barreled over her the instant he'd stepped into the E.R.

His manner had been distant yet polite. After what

she'd done, that was probably more than she should
have expected.

Her wrists were stiff with gauze, but at least the
earlier pain had dimmed to a throbbing ache. She still
felt detached, empty. As if there was no substance to
her body. Except for when Ben had been here, and
then everything inside her had come alive.

She didn't want to go to sleep. Not only because she
was afraid she might dream about him, but also
because she was afraid she might not wake up. Still,
the strain was too much. She tried to stay awake but
felt herself drifting off.

She knew it was a dream as soon as it started. She
was on duty in a well-known department store that was
rapidly being engulfed by a blaze. Somewhere a child
wailed. Moving as quickly as possible, she followed the
sound to the back of the store. No one was there.

She heard her captain's order to evacuate, and she
turned to leave. Eruptions of heat and sparks and fire
boiled around her, beneath her, snatching her down
into a quicksand of hell.

Blinding gray smoke obliterated her flashlight
beam. Someone grabbed her ankle, and she reached
down to help them. Instead of a person, she gripped a
ball of flame, a living incinerator that writhed around
her hands like vines.

Her flesh burned as if bare. Where were her
gloves? Frantic, she tried to beat off the flames
ripping at her hands.

It was too late. The fire peeled off the first layer of her skin, chewing through the flesh, searing her nerve endings.

She shot bolt upright in bed, gasping for air as a cold sweat slicked her spine. Unbearable agony drew her hands into cramped, closed fists. Something was wrong. She needed light.

Flipping the switch was excruciating. She turned her hands over and cried out. Blisters covered her palms. Blood-red bubbles of skin from the bases of both palms to the tips of her fingers.

Tears blurred her vision. She dried her eyes on the sheet and looked again.

A dizzying heat washed over her as she stared at her palms, then touched them. Only smooth flesh, undamaged by fire. There were no blisters. None.

Chapter 2

If there were any reason that would make Ben even less eager to see Cass than he had been yesterday, this was it.

The answers he'd gotten from the other firefighters at the scene were forming a picture that hollowed out his gut. So far, everything he'd found pointed to Cass's "accident" as being a premeditated act.

By the time he had seen her at the hospital the first time, it was three in the morning. The hours since then had been spent at the scene or interviewing witnesses well into the afternoon. After grabbing a sandwich for supper, he returned to the hospital.

His eyes were gritty from fatigue, and he needed sleep, but he knew he needed to talk to Cass first.

The door to her private room was open, and he paused outside. Flowers and balloons crowding the wall-length windowsill made the space look and smell like a flower shop. He rapped on the door. "Hello?"

"Ben? Come in." She barely sounded hoarse today.

He stepped inside and found her sitting up in bed, wrists still bandaged. Her thick hair was down, sliding around her shoulders in a silky cloud.

Not wanting anyone else to hear what he had to say, he closed the door. He caught a whiff of soap and shampoo, and was unable to tear his gaze from the heavy satin of Cass's hair. He wanted to bury his hands in it, his face. Cutting off those thoughts, he shifted his attention to her.

"How are you feeling today?"

"Not too badly. My throat hardly even hurts. The burns are healing quickly." She glanced at her hands, then curled them into fists, a strange look crossing her face. "The nurse helped me wash my hair and take a bath. It's good to get rid of the smoke smell."

Her clean fresh scent teased him as he took in the dewy skin of her face and neck. Instead of a hospital gown, she wore her own sleepwear—a red tank top that hinted at her deep cleavage, and he knew that, under the sheet, she had on the matching polka-dotted red shorts. She cleared her throat, and he realized he was staring.

Jaw tight, he forced his attention to her face. He wasn't the only one affected, he realized, as he caught the awareness shimmering in her eyes.

She lifted her chin. "The doctor said I can go home in the morning, but I have to come back for a check-up in a week."

Ben dragged a hand across his sweat-dampened nape, determined to channel his thoughts back to the case. "That's great. Still pretty unbelievable, but great. You're lucky."

"This whole thing has been so bizarre," she murmured.

"Yeah." Standing at the foot of her bed, he suddenly became aware of the dirt and ash on his jeans and navy OCFD T-shirt. He should've showered and changed before coming here, but his suspicions were so strong that he had cared only about getting to Cass. "There are some things I need to touch base with you about."

"Did you find out about that firefighter? Who he is?"

"I still don't know. None of the other firefighters or the incident commander saw the guy."

"You mean I was the only one?"

"Yeah."

She stared down at her clasped hands, brushing her thumb back and forth across the opposite palm. "Maybe I hallucinated him."

"Are you saying you're unsure now of what you saw?" If she were, it could be a result of her dead-but-not-dead experience. "Cass?"

"I'd just hoped someone else might have seen him." She rubbed at her palms again. "It's just that I wouldn't blame you if you didn't trust me."

"What happened between us doesn't have anything to do with this fire," he said stiffly. "It's in the past. Leave it there."

Her mouth tightened. "All right."

He felt like hitting something. Why did she have to bring up their past? It had no relevance here. He wouldn't let it. "I found a length of rope near where you fell. Do you remember seeing it?"

"No. Do you think it had something to do with my accident?"

"It was tied to the beam that fell on you, and the construction foreman hadn't seen it before. He said there was no reason for it to be there."

"That's strange. I don't get it."

He might as well tell her all of it at once. "The beam that fell on you was cut."

Apprehension crossed her face.

As matter-of-factly as he could, Ben continued. "The reason that beam fell on you wasn't because it was weakened in the fire. It was because someone cut a notch in it and pulled it down with the rope."

She blinked. "To deliberately hurt someone?"

"Not someone," he said grimly. "*You.*"

The color drained out of her face. "Why would someone want to hurt me?"

She had to be thinking about her brother. Ben sure was. "We need to figure that out. You're sure this mystery fireman motioned you over?"

"Yes."

"Is that an area you would've gone to if he hadn't?"

Massaging her hands, she shook her head. "No. Those offices had already been checked and cleared. We were ordered out."

Dread snarled Ben's gut.

Her troubled gaze pinned his. "So that fire was arson."

He hated that she was coming to the same conclusion he had. "Matchbook and paper starter. Most likely the arsonist set the fire, then waited, wearing firefighter gear, for y'all to arrive on the scene."

She looked horrified. "He was waiting for *me*?"

"It appears that way. Your name is on your turnout coat, so it wouldn't have been hard for him to blend in and keep track of you."

"Whoever it was could've found out my schedule and set the fire knowing I'd respond to the call."

He nodded, concern mixing with anger.

"Lee could've found that out," she whispered.

Ben's jaw locked. He wanted to stop whoever was doing this, not only because it was his job, but also because Cass was the one being threatened.

"No one else saw him." Horror crept into her voice as realization set in. "He made that beam fall on me."

"I have no proof it's your brother."

"It is. I know it." Tears filled her eyes.

Everything inside him urged him to hold her, but he knew how stupid—and unwelcome—that would be.

"Is there anyone else who might want to hurt you?"

"I hope not. I don't think so."

"Has anything strange happened in the last few months?"

"You mean besides that whole freaky thing yesterday when I came back to life? No."

"No one's threatened you at a scene? No trouble at work?"

"No."

"What about dating?"

Her eyes widened. "What does that have to do with anything?"

"Maybe nothing." He wanted to know, that's what, but the truth was that it also might matter. "Have you been seeing anyone? Had a bad breakup?" Thanks to their history, he knew that was a definite possibility.

"I haven't been seeing anyone. Not since… No."

"Anyone asking you out who won't take no for an answer?"

"Nothing like that."

Ben told himself the reason he was relieved was because it narrowed his suspect list, but that was a lie. He was glad she hadn't drop-kicked him and immediately hooked up with someone else. Which meant he was letting things get too personal.

His shoulders went tight. "I talked to Lee's parole officer again on the way over, and he's heard nothing. There's a warrant out to pick up your brother, but he's still MIA. When you get out of here, you can't go home."

"Where am I supposed to go?"

Ben noticed she kept rubbing her hands nervously. No wonder. Someone had tried to kill her. He wanted to be the one to protect her, but he couldn't be. He wasn't going to let himself cross a line he might not be able to recross. Things between them had to stay professional.

"For a while, you'll need to stay somewhere besides your house. What about with friends? Maybe Jana and Tim Daniels?"

"No. Lee knows them. If I stay there, there's a chance they could be hurt. I don't want that."

"Okay." He would feel the same in her place, but he didn't know an alternative.

She was silent for so long that his mind started working in a direction he didn't like. He could stay with his brother until this was over, and Cass could stay at *his* place.

He didn't want that. She was already in his head; he didn't need her flirty scent in every inch of his house.

"I can stay at the firehouse," she said. "It won't matter that I'm not cleared to work."

"That's a good idea." Both disappointment and relief charged through him. The fire station was manned 24/7. No one could walk in or out without being noticed. "I'll talk to your captain, too. I want him to be aware there's a threat."

She massaged her hands again.

"Your hands okay? Should I get a nurse?"

"No, they're fine." She shoved them beneath the sheet. "Do I have to go into hiding?"

"No, but if you need to go somewhere, don't go alone. I'm not the only one looking for Lee, so we'll find him. It just may take a while."

The anxiety in her eyes hit him hard. Even though her staying at the firehouse was the best solution, it didn't feel like the *right* one. Even so, he refused to let this be about anything except the job.

He'd ridden in that rodeo before. More than once, since their breakup, he'd been glad he hadn't asked her what he'd originally planned the night everything fell apart between them. Not to move in with him, but to marry him.

As it was, she hadn't been able to get away from him fast enough.

Yeah, he was keeping as much distance from Cass as possible.

He wasn't going to let her get hurt, but he also wasn't going to let her hurt *him* again.

Ben's visit was still fresh in Cass's mind the next day. Someone had tried to kill her, and her brother was a likely suspect. And if that weren't enough to have her reeling, there was her reaction to Ben to contend with. Just because he still got to her, that didn't mean she'd been wrong to leave him.

Tension whipped her nerves taut. She was glad to be

out of the hospital, although she wished she were home. Unable to return there at all, she had asked Jana to bring some clothes and toiletries to the firehouse. She wished she were staying with Ben, but it was better that distance remain between them. Being around him could make her second guess her decision about breaking things off.

She still wanted him. She couldn't call her body's reaction to him anything *except* want. The way he'd looked at her in the hospital had put her hormones on simmer. Her pulse hitched as she remembered the undisguised desire in his eyes.

Did he feel anything except lust for her now? If so, she couldn't tell.

As she finished the kitchen cleanup for the guys who'd answered a call, the television blaring, a local news anchor broke into the programming to report an arson fire at Mercer's department store. The blaze had claimed the life of a child. Every detail slammed into Cass like a two-by-four.

Everything was exactly as she'd dreamed last night.

Sweat broke out over her whole body. She sank into the nearest chair and put her head between her knees to keep from throwing up.

Her stomach began to cramp as a theory formed. The vision of that fire had happened after she'd died and been resuscitated. It had to be related to that.

Could this be possible? Had she really seen a fire before it happened?

* * *

Cass told herself that seeing the department store fire before it happened was a fluke. But when she saw another arson fire the next morning—this time without falling asleep first—and learned hours later that it, too, had happened, she called Ben and asked him to come to the firehouse. She didn't want to, but she had to.

As they sat in his white SUV, night settled over the city in sooty layers. It was too hot to talk outside, and she didn't want to discuss this in front of her fellow firefighters. Ben's vehicle was the best place for their conversation.

Cold air blasted from the vents. He angled his broad shoulders into the corner and draped one big hand over the steering wheel.

The sleeves of his white dress shirt were rolled back to reveal strong forearms. Crisp black hair showed in the vee left by two open shirt buttons, and he wore navy slacks. Typically, he wore a suit only when testifying in court.

He shoved a hand through his short dark hair, the fabric of his shirt pulling taut across his muscular upper arm. Dark blue eyes zeroed in on her. "You sounded shaky on the phone. You okay?"

"Yes." *For a freak.*

His eyes glittered like dark glass in the shadows. Her gaze slid over his corded neck, the strong line of his throat. She was hit with the urge to put her mouth there. Kiss him. Lick him. Like that would ever happen again.

Quietly he said, "You don't look like you've gotten much sleep since leaving the hospital."

"I haven't." *And you're getting ready to find out why.* She took a deep breath. There was no good way to do this. "Let me get all this out before you say anything, okay?"

Eyes narrowing, he hesitated then nodded.

"I was… After I…" she began haltingly. How did you tell someone who dealt in hard evidence that you saw fires before they happened?

She plunged in. "Since the accident, I've had these…episodes. It's like I'm at a fire. I see the location, the victims…all kinds of details."

She touched her hands, still astonished that there were no blisters there. No way was she telling him about those. She already sounded like a crazy person. "But these aren't dreams. The most recent one happened when I was wide awake. The first one was in the hospital. I saw the fire at Mercer's department store."

Ben straightened, coming to attention at her words.

"At first I thought it was a nightmare. Then I heard about it on the news. Everything about it was exactly what I saw."

Her voice began to shake. Hearing herself talk about her visions aloud, sharing it with Ben, unsettled her even more. "I didn't know what was happening until I saw the news and realized—" Was she really going to say this out loud?

"Realized what?"

Every doubt, every jeer she'd uttered to herself, was in his tone. "That I'm seeing fires before they happen."

The silence was immediate and heavy with disbelief. Drawing out until her nerves stretched taut. "I know it sounds like voodoo witchy stuff, all right?"

He said softly, "It sounds like post-traumatic stress disorder."

"I thought about that, but how could I know details like the specific building or what was inside or the victims if I hadn't really seen those fires?"

"Because of your brother," he said bluntly.

"What about him?" Then she understood. "You think he's the arsonist and he's telling me what he's going to do? You can't be serious!"

"It makes sense."

"No, it doesn't! He hates me. He's not going to confide in me."

"Confide, no. But he might give you the information in order to put you in a bad position, to compromise your job."

Stunned, she stared at him. "Well, he isn't! I just told you how I know about these fires. I don't see who sets them or how they start."

"Okay, when's the next one?"

"What?"

"When's the next fire?" he challenged. "And where?"

"I don't know! This hasn't been happening long

enough for me to figure it out. This seems just as weird
to me as it does to you, believe me." Probably more so,
thanks to the blisters that came and went. She didn't
blame him for his doubt, but it irritated her anyway. "All
I know is these fires took place hours after I...saw
them."

A muscle pulsed in his jaw. "It would be under-
standable if you wanted to share information about
Lee without actually informing on him. I know how
you beat yourself up after testifying against him."

"That isn't what's going on." Her voice cracked.
How could Ben think she would cover for an arsonist,
even her brother? Especially since she'd been the one
to turn him in three years ago. "Maybe it *is* him, but I
don't *know* that."

"You're telling me everything?"

"Yes," she lied, thinking about the blisters.

Apparently she'd hesitated too long, because he
pinned her with those piercing blue eyes. She held his
gaze, trying to appear calm even as her heart slammed in
her chest. She fought not to blurt out the rest of the story.

His gaze was sharp, ruthless. "What do you think I
can do with this information? Am I supposed to wait
until you get one of these dreams or visions or whatever
they are, then put out a call and ask for extra men to
watch whatever place you claim to see?"

"I don't know what you should do." Nerves wound
tight, she rubbed at her hands again. They were stiff and
sore. "I don't know who it is, and I don't know when

the next fire will be! Maybe nearly dying *did* leave me with brain damage, but I thought I should tell you what was happening. I couldn't keep quiet, knowing my information might help prevent a fire or stop one before it kills someone else."

She told herself Ben's skepticism wasn't personal. The story *was* fantastic. It was happening to her, and even she couldn't believe it.

She looked him in the eye. "I wouldn't lie."

"I know that." There was no hesitation, no doubt. "But this is pretty damn hard to believe."

"I'm having a little trouble with that myself." As certain as she was that she was seeing fires beforehand, the knowledge still rattled her. She wanted to throw herself in his arms, but was so shaken by how much she wanted that—and by the whole conversation—she opened the car door to escape. A wave of steamy air hit her face. "Thanks for coming."

Before she could move, her cell phone rang.

It was the groundskeeper at the cemetery where her father was buried.

"What's wrong?" Ben asked when she hung up.

He was the last person she wanted to tell, but she couldn't stop herself. "My father's headstone has been vandalized. I have to go to the cemetery."

"I'll drive you."

"No." She would call Jana or Tim.

As she began to slide out, Ben cupped her elbow. "You aren't supposed to go anywhere alone."

Off balance, she started to argue, but she just didn't have it in her. "Thanks," she said in a half whisper, and pulled the door closed.

Lee resented their father, and this act of vandalism, so close on the heels of the fires, felt to her like further proof that her brother was the arsonist. Her stomach sank.

"I think it's Lee," Ben said.

His hand felt hot on her flesh, but she tried to ignore that as he went on.

"But if it *is* him, and this is his way of telling you he's behind these fires, why not just contact you instead of playing this game?"

"A question I'd like to have answered, too."

He removed his hand and put the SUV in gear. "I'm sorry, Cass. For all of this."

Nodding, she stared out the window.

She wasn't sure what she had expected when she told him, but it hadn't been him accusing her of covering for her brother.

Or him offering to go with her to the cemetery. She shouldn't read anything into that. His presence was for her protection, for the case.

She suddenly, fiercely, wished it were about her.

Chapter 3

Seeing fires before they happened? If Ben didn't know better, he would think Cass was on drugs. Or having an allergic reaction to something they'd given her when she left the hospital.

But she'd never done recreational drugs, and he knew the doctor hadn't prescribed anything, so there was nothing to cause an adverse reaction. Apparently the trauma she'd suffered had affected her more deeply than she'd first let on. Maybe some part of her brain really had been damaged. Regardless, she was upset, so it had seemed only right to insist on driving her to the cemetery.

What did she expect him to do about her claim that

she "saw" fires before they happened? What *could* he do? For right now, he would start by not letting her out of his sight.

A fierce sense of protectiveness swept over him, but he dismissed it and told himself that what he felt was responsibility. She was a victim, a witness. Right now, she happened to be part of his job. That didn't mean she was part of his life. He had to be careful not to get sucked in again.

His doubts about her getting information from some kind of vision had nothing to do with the fact she'd dumped him, but with plain old disbelief in that kind of paranormal crap and with her low-life brother being a convicted arsonist. It made sense that Lee Hollister was the torch and tipping Cass off as a means to taunt her. To show her that she couldn't stop him. And in Ben's opinion, her turning Lee in three years ago was reason enough for her not to turn him in again. The whole ordeal had been hell for her.

No matter where Cass got her information, there was no doubt she was certain of it. Just as there was no ignoring the fact that she was afraid. She'd probably expected him not to believe her story, but if what she'd told him could save a life or stop a fire, he couldn't afford to dismiss it.

Though he had no proof, he still suspected Lee was the one who had started the fire and rigged that beam to try to kill his sister. The SOB needed to be sent back to prison for good, before he made another attempt on

Cass's life or started more fires, and Ben wanted to be the one to send him on that one-way trip. Right now, the best chance Ben had of finding the bastard was to spend more time with Cass.

It was the best and most logical thing to do. And the worst. Being near her drove him crazy. Her soft floral scent scrambled his thoughts, and he couldn't help remembering the sweetness of that honey-and-cream skin—her neck, her breasts, her thighs. He wanted another taste. *Man, don't go there.* Pure torture.

Once they reached the cemetery, he followed her directions around a curve and parked on the side of the asphalt road. Regularly spaced light poles put off a filmy glow as Ben and Cass passed neatly tended plots. The light swam with shadows, making the ground appear to move, though that wasn't what had the hair on Ben's neck rising.

It was the heavy feel of the night. Silent...still. Threatening. Oklahoma was rarely without wind, and its absence, combined with the steamy temperature, made the air a dead weight. The way it was in the seconds before a tornado.

The groundskeeper was waiting patiently next to Mike Hollister's headstone, aiming his flashlight so the beam fully illuminated the grave marker's stony face.

The rectangular stone, arched at the top and made of gray granite, was all but destroyed. Cass drew a sharp breath. Ben could practically feel the hurt well up inside her. Chunks of rock had been gouged out, leaving holes that gaped like empty eye sockets.

She knelt, touching the damaged facade.

"Looks like someone took a sledgehammer to it," Ben said.

"Dad's name is gone."

The word *Father* had been obliterated, as well. The crime was clearly personal. In Ben's opinion, Lee had to be responsible. Who else had motive? Who else hated the dead man so much?

In the glow of light, with her head bent, Cass looked small, alone. Anger burned inside Ben. When they had been together, she had sometimes talked about her brother's bitterness toward their father, how he'd never had the balls to tell the old man he didn't want to be a smoke eater. Cass had excelled at fighting fires, though, making Mike Hollister proud. And Lee even more resentful.

The groundskeeper said he'd already viewed the security tape, but the cameras hadn't gotten a clear image of the vandal. Even so, he apologized for not catching the culprit.

As the man walked away, Ben thanked him. He expected to hear Cass do the same, but when she said nothing, he looked down at her.

Moonlight limned one side of her body, turning her profile a cool silver. She was staring straight ahead, eerily motionless.

"Cass?"

No answer. She didn't so much as twitch a muscle. It was as if she didn't hear him.

Concerned, he stepped closer. "Cass?"

She gave a keening moan and gripped the headstone, doubling over.

What the hell? Ben lunged, hooking an arm around her waist to catch her before she pitched facefirst into the granite.

He fell to his knees, and she sagged into him. "You okay?"

She didn't answer. Beneath his hold, her muscles were locked tight. Her breath sawed in and out of her lungs, and her pulse was hammering so hard in her throat that he could see it even in the dark shadows. There was a sheen of perspiration on the curve of her neck. Ben's heart kicked hard. What was going on? Was she having a seizure? People with head trauma did that sometimes.

Sobbing, she drew back and thrust her hands toward him. "Look! Look at my palms!"

He did. And sucked in a breath that knifed painfully through his lungs. He told himself the light was playing tricks on his eyes. He couldn't be seeing what he thought he was.

"I saw another fire," she whispered.

Ben couldn't look away. Her palms were covered in blisters, open pockets of boiled skin.

What was he seeing? What the hell was going on?

Tears streaming down her face, Cass demanded hoarsely, "Get your cell phone. Quick! Take a picture."

Operating on reflex, barely aware of moving, he whipped the phone out of his pocket, flipped it open and clicked a shot of her palms.

"Another one," she choked out.

He did, then paused. There were no blisters. Thinking there must be a problem with the viewfinder, he lowered the phone.

She lifted her hands, palms up. "They're gone."

Gone. Just like that. He stared hard, his brain numb. Adrenaline shot through him, and he rose, helping her to her feet. "Are you okay? Let me take you to the emergency room."

"I'm fine. I just need a second to get a hold of myself."

"I might need more than a second," he muttered, moving her away from the headstone. He slid an arm around her waist and steered her toward his SUV. "You need to sit."

He wanted to make sure nothing else was wrong with her. He hadn't just seen what he thought he had. He couldn't have.

"I'm fine. Really."

She didn't look fine. She looked afraid, defeated.

He kept his arm around her in case she started to tumble again and he needed to catch her. Hell, someone might need to catch *him*. "You don't seem surprised by what just happened."

"I'm not. It…it happened before, too."

She trembled, and tears ran down her cheeks. Ben

didn't know if she was even aware of them. He opened the passenger door and set her carefully on the edge of the seat to face him. "How many of these episodes have you had?"

"Three now."

"You've gotten blisters every time?"

"Yes."

"Are they always this bad?"

"Yes. They haven't gotten worse. I guess that's good."

"Let me see your hands again."

She reluctantly obliged.

Staring at her palms, he shook his head. Her flesh was smooth. There wasn't even a hint of redness. How was this possible? He'd seen those blisters, seen how badly burned her hands had been.

She believed her near-death experience had something to do with these episodes. He couldn't prove differently.

Son of a... Ben felt disoriented, as if he were trying to find his way blindfolded along the edge of a cliff. Something weird was definitely going on, and neither of them could explain it. Maybe there *was* no explanation.

He gently brushed his fingers across one of her palms. "Does this hurt?"

"No." She tugged her hand free of his hold.

Her skin was damp with sweat, and he lifted a hand to push a stray lock of hair away from her face. She stared up at him with those deep green eyes, searching his face. For what? Reassurance, maybe? He didn't have any.

He became aware then of how close together they were standing. Her flirty scent had his nerve endings throbbing. His body went tight.

He wanted to touch her petal-smooth skin, her warmth. He needed to feel her. Comfort her.

Damn, he needed comfort himself.

Her voice cracked. "Lee destroyed Dad's headstone. I know it was him."

The devastation in her face cut Ben deep. He pulled her close and wrapped his arms around her.

Burying her face in his shoulder, she gave a choked sob. Hesitantly, her hands rose to his waist, then slid around to splay across his back as her tears dampened his shirt. She held on, her breasts flattened against him, her head tucked beneath his chin.

Her skin-warmed scent settled in his lungs, chiseled away at his control. He should release her, but he couldn't make himself do it.

After a moment, Cass lifted her head, swiping at her tear-stained face. "Sorry. I lost it there for a second."

"You're entitled," he said gruffly. He forced himself to let go, although he couldn't help touching her cheek as he withdrew.

Looking uncertain, she inched back on the seat. "Do you believe me now? That I'm not getting the information from Lee?"

"Yes." Lee might be the torch, but Ben was sure now that Cass wasn't covering for him. She couldn't have faked what he'd just seen.

"He has to be the one behind everything. I can't believe he hates me this much."

"Neither can I," Ben said grimly. He wanted to get his hands around Lee Hollister's throat and squeeze. Before he registered the thought, the words were out. "I won't let him hurt you."

Surprise flared in her eyes as she nodded. As Ben stared down into her face, he inwardly cursed. He was going to protect her, and somehow he had to do it without getting tangled up with her again.

The return trip was short. She refused to go to the E.R., and Ben admitted there was nothing to show the doctors anyway. He was still stunned over what he'd seen happen to her hands. He wanted to help her, but he didn't know how he could, how *anyone* could.

She sat quietly, gazing out the window as they passed trees and houses and city streets. Light from the streetlamps flashed in and out of the car as they drove. Occasionally she would glance down at her hands, then clasp them together.

"Are you going to file a police report about the headstone?"

"I guess, although I don't know that it will do any good."

He studied her profile. "How do you feel? Head-ache? Pain anywhere?"

"No."

"Tell me what you saw," he said quietly.

"The fire's at an office complex." Her voice was flat. "A new one, northwest of the city, around MacArthur and Memorial."

He knew the area. "One of the finished ones?"

"It's nearly finished. It's across from the bank that's open for business. The fire originated in a small closet."

"So maybe the construction people left some flam-mables—paint, cleaner, stuff like that?"

"Maybe." She rubbed at her hands, her voice growing agitated. "I hate this. If I'm going to see these things, why can't I see when they'll happen? Or who's doing them? I have no control over it at all."

"You don't need to know when or who. What you saw is enough for us to do something this time. Since we have no idea when it might happen, we need to make a plan."

She nodded.

"You saw the first fire six hours before it happened, and the second one more than ten."

"Right."

"I can't put a crew on standby for this." He felt, rather than saw, her tense. "But I can do some surveil-lance on my own."

"Like a stakeout?"

"Yeah."

"That's a good idea." She seemed to relax a bit. "I'm coming, too."

The last thing he wanted was to sit in six feet of space all night with her next to him, smelling her, close enough to touch her, but she was right. She needed to be there. And for all he knew, she might need *him* to be there. What if she had another episode? She shouldn't go through that alone. Besides, the sooner he caught this torch, the quicker he and Cass could go their separate ways.

He pulled up in front of her fire station to let her off. After picking up some things at his office, he would return for her. He asked her to bring her camera for backup pictures and something for them to eat.

"All right." She massaged her hands, and he couldn't help reaching over to cradle them in one of his.

"Do they hurt now?"

"No."

He brushed his thumb across her palm. He still couldn't believe there was no evidence of the blisters that had ravaged her hands. "You rub them a lot. Is it because they're tender?"

"No, they don't feel any different than normal." She tugged her hands from his hold and slid them under her thighs. "I want this to stop."

"Yeah, I imagine you do."

"I'll feel better if we can actually prevent a fire. What if we sit there and nothing happens?"

"We'll consider ourselves lucky."

The sight of her wan features pulled at something inside him. He squeezed her leg. "Don't think about what's bad. Think about what's good. We know the location, thanks to you. If we're there when the fire starts, that gives us a head start on calling dispatch, maybe even stopping it before it starts."

"True." She sounded exhausted.

"Are you sure you're up to this? You've been through a lot. Maybe you should rest."

"A child is dead because of this arsonist. I want to do something. I *need* to."

And this would give her some sense of control.

"Will you have to get approval for the stakeout?" she asked.

"Yeah." She knew he would, so why was she asking? He cocked his head, waiting.

She averted her eyes. "Where will you say you got your information?"

She was afraid he would reveal her secret. "You don't need to worry, Cass. I'll say I got a tip, and if I'm pushed, I'll refuse to disclose my source."

The relief in her face was so great that his chest ached.

Her voice shook. "Thanks for keeping it between us. Of course, no one would believe you if you *did* tell."

He couldn't argue with that. He still wasn't sure he believed it himself.

She made a frustrated sound. "Who gets cursed with stuff like this? Freaks, that's who."

"You're not a freak. I don't understand what's happening, but you're not a freak."

"I want it to stop. Why won't it stop?"

Fear vibrated in every line of her body, and Ben's only thought was to make it go away.

"Hey." He slid his knuckle beneath her chin and turned her face to his. "I know this is scary as hell, but you're going to be able to do something about this fire. That's good."

She didn't look reassured. He smoothed her hair back, grazing his thumb against her cheek. "We'll figure it out."

"You'll help me?" Turmoil darkened her eyes.

He nodded.

"Thank you." Her gaze dropped to his mouth, and danger signals flashed.

When her breath feathered against his lips, he knew she was going to kiss him. And he knew he should stop her.

The first brush of her mouth zinged him to his toes. It was too much. It wasn't enough. He wanted a taste, just one more taste of her.

He settled his mouth on hers and gave in to the hunger that had been building inside him. In an instant, her spicy sweetness, the slick heat of her tongue, overrode every thought. She made a sound in the back of her throat, and whatever restraint he had snapped.

Locking his free arm around her waist, he dragged her closer, cursing the console between them. One soft hand curled around his neck. The full press of her breasts, her soft floral scent, had the blood pounding through him. He took the kiss deeper, urging her into him.

He'd missed her. The way she fit him just right, the teasing stroke of her tongue, the *feel* of her. It took several seconds for him to think past the heated rush of his blood.

Cass was the only woman he'd ever wanted to marry. And he'd been nothing more than a rebound. She hadn't said that, but it was true. The thought penetrated the lust-filled fog in his brain. He remembered the pain. And the anger. They hadn't worked the first time. No reason to think they would now.

He pulled away, breathing hard, his body hurting. "Stop, Cass. Stop."

The dreamy look in her eyes nearly had him saying forget it and pulling her onto his lap. But that would be stupid.

Her mouth was wet from his, and she touched it with trembling fingers. "Ben?"

Her husky voice had his muscles clenching. He started to tell her the kiss meant nothing, but damn it, it *did* mean something.

"That was a bad idea," he said. "We're not going back there."

The pain in her eyes struck hard. He wanted to tell her he didn't mean it, but the truth was, he *had* to mean it.

"You're right." There was a mix of anger and resignation in her voice as she opened her car door. "I'll be ready when you come back."

Ben started to argue, then reminded himself that she had a stake in this, too. And he needed to stay nearby in case she had another vision or ran into her brother.

She shut the door firmly and hurried up the fire station's drive, her shadow lengthening in the floodlights shining from above the door. In seconds she had disappeared from sight.

Sharp-edged desire clawed through him. He wanted her, but being with her would never be just sex for him. For every man there was a woman he couldn't walk away from, and for him that woman was Cass Hollister. She'd done the walking last time, and he'd been feeling the pain of it all over again since seeing her in that hospital bed.

He groaned, dropping his head back against the seat. Why had he let her kiss him? Why had he kissed her back? Now he'd had a taste of her, and it was going to torment him.

He'd been kidding himself to think he could treat her like any other victim. She wasn't just any victim. She was the woman who'd ripped out his heart. That was what he needed to remember.

Chapter 4

The man could still make her melt. Cass had ordered herself not to think about that kiss. She lasted ten whole seconds before the memory was all over her. He wanted her, but he'd said they weren't going back there, and she knew he meant it.

Now, sitting with him again in the SUV, her body still tingling from his kiss, he was aloof. She reminded herself that however cold he was now, he'd been there for her earlier when she'd needed him.

He'd changed from his slacks and dress shirt to jeans and a black T-shirt that molded to his broad shoulders and flat stomach. Soft, worn denim hugged his powerful thighs. He smelled good, like mint and shaving cream. His left hand was draped over the steering wheel; his right rested on his thigh.

As much as his kiss had wound Cass up, something else was zinging along her nerves now. After placing her camera on the console, she slid a pink slip of paper out of her shorts pocket. "There was a message from Lee when I got to the firehouse."

"What?" Ben's head whipped toward her. "What kind of message?"

"Just to say he was checking on me." There was no telling what that meant, and she shuddered. Her brother could be watching her. Or maybe he just wanted her to think he was.

"You're sure it was from him?"

"Yes. He left his name. Isn't that helpful?" she choked out. "I called his parole officer, Hugo. He still hasn't heard from Lee or seen him."

Ben cursed. "You okay?"

"Yes." Just looking at his mouth roused a tickle in her stomach. "At least he didn't come to the firehouse, although that might've been better. If he had, we'd know for sure he was in town."

"My gut says he is, and yeah, I know that doesn't prove anything."

He took the ramp from Britton Road onto northbound Hefner Parkway. "We'll find him, Cass. He's probably still in Oklahoma City and watching you, just like he wants you to think." Ben exited on Memorial Road then took the Kilpatrick Turnpike west. "I haven't had a chance to print the picture of your blisters yet."

"That's okay." The memory of her ravaged palms made her slightly nauseous. And no matter what Ben said, she felt like a freak.

He hitched a thumb toward the backseat. "I brought the files on the two fires you...saw before they started."

Cass unbuckled her seat belt and turned in her seat, leaning over to grab the folders. As she eased back down, she felt Ben's gaze on her backside. Sensation fluttered in her belly again.

He hit the overhead light as she opened the files and read. "The first one was started with a matchbook. The second with gasoline. The torch didn't even try to hide the gas can.

"We didn't get any prints at either site, so we still don't have a solid lead. I interviewed people in the area, but no one saw anything."

She exhaled in exasperation. "Since the blazes weren't started the same way, how will we know if one person is responsible for them?"

"We won't for sure until we catch him, but I think it's one torch. Just call it my gut again."

A sudden frustration surged through her. Why couldn't this...curse, gift, whatever it was, go away as suddenly as it had come? On second thought, if she had to die again in order to get rid of it, forget it.

Ben drove up to a complex of four quadrants, each one hosting a single strip of three offices, some of them already open for business, judging by the signs. "There's not much around here we can use for cover."

She scanned the well-lit parking lot and the empty field beyond, which was dotted with pine trees and scrub brush. Bradford pear trees lined the median dividing the complex into its four sections.

At the second quadrant, Ben drove over a curb, positioning his SUV behind a completed office that sat diagonal to the nearly finished building Cass recognized as the scene of the next fire.

"We won't be immediately visible here," he said as he killed the engine. "Can't run the air conditioner, so you should roll down your window."

Cass did, wondering if her coming had been a good idea. Who knew how long she would have to sit here with Ben and remember their mind-blowing kiss. And realize for the hundredth time just how badly her judgment sucked. Her ex-boyfriend had been a dirty cop, and she'd never suspected a thing. She'd stayed too long with a guy who was a jerk and run from the one who wasn't.

Ben grabbed his camcorder case from the backseat and pulled out the charger for the extra battery, then plugged it into the cigarette lighter.

"The other fires I saw were at night," she said. "Hopefully this one will be, too."

Nodding, he aimed the camera, then repositioned himself to get another angle. Once he was satisfied, he leaned back against the seat.

After they ate the sandwiches Cass had brought, they sat quietly. The night sounds of crickets and locusts swelled around them. From the nearby expressway, she could hear the whoosh of passing automobiles.

Maybe she was paranoid, but Ben seemed determined not to touch her in any way. He had pulled back from the glancing brush of her fingers when she'd handed him a sandwich, and again when she offered him a bottled water.

In spite of that—or maybe because of it—she was acutely aware of him. His long fingers resting on the steering wheel, the small space separating his big frame from hers, his body heat. The urge to kiss him again surged inside her. And when she caught his gaze on her mouth, awareness drummed against her already ragged nerves.

In the shadows, his blue eyes looked black, sultry. Even with the window open and the smells of grass, fuel and dirt in the air, she caught his masculine woodsy scent. Sitting a foot away, wrapped in darkness, the drift of his body heat was almost palpable against her skin.

Her heart hurt thinking about how right their kiss had felt. And how he had pulled back. "I'm sorry if I was out of line earlier."

The way his eyes narrowed told her he knew exactly what she was referring to.

"It's okay." His words notwithstanding, his tone clearly said "drop it."

"It only occurred to me later that you might be seeing someone."

He shifted his gaze out the windshield, his body rigid, his profile softened by the night. Silence swelled between them. Had she ruined everything? Even the smooth way they had been working together?

"I wasn't trying to make a move on you. Or, well—" She gave a nervous laugh. "That wasn't my intent. Things got out of hand. I just needed—" *You.* She bit back the word. "A friend."

He looked at her, eyes glittering hotly. The mix of light and shadow shifting across his face made him appear harsh, intimidating.

She tried not to squirm. "I guess I just wasn't thinking."

"Forget it," he said gruffly. "I know you were upset by the episode at the cemetery."

"I didn't mean to do it, but I'm not sorry."

Wariness flared in his gaze. "What am I supposed to say here?"

"Nothing." A nervous breath shuddered out of her. "I'm just…clearing the air."

She might as well face up to everything. "And while I'm on the subject of things neither of us wants to talk about, I don't think I've ever apologized for walking away from you. Running away is more accurate, I guess."

His gaze moved over her face, lingered on her mouth. Hope ballooned inside her until he broke the moment by picking up the camcorder and staring through the viewfinder.

Before now, she hadn't allowed herself to consider the possibility that they might still be together if she hadn't panicked at the first sign of commitment. "You ever wonder what might've happened with us?"

"No." Despite a brief hesitation, he sounded certain.

Was he relieved now that she hadn't moved in with him? "At the time, I didn't realize how much I was hurting you. All I thought about was—"

"Getting away," he grumbled. "Yeah, I picked up on that."

"I was messed up, Ben. Did you understand why I left?"

"You didn't trust me not to hurt you."

"No! It was because I didn't trust myself. I was worried about making another mistake that would hurt both of us." She hated that he ever believed he'd been at fault. "After Mitch was busted, I was afraid to rely on my judgment about anything." Her boyfriend of nearly two years had been a dirty cop on the take and she had suspected nothing until his arrest.

"Then you and I met three weeks later, and I fell hard for you. And fast. I left because it scared me."

His eyes narrowed.

Since he was listening, Cass tentatively continued, "Have you been able to forgive me?"

Tension strummed across her nerves. The sweat slicking her palms had nothing to do with the hot July night and everything to do with the big man sitting less than an arm's length away.

"Yeah. And I think you were probably right. We moved too fast."

Did that mean he hadn't felt as strongly about her as he'd thought? She had no right to feel disappointed.

"I figured I'd done something," he admitted hesitantly. "For a long time, I wondered what, then I realized it wasn't really about me. Not for the most part, anyway."

"None of it was. There was nothing bad about you." She folded one leg under her. "You were great."

He stared at her mouth, then, with an impatient shake of his head, dragged a hand down his face. "I pushed. You weren't ready."

"I *wasn't* ready, but you didn't push. I accused you of that because I was afraid. I didn't believe my feelings for you could be real, not so fast. I wasn't sure if what we had was only physical. If I made you feel my problems were about you, I apologize for that, too." She took a deep breath. "Being with you was the only right thing I did during those months after Mitch."

"Not right enough, I guess."

She managed not to reach for his hand. Tension was already palpable. Touching him wasn't a good idea. "You've been there for me since all this weirdness started, and I appreciate it. You're a great guy." *And I was an idiot to throw that away.*

"I like you all right, too," he said gruffly, looking uncomfortable at the compliment.

Her pulse skittered. For an instant she saw a raw hunger in his eyes. Then it disappeared as he shifted his gaze back out the windshield. The desire she'd glimpsed prompted her to ask, "So…did I step on another woman's toes when I kissed you?"

"No."

Did that mean he was seeing someone, but not seriously? Or that he wasn't seeing anyone at all?

Frustrated, she searched his face. She could tell nothing from his neutral tone, but she certainly saw no hint of the skin-tingling desire she'd seen earlier. He'd moved on; she had to do the same.

"Can we start over from here? As friends?"

He shifted until his gaze held hers once again. Indecision and doubt flickered across his face. Regret swept through her.

The leashed energy in his body told her that he was restraining himself, but the shrug he gave was nonchalant. "Sure, friends."

She'd thought addressing the kiss and the issues between them would erase the dissatisfaction that had gnawed at her since seeing him again, but it hadn't.

Suddenly he leaned forward, grabbing the video camera.

Snatching up her own camera, Cass whispered, "Did you see someone?"

He turned the camera on and looked through the viewfinder. "Some*thing*. Not a person." Then, "Smoke!"

Cass saw a sudden orange glow in the building they were watching. A heartbeat later, flames crawled out two side windows.

"Damn it!" Ben sprang out of the SUV, still holding the video camera. "Check the other buildings!"

He took off running as Cass scrambled out behind him. Sprinting toward the nearest building, she fumbled her cell phone from her pocket and dialed 9-1-1. She pounded on the door of a dentist's office, yelling for anyone there to get out, then moved on. Due to the late hour, no employees were likely to be around, but vagrants were a different story.

Moments later she heard sirens, then the blaring horns of fire trucks. There was no sign of anyone, which meant the torch had either come and gone before they'd arrived or had eluded their notice.

The firefighters were soon directing water on the blaze. By the time Cass finished checking the last building, the fire was out.

An hour later, after giving their information to the incident commander, Ben dropped her off at the firehouse. He wanted to start his investigation immediately and promised he would let her know what he found.

As she walked inside, she hoped he would find something to indicate whether Lee was responsible for tonight's fire or any of the others.

But upstairs, in the women's bunk room, she was the one who found something. A walnut plaque with gold engraving lay in the center of her bed, with a small piece of paper taped to it. A sudden inexplicable dread pounded at her as she drew closer. She recognized that plaque. It was an award from the city to her father for distinguished service. One of several awards he'd been given, all of which she kept at her house.

Legs going numb, her gaze slid to the attached paper.

What did you think about the fire show tonight?

It was her brother's handwriting. How had he walked into the firehouse unnoticed? How had he known she wasn't here?

He had to have been watching her. Did he know she had seen his fire before it started? No, he couldn't.

Shaken, she stared at the plaque. Her brother was messing with her mind. Again.

It was 3:30 a.m. when Ben picked her up at the station. "You all right?"

"Yes." He'd asked her that same question twice when she'd called him about finding her father's award on her bed. Of course she'd been rattled then, but she was calm now. Mostly.

Ben insisted it would be a good idea to check her house for evidence of a break-in, even though Cass felt sure there would be none. Her brother would know how to get inside their childhood home without force.

Sure enough, they found no signs of unlawful entry

at the three-bedroom house where she and Lee had grown up. She unlocked the door and followed Ben inside.

"After I found the plaque, I called Lee's parole officer again. I probably should've waited until he got to the office, but I couldn't, so I tracked down his home number. Hugo said he still hasn't seen or heard from my brother."

"Not surprising," Ben muttered.

"He also said he was keeping notes of everything."

"That's good. His account will support ours."

"I woke the guys, and they all said they hadn't seen anyone come in or go out of the firehouse. Did you find anything at the scene?"

"It was definitely arson. Found the base of a lamp and shattered lightbulb glass. I'll have to check some samples to be sure, but I think the lightbulb was injected with gasoline, then the lamp put on a timer. That allowed the torch to get far away, giving him an alibi. When the bulb got hot enough to explode, it ignited a nearby trail of gasoline."

"So everything could've been arranged hours before we got there."

"And probably was."

Frustrated, she huffed out a breath. "Why couldn't I have seen *that* in one of my visions?"

None of Cass's family pictures or furniture was disturbed. Only the one plaque was missing from her father's collection.

There was nothing suspicious until they stepped into the dining area, where a framed photograph of her and her father lay on the table. Next to it was a key.

Chilled, she turned to Ben. "He's been here."

"How do you know?" He came up beside her, his arm touching hers.

"The photograph is out of place. It's my favorite and Lee knows it." For one second she let herself lean into him. She gestured toward the table. "Plus, that's my extra house key. The only other person with a key is Jana, and she wouldn't come here unless I asked her to, and she wouldn't leave her key. Lee would be able to figure out where to find the spare key. I know that isn't enough for you, but it's enough for me." She wrapped her arms around herself. "It's Lee."

"I sure can't prove it isn't," he said stonily.

Nothing else in or around the house was disturbed. Ben sealed and marked the photograph and key in separate evidence bags, saying he would have them checked for prints.

She didn't want to go back to the firehouse, but she certainly couldn't stay here. Maybe a hotel.

Taking a last look around Cass's small house, he wrapped one hand around her upper arm. "You're coming home with me."

In some ways, she would feel safer with him. In other ways, she wouldn't. Especially after their kiss. "Do you think that's a good idea?"

"Doesn't matter if it is or not. Your brother isn't getting anywhere near you."

The tight line of his lips, the burning resolve in his eyes, told her not to argue. So she didn't.

Chapter 5

Cass couldn't sleep. She was hot. She was mad. She wanted to pound Lee. And she just plain *wanted* Ben.

Part of her thrilled to his protectiveness, but another part of her chafed. His hauling her home with him made her want more than friendship. Especially since memories were everywhere.

She remembered making love in front of the fireplace. In the kitchen. Their first time had been in the hallway outside his bedroom. They had dated for about two weeks when he brought her to his house after his family's annual Labor Day cookout. As he was showing her around, he kissed her and it just happened.

She could still feel the uneven texture of the wall at

her back, the plush carpet between her toes. His mouth *all over her*. The recollection caused a flutter low in her belly. Exactly what she didn't need.

Cass got out of bed. Eyes adjusting to the darkness, she padded barefoot down the carpeted hallway to Ben's living room. The guest bedroom was on the other side of the house from his, so at least she wasn't worried about waking him. Moonlight drifted over the fireplace and mantel, and the dark blue recliner at one end of the navy tweed sofa.

She crossed the taupe carpet and stopped at the French doors leading to the back porch. Built-in bookcases lined the wall to her left, adjacent to a fireplace. Sweat dampened her neck, trickled between her breasts. She lifted her hair and twisted it on top of her head, fanning herself with her free hand.

Her brother was out there somewhere, watching her. Waiting for something. What? Thinking about the award he'd taken from their childhood home, the key and photograph he'd left, had tension knotting her shoulders. She didn't want to believe Lee was the one setting fires and tormenting her, the one who had tried to kill her, the one who had killed a child, but she knew it was him. He had motive, means and opportunity. Who else could it be?

She'd been so glad it was Ben who'd been with her at her house. Beneath the desire, she felt safe with him and always had. Another realization she'd come to in the months since walking away from him.

The throb that started in her veins every time she

thought about him had her moving to the fireplace. She released her hair and dragged it over her shoulder. A framed photograph of Ben with his brother, Jeff, sat on the mantel. The candid shot of the pair laughing clearly showed the closeness between them.

She and Lee had once been close. Until he'd failed the fire academy and their relationship had become a twisted competition.

"Cass?"

Jumping, she whirled at the sound of Ben's deep, sleep-roughened voice.

"Didn't mean to startle you."

"That's okay. I'm sorry if I woke you."

"You didn't. Wasn't really getting much sleep." Dragging a hand down his face, he moved into the room and stopped behind the couch.

Pale light washed over him, bringing his bare chest into sharp definition. The dark shorts he wore emphasized the bands of muscle across his stomach. His gaze roamed over her, making her keenly aware that she wore only panties and one of his T-shirts. She felt a rush in her blood.

"You see another fire? Are your hands blistered?"

"No, I'm fine." He sounded so matter-of-fact. As if he were asking about a headache.

Her emotions rocketed between anger and lust. If she stayed out here with him, she wasn't sure she could hold herself together.

He stepped around the sofa and walked toward her.

Light and shadow skimmed over his wide shoulders, the flex of muscle in his arms and legs. The sight of his deep chest, the black hair that thinned between his breastbone and toward his navel, had her swallowing hard. An ache started at her center. She should go back to bed. Right now. Alone.

He stopped a foot away, his eyes gleaming in the dim light. "Is Lee the reason you can't sleep?"

"Partly." She wasn't about to tell him that he was the other reason. "I don't understand why he's doing this. I know he wants revenge for whatever he thinks Dad did to him and for my helping to send him to prison." Her voice cracked. "But he could take out plenty of resentment without setting fires and…and killing a kid."

"He won't get close to you again." Ben shifted, coming nearer and sparking all her nerve endings. He smelled like a summer night. He was all muscle and hard man and power.

She dug her nails into her palms to keep from touching him.

"Until we catch him, you won't be alone," he went on. "I'll be with you, or a cop will be assigned to protect you. The fire chief okayed it, and so did the chief of police." He toyed with a strand of hair lying over her shoulder.

Trying not to look at his mouth, she focused on the hollow of his strong throat. "Staying with me 24/7 will drive you crazy."

"Probably," he murmured. He didn't look as if he minded.

Easing close enough that she felt his body heat, he braced his left hand on the mantel just above her shoulder. "Every time I think about Lee in the firehouse, how easily he could've gotten to you, it makes me furious."

"Same here." Her pulse thundered wildly at Ben's nearness. "And he scares me."

"I won't let anything happen to you, Cass."

She wanted to throw herself at him, wrap herself around him. Naked. All she said was, "Thanks."

"Mmm." His gaze drifted over her, triggering points of sensation under her skin.

Go. Now. Her mind screamed the words, but she couldn't move.

"I made a mistake."

She stilled. "By bringing me home with you?"

"No, not about that." The low gruffness of his voice made her shiver. Fierce emotion blazed in his eyes. He looked almost savage. Dangerous. Her pulse skittered.

"About saying I wanted to move on as friends. That's not going to work for me."

Her heart sank. He really hadn't forgiven her for what she'd done. "I understand. I'll go tomorrow."

She had no idea where. Sadness tightened her throat.

"I want more than that."

At his husky words, she blinked. "What?"

He angled his body so she was backed into the mantel. His other hand clamped over the dark wood, caging her in.

Hardly daring to breath, she glanced to either side. His hands were big. His forearms were corded with muscle, dusted with dark hair. He leaned in, his body not touching hers, yet raising prickles of awareness clear down to her toes. Need tugged low in her belly.

He couldn't mean what she thought he did. Their kiss hours ago had scrambled her brain. She was misreading the signals. "You want more what?"

"You." He bent his head and brushed his mouth against hers. "I want more of you."

"Oh." A little wobbly, she hooked a hand into his waistband to steady herself.

The light scrape of her nails against his abdomen had all the muscles in Ben's body clenching. The moonlight covered her like a veil, giving her skin a translucent glow.

Her eyes darkened. "Really? But you said—"

"I was wrong."

After a long moment that had his nerves winding tight, she asked softly, "Are you sure?"

"Oh, yeah." The fact that she had hurt him was fading into nonexistence next to the raging intensity of desire. After learning her brother had somehow gotten into the firehouse, Ben's protective instinct had kicked into hyper-mode. That tipped the scales for him.

He'd tried to forget that kiss, tried to forget *her*, but their time together in his vehicle had weakened his restraint. When he'd seen her standing there in his T-shirt, the curve of her body outlined in the moonlight, her full breasts pressing against the thin cotton, he'd said to hell with it. He had to get his hands on her.

In the seconds since he'd told her what he wanted, she hadn't tried to leave. And she hadn't pushed him away. That and her slightly parted lips were enough invitation for him. He kissed her again, harder.

Her arms went around his neck, and he slanted his mouth over hers, going deeper into that velvet heat. While they had been checking her house for signs of a break-in, an urgency had built inside him. Now, with her finally in his arms, it leveled out.

Breathing in the subtle scents of her soap and his, he homed in on the layer of cotton between them, the pressure of her nipples against his chest.

One hand curved around her nape. He skimmed the other over her bottom to the back of her thigh, dying to feel more of her. He picked her up, and she wrapped her legs around his waist.

Cradled by her thighs, all his blood rushed south. Her hands were in his hair, her mouth was hot on his. If possible, his sex grew even more rigid and his legs grew weaker.

Still carrying her, he moved to the couch and sank down, his knee bumping the coffee table. Without breaking the kiss, he buried his hands in her hair and ravaged her mouth. Thick silky locks tickled his thighs when he nudged her head back to rake his teeth down her throat.

She wiggled, fitting herself to him. The low sound

of pleasure that escaped her flicked his nerves like a whip.

Half-dazed by the honey-sweet taste of her mouth, the delicate scent of woman and soap, he reached under the thin T-shirt, skating his hands over her bottom, the gentle flare of her hips.

She pressed down hard on his erection as she dragged her mouth along his cheek to nip his earlobe. When she sucked at a spot low on his neck, he hissed out a breath. Despite the coolness of the room, sweat dampened Ben's chest. The only sounds in the house were their labored breaths and the occasional moan.

He slid his fingers around to her rib cage and palmed her full breasts. She shuddered in his lap, making him even harder. Thumbing her tight nipples, he pulled back from the kiss, shoving up the shirt so he could see her plump creamy flesh.

Her breathing was as labored as his. Her eyes fluttered open, and the total surrender there nearly had him ripping off her underwear. Lashes lowering, she watched him touch her, and that charged him up even more. Even in the silvery light, he could see the flush of arousal on her skin. Could feel it, too.

She fit him the way she always had, the way he knew she would. He pressed a hot, openmouthed kiss on the swell of her breast, then slid his tongue to where pale flesh met rosy-pink.

As he closed his mouth over her, she touched his face. "Ben," she rasped.

Heat shot through him. He knew what she liked. How fast, how slow. Every damn thing about her, but he didn't know how long he could hold out. When she slid her hands to his waistband and pushed down his shorts and boxers together, he nearly lost it. He eased up, and she scooted back on his thighs to tug the garments far enough out of the way to free him. She wrapped her hand around him, making a soft sound that chewed at his tenuous control.

He swept one hand up her sleek outer thigh, then inside to dip his fingers into the burning hot crease where her hip met her groin. She moaned or he did. He couldn't tell, didn't care. Man, she made him hurt to be inside her. Now.

She went up on her knees, reaching to push off her panties.

"No," he murmured against her breast, hooking a finger into a leg opening and pulling the lacy fabric to the side.

The silky liquid heat against his knuckle told him she was ready. With his free hand, he grasped her hip and pulled her onto him. She sank down with a gasp, her arms tightening around his neck. For a second, his vision blurred. She rested her forehead against his, his name spilling from her throat in a ragged plea.

When she moved, Ben caught her rhythm, fast, intense, almost desperate. He wanted to protect her, claim her. Take her. The stroke of his body inside hers, the tease of her breasts, the friction of her panties rubbing against both of them, splintered his control.

Gritting his teeth, he managed to hold off his own release until he felt her inner muscles clench around him, and then he let go.

Over the next three days, Cass and Ben settled into a rhythm. They jogged in the mornings and ate together every night. When Ben went out to check leads or deal with other cases on his desk, an OCPD officer stayed with Cass.

She hadn't had a vision since the night they'd first made love. Ben had remarked on it that morning, and she had told him not to jinx it by talking about it.

An hour ago, he'd come home from a night of working a fire scene, talked to the cop assigned to her, then eaten. It was nearly noon by the time he took a shower. Cass debated going in with him, then plopped down on his big oak bed to wait, one finger tracing the pattern in his blue plaid comforter. The familiar gray walls and white trim were reassuring, a constant in her upside-down world.

Being here made her feel shielded from her brother and the visions. She felt as if she belonged here, although she wasn't about to tell Ben that. She was afraid he might say what was happening between them didn't mean to him what it meant to her.

He walked out of the bathroom, his hair still damp, his boxers riding low. Her gaze slid down his dark-haired chest to the flat of his stomach. He grinned and flopped down beside her. Shifting to his side, he propped himself up on one elbow and hooked an arm around her waist to pull her to him. "Hey, gorgeous."

"Hey."

After a long kiss, he rolled to his back and arranged her body half on top of his. "The picture from the cell phone is still where I left it on the kitchen counter. Have you looked at it since I brought it home?"

"No. I'll look at it when I follow up with Dr. Hill tomorrow." She nuzzled his neck, inhaling the delicious scent of man and soap. "Let's not talk about that."

"What do you want to talk about, then?" His voice was gravelly with fatigue. He slipped a hand under the hem of her red spaghetti-strapped T-shirt, tickling the small of her back.

"Nothing." She raked her nails up the inside of his thigh and felt a muscle jerk beneath her touch. "I don't want to talk at all. Unless you're too tired to get naked."

A laugh rumbled out of him, and before she could blink, he had her on her back and was pressing himself against her. "Does that feel tired to you?"

"Yes. Maybe you should rest." She laughed. "Let's take a nap."

"Not until you finish what you started, woman." The husky growl of his voice shot heat straight to her toes.

He brushed his lips across her forehead, her eyelids, her cheeks, before slowly seducing her mouth.

She ran her hands over his hard wide shoulders as he dragged his mouth to her ear, his hot breath causing a shiver deep down inside. Just as she had last night, Cass wished he would ask if she wanted more than this, but she knew he wouldn't.

Which was fine, she told herself, as he peeled down her ribbed knit top and curled his tongue around one nipple. A shiver rippled through her. She slid her hands into his hair, giving herself over to the feel of his hot mouth on her, his heavy weight pressing her into the mattress.

Easing to one side, he undid the button of her denim shorts, and brushed his thumb back and forth just inside the waistband of her panties.

Her breathing broke. "Ben."

He looked up, blue eyes glittering. Dark color streaked his cheekbones. With his blunt fingertips, he nudged her hair back and stroked her face.

The scent of soap and musk settled in her lungs. His touch was like a drug, drawing her into a place where there was only sensation. The solid angles of his body next to her softness. The crisp hair of his chest tickling her skin. His gentle finger down her neck. The brush of a knuckle along the full undersides of her breasts.

There was no mistaking the possessiveness blazing in his eyes, or the tenderness and desire.

Throat tight with emotion, she framed his face in her hands, skimming her thumbs along his lightly whiskered jaw. Covering her mouth with his, he eased his palm into her panties and cupped her. She arched against him, murmuring encouragement.

Abruptly, a flare of orange burned across her mind.

Cass's pulse spiked, and her legs tightened reflexively around his hand. No! Not now!

Fighting the vision, she focused on Ben's hot tongue tasting her body, on the intimate way he massaged her. Another fiery image flashed in her brain.

She refused to let it take her this time. Trying not to panic, she locked her gaze with his. Hoping their connection would be strong enough to stave off the vision, she kissed him roughly, almost desperately.

Not now. Not now. Not now.

Powerless, she felt herself sliding away.

And then she was standing in the middle of a fire. Flames shot toward the ceiling. Gray and white smoke swirled around her. Crayon drawings were taped to walls painted with a safari motif. Small desks, illegible words on a chalkboard. A clock above the door.

The flames lashed at her hands as she dropped to her stomach, searching for an escape.

Alarms clanged through the building. Oxygen tank weighting her back, Cass crawled into the hallway, relieved to see no children. She searched frantically for a red exit sign, her hands beginning to roast. Where were her gloves? As she looked down, her skin peeled back.

"Cass! Cass!" Ben was shaking her, yelling her name.

Disoriented, terrified, she stared dumbly at him. Her palms throbbed in white-hot agony. Ben still lay on top of her. And her hands still held his face. Her bloody blistered hands.

Crying out in horror, she jerked them away.

Agony shot up her arms. Panic nearly choked her.

Cass's breath jammed in her chest. Ben sat up, scooping her into his lap. One strong arm curved around her waist. His other hand pressed her head to his chest.

Uncaring how much it hurt, she drew her hands against her body so they wouldn't touch him. Finally the pain began to fade.

And there was Ben, solid, steady, holding her tight against him. "Are you okay?"

She nodded jerkily.

"Let me see your hands."

"N-no." Tears burned down her cheeks. It made her stomach churn that this had happened now. *In bed with him.*

She trembled, dragging in air as Ben sat her beside him. He smoothed her hair away from her sweat-dampened face. "I'm going to get a wet rag, then I want to look at your hands."

As he moved into the bathroom, she stared down at her palms, relieved to see that they were fine, then, in the next second, she was furious.

During sex! If the visions could hit her at a time like this, they could happen anytime. Anywhere.

Pressure squeezed her chest. She was a sideshow freak, and she might have to deal with these hideous episodes the rest of her life.

She managed to get to her feet and tug on her shorts. Legs shaking, she readjusted her T-shirt. He was taking a long time. Why wouldn't he? He was probably repulsed. And as disturbed as she was.

When he returned with a wet cloth, she couldn't look at him. Very gently, he examined her hands, kissing her palms before running the rag softly over her face.

Tears stung her eyes.

"Tell me what happened."

She tried to control the tremor in her voice. "One minute we were kissing, then I was in the middle of a fire. At a nursery school. Flames everywhere, but there were no children. And the next thing I knew my… hands were on your face. My…disgusting hands. And you were staring down at me, white as a sheet."

"You scared the hell out of me."

And probably sickened him, too. She choked back a sob and stepped around him.

"I hate that I couldn't help you." He watched her pace the width of his room.

She waited for him to say more, to distance himself from her. When there was only silence, she dared a look at him.

Concern shadowed his eyes. But even if he weren't revolted now, what about next time?

"I can't do this. I thought I could, but I can't."

"Can't do what?"

"Be with you."

He went still. "Cass."

She resumed her pacing. "How can you stand to look at me? I'm a freak!"

"Stop saying that." Snagging her elbow, he held her in place, waiting until her gaze met his. Her eyes were wild, fever-bright. His chest ached. Ben stroked her cheek, and she jerked away as if it hurt to be touched. "You're not a freak."

"The fact that I might go into some kind of… trance while we're having sex says I am." She put a hand over her mouth. "This is horrifying in so many ways, I don't even know where to begin. I can't put you through that."

"Stop." He took her shoulders. "There's no reason to walk away."

"No reason? I'm terrified at the thought of being naked with you and that happening again. I tried to stop it, and I couldn't control it at all. What if I have these episodes the rest of my life?"

"We'll deal with it."

"Haven't I put you through enough?" Her voice was bitter as she turned away.

He wrapped his arms around her from behind. "Cass."

She stiffened.

"Listen to me." Ignoring the rigid line of her spine, he nuzzled her petal-smooth cheek. "It scared you. It scared me, too, but it's over."

"For now." She dashed a hand under her eyes. "But

you…you can't get involved with someone who could go zinging off into a trance any second."

"We're already involved." He tried to remain calm. "And we can handle this if we do it together."

"Ben." Her voice cracked. "I can't."

Anger flared. He dropped his arms and stepped away. "You mean you *won't*."

She was upset. He didn't blame her, but getting rid of him wasn't the way to deal with it. That seemed to be her answer to everything.

Which pissed him off. Hands curling into fists, he fought to keep his voice level. "You're using what just happened as an excuse."

She turned, looking confused. "An excuse for what?"

"To take off. I thought we were past that. You think I'm getting too close, so you're ready to run."

"This isn't about that at all."

He ignored the pain in her eyes. "If it weren't, you'd want us to work this out together."

"You have no idea what you'd be signing up for."

"Neither do you. Something could happen to me, too. I could get hurt or sick, so what's the difference? You're running because you feel you're getting in too deep with me, and it scares you."

"What if…the visions start coming all the time? And not just when we're alone but out in public? I'd become a burden."

"You wouldn't be more of a pain in the butt than you are right now," he muttered.

"No?" Her eyes flashed. "What if sometime we're together with your family and I zone out? What will you tell them? 'Oh, by the way, she has—'" she hooked her fingers in the air "'—*visions*. Just give us a minute.'"

"Stop it." He wanted to shake her, so he braced his hands on his hips. "Cut the bull, Cass, and call this what it really is."

"What do you mean?"

"You can't commit. Or you won't. Things have been going great, and now you're running out on me. Just like last time."

Hurt darkened her eyes. "That was different."

His jaw tightened. He knew his next words were harsh, but he had to get through to her. "We get to a certain point and then you can't seem to get any further. You don't try to work through things. You leave."

"I'm doing this for you."

"Enough!" He yanked his jeans off the floor and jerked them on. He had to get out of here, had to cool down. "We're not doing this right now."

"*What?*" Disbelief, then anger, streaked across her features.

He tried to gentle his voice, but even *he* flinched at the roughness of his tone. "We need to step back for a minute, then talk about this later, when it isn't so fresh."

Chin tilted mutinously, she plainly wanted to argue, but after a long minute, she gave a sharp nod.

Ben wasn't dumb enough to feel relief. She had

something wedged in her brain and wouldn't let go, but for now, they had to take a breather. "You saw the next fire. That means we need to get there. Tell me where."

As he pulled on a navy T-shirt, she said, "Button-wood Pre-school. The name was written above the blackboard. And I saw a clock."

"A clock? You haven't seen anything like that before."

"It read five-fifty-six. Do you think that matters?"

"So far, all the stuff you've seen at the other fires has been accurate. That could be a.m. or p.m., though."

He fastened his jeans and grabbed his tennis shoes as she put on her own shoes. They would deal with this fire. Then Ben would deal with her. "We'd better get moving."

Color high, mouth tight, she silently followed him out the door.

After gathering what they needed, they drove to the preschool on the far west side of Oklahoma City. The air hummed with tension.

It wasn't until they reached the school and had their cameras set up that she spoke. "Why are you fighting me on this? Breaking up is the best thing for both of us."

"It's the *easiest*," he emphasized harshly, trying to be patient. "Not the *best*."

"I think I'm doing the right thing."

"You thought that last time, too. Easy, hard, it doesn't matter. I'll tell you this. I'm not letting you go, and you need to find a way to deal with *that*."

Chapter 6

The school building was constructed as an open-ended rectangle with a grassy berm in the center leading to the playground. The corner of the roof where Ben and Cass sat hidden afforded a view of all the classrooms on both sides of the structure.

They hadn't spoken for the last two hours. Ben was still fuming because Cass was again trying to bolt. From the rigid set of her shoulders, she was still upset, too. Probably about his telling her how things were going to be.

He knew the visions were traumatic. And, hell yes, the mid-coital episode had freaked him out, too. But neither of those things was a reason to dump him.

Again. He knew she had feelings for him. What he didn't know was how to make her trust them. Frustrated, he admitted to himself that he might have pushed too hard.

Catching a movement out of the corner of his eye, Ben scanned the grassy area between the long sides of the building. There it was again, a motion in the shadows beneath the eaves in the glare of the late afternoon sun. He turned on the video camera.

A couple of feet from him, Cass sat with camera ready. As they watched, the form moved. Something whizzed through the air and crashed through a window on the opposite side of the building. Cass snapped pictures as Ben followed another blur with the video camera. Glinting in the light, the object hurtled through the broken window, landed inside and exploded.

Molotov cocktail, Ben registered, as Cass called 9-1-1. The camera's zoom on its most powerful setting, he followed the suspect as he ran away from the building and onto the playground. When the culprit stopped to look back at the flames now curling out the broken window, Ben could tell it was a man. "We got him."

The man took off again, weaving through a swing set.

Beside Ben, Cass continued to take pictures. "I can't tell if it's Lee."

Ben kept recording until the suspect disappeared into a stand of trees.

Thanks to the approval he had gotten to put the nearest firehouse on standby, trucks rumbled into the parking lot within mere minutes.

He and Cass gathered their empty sandwich bags and water bottles, then climbed down the ladder they'd leaned against the side of the building.

As the firefighters rolled out hoses and rushed toward the flames, Ben updated the incident commander and replayed the video for him and Cass. Though they all agreed the suspect was male, none of them could distinguish specific features.

He and Cass gave their statements and left the scene. As they drove, Ben arranged for the cop guarding her to meet them at her firehouse. Once she picked up some necessary paperwork for her doctor's visit, Officer Giles would take her for a checkup at the emergency room.

As she slid out of the SUV, Ben knew that things between them were still strained. He didn't like it, but he figured he'd said enough for now.

He cleared his throat. "Hopefully, the police lab will be able to get a clear image once they blow up the video."

She nodded.

"Giles will take you back to my house after you see Dr. Hill. I'll call you as soon as I learn anything."

"Great." She closed the door and turned toward the firehouse.

As he drove away, he glanced in his rearview mirror until she disappeared from sight. His chest hurt. He'd finally convinced himself to let her back in, and now he might have sabotaged the relationship. Maybe he'd been too caveman back in his bedroom. Had he screwed up everything? What if he had run her off for good?

About two minutes later, his cell phone rang. Glancing at the screen, he saw it was Cass and answered, hoping she would tell him she'd decided he was right. Or that she was at least willing to try. "Hey."

"Ben?"

The slight tremor in her voice had his spine turning into steel. "What is it? What's wrong?"

"My brother—"

"Come to Cass's house," an unfamiliar masculine voice said. "And bring the video."

Damn it, how had Lee Hollister gotten to Cass?

"We'll make a swap."

"Let me talk to her," Ben snarled.

"Come alone."

"Don't hurt her, you sonova—"

Click. Dial tone.

Ben cursed as rage hazed his vision. It took him a moment to react, then he made a sharp U-turn and drove like hell to Cass's home. On the way, he called for police backup, then fire dispatch, warning both of them to keep their distance, and to run without sirens and lights, so Lee wouldn't spot them. How had Hollister gotten close to her at the firehouse? Where was Officer Giles?

Fear cut straight through Ben. There had been no time to book the video into evidence, no time to make a copy. He just hoped there was time to reach Cass before her pyromaniac brother finished what he'd started at that downtown hotel.

"He'll be right over." Cass's brother dropped her cell phone beside her on the leather sofa.

He had forced her into her Mustang by drilling a gun into the side of her head. A gun that likely belonged to Officer Giles—and she could only hope that Lee hadn't killed him to get it.

Cass refused to cry and focused instead on fury. Some part of her had wanted to believe he hadn't been the one who tried to kill her, but the weapon he stuck in her face crushed that hope.

"Why use the house where we grew up, Lee?" She had to do something, but what? Her hands and feet were bound with duct tape. "Why not someplace where people won't recognize you if you're seen?"

"Everything started here." Her brother's eyes, the same green as hers, glittered like shards of glass. They also shared the same ginger hair color, but that was where the similarities stopped. He had always been the more introverted, and as they grew older, he became more so, to the point that, before going to prison, he'd withdrawn from most people. "This is where it's going to end."

The bitter finality in his voice had panic flaring. She struggled against her bonds. Ben was coming, and he would be in danger, too. "How did you know it was us who had video of you? We saw you run off."

"I always hang around for a while and watch my fires. I saw y'all come down off the roof."

Of course he'd stayed to watch, she thought. Typical firebug behavior.

"How did y'all know I would be there?"

"We didn't."

"But you knew there would be a fire there. How?"

Because I saw the whole thing beforehand. Aloud, she said, "Things will go easier for you if you turn yourself in."

"I'm not turning myself in, and you won't be doing it again, either." He moved to one of the oversized burgundy chairs at the foot of the couch and bent to pick up something from the floor.

"So this is about me doing the right thing and turning you in when you were setting all those fires?"

Walking past her, he carefully set a small food storage container on the end table closest to Cass, then shoved his face into hers. "Being disloyal isn't the right thing. You took me out of commission. Now I'm doing the same thing to you."

His words roused a greasy feeling in her stomach. Had he spent the last three years in prison thinking up ways to hurt her? "So it *was* you who tried to kill me at that hotel fire?"

"I still don't know how you survived that beam falling on you. The paper said you died and came back to life. What a crock."

Hoping to think of a way to convince him to discard

his plan, she tried to keep him talking. "That was you I saw there, wasn't it? You wore turnout gear, and no one even noticed you didn't belong."

He gave a smug smile as he eased between their father's tan recliner and the end table to the wall covered with awards.

"The night you left that plaque at the firehouse, how did you know I wasn't there?"

"I was watching you. Saw that fire investigator drop you off then come back to pick you up."

That was because she'd told him about finding the plaque. Her stomach knotted. "How did you manage to get in without anyone noticing?"

"I waited until they were watching TV then snuck behind the fire engine and went upstairs. I left through your bunk room window."

He gestured toward the many plaques and mounted medals on the wall.

"What did you get when you turned me in? Some kind of commendation? Why isn't it here on Daddy's wall of fame?"

"You know you can't get away with this." Cass pulled against her bonds, the tape biting into her wrists. "You'll go back to prison. Even longer this time."

"I'm not going back to prison, little sister," he snarled. "Once I get that video, I'm outta here. With no loose ends."

He was still planning to kill her, she realized. How had things gone so wrong? Heartsick, fear growing, her throat tightened. "Stop this, please. You said you didn't kill Officer Giles, but you did kill a child at that department store. That's murder, Lee."

He slipped the policeman's gun into the waistband of his grimy jeans, gesturing at a dark walnut plaque. "Do you remember when he got this Distinguished Service Award? Right after I washed out of the fire academy. Good timing, huh?"

"Lee." She knew he blamed their father for almost everything. Lee had never wanted to be a firefighter, but he had lacked the self-confidence to tell gruff, blustering Mike Hollister so. As a result, her brother's resentment had grown deeper every year. "You can get away without involving anyone else."

"As soon as that fire investigator gets here with the camera, I'll be gone for good."

Cass wanted to scream from the frustration and fear of being unable to keep Ben away and safe.

Suddenly an image of flames shot through her mind. Staggered by the unexpected flash, she tried to fight, but she barely had time to acknowledge it before she was yanked into the vision.

This one was different. The blaze was already out. Smoke was funneling out through a ragged hole in the ceiling. Wood and glass littered the floor. Furniture and walls had crumbled into crackling piles of ash. Her gaze scanned a scorched leather sofa, a charred fabric recliner. Her dad's recliner. She was looking at her own living room! She saw Lee, then the vision ended.

Dazed, she blinked. The agony in her palms had her hands clenching into fists. Why had she seen the scene of a fire that had already burned?

"Hey!"

Lee's voice startled her out of her thoughts. He narrowed his eyes. "Did you just black out?"

"No."

"What's wrong with you?"

"Nothing." Her hands throbbed, but the pain was already fading.

After a long moment, Lee turned back to the awards, touching them in turn. "Meritorious service award. Twenty-five-year service award. Firefighter of the Year—twice."

He removed a light oak plaque distinguished with a brass OCFD badge. "Fire Chief's Award."

Making a sound of disgust, he came over and opened the plastic storage container he'd set down near her and removed a dull white jelly-like cube.

What was it? Cass wondered, her emotions zipping from anger to fear and back.

He carefully pressed the pliable material to the brass plate engraved with their father's name. From his left pocket, he took a slender metal cylinder about two inches long and crimped at one end.

Apprehension clawed through her.

With a small smile, he stuck the metal piece into the gelatinous substance. "Explosive."

Explosive? Cass thought frantically. So was that

metal thing a blasting cap? It must be, although it looked unlike any of the few she had seen.

"Made it myself from bleach and salt substitute. Slick, huh?"

Suddenly she understood why there hadn't been a burning fire in her vision. Because it wasn't a fire that would destroy her house. It was a bomb. Her stomach turned. She didn't know her brother anymore, if she ever had. She fought against the band of tape around her wrists. The adhesive rubbed her skin raw.

"I just can't figure out how y'all managed to get to that fire before it even started. Like you already knew where it would be."

She had, but she was not telling him about her visions. No way. "Just lucky."

"Not so lucky now, huh?"

Ben would be here soon, and Lee would kill him, too, she thought. Nauseous, her skin peppered with cold sweat, she realized she'd made an awful mistake leaving Ben the first time. And she'd nearly done it again. Now she might never get the chance to tell him how wrong she had been.

Lee centered the plaque in the seat of their father's well-used chair. The corduroy fabric was frayed in places, and Cass knew the chair should be thrown out, but she kept it for sentimental reasons.

A sound came from the kitchen. The groan of a floorboard. Oh, no! Ben.

Lee's gaze shot to the dining area. "Ah, you're here, Investigator."

Cass figured Ben had tried to sneak in and the stupid floorboard had creaked. It had always creaked. Her brother would know immediately the noise wasn't caused by anything except another person.

She couldn't bear to think that Ben was about to be killed because of her.

"Get in here or I'm going to hurt her," Lee demanded.

"He can leave the camera for you," Cass argued. "He doesn't have to come in here."

"Yeah, he does." Lee raised his voice. "Investigator, if I don't see you in three seconds, I'll shoot her."

Ben stepped into sight, and Cass nearly cried.

He glanced at her, concern dark in his eyes. "You okay?"

She nodded.

"Let her go, Hollister," Ben said. "I have what you want."

"Lee," Cass begged. "Let him leave. Please."

"Shut up!" Her brother's gaze swung to Ben. "Where is it?"

Ben held up the video camera as he moved into the living room.

"This doesn't have to end badly," he said.

"It isn't going to end badly for me." Gesturing with the gun he'd stolen, Lee directed the other man toward the middle of the room. "Walk over, put the camera on the coffee table and step back."

"He's planning to kill both of us," Cass said.

A muscle flexed in Ben's stony jaw, but he did as Lee ordered, edging between the leather chairs at the foot of the couch. Angling his body, he kept both Cass and her brother in view.

She tried to communicate with her eyes that she'd had a vision. Staring intently at Ben, she lifted her hands, turning her palms up as much as the tape biting into her wrists allowed.

Ben read the urgency and fear in her eyes. She was trying to tell him something. When she made a show of looking at her palms, he knew she'd had a vision. "Here?" he asked.

"Yes. It's not a fire."

Lee looked from Cass to Ben. "What are y'all talking about?"

Not a fire? Scanning the room, Ben tried to figure out how Cass's brother planned to get rid of the place and them along with it. His gaze snagged on the award resting in the chair, and he cursed under his breath.

That was plastic explosive with a blasting cap! But there was no fuse attached. If Lee wasn't using conventional means, such as a match or a lighter, how was he going to set it off?

The other man slid something out of his pocket. A red dot of light skipped around on the carpet.

Alarmed, Ben realized the SOB had a laser detonator and could use it from outside, a good distance from the house. Adrenaline spiking his blood, he moved on sheer instinct. He flipped his wrist, firing the video camera like a Frisbee right into Lee's face. The unexpected blow was enough to make the other man flinch and stumble, then fall backward to the floor.

Ben wasted no time. Kicking aside the coffee table, he grabbed Cass and threw her over his shoulder in a fireman's hold, then headed for the nearest exit—a sliding glass door leading out to the covered patio. Shoving it open, he ran as fast as possible while carrying her. He crossed the yard, heading for the back chain-link fence.

A muscle cramped sharply in Ben's side. Glaring evening sunlight stung his eyes. Cass stayed still, helping him keep his balance. Sweat trickled down his temple, into his eyes.

An explosion rocked the house.

Deafened by the thunderous blast, Ben threw himself to the ground, turning so that his shoulder, rather than Cass's, hit the summer-baked dirt. He rolled, putting her beneath him.

As another explosion shook the earth, he curled his body around Cass. Debris rained down. Fiery sparks, wood and shards of glass pelted his forearms and neck.

Then the boom began to fade. As the buzzing in his ears dimmed, he heard the crackle of flames. Heat and smoke rolled toward them like a tide.

He got to his knees, checking over his shoulder. The center of the house had collapsed in on itself. While the firefighters who'd trailed him rolled up and trained water on the structure to drown any burning embers, Ben hurriedly helped Cass to her feet and worked the tape off her wrists.

She was shaking, her red-rimmed eyes huge in her pale face. She gripped his hand. "Lee?"

No one could have survived that explosion, and Ben was damn glad Cass hadn't been the one inside. Grimly, he shook his head.

They would never know if Lee had accidentally triggered the detonator or not.

She choked back a sob and grasped his shoulder as he knelt to unbind her ankles.

The paramedics checked them both and released them. Then they gave their statements to the incident commander, the fire investigator and the OCPD detective who would work the case together, because a death was involved.

As Cass stood alone under a tree, she hurt over the loss of her home and her brother, and over what her brother had become, but she knew that in reality she'd lost him long ago.

She looked up, and her gaze tracked Ben to where he stood talking to the incident commander. She caught his eye, but he quickly looked away.

Afraid she'd lost him for good, she walked over toward the ladder truck where he stood with a burly red-faced man, hoping she wasn't too late to tell him she'd been wrong to try to leave again.

She wanted to rush over and hug him, but she wasn't

sure what kind of reception she would get. Her hands trembled as she asked, "Can we talk?"

Heat flared in his eyes before they shuttered against her. "Do we have something to talk about?"

"I hope so."

At her words, Cass saw a vulnerability in his eyes that stunned her. Until that moment, she hadn't realized how unsure he was of her. He hadn't expected her to stay.

The fact that he believed she had walked away again left her with a hollow ache.

Tentatively, she reached out and took his hand, encouraged when he didn't pull away. Still, he wore the same reserve he had when visiting her in the hospital. She caught a whiff of his clean sharp scent beneath lingering smoke.

"I'm sorry about your brother."

"Thank you," she said, her voice cracking. "But I really lost him a long time ago. I was afraid I'd lost you, too. I'm so sorry, Ben. I was such an idiot."

His gaze sharpened.

"You were right. What happened when we were in bed made me panic. I couldn't imagine going through that again or putting you through it. When I said I couldn't be with you, I thought I was protecting you."

A muscle flexed in his jaw as he stared at her skeptically.

Her voice thickened. "I didn't realize how deeply I was hurting you."

She wanted him to say something, but he remained quiet, his expression inscrutable. Every long silent second scraped against her nerves like a blade.

Had she completely ruined things between them? How could she convince him that she meant to stay? "I—I know I made a mistake when I left eight months ago. I knew how I felt, but I wasn't ready to accept it then. Am I too late? Can you forgive me?"

He said nothing. Dread knotted her stomach. "Ben?"

He caught her hand and pulled her around to the other side of the ladder truck. Hidden from view, he backed her into the vehicle. "Yes, I can forgive you. And I'm sorry, too. About what I said earlier. Or, actually, the way I said it. I realize the caveman approach might not have been the best way to handle things."

She thought of how she'd hurt him, how she'd nearly lost him. All she wanted was to kiss him, but there was something she had to say first. "Your approach was better than mine."

He braced one arm over her head and curved the other around her waist, fingers caressing her lower back, heating her blood. "I thought I'd run you off. Screwed up everything."

She looked into his eyes and felt her heart catch. She didn't want him to doubt her ever again.

"I was afraid to trust my feelings before, but not now. I love you."

His eyes flared hotly. "Does that make you want to run?"

"No. It makes me want to stay."

He stilled. "No matter what?"

"No matter what."

His hand flattened on the small of her back, urging her into him. "Even if you see another fire?"

"Even if." She was disappointed that he hadn't said he loved her, but she knew it might take him a while to believe she was sticking around. "About that. The vision I had in my house was of a bomb, not a fire. The only thing those fires and the bomb have in common is Lee. I never saw blazes started by anyone else, so perhaps I saw the things I did because Lee's my brother. Maybe whatever happened to me at the hotel fire happened because I was supposed to stop him."

"So you think the visions might stop?" Ben pulled her closer.

"I hope they will. It's just a theory, and it may be completely wrong. But if I do still have these episodes, I don't want to face them without you. Although if one hits during sex, I'll probably freak out again. At least the first few times."

"That's okay, as long as you don't take off."

"I won't. Ever again."

The tension drained out of him. His lips drifted over the curve of her cheek. "I love you, too."

A sense of rightness she'd never known before warmed her. Her feelings for Ben were different than anything she'd felt for any other man. Deeper. *More*.

"Say it again," she said dreamily.

He nudged her chin up with one knuckle, blue eyes burning into hers. "I love you."

"It's a good thing, because I'm not going anywhere. Think you can deal with that?"

He laughed, murmuring against her lips, "Oh, yeah."

* * * * *

A KISS OF FROST

MICHELE HAUF

Dear Reader,

So who says Nocturne heroes need to be all dark and
creepy and stalk the shadows? A man who can chill you
with a glance, yet warm you with his touch intrigues me.
We all love Jack Frost for the fancy patterns he leaves on
our windows, but did you know about his darker side?
I hope you'll enjoy getting to know my version of the
winter god as much as I enjoyed writing him.

I have a passion for snow! I admit that living in
Minnesota all my life has made me a connoisseur of
snowflakes. I can do without the cold, but seriously, I can
spend hours studying snowflakes. I'd love to take up my
heroine's hobby someday. Maybe I will.

Michele

Michele Hauf has been writing for over a decade and has published historical, fantasy and paranormal romance novels. A good, strong heroine, action, adventure and a touch of romance make for her favourite kind of story. (And if it's set in France, all the better.) She lives with her family in Minnesota, and loves the four seasons, even if one of them lasts six months and can be colder than a deep freeze. You can find out more about her at www.michelehauf.com.

To Maria Alby. Yes, we've known each other since birth, but there are still things about you that surprise me and make me smile.

Chapter 1

*"If I am too cold for human friendship—I trust
I shall not soon be too cold for natural influences.
It appears to be a law that you cannot have a
deep sympathy for both man & nature.
Those qualities which bring you near to the
one estrange you from the other."*
　　　　　　　　　　　　　　—H.D. Thoreau

*"Sex is like snow, you never know how many inches
you're going to get or how long it will last."*
　　　　　　　　　　　　　　—Unknown

After a fierce night of wind and snow, the world
awakened enchanted—a sea of glittering ice crystals.

Sun shimmered across the billowing expanse of snow smothering the ground. Too bright to the mortal eye, the brilliance dazzled.

Vilhjalmur Frosti did not blink. Footsteps crackled as he glided along the crisp lace of ice crusting the tire ruts in the country road. In his wake, frost crystallized upon the mixture of dirt and snow.

Focused and direct, he moved through the air, alerting a mouse with his ominous chill. Formed completely of frost, he wore a human shape, instead of his usual particulated form.

He eyed the log cabin perched in a shallow valley. Smoke rose from the brick chimney, captured in cumulous puffs in the below-freezing air. The gravel road leading to the home bore a single set of tire tracks, where noxious rubber fumes yet lingered.

The industrialized mortals gave little concern toward nature, to the wildlife, why, to the very air they breathed. They were killing themselves.

They were killing this planet.

But he did not make judgments. Frost had been given his orders; he was an assassin.

Old Man Winter targeted environmental offenders, and Frost served his master accordingly. His icy touch delivered a powerful warning to those mortals who would tamper with the course of nature. If the warning were not heeded, a slow, painful death followed.

His current mark lived at the edge of the Boundary Waters Canoe Area Wilderness of northern Minnesota. Over a million acres of forest, streams, cliffs and crags, gentle hills, beaches and meadow capped the top of the state.

A whiskeyjack *whee-ahhed* deep from within the needles of a pine tree. Frost liked it here. The majority of it was pristine, if he overlooked the emissions from snowmobiles.

Stopping at the bottom of the drive before the log cabin, he leaned against a paper birch across the road from a steel mailbox. *Wilson,* read the name on the box.

The squeak of a door alerted him, and someone stepped outside the cabin. The mortal was swaddled in a hip-length winter coat. White fur edged about the neck and hem, yet it wasn't zipped closed. And the body beneath was barely clad.

A hiss of frost twinkled in the air as Vilhjalmur leaned forward to study the mark. Was that pink lace?

The tall, slender mortal strode down the drive toward the mailbox. A thin strip of pink lace hugged narrow hips and from there, the bare legs dashed forever until they disappeared into heavy buff snow boots edged by fur.

About the furred hood thick waves of vibrant hair bounced with each step. More pink lace tried to contain breasts as round as—

"A female," he murmured.

His voice would not be heard on the mortal level unless he wished it. Instead, it carried from his mouth on a dazzle of frost.

A sniff of the air detected the mortal's scent. Young, strong, he sensed no physical afflictions in her makeup. Beyond the mix of salty flesh and clothing fiber, he detected an unrecognizable sweet scent. The elusive odor teased at him.

Frost imagined dashing his tongue out to taste the tempting sweetness. But he could not consume tastes or food. No worry, smells served him all the information required to move through this mortal world.

Rarely did Frost consider the crime before he struck—but he'd never had a female mark before. What could this woman possibly have done to merit his deadly attention?

A glossy crust of ice held the mailbox door stuck. The woman tugged and then beat a fist on top the metal box. Ice crackled and fell into the snow beside her boots.

She touched the side of the metal box—laced with Frost's handiwork—and pulled back quickly. "Freezing," she muttered.

He nodded appreciatively. As if his work would be anything but cold.

"Duh. Like you expected it to be tropical this morning, Kate?"

Frost winced. How he loathed knowing their names. Didn't necessarily make the task more difficult, but, well—*Kate.* The name did land crisply in his brain, and he liked brisk, fresh, crisp things.

When she bent forward to inspect the innards of the

mailbox, the coat shrugged high to expose her derriere. Pink lace edged the pale peach smoothness of her flesh as if frost hugging an exposed river stone.

Frost sucked in a breath—a cold breath, unlike the backside wiggling before him.

Mortal flesh was warm, dangerously so. He could adhere to it in his natural particulated frost state to induce frostbite. Yet a touch while he was human-shaped could transform him to mortal form, fleshed out and solid. It was an interesting state of glamour, but one he rarely employed.

He stepped forward, moving stealthily. The mortal would not see him. He blended with the snow as easily as he insinuated the elaborate frost pattern painting the cold metal box.

He was everywhere, and yet right now, he leaned over her shoulder—*Kate's* shoulder—curious about what was inside the box. The visceral scent of her invaded his particles.

She straightened quickly. The move brushed her coat sleeve against his arm. He didn't flinch; it hadn't been flesh-to-flesh contact. No danger.

A toss of her head swept shiny long hair over his face. And he felt her warmth.

Grasping his face, he pulled away his hand to find it transforming. Color radiated through his fingers. Mortal skin. It tickled across his veins, tightening, growing…not cold.

The woman turned.

Frost dashed to the snowbank and plunged in his hand, and to be safe, his face. The transformation halted. Once again, he was frost.

"Huh." She shrugged a hand through her hair and the strands caught the sunlight and flashed copper and red. "Felt like someone touched me. What a nut. Must need a visit to town, to communicate with real people for a change, instead of staring at the computer all day."

With a slap, she shut the mailbox and then shuffled back inside the house.

Frost rushed after her, his form particulating and fixing to the large paned window at the front of the house.

He observed her through the window, setting the mail on a table and slipping off the coat to toss over the back of a sofa. She wore but underthings.

Mortals did not appeal to him. They were beings who populated and contaminated this world. Sure, his handiwork delighted and intrigued them. Mortals required entertainment. He, an assassin, was loved by billions.

On occasion he did observe children building castles in the snow or sliding gleefully down a snow-packed hill. The sight touched him in a manner he couldn't articulate. But he tried not to think on it.

But no interest. Absolutely none. Detachment from emotion was keen to his survival. And mortals were nothing but masses of blithering emotions. The tragic looks their faces held when he covered their crops or carved jack-o-lanterns? Pitiful.

The woman inside the cabin stretched out her arms. The delicate pink lace drew his focus. A breath lifted her breasts, barely covered by the bits of fabric. Two points of hardness, one on each breast, fixed his stare.

"Stop it, Frost," he cautioned. "She's a mark. And you have failed."

He'd had the moment, by the mailbox, to touch her with his frosty death. And he had not. He had never disobeyed a direct order for elimination. And had no intention to do so this time.

So why the pause now?

She bent over a table, sorting through the mail. Could those breasts be as soft as they looked? If she leaned farther forward, they might spill out from the tiny bits of pink and lace.

He lusted. Often. Lust was satisfied by his frost folk—all gods had minions. But no frost faery had ever looked so inviting. So lush. As if a feast to quench an ache he could not name. Right there, in his core.

Perhaps this mark required surveillance before he completed the job.

Kate collected her mug of hot chocolate and snuggled into the easy chair before the fireplace. An hour earlier she'd hauled in three pine logs and started a blazing fire. A bright red fleece blanket wilted about her shoulders and thighs. The radiant heat stroked her bare legs.

The quick trip outside in her undies was always brisk fun in the morning.

Weird, though, the feeling she'd gotten while standing at the mailbox. As if someone had run fingers through her hair. Of course, that was ridiculous, considering she lived fifteen miles from the nearest main road and was surrounded by a good fifty acres on all sides before she saw another house or cabin. Kate communicated with moose more than men.

A glance outside was blurred by the incredible frost pattern on the window.

"That's a lot of frost." She got up to check it out.

The older single-paned window tended to collect condensation, which froze into gorgeous frost patterns. Despite the heat loss from the window, Kate was always happy for a photo opportunity.

Grabbing her digital camera, which she kept on the table near the front door for quick shots, she snapped a few dozen photos of the elaborate arabesques and filigree dancing across the window.

"Now I've begun to work, guess I'd better get bundled up and head outside."

Chapter 2

Kate sat outside, across the road from the cabin, her equipment set up near the sharp needle border of a snow-frosted blue pine.

Her microphotography setup included a digital camera, microscope objective, aperture, field lens and color filters, all securely mounted in a portable hard-shell case she could lug around as a backpack.

Her work uniform was a white Arctic Cat snowsuit, Thinsulate gloves and a ski cap. Underneath, she wore thermal long underwear, a thin sweater and jeans. Layers, the only way to go.

The day was bright and brisk, a balmy twenty-two degrees—perfect temperature for capturing the larger and photogenic plate snowflakes. She could sit out here for at least an hour, snapping away, before a warming trip inside was required.

Yet no work could be done until—

It started to gently snow.

Kate tilted back her head to catch the first flakes upon her smile. Cold kisses melted and trickled over her skin.

Thrilled with her luck, she held out a chilled microscope slide to catch a few flakes. Using a small artist's paintbrush, she pressed the specimen firmly to the slide to reduce air pockets. Placing the slide immediately under the microscope and choosing red and blue color filters, she then began to snap away.

She was photographing snowflakes. Or so that is what Frost guessed after observing her strange machinations.

What did this mean? On an earth-threatening scale he couldn't determine the danger. Did she use harmful chemicals in her processing equipment? If so, it could hardly be enough to threaten more than a few square feet of air space. Nothing when compared to a giant shipping rigger dumping oil in the Atlantic Ocean and killing tens of thousands of wildlife and contaminating the water and shores.

There had to be something he was missing. Perhaps this activity was merely a foray, an aside from what she really did. Yes, he must continue to observe. Soon, the

woman would reveal herself—and her evil deed—
to him.

That sweet scent still lingered about her like a
frothy mist of ice crystals that form after laughter in
below-zero air.

Frost did not allow himself to be intrigued by mortals.
Not much. The few needs he decided were emotional—
lust, humor and challenge—were met by his folk.

Thinking of which, where were his frost faery
underlings, his folk? He didn't sense them near, and
they should be everywhere with the bright sun and the
low temperatures.

He blew into the air, which produced hundreds of
tiny beings, each a glint of frost sparkling in the sun.

Get to work, he mentally commanded, and then
parted the heavy pine fronds to continue observation.

The woman shivered as his folk landed her shoulders and skated over her face. She rubbed a gloveless
hand across her cheek, then held it there a moment.

"It's cold enough for frostbite," she muttered.
"'Spose it is time to take a break."

It took her a while to pack up the elaborate camera
system and hook it onto her back. Soon enough she
headed for the road, her fur-trimmed boots clomping
down one of the frozen tire tracks.

Ready to dash from her path, Frost saw the box
balanced on top of her stack slide. In frost form, yet
human shape, he dodged to catch it mid-air. But he
overlunged, and caught a hand against her throat.

Something bit him. No, not a bite, but the jolting touch of mortal warmth.

They both toppled and went down in the snowbank edging the road. Boxes and equipment sank into the plush snow.

The woman let out a yelp and landed, sprawled on her back, her body sinking in the snow. "What the hell? Where'd you come from?"

Realizing with a start the touch of her had warmed his frost to human flesh, Frost quickly worked a glamour to clothe himself in appropriate attire. Gray ski coat and leggings, hat, gloves and—cross-country skis would serve an excuse.

"Sorry," he said.

The sound of his voice, spoken in the mortal realm, and rarely used, always startled him. He cleared his throat and straightened, jamming both ski poles into the snow. "I saw your things start to fall and tried to help. Guess my skis got in the way."

With no stable surface to push off, each press of her hand into the snow sunk her in deeper. He thought of offering to help her, but the idea of touching her again put him in an awkward position. He shouldn't allow a mortal to see him like this. Yet, to dissipate to frost would startle her even more.

Finally, she rolled forward, crawled a bit, and then stood.

"Don't get many skiers down this way," she said. "Are you lost?"

"Maybe." He frowned. *Entirely too much conversation.* And yet, how else to discover her evil truth? "Is that your cabin?"

"Yes." She studied him, from the tight-fitted ski cap all the way down to his boots. The look on her face wasn't exactly accepting. Wary? The chevron arch of her brow captivated Frost.

"You've some snow on your cheek." She pointed to his face.

He touched his cheek, but felt only human flesh, which was entirely too warm for his taste.

"Maybe not. Looked like ice. Anyway! I'd suggest backtracking a couple miles and heading east." She gestured over her shoulder. "That'll take you to the trail that circles the lake. It's a beautiful trek when the sun is shining."

"Great." But he wasn't about to leave until he learned more. "First I'll help you pick up your equipment. It's the least I can do. What is all this stuff?"

"Photography equipment." She knelt and inspected the boxes, no doubt checking for damage. Then she turned and offered a gloved hand. "Kate Wilson, resident snowflakologist."

"Vilhjalmur Frosti," he offered in return.

"Now that's a Scandinavian name if I've ever heard one."

"So it is. Please call me Jal, Kate." He bent to gather the largest box from the depths of loose snow. It was surprisingly heavy, and he wondered how the delicate woman could handle the weight. "And do explain what a snowflakologist does."

"It's a self-titled profession," she said.

The smirk in her voice made him smile—slightly. Curious how her mood changes manifested as his own. He never smiled. It wasn't necessary.

"I went to school for meteorology but could never get into tornadoes and summer droughts. I'm a cold girl."

"You are?" His kind of woman.

"Yes, I mean, I prefer cool temperatures. I do research and studies and write related papers to make it all look good, but it all comes down to me, a camera and snow. I take pictures of snowflakes."

"Huh. That's all?"

"What, you think I'm crazy like the rest of my family and friends? There's nothing whatsoever wrong, eccentric or even boring about studying snowflakes. Someone has to do it."

"Perhaps so." Jal left the skis stuck in the snowbank near the road and, both arms grasping a box, walked behind Kate. "Doesn't seem all too threatening to the environment, your work."

"Why would it be?"

"Do you use harmful chemicals?"

"Nope."

"Do you raze large areas of forest to pursue your profession?"

"Nada. Are you a tree hugger, Jal?"

He matched her pace. "Can't say I've hugged any trees lately. But I am concerned for the environment."

"Well, don't worry about me. I wouldn't harm a snowflake. Er, beyond the induced melting that occurs from the lighting I use. There's bazillions of flakes to go around, so a few here and there—ah, heck. I reduce, reuse and recycle more than most."

They arrived at her front door and she held it open with a hip.

"If you'll set that box inside," she prompted.

Jal paused over the threshold. The air inside must be fifty or sixty degrees warmer than outside. Certainly he could survive warmer climes. He ventured to Florida to cling to bright, sweet oranges on occasion. Yet he'd never tested heat in this human form.

That wasn't what kept him hugging the crisp, icy kiss of winter. What stalled him was the thought that beneath the slim-fitted white snowsuit Kate wore pink lace. Maybe?

He could hope.

What are you thinking, Jal? This isn't like you. Do the job. Now's your chance.

"I don't bite," she offered, and left him standing against the open door to set her stuff down on a woven rug. "Have time for some hot chocolate before you head back out?"

"Hot chocolate?"

"Are you sure you're from this planet, Jal?"

"Of course I am. What makes you think I'm not? I

know hot chocolate." Maybe. He knew chocolate; it was a sweet mortal treat. So the hot version must be...hot and sweet. Ah, so that was the scent he detected on her. "I thank you for the offer, but I shouldn't intrude."

"Got to get back to the trails?"

"Probably. Well, surely."

She took the box from him and set it aside on a table that stretched before the window. "Well, then, you'd better get going before you let all the cold air in."

Like him? Even now, as he appeared *in the flesh,* he knew his body was of chilled air, not blood or skin or hair, as she was.

He was a god. She was human.

Suddenly the differences between the two of them became incredibly painful. He located the strange ache in his core. Jal clutched his chest.

"Jal?"

"Sorry. Right. Cold air. Wouldn't want to mix with your warm. Shouldn't. Can't, really. Uh, fine then."

What was wrong with him? He didn't do conversation with humans.

"You ski this area often?" she asked.

"Probably."

She smirked and shook her head. "Well, if you get a hankering for hot chocolate, you know where to find me. Thanks for helping me with my stuff."

And the door closed on him. Jal stared at the solid wood door, but he didn't see anything because his senses were deluded with the mixture of Kate's sweetness, the dry warmth of the smoke that had clung to the corners of the room, and the intriguing fruity smell he could guess had been on her hair.

"Woman," he said. "Nice."

And though his vocabulary had taken a strange plummet, Jal could hardly care. This mission had taken a strange turn. He didn't want to kill the mark.

He wanted to learn her.

Chapter 3

Kate peered over the rim of her glasses at the computer screen. Digital shots loaded and appeared in thumbnails on the iPhoto program. She'd taken over a hundred shots this afternoon. Most would be blurry, smudged or of broken flakes. Usually only a quarter of them would prove useful.

Snow was a finicky subject. Though she'd mastered the art of capturing individual flakes, and working quickly before they began to melt under the lighting, she was a slave to nature. If a particular snowflake didn't want to be photographed, it wasn't going to happen.

She would catalog and do a data scan on her shots later.

Right now, she clicked open the first shot of the frost pattern she'd taken from the front window. At six-hundred dpi the frost pattern revealed its intricate structure, plumed and lacey and curling as if dancing across a rink.

"More detailed than a snowflake," she said with admiration. "And such elaborate designs. Jack Frost really is an artist."

She traced the computer screen, drawing her fingernail along a graceful coil that exploded into a multitude of spiky frost ferns. It was weird, but the pattern spoke to her. Like art hanging in a museum that drew the viewer to make conclusions, form ideas and feel real emotion, this frost pattern did much the same.

Of course, nature had been speaking to Kate since she was a child. She hadn't known she'd seen the world differently than others until a kid at school had laughed at her for describing a tree as pulsing with orange energy.

Snowflakes she saw in dimensions and with color, just as her micro-photographs proved.

"Sexy," she decided of the frost pattern. "And noble."

And then she laughed, because she did this so often with her snowflake pictures.

"Good thing I've secluded myself far from mankind or they'd come after me with a strait jacket. I can hear my mother now. 'You'll never meet a man wearing one of those ugly snow jackets. It has no style. It doesn't show off your curves'."

Before her death, Kate's mother had been desperate for Kate to announce she'd met *the one*. Not because she wanted grandchildren or for Kate to actually be happy. No, Claire Wilson had wanted her daughter to find a man so she would fit in, become status quo and be less odd. Perhaps a man would steer her away from that silly photography career she pursued. Snowflakes? Ufda!

"Never," Kate declared defiantly. "I love snow too much to let a man come between me and it. I am the snow queen!"

And then she shook her head at her theatrics. The childhood dream never abandoned her. One of dancing across the snowdrifts clad in a gown made of snow, and she, the queen of all snow. Snowflakes would fall from her hair and storms were lifted with her fingertips.

Yeah, it was silly, but she'd dreamed it so often there were times she couldn't avoid a wistful sigh at her un-queenlike reality.

"Good thing Mother never knew about my crazy imagination."

Yet Claire Wilson had known about Kate's strange way of seeing the world. Her parents had taken her to doctor after doctor once Kate had innocently explained she'd seen the blood flowing through the veins of a maple leaf. (She knew it wasn't blood, but that's how it had come out when she'd been six.)

It wasn't synesthesia—as a few doctors had concluded—but Kate finally settled into the diagnosis and allowed her parents to believe that, if only to stop the incessant medical visits. Synesthetes saw voices in color and heard sounds when they tasted, and various other cross-references between their five senses.

Kate saw the world with all five senses, and none of them crossed. Everything was just *greater,* possessed more depth, shine, color and essence.

Kate was regretful she hadn't been able to give her mother the one thing she desired—pride. Even Kate's degree in science bore little weight to her mother's desire to see her fall in love.

Kate had never told her mother marriage was not important to her. Independence always topped her list.

"If I can find what I'm looking for out there amongst the snowflakes, then I'll be one rich lady, and I can build my own castle in Alaska and travel the world. And…maybe someone will finally believe me."

Because that is all she truly wanted. Someone to accept her for what she was—different, and happy for it.

With one last touch of the frost pattern on the screen, she turned off the computer and set her reading glasses aside.

The crackling fire shed the only light in the open-floorplan cabin. A narrow kitchen stretched along the west wall; the ceiling over the breakfast bar was hung with dozens of sparkling crochet snowflakes. The living room and her office space mastered the center of the cabin. And her bed sat against the east wall, two steps up from the main floor. The hearth heated the entire area so long as she kept it stoked.

Once her parents' cabin, and inherited upon their deaths, Kate loved the vast open space which still managed to be cozy and relaxing. Sure, it would be cozier with a man stretched out before the hearth, a wine goblet in hand, and a sexy glint to his smoldering eyes.

"His eyes." Kate recalled the cool, blue gaze of the skier. Like chilled indigo liquid pressed under glass. Far from smoldering, but intriguing in their own way.

"Jal? A weird name." Yet she couldn't recall the longer version he'd first given her. "Handsome, in a pale, Norse god kind of way. Lots of muscles. A little awkward with conversation though."

For a moment, standing out on the road, she could have sworn his cheek had been made of snow or frost. It had gleamed with silver and dazzling crystal, much resembling the snowflakes she photographed.

"A trick of the sun," she said, dismissing it, for no one was made of snow. And she didn't see people as she saw nature. They were plain, flesh and hair and clothing.

Standing in the doorway, vacillating whether or not to come inside, Jal had appeared starkly out of his element. She wasn't that scary, was she?

"I'm far too trusting," she admonished.

Attribute that to Minnesota nice and the small-town attitude of leaving one's door unlocked and greeting strangers with a smile. Yet a woman living alone and so far from a city—and a quick response police team—couldn't be too careful.

On the other hand, if he'd wanted to harm her, he would have done so. No, Jal Frosti was okay. Sensuous lips and eyes. Tall and noble, he'd looked like a winter warrior stalking his lands when she'd first crashed into him. Perhaps he'd been out surveying all he owned.

"Oh, Kate, you and your imagination."

With a twirl, she spun to land her bed and wrapped herself up in a thick homemade quilt. Tonight, if dreams went well, the snow queen would meet her Norse warrior.

She was doing it again. What benign form of natural catastrophe did Old Man Winter believe Kate Wilson would cause? Harming a few snowflakes? It was beyond Jal's comprehension.

So he followed her again.

Warmer today by a few degrees, the sky was crisp and bright. Kate snow-shoed around the bank of a shallow stream, and settled her equipment in a gorge edging the iced stream. A trembling couple of gold-finches grazed the cones dangling from the fragrant pines bordering the stream.

Jal's cousin, Ice, had worked a fine job over the stream and along the hem of snow that hung thirty feet over Kate's head. Clear icicles stabbed down in a jagged spine that sparkled even in the cloud-subdued sunlight. Oblivious to his presence, she focused on the camera and her delicate six-branched subjects.

"Snow would get a kick out of this," he murmured.

Maybe. The Snow goddess had proven rather bothersome of late. She did not welcome Jal's conversations and frequently destroyed his creations and folk with her own raging blizzards. Much more so than was necessary.

Females. Was a man supposed to ever understand the complex species? For that matter, he often wondered about the entire human race. Why was it that some were so happy and others were not?

Moments like this Jal became cautious with his thoughts. It never served to wonder too much. Yet, wonder he did.

Was it because humans had *things?* Things that appeared to make them happy? Because he'd noticed those who smiled most possessed something material.

Kate's smile intrigued him. Wonder what made her happy?

Jal moved closer, to see exactly how Kate managed to handle her delicate subjects. Her cheeks were rosy. His folk had been at work.

Sliding his palm through the air, he invoked a screen of frost, imbued with a message his folk could plainly read. *Hands off the woman.* And he blew, sending it through the air. The delivery shimmered and tinkled softly, but the tones would be understood for miles around.

Jal dashed a finger across Kate's cheek. She startled, head jutting up from her work.

Fleshed as a human, he quickly assumed mortal costume, ski poles in hand.

"Oh!" She turned and stood. "Jal, I didn't hear you come up on me. You're like a snow fox sneaking about."

"Didn't mean to startle you." He tugged off the wool cap because the warmth threatened him. A shrug of his fingers through the short, spiky hair felt strange. This human form did prove unique, if a trifle heavy. "I saw you here by yourself and thought to see what it is a snowflakologist does. You taking pictures?"

"Yep. Almost ready to call it quits for the day. My cheeks were getting alarmingly cold, but now, they're not so bad." She pressed the back of her fingers to both cheeks. Indeed, the impending frost-bite had receded.

Jal's folk always obeyed.

"I'd offer some hot chocolate—" she shook a silver thermos "—but I just drank the last drop. I like your hair."

He brushed his fingers over it again.

"It's so white, but almost silver," she said. "Nice."

Silver hair? Worked for him. But she lingered on it, as if discerning its makeup. He'd never been studied so thoroughly before. The attention twanged at the weird ache in his chest.

A diversion was required. He gestured to her equip-ment. "So how does all this work?"

"Oh? Sorry, I was staring. You're just so...well,

you're a handsome man, Jal. Come around here, and I'll let you watch. First I capture a specimen."

She picked up a clump of loose snow from the ground and flicked a paintbrush through it.

"I work fast," she explained. "The flakes melt quickly." She slid a rectangular piece of glass within the elaborate mechanical setup. "But there. See?"

He leaned in, his cheek but a breath from hers. "That's it? Where's the picture?"

"It's all digital. I'll load them onto the computer when I get home. I've a copy of my first book in the box here..." She fished out a small hardcover the size of a pocket notebook and opened it and handed it to him. "Published last year. At the moment, I'm working on a coffee table book."

He had no idea how one would tote around a book the size of a table, but if it worked for her, it was fine with him.

Jal browsed through pictures of snowflakes set against a light blue background. The actual snow crystal appeared on the page in red, blue, yellow and clear. Interesting. But not so impressive. This was a flat picture.

"And what is your purpose in creating all these pictures? Cannot human—er, other people, like you, simply walk outside if they wish to view snow? And in three dimensions?"

"Yes, but the naked eye can't pick out such detail. Or so I've been told."

"You've been told?"

The frost blush on her cheeks deepened. "I...see the world a little differently than most. These pictures? The human eye cannot see a snowflake this vividly, but it's how I always see them. Weird, I know."

"Not weird, but interesting. So you're bringing the beauty of nature to those who cannot see it firsthand."

"Exactly. Actually, I'm on a quest."

"Tell me." This was it. She would reveal her ulterior motive and then he must act.

"Promise you won't laugh?"

If he should, the air would freeze and her cheeks would take on the frost. It would be a pity to damage the smooth, rosy flesh. "Promise."

"I'm trying to find two snowflakes alike."

Jal scoffed. "Impossible."

"Improbable, but not impossible. I've done the math. The odds of finding two identical snowflakes are astounding, but I am determined. I've a million dollars waiting for me should I be successful."

He had no idea the value of a million dollars. Her task was ridiculous, yet far from dangerous to nature. Was it possible Old Man Winter had gotten the mark wrong?

"Best of luck to you," he offered. "If it is what you are passionate about, then you should continue."

"Yes, passionate." Her lashes lowered and she smiled as she looked to the side. "Passion is good." She unzipped her jacket and tucked the book he held inside a pocket. "Whew! This feels good, the cool air." She spread her jacket wide and tilted her head back as if to cool her flesh. "Isn't the sun amazing today, even in the dead of winter?

"Sure."

"It takes a lot to impress you, doesn't it—"

The thump of darkness startled Jal. Smothering snow had thundered down from above, and crushed he and Kate into a tight, squeezing grip.

Chapter 4

As soon as the heavy, wet snow contacted Jal's human flesh, he transformed to frost. And that form made digging Kate out from the snow tricky. All effort went into focusing his energy to strengthen his crystal structure.

The heat of her wasn't helping his rescue efforts. Her body temperature melted his crystals. With a forceful breath, he drew up a thick layer of hoarfrost to cover any part of fabric, hair or flesh.

Using the sturdy structure of the hoarfrost, he formed fingers and worked at the snow. The camera and microscope, possibly broken, he set aside. And when he dug around Kate, he listened near her mouth.

Still breathing. The weight of the snow had stretched the jacket off her arms, exposing too much flesh. Her lips were blue.

He attempted to lift her, but her shoulder slipped through his frost fingers.

"Cursed crystals. Jal, get it together."

Touching her cheek, a minute trace of warmth infused Jal's system with the glamour to take on human flesh—and muscle and strength.

Now he lifted Kate with ease over one shoulder. Unlike his cold ichor, blood flowed through her veins. Blood that needed to be kept warm. But how—

"Fire." What could kill him could save her.

He dashed over the loose snow. Deftly, he slid across a plank of thick ice, gliding until he landed on the road.

Jal entered through the unlocked cabin door, but paused as he caught sight of the hearth at the far end of the room. Simmering embers glowed within a pile of gray ash. He had no idea how to coax those embers to flame nor must he attempt it.

Instead, he laid Kate across the couch that sat but eight feet from the door. Cold air breezed through the open doorway. She groaned and moved a trembling hand.

"Kate, are you hurt?"

The coat flapped away from her chest. A wedge of snow fell from the crease of her elbow and landed the wood floor. Her entire body shook.

Jal tugged off her suede boots and tossed them aside. He hovered his hands over her torso. She needed a blanket, some form of insulation to keep her body heat from further escaping.

"I'm fr-freezing," she managed. "Wh-what h-happened?"

"A massive amount of snow dropped from the cliff overhanging the gorge."

Now he thought on it, it was strange something like that happened on such a cold day. On the other hand, it didn't take a large rise in temperature to loosen the crystal integrity of snow and make it unstable.

Kate rubbed a palm over her stomach. The movement lifted her red sweater and exposed bare skin.

"Wh-what are you doing, Kate?"

"Gotta warm up. I'm so cold." In proof, her teeth chattered. "Pu-please…hug me? I need your warmth."

His warmth? Not something he'd ever heard before. Was it even possible? Why, he embodied the opposite of warm.

"Jal, please."

Her shivering lips were actually blue. Should not being in this oppressively hot house serve the warmth her body required?

Trembling fingers reached for him, gripping at the dangling zipper on his ski jacket and pulling it down.

"Come here, no t-time to be modest. You were trapped in the snow, t-too. Body heat is the best cure for hypothermia."

Not if the man you're hugging is the master of frostbite.

But while Jal's mind protested, his glamorized human body leaned in and allowed whatever was about to happen…happen.

"Don't worry," her words trembled out. "I trust you. You rescued me, so I believe you don't wish me harm."

"Harm? No." Not at this moment.

Kate's arms slid around his body. The searing heat of her startled him. He flinched, but then the novelty of the moment settled his anxiety.

He pulled her close and she wrapped her legs around his hips and her torso snugged firmly against his. The sensation of woman and the sweet smell of her overwhelmed any apprehension to her body heat. The clothing between them did little to disguise the curves of her breasts, the hard plane of her stomach. The squeeze of her legs, drawing him closer, demonstrated desperate want for…

This human wanted? Yes, warmth. It would make her happy. And he realized, for the first time, that different situations required different means to happiness. Interesting.

Tentative, Jal nuzzled his nose into Kate's hair. The cool strands were slick and soft, like a fine fabric the Summer gods would value highly.

Mercy, what was this? He felt so…

Well. He *felt*.

Was this what happiness felt like?

"Oh, that's good." The shiver had left her voice; now it was deep, whispery.

"Good? So this…makes you happy?"

"Yes. Warmth is happiness." A hand slid up and down his back beneath the jacket and against a shirt thinner than Ice's finest creations. "You're pretty cold yourself. But I'll warm you up."

"Sure. Uh…"

"Thank you for getting us out, Jal," she said, her breath hot against the base of his neck. "That was the freakiest thing. Like a mini avalanche. Things like that don't happen in Minnesota."

No, they did not. And no amount of sensory overload could erase the disturbing thought from his mind. Had Snow purposefully intervened? Why?

"I have this weird ability to survive freak accidents," Kate muttered. "Like my parents."

The warmth of her gushed over his neck, permeating deeply. How could breath feel so luscious? "Oh?"

"Yes, but they're gone now. Three times a charm, but the fourth? Deadly. So! Nice way to get to know a person, eh?"

He peered down into eyes the color of new grass. It was as if he held a piece of spring—and spring was never his favorite season. Yet if it was appealing as Kate's eyes perhaps he'd overlooked the value of the season.

"Jal? What's wrong? Are you getting warmer? You still look so cold."

Was he getting warm? Not a good thing. And yet, what he did next would surely be his undoing.

Leaning in, Jal brushed his lips across Kate's mouth. Her soft skin tickled his. Millions of tiny light beams sparkled through his system. The minute touch spread through his shoulders and arms, down his torso and legs, to his very toes. He wagered the sensation even entered his ichor, for all of him seemed to effervesce.

He knew what a kiss was. If he wished to sate his carnal desires, he chose a frost faery to service him.

But Kate Wilson was not made of frost, nor did she chill him to a tremulous and satisfying climax. She... stirred him. She made him feel things he'd never experienced. Warmth. Wonder. Perplexity.

Happiness?

Asking a complete stranger to hug her was about the most forward thing Kate had ever done. But it had been medical necessity, a matter of survival.

Okay, so she hadn't been knocking on death's door—but still.

And he had been the one to kiss first.

Now Kate wrapped her arms around Jal's wide shoulders and climbed onto his lap as he knelt before the sofa. His perfect mouth explored her lips carefully, not too insistently. The gentle approach fired her desire.

Two years ago, her friends had all laughed when she'd announced she was packing up and moving to her parents' cabin. So far from civilization, they'd whined.

And men! There were no men up there, save for rednecks and outdoorsmen.

Kate hadn't missed anything that a vibrator couldn't take care of.

Until now. She'd missed the contact, two bodies discovering one another. The delicious giddiness of the first kiss.

Crushing her mouth over Jal's, she fit her body to his hard, muscled chest. Her nipples jutted beneath the sweater. She crushed her breasts to him, wanting him to know how much he turned her on.

She glided her fingers through his silver hair, noting it was cool as pine needles. He did not warm as quickly as she had. Hell, fire flooded her veins on licking torrents. This man could bottle his heat, sell it as emergency frostbite cure and make a fortune.

"Kate." One finger flicked her nipple through the sweater, but it hadn't been intentional. In fact, he flinched away at that touch. There was something innately innocent about the man, and yet, he was strong and brut as the warrior she'd first imagined him to be. "You're so hot, Kate."

Blowing stray strands of hair from her face, Kate smiled at his curiously stunned expression. "Thanks. I try."

"Maybe a little too hot." He pushed her up onto the couch and stumbled backward, catching himself as he tripped over the ottoman behind his legs. "I should be going. Your equipment!" He shrugged down the sleeves of his coat and blew out a huff, as if sweating. And he likely was. He'd certainly turned up her thermostat. "Gotta go!"

Never had a man dashed from her arms. Kate could but sit, stunned, as she watched Jal high-tail it out of her cabin and slam the door behind him.

"Huh." She toed the fur rimming one of her boots. "I thought the kiss was pretty good, myself. What's his deal?"

As soon as Jal hit the snow his body transformed and the glamour of mortal clothing slipped away. In particulated frost form, he raced through the air, the brisk chill reviving and sharpening his soggy instincts.

He'd kissed the girl!

An exquisite, hot, mortal woman whom he had been sent to assassinate for reasons that still eluded him.

What had become of Vilhjalmur Frosti, the cold, emotionless assassin? He wasn't using logic, he was…he was thinking far too much. Thinking about humans and their quest for happiness. Following the strange ache in his chest until it had led him to Kate.

By all the snows, that had been superb contact. Flesh to flesh. The infusion of her heat had scurried through him, exciting parts of him and awakening a stirring he still felt in his groin even though he wasn't in human form.

"You're being foolish," he chided as he landed the camera equipment and flaked across the metal into frost.

Breathing out frost crystals, he summoned myriads of folk. The miniscule crystals attached to the camera and equipment and soon it was lifted into the air. The entire assembly swiftly made way to the stoop before Kate's cabin.

Dismissing his folk with a sigh of gratitude, Jal, still of frost, formed human shape, then stepped to the front window and breathed over the glass. Curls and arabesques formed a grand design. It was all he could offer.

Chapter 5

Kate sat upright, instantly awake, which she attributed to her inner clock being averse to lingering in bed. In the bathroom, she splashed her face with water. An exaggerated shiver had her bouncing down the hall to adjust the furnace up a degree. The temperature had dropped noticeably overnight.

Stepping into her boots, she then shrugged on her coat, without zipping it but instead tugging it tightly closed, to trek outside and around back of the cabin for firewood.

She found her camera and equipment on the front step. A cursory check couldn't determine how badly things might have been damaged, but it would certainly set back her quest.

Setting the equipment inside the house, she then glimpsed the glint of morning sun against a bizarre coating of frost on the front window.

"Wow, that's just…it covers the entire window."

Boots crunching across the compacted snow, she approached the glass, marveling at the artwork. Normally frost clung to a corner, not the entire window.

Stepping back, Kate realized the frost pattern became less a frenzied mix of sharp dashes and coiling curls. It seemed to spell something…in reverse.

"Sorry?" Kate blinked. No, she couldn't be seeing things right. "I am not a pig and spiders do not come out in the wintertime. It's your imagination, Kate."

She went back inside, forgetting about the firewood, and trying to forget the window—but she couldn't resist a glance over her shoulder. The word read in the obverse now. It really did say *Sorry*.

"Not dreaming. But maybe touching insanity."

Instead of taking a picture, Kate searched for the red plastic ice scraper and found it under a glove by the door. Racing outside, she stroked frantically across the glass until her face was covered with melting frost crystals and water dribbled down her chin.

"You are not going insane, you are not going insane," she declared loudly. Turning, she found Jal sitting on her front step.

"I am going insane," she muttered, clutching her stomach and wielding the ice scraper weapon-like before her. "How do you do that? Always appearing out of nowhere? Skiing so early?"

The silver ski suit made him a fashion model fresh from the pages of *Vogue*. No jacket or gloves, not even a cap for his silver hair. The Nordic warrior had transformed to some kind of ice god. Had he not flesh he would have blended into the surroundings.

And yet, today his eyes sparkled as if ice. They had depth, and colors glinted within the crystal orbs much as icicles hanging from a rain gutter did.

She was seeing things that weren't there again. Only nature appeared so vivid and fathomless, humans were plain.

Yeah, keep repeating that, Kate. He's plain. He's not different or intriguing, or, hell, sexy.

Had she just kissed him yesterday? Yes, and she'd do it again if he let her.

"I couldn't stay away," he said, drawing her attention from his crystal eyes. "Why did you scrape off the frost? Don't you find it pretty?"

"I do." She looked at her handiwork. Long scrapes obliterated the clingy frost. "I just…it covered the entire window. I couldn't see out."

Yeah, and pigs do not talk to spiders. Just keep a cool head, Kate. "It is pretty, the frost. It speaks to me."

"Really?" He stood, propping a hand on the ski he'd stuck into the snow bank. Could a man get more good-looking? Forget *Vogue,* he was *Men's Health* cover material with a blurb line promising killer abs by utilizing a cross-country ski regimen. "What does it say to you?"

"It says beware men who run from my kisses."

Right, Kate. Be smart. Living alone in the middle of nowhere. Flick on your stalker radar, and pay attention. "I should go inside."

"Does it offer any warnings about women romping about in their underthings in eighteen degree weather?"

"It's not eighteen degrees. It must be close to thirty. It's a beautiful day."

"It's eighteen there in the shade of your house. And you're going to catch a chill soon if you don't zip up that coat."

Oh, yeah? So Mister Fashion Model was going all Doctor Chicken Soup on her? She *should* zip up. She wore a camisole and panties, and it was cold. But looking at Jal warmed her by ten degrees.

"I don't know where you come from or what your deal is." She stepped up to him, her boots crunching the snow like Styrofoam and stroked a finger down the sleek smooth silver fabric. He should talk. His jacket was unzipped and it revealed a thin blue sweater to match his icicle blue eyes. "But you're here, and you intrigue me."

"Like your snowflakes?"

"Yes, they all appear similar at first glance, but when you really study them, and see the makeup of each individual flake, you discover something truly wonderful."

Jal looked down and to the side. Shy? Well, she had a cure for that.

Kate tilted up on tiptoes to meet his mouth. His lips were cold, but so were hers. "You think I'm too hot for you? Am I cold enough now?"

"Cold enough," he murmured and then made the kiss his own.

Wintergreen coolness and Sunday afternoon snow slides filled Kate's thoughts as she indulged in the kiss. One reason she loved winter so much were the many ways a woman could warm up. Snuggled up to a handsome stranger. Breathing his cool breath. Drawing in his air, which tickled the back of her throat with the brisk bite of winter.

His flesh was cold, as icy as the skiwear looked. Yet, the coolness of him proved more exotic than a tropical vacation beach. Were she a snow goddess she would crown this man her snow king.

"So tell me more about yourself," she said, forcing herself up from the kiss. The back of her throat felt sore, as if she'd swallowed tiny ice shards. Could a cold be coming on?

"Do you really need to know?" He kissed her jaw, and glided snowflake kisses down her neck.

"Not really." Her nipples were harder than rime on steel. Jal landed on them with soft, nuzzling caresses from his mouth. "Oh, yes, that's...yes."

She lost her balance and, feeling herself fall, tugged Jal down with her. They landed the snow bank before her front window. Kate's jacket splayed wide, and the crisp skitter of snow crystals tickled her bare thighs and throat. But she didn't feel the cold. Not with Jal's mouth moving down her stomach to nibble at the lacy hem of her camisole.

He swished snow across her abdomen, and followed with hard kisses, and then lighter, tickling ones that licked away the droplets. Kate giggled and slid her fingers through his cool, short hair. She moaned sweetly as his explorations landed on her lace panties.

He breathed upon her mons, a chilly touch that made her shiver.

"Very hot," he said. "You tempt me beyond my safe zone, Kate Wilson."

"You have a safe zone?" Spreading out her arms, her fingers dug into the snow and the packed crystal flakes melted against her palm. "I thought only women were concerned about stuff like that. I don't have any zones I want to keep you away from."

"Be that as it may."

He'd journeyed back up to her lips, which was a little disappointing. But then really, what did she expect on their first makeout session?

"The speed of my attraction to you cautions me," he explained.

"You like to take things slow?"

"I'm not sure. Do you?"

"Slow is better for someone you hardly know. This is good, lying here in the snow."

"Does it make you happy?"

"It does, in a slightly twisted wouldn't-this-be-much-better-inside kind of way."

"Your cheeks." He touched one and then the other. "You'd best get inside."

"Only if you'll come with me. And promise not to run."

He drew in a heavy breath. "Can't do that. I have... work to do."

"You work around here? In the Boundary Waters?"

"Yes. Er...surveying."

Surveying all his lands. A grand fantasy she'd formed upon initially bumping into him but probably more like surveying specific trees or landmarks for the local DNR office.

"Can you come back after your work is finished?"

"I'd like that." His hair prickled her cheek as he leaned in to whisper against her ear. "A kiss to keep me in your thoughts."

This kiss crackled brightly upon her mouth. Winter frost to springtime. Yet again, at the back of her throat, the ice of his breath scratched.

Jal left swiftly again. Grasping her throat, Kate sat up and watched as he wandered down the road, skis slung over one shoulder. Whistling.

A glitter of frost crystals misted in his wake. The myriad colors dazzled. Probably snow stirred up by the wind as he briskly passed. Except, it wasn't windy.

"To do survey work?" Kate tugged her coat tight across her stomach. "There's something strange about that man. But whatever it is, I don't want to know."

Stupid, she knew. Maybe it was the childhood snow queen inside of her that wanted this fantasy to be real. More likely, it was the cool prickle of Jal's kiss lingering on her lips.

"Why?" Jal asked as he paced before the great and mighty Old Man Winter. "I need a reason for this job."

"You've never required a reason before," sounded in Jal's head.

Old Man Winter did not so much speak as rumble his thoughts through the air. The god was without form and appeared to Jal as a brilliant whiteness and so cold. He liked the feeling of strength and utter domination the winter god possessed. And he feared it.

"True, I never question my orders. You have always sent me after the deserving, those mortals who will never understand, who must be removed from the food chain before they cause great harm. I've been busy of late."

"You do fine work."

Jal shimmered brightly to show deference to his master. Humans considered him a mere artist, creator of frilly frost patterns. Old Man Winter offered him the respect his work deserved.

"Kate Wilson threatens no part of the natural world I can figure," Jal said. "She spends her days photographing snowflakes. I can only imagine her images, when presented to the world, would *increase* an awareness for the beauty of nature and not harm it."

"Enough! If you think to disobey an order, than I shall see to crushing you, Vilhjalmur Frosti, and wiping this world free of your presence."

Jal shuddered, his essence crackling smartly. "No, no, I—it will be done. Well met, Old Man Winter. I leave you with all respects."

And he shimmered away from Nordika, entering the mortal realm at the North Pole where all time zones were accessible with but a step. There was work to be done, frost folk to be dispatched throughout the Northern hemisphere.

But instead of ensuring the world was covered with frost, Jal ruminated on something Kate had said after he'd warmed her following the avalanche.

I have a weird ability to survive freak accidents, my parents, too.

How many times had she been destined to perish, only to survive? Surely one so strong was meant to be in this world. She practiced a benign profession. And her goal? To find two snowflakes the same. Impossible. No mortal being could ever catalog all the snowflakes in the world. And Jal knew she would never find duplicates.

Kate would harm none.

But he could not disobey Old Man Winter.

He needed irrefutable proof, though, before he ended the life of one of winter's most stunning inhabitants.

Chapter 6

The database Kate had designed to compare snow-flake photos ran them through dozens of comparison checks, using a mathematical equation to delineate the various branches, spikes, dendrites and columnar structures. There was a surprising variety of basic snowflake shapes, and this program put each photo through the rigors. It was a long process and worked through the night on Kate's daily photographs, producing a printed report by the morning.

Looking over the printout assessed the usual results. Still no luck. But she was determined.

Two snowflakes alike? The mathematical possibilities ruled out the minutest potential. If ever she were to find a match it would probably be one of the hexagonal plate types of flakes. They possessed but a length and width and were simple crystals that looked like a tiny clear hexagon.

The idea of finding matches had always intrigued Kate. It was an obsession.

Surely as a child growing up in rural Minnesota who spent her days outside digging in the white stuff, making forts, sliding, snowballing and snowmobiling, she hadn't any choice but to like snow. It was marvelous. It was delicate, gorgeous and breathtaking. It was not the flat white star design that most believed, but snow had depth, color and intensity. At the same time it could be dangerous, angry and life stealing, as she had learned yesterday.

And Kate wanted to master it.

When a physics professor from her alma mater, the University of Minnesota, had offered her a million dollars to find a match, she'd taken the challenge.

It fueled Kate's blood to master a challenge. She'd graduated from the university two years ago. With a BS in Science and a Masters in meteorology, she had initially toyed with the idea of being weather girl for a local television station. She could do the fake smile, yet the long hours and her lack of interest in summertime weather, had nixed that plan.

A million dollars could buy some land in Alaska and allow her to travel the world's Arctic landscapes, further increasing her photographic portfolio. She didn't need fame, but she did like her independence. Money could make a woman very independent.

Setting aside the printout, she browsed the photograph thumbnails.

"If snow had a personality," she muttered as she looked over one of the pictures from yesterday's shots, "it would be a sexy young woman with a vengeance for an ex-boyfriend. Teasing, playful and alluring, but don't mess with me, mister."

Kate smiled and glanced to the frost-free front window. "As for frost? I think he'd be rather secretive, a little arrogant and icy cool."

The touch of Jal's kiss tickled a shiver of remembrance up her spine. "Yes, a lot like him."

"Hey, Snow, long time no talk."

Jal wandered the elaborate quarters Snow kept in Nordika, where the winter gods resided. Unlike his own home of ice and frost, Snow's home resembled a mortal's residence with paneled wood walls and thick, cozy sofas and even a fake fireplace at the end of the massive room.

"Frost," the Snow goddess acknowledged. She did not look up from her focus on what looked like a wool scarf fashioned from red yarn.

"How's things?" he asked, unsure how to approach the goddess with the real question. She'd been cranky lately. And yet, he had never been one to avoid seeking truth. "Crush any mortals beneath avalanches lately?"

"If only," she said, and sighed out a cloud of flakes.

"How about crushing them beneath minor drops of snow in gorges that shouldn't normally see such an accident?"

Snow spun around, arms crossed over her chest. Her long white hair crackled and mists of snow furled out from the strands. She wore a human shape—all of snow—just as Jal focused his form to resemble a human shape, yet he remained all of frost.

Snow smirked. "She dead?"

"Kate Wilson? No, I dug her out."

"Look at you." She strolled past him. "Playing with the humans. What were you trying to prove with that heroic rescue, Frost? That you're better than me? You know you're not."

"I...hmm." Technically he did rank lower than Snow. She was right below Old Man Winter, followed by him and Ice, who were equals. "Why do you think Old Man Winter ordered the hit on her?"

She shrugged. Snow glittered from her shoulders and piled at Jal's frost feet.

Her silence raised his suspicions.

"Old Man Winter didn't order the hit, did he?"

A snow brow arched wickedly above her eye. "Of course he did."

Right, but Snow had her fingers in the brew, he felt sure. "Old Man Winter ordered the hit. Yet when I couldn't do it, you thought to take matters in hand."

"You're very perceptive, Frost. I guess that ends this conversation. Good seeing you. Ta."

"Not so fast." He gripped her by the throat. Frost hardened the crystal structure of her snow. She cracked out a wheeze. "What are you up to, Snow? Kate Wilson is not deserving. She is of no concern to nature."

"She is."

Blasted in the face with a storm of flakes, Jal released Snow's neck and choked on the swallowed litter of snow. So she was going to play things the hard way?

"Looking a bit melty around the cheeks, eh, Snow?"

She delivered him an icy glare.

"I can fix that for you." He blew frost crystals at her, and her cheeks hardened to rough rubble of rime.

Snow couldn't move her jaw, yet rage exploded from her in a storm that swept the room and swirled about Jal. He was accustomed to snowstorms, but not his own personal blizzard. Pummeled in the chest, he took the weight of the goddess's anger. Limbs splaying, he stumbled backward.

"Two snowflakes alike?" she growled. "What does she think she's doing? Do you know how that makes *me* feel?"

"You feel nothing!"

"I feel—" The Snow goddess snapped up and stomped away.

"It'll never happen." Spitting at the snow that poured over his face, he struggled not to swallow it.

"Of course it won't." She reformed ten feet away. All of snow, yet shaped as a gorgeous female, she had never attracted Jal beyond respect and admiration for the beauty she created. "But the humiliation of what she's doing must not go unpunished."

"So you want to kill this woman because you feel threatened by something you know will never occur?"

How *did* the female mind work? Their mysterious behavior baffled him.

"There's got to be something more," he urged. "Kate's offense to you is not worthy of death when compared to a deforestation crew plowing down thousands of acres of rain forest to make superfluous products for demanding consumers."

"I've never known you to be judgmental, Frost. What's up with that?"

Yes, what had happened that he was so quick to defend one human over another? This wasn't him. He didn't care.

Did he?

"Regarding this particular mark," Snow warned, "I'll be the one to decide the worthiness of offense."

"You've no right!"

What to say? How to pry out what he sensed lurked within the goddess beneath the surface of her hard snowpack exterior.

"Your work is splendid," he offered, tempering the sly tone in his voice. "Always much finer and more gorgeous than anything myself or Ice could ever produce."

"Naturally." She flipped back a storm of hair over a shoulder and picked up the scarf from the back of the brown velvet sofa.

"Did you make that?" he tried. "It's for warmth, isn't it?"

"It is." She toyed with the fringed hem of the object, a bit too concerned over a mortal product designed to prevent the chill of snow.

Snow paced across the room, which took her far from Jal in but a few seconds, and then as quickly, back to his side.

Snowflakes sifted about her as she bowed her head. "Have you ever been in love, Jal?"

Love? He'd heard the word. "Why do you ask?"

That she shrugged again struck him deeply. So human the goddess's gestures. It disturbed him to wonder at her actions.

Love? It was something similar to lust, but emotion-based.

"Doesn't matter," she finally said. "But I will tell you this. *She* was supposed to be the next Snow goddess."

"She? Who?" And then he instinctually knew. "But... are you sure? Why then would you seek to destroy her?"

"Jal, you forget your younger years as your time draws near."

Indeed. Gods did not measure time with days, weeks or hours. And yet, each of the winter gods served a short service to the world. But his memory failed him as to length.

"Every thousand mortal years," Snow began, "a chosen changeling child is born in the mortal realm and instantly orphaned. As we were when you and I were born. The gods then take that child into their care and train him or her to replace the current Snow or Ice or Frost."

"Yet it seems I spent some time as the former Frost's folk…"

"You did. You don't recall much of that servitude. It would destroy you were you to have recall of such menial labor."

Yes, and a short span of existence, as well. His frost folk generally survived the trip to the mortal realm, did their deed, then evaporated or melted.

"So Kate was to be the next Snow goddess?"

"Yes, but something went wrong. She wasn't orphaned following her birth. Not even after the Universe attempted to kill off her parents three times."

"She did…" Jal stopped his confession…*mention something like that.* That she and her parents had survived freak accidents. "So what does that mean? Why kill her now?"

"Because!" An explosion of snow surrounded the goddess at her outburst, settling to drifts about her ankles. "I am bored of this job, and now I must wait another thousand years for another changeling to be born. I cannot *conceive* another thousand years. I'm ready for the mortality granted me when I step down from my servitude. I want to be human, Frost."

Human? A strange desire. A concept he could not quite comprehend. And yet, touching a human was marvelous.

"And you think killing Kate Wilson will clear the way for a new Snow goddess to be born?"

"Yes."

"Have you proof?"

"No, but it makes sense."

"I won't allow it."

"Why? Are you in love with the human? You are." Her eyes glittered with perfectly formed snowflakes, a disconcerting dazzle Frost had to look away from or become enchanted.

"I don't know what love is," he murmured quietly.

"You do, you just don't realize it yet."

Jal opened his mouth to reply, but instead looked aside, crimping his brow. He wasn't sure what he knew, actually. What Snow had said…he had been born to the mortal realm?

"Love or not, she needs to go," Snow snapped. "That's all there's to it. And so what if my folk have been making copies of flakes? It's not worth the effort relentlessly crafting new ones. I tell you, there's only so many ways to shape a snowflake."

"You *are* making copies. So then—" If Kate were diligent her research could be successful.

And the harder Kate pursued that goal, the more vigorous Snow would hunt her.

"You'd sacrifice being a goddess for mortality?"

Snow flicked a few flakes through the air at him and winked. "In the dazzle of a snowflake."

Chapter 7

After a bath, Kate donned a thick white terry robe over a matching black bra and panty set. She liked sexy lingerie. What woman did not? It made her feel great to know beneath her bundle of winter sweaters and long johns and coats and scarves and mittens, the next-to-nothings hugged her skin. Like her body wasn't going completely to waste out here, so far from hot, sexy single men.

It had been her choice to seclude herself. And it wasn't as though she was a hermit. A trip to town once a week found her spending the day, buying groceries, chatting in the café with friends and stopping by the small, but resourceful library. And she never turned down the opportunity to chat with a handsome man.

A lot of strangers visited the town of Ely; it was a tourist hotspot for hunters and outdoor sports enthusiasts headed into the Boundary Waters. This time of year, there were plenty flannel-clad beefy types to choose from, and even a few uber-ripped snowboarders. Sometimes, after a chat, she went out to dinner with the guy. And when in the mood, she even went with the occasional man back to his motel room for sex.

She was a modern woman who didn't need a boyfriend but did enjoy sex. The bonus was the connection and conversation. Most laughed at her profession, or said, "No, really, what do you aspire to do with your life?"

She was aspiring right now, thank you very much. The scientific implications of finding two identical snowflakes could disclose itself to global warming, or who knew what else. She wouldn't know until she found that elusive pair.

Tracing her hand through the air before the window in an arc to match the sweep of frost, she caught a blur of motion out near the window. A bear? The woods were filled with them, though this time of year they should be hibernating. Could be a moose, yet they rarely ventured so close to humans.

"Maybe a raccoon," she said as she opened the door to inspect. And there he sat on the front stoop.

"Should I be worried you've become my stalker?"

"Only if my frequent visits disturb you." Jal turned and beamed a cool gaze up at her. "Do they?"

"No, surprisingly…no. If I'd met you in town—"

She would have followed him to his hotel room. "Want to come inside? Or am I right in guessing you like the cold as opposed to the cozy warmth of my home?"

"It's a beautiful evening. The moon is low and full."

Indeed the deep blue night sky was punctuated with a brilliant silver moon and stars too numerous to count.

"Grab a coat and join me, Kate."

"Be right there."

Shuffling her bare feet into the knee-high furry boots lined up by the door, Kate wondered how many levels of disturbing this strange dating scenario qualified for. The few times she'd seen Jal she had been clad in but underwear—as she was again. He seemed to exist in fifteen-degree weather as if it were mere air conditioning. And she was pulling on a jacket over her robe to go sit on an icy cement stoop.

Because the man was hot, and she wanted another kiss from him.

So maybe she was crazy. She'd be sure to leave this little affair of the deranged off her Christmas letter to friends this year.

The thermometer had settled to the teens, and Kate knew she'd last but a few minutes outside without thermal leggings and a cap and mittens. But she counted on some snuggling to prolong the minutes.

"Besides," she muttered, shoving her hands in her pockets, "I'm a born and bred Minnesotan. If I can't take the cold then I should pack up and move."

Heck, it was the one real bragging right Minnesotans had, and Kate was not averse to use it when it suited.

She stepped out and sat, tugging her coat low to sit on. "The sky is gorgeous," she said. "You don't see stars that bright in a big city. Must be the cold air."

"I like the cold air."

"I guessed that."

"You do, too."

She dipped her gloved hand into the loose snow shoveled high by the step and formed it into a snowball. "Love it, couldn't imagine a world without it." A toss hit the mailbox with a clang. "But I do respect the awesome power of nature and its swift ability to render we mere mortals helpless."

"Yes, a mere mortal." He turned his gaze onto hers. So pale, and seeking, piercing her with an intensity that read her like a scanner, documenting every portion in minute detail. In the darkness Kate was unable to see the dimension of color in his eyes, which was a good thing.

"What are you looking for, Jal?"

"I'm not sure," he said. And he meant it. "I don't believe I've ever looked at eyes the color of yours."

"They're just green."

"They are spring. I don't much like spring."

"I suspect you don't. I could close them." She did so, and leaned into his body to mine some of his warmth. No such luck. The shiny ski jacket held the cold. "Now what do you see?"

"Moonlight on copper." Fingers slid over her hair. "Pure beams of light on pale flesh."

The touch of his ungloved finger made her flinch, but she kept her eyes closed as his fingertip traced the brow of her nose, and under her eyes, and then tickled an icy thrill across her lips.

"What are *you* looking for, Kate?"

She smiled and dipped her head into his palm. "The Norse warrior, I guess."

"I don't understand."

"You don't have to. It's a silly dream."

He nodded, cleared his throat. "Why do you exist, Kate?"

"That's a pretty deep question, Jal."

"I just wonder about things."

"All right then. I exist…" Man, he'd jumped to existential in a flicker. He hadn't struck her as the sort, but she was all for humor especially since she was starting to shiver. "Because I was born."

"Why?"

"Why was I born?" An even quirkier question, but it didn't take much thought. "Because my parents were in love."

"Ah. Love. Tell me about love."

"The long version or the short?"

"Short. You're starting to shiver."

"All right. You want to know why I exist? Love is what it's all about."

"Really? Does love…make you better? More worthy?"

"I don't think so, but it certainly feeds your soul." She snuggled up to him. "Speaking of feeding one's soul, I would like another kiss because I'm starting to really feel the cold."

"My kisses can never make you warm, Kate."

"You are rather chilly. Most guys are warmer than girls. Cold-blooded, probably. But you're wrong about your kisses not making me warm. They light a fire in my veins."

"Impossible."

"You say impossible a lot." She took his hand and held it to the side of her neck. So cold, his flesh, and yet, the sting of it ignited her inner flame. "Are you so unaware your kisses render me hot and bothered? Jal, you undo me."

"With a simple kiss?"

"With a kiss. With your touch. With your presence. I don't know what it is about you, but it's like the frost I find on the window each morning. You speak to me in a language that needs no words."

"But you scraped the frost pattern away. Maybe you'll want to scrape me away if I touch you too much?"

Was the man simple? Perhaps he didn't date a lot of women. It was possible, for his oddness.

"Touch me, Jal, and see how quickly I pull you closer."

"I'd love to touch you all night, Kate. But there are things about me you would never understand."

"Try me."

He hung his head. Considering a confession? "Not tonight. But another kiss in the moonlight, if you please?"

"Yes. No."

Kate stood and tugged the coat tightly across her stomach. She may be open to strange men, but she wasn't desperate, or a glutton for frostbite.

"No more kisses in the freezing air. I like winter, but not enough to suffer frostbite. If you want to kiss me again, Jal, it's going to have to be inside."

She held the door open for him. Heat from the hearth fire crept over her cheeks on seductive waves. She wanted to melt with the sensation, drip from her clothes, and drown in Jal's kisses.

Jal stood and peered inside her house. What was he afraid of?

"I don't bite," she tried.

He smiled, weakly, and stepped across the threshold, then captured her in an embrace against the door. Fine with her. They were inside. Mostly.

Sensing an oncoming kiss, she pressed her fingers to his cool lips. "Do you live around here?"

"No."

"Then how do you get to my cabin? It's fifteen miles from town. You don't drive. Are you a cross-country skier?"

"Why all the questions? I thought you wanted to kiss."

"A girl's got a right to ask questions of a man standing closer than close, and well, what is it with us that you've seen me in my underwear more than actual clothes?"

"They're very pretty," he said, and tugged open her coat. "Black lace and pink ribbons. You speak of being undone. I don't know what it is you do to me, Kate, but whatever it is, it feels good. Right here." He touched his chest, and then reached for the same spot on Kate's chest. "Can I touch you here, where your flesh curves?"

She caught his hand as he moved in for the play, and rubbed his fingers vigorously between her palms. "You're cold as ice, buddy. No touching until you warm up."

"I thought you liked my cool kisses?"

"They're awesome." She blew over his fingertips, smiling as he flinched playfully. "But some touches shouldn't be so cold. There. Still cool, but much better."

He snuck a kiss, and smiled against her mouth as his hand moved in for adventure. The cool electricity of his touch, there, between her breasts and tracing the curves, made Kate suck in a breath. She must be thirty degrees warmer than the man.

Delicate coolness trickled over the mound of her breast. Her nipples tightened.

"Hot chocolate," he whispered in her ear. "I smelled it on you that first morning out by the—er, when we first met. You're the sweetest thing, Kate. The sweetest thing I've touched. The sweetest kiss."

He splayed a hand over her breast and massaged her nipple through the black lace.

"So I'm a sweet girl. You know, that's not necessarily a compliment."

"It isn't?" He leaned down to kiss where his fingers pinched her nipple.

"Oh, that's good, that's…"

"Sweet?"

"I don't want to be sweet, Jal. I want to be—"

"So hot."

"Yes."

"Sticky with need." The shivery trail of his touch glided across her bare stomach, circling her belly button.

Though he was noticeably cool, fire blazed in the wake of his explorations. And when he tugged her lace panties over a hip and slid his hand behind the lace, Kate tossed back her head and moaned appreciatively.

"You like this?" he murmured against the lace of her bra. Two of his fingers found a rhythm and massaged her aching, moist sex. "Here is where you truly are fire. It's the only fire I can ever be near. You burn me, Kate."

His rhythm increased, and while he dizzied her senses with an exquisite mastery, he scattered nipping kisses from breast to breast. Felt like sharp snow crystals pinging her skin. Very sexy. Uniquely Jal.

Kate clung to the back of the sofa. The heavy parka slid from her shoulders down to her wrists. Jal's ski coat slithered against her thighs. She wanted to arch farther back, opening herself completely to him, but when climax verged, she snapped forward, wrapping herself about Jal, squeezing her thighs around his hand and crying out against his neck.

If two bodies could mist, theirs did. Kate's heat simmered across Jal's cool flesh. Tendrils of steam coiled about their half-clad embrace. Jal kissed the crown of Kate's head and held her until the final shudders of her gorgeous climax slipped away.

Frost faeries never came like this. They usually shuddered to bits, literally, at climax. A dissatisfying end to his quest to slake lust.

He licked Kate's fire from his finger. Delicious, but so hot. Too hot for him?

Unsure, he looked to the door. Not completely closed, a wave of cool air hissed across the side of his face. His flesh, this human flesh he wore appeared vividly bright, growing deeper in color, blazing like fire.

Kate could not know how dangerous it was to touch her. Yet he was torn between racing for the door and dipping his head down to suck one of her nipples into his mouth.

When she tugged insistently at the fly of his ski pants, he quickly decided.

"Until we meet again," he whispered and tipped up Kate's chin to kiss her on the mouth.

"No, you can't leave. Stay, Jal, we've only just—"

Another kiss stole away the plead he couldn't bear to hear. This is how it had to be. He didn't do things like this with humans. It destroyed his focus.

Could she melt him? Was that why his chest ached so fiercely?

"I've business," he summoned the lie. "A flight to catch."

"No."

Even as he unwrapped her legs from around his hips, she kissed him, teasing him back into the flame. Hell, he wanted to find his satisfaction. Was there happiness in making love to Kate? He craved it. But he couldn't know how long before being inside this toasty home would harm him.

"I'll return when I can."

And he kissed her wanting mouth, quickly, wistfully, and then turned and walked out.

He cleared the drive and entered the forest before plunging himself into the snow and reviving his natural state. It took longer than usual for the human costume to release its heat and begin to crystallize into rugged hoarfrost before finally particulating into fine crystals.

"She will undo me," he thought, as he took to the air.

Chapter 8

He'd done what he must to get himself out from Kate's death embrace. Yes, her warm, wanting body could prove deadly. Maybe. Well, he wasn't exactly sure.

So after Jal finished a minor job on the peak of the Alps—taking out a Fortune 500 boss who was single-handedly responsible for clearing thousands of acres of rainforest—he headed home to Nordika to find Ice.

His cousin Ice was an easy-going fellow who had taken Jal under wing, so to speak, when he'd first been deemed Frost, and had shown him the ways of their kind. Ice was always wrapped within the arms or legs of a sexy ice faery. If Ice wasn't freezing the entire northern hemisphere, then he was having sex. Something about a constant ice-hard-on...

Frost was relieved to find his cousin kissing a giggling ice faery *goodbye* as he arrived at his estate. A swanky palace completely of ice, accented with hematite columns polished to a chrome gleam. The ice god lived the high life.

"Frost, my man." Ice, still in the human-shaped ice form he assumed to have sex with one of his folk, offered an open-armed gesture.

Jal reformed his crystals into human form and leaned in for a brief hug from Ice. He didn't touch the god long; his frost hardened and began to crack. There was a reason neither of them had ever considered shagging Snow. Neither wanted to risk rearranging their crystal structure.

"She was gorgeous," Jal commented on the slender faery who likely dispersed into thousands of diminutive ice folk the moment she'd left the palace.

"I never do anything less than gorgeous, man. So what's up with you? I saw your work on the Brooklyn Bridge last week. Cars sliding this way and that while photographers scrambled to take pictures. Splendid!"

"Thanks. I was pleased with that creation myself. But you! That lobster boat in the Atlantic the other day?"

"Froze it in place right in the middle of the ocean. Sweet, eh?"

"Nice." Jal strode along the wall formed by a crisscross of laser-precision ice bars. "You are the master, Ice."

"You know it. No one ever poked an eye out with a frost pattern. You need an icicle for that."

"I concede to greatness," Frost said and offered a mock bow. He snapped a finger against an ice beam and it rang as if fine crystal. "So, Ice...you talk to Snow lately?"

"Are you kidding? That female is just nasty lately. I think it's that time of the century, you know? Crabby and belligerent, and all in your face about any little thing. No, I've kept my distance."

That time of the century? Jal smirked. "She's influenced Old Man Winter. Actually got him to somehow order me on a superfluous hunt."

"The chick who's looking for two identical snowflakes?"

"You know about her?"

Ice grinned a clear smile. "She used to skate on me when she was younger. Nice legs on that Wilson girl."

"Yes, they are rather fine."

And when wrapped about his hips, all the finer. Jal touched the icy sail of a decorative crystal ship, imbuing his frost across the frozen water. Recalling Kate in his arms made his thoughts so warm, he wasn't sure if he'd start melting right here. "She is exquisite."

"Frost, I know that tone."

"What tone?"

Ice's frozen grin grew even wider and he winked.

"You're lusting after a human woman. Those snow-flakes in your eyes are the closest things to stars we'll ever have."

"Nonsense. I am detached and uncaring."

"You want her, I know it."

Frost sighed out crystals. "So what if I do?"

"Long as you don't get too close, is all I'm saying."

"Too close? Ice, I've kissed her."

"Nice." The god rubbed his chin with ice fingers. "What did she think about that? You being colder than outer space and all?"

"She didn't mind it. Ice, it felt like fire to kiss her."

"That is not good."

"Not real fire. In here." He clapped a palm over his chest. Frost crystals scattered to the ice rink floor. "Right here…it…it aches. Whenever I'm around her. And even when I'm not. I feel like I…want something. Like right now? I can only think about returning to the warm cabin and kissing her again and touching her, and—but I can't."

"Why not, man? Sounds like fine recreation from the death and karmic-repayment bit to me."

"We Winter gods can't touch human flesh for long, can we? I've never been attracted to a human before. This is the first time I've touched one and have not given them frostbite."

"Because you were in human flesh form."

"Yes, but Kate's warmth… Won't it destroy me?"

"Ah, you're worried about a major meltdown. Won't

happen, man. Trust me. She might send your mercury popping through the glass, but you don't need to worry about melting if you have sex with her. Trust me. So long as you cool down as quickly as possible after the fun, you'll be fine."

"Sounds like you've experience with this."

"Maybe. See, man, touching the woman's flesh can melt you. Slowly. Not so quickly you can't do it with her for a good while before you start to feel sort of…squishy." Ice averted his gaze south on Jal's anatomy, and then quickly glanced away. "You'll know what I'm talking about when that happens. Anyway, if she can take your chill, I'd say go for it."

"I won't give her frostbite in any uncomfortable places?"

"Not unless you want to."

He could induce frostbite when in frost form, which wasn't going to happen around Kate. Never. Besides, he'd touched her intimately without causing anything more than orgasm. What a spectacular success that had been.

Ice snapped his fingers smartly, focusing Frost's attention. "It's not the warmth of a human we Winter gods need fear, but emotion."

Jal mouthed the word, "Emotion." He nodded, though he wasn't entirely sure what Ice meant.

"It's a killer," Ice said. "When you start feeling and pining for the woman. Like that ache you're talking about? It's your heart, man. Trust me, we gods do have hearts, and we can love and hate with the best of them."

"I thought we only lusted?"

"That's what you've been led to believe. If you don't know love than you need never fear it, right?"

"Snow mentioned love. I'm not sure what it is. But if it's this ache inside, then I don't want it to stop."

"Razor ice," Ice swore. "You're already falling for her."

Frost clapped a hand over his chest. "Falling?"

"In love, Frost. Love. To whisper *I love you* to the woman—and mean it—could be your death. She's not like you and I."

"I know that. She is flesh, and I am not."

"Exactly. We were meant for Nordika, she for the mortal realm. If you lose your heart to her, then it's as if you've ripped it out and left it to melt on her doorstep *in springtime.* That part of you doesn't belong in the mortal realm. It *can't* belong there."

"So I can never have love?" What had she said? *Love feeds your soul.*

"Hell yes, you can. Hook up with one of your frost folk. Not that I'd recommend falling in love with one of those silly bits, but you know."

No, he wasn't interested in the vapid, unfocused frost folk whom he conjured to serve him both out in the mortal world, and here in Nordika on a more intimate level. They never lasted longer than a day or so.

"So I can give Kate physical pleasure, but I can never give her my heart?"

"Exactly."

"Shouldn't be too difficult. I have sex with my folk all the time. They come. They leave. I never think about them again. I can do this." No problem. Love would be experienced, and then onward to the next challenge. "Thanks, Ice. It was good talking to you."

"Yeah, man, no problem. Hope to see you again."

Jal walked out of the palace, yet didn't hear Ice's last words. "Think that one's a goner, he is. Wonder how soon it'll take to find a replacement for Frost?"

A bowl of chicken noodle soup sat cooling near the computer monitor. Kate's throat was scratchy, as if she had a cold, yet she felt great. No body aches or sniffles. She hadn't any cherry lozenges to suck on, so soup would have to serve.

She had catalogued yesterday's photos. Now she sat staring at the image of the frost pattern she'd snapped days earlier.

"Sorry? It really is there in the frost. A word. But why *sorry?* Who would want to apologize to me? Did Jal trace the word into the glass?"

Frost could be manipulated to form designs on windows and metal surfaces by introducing scratches or even finger smears. She had tried a few times and had created geometric designs. It had made for a cool eighth grade science project. There were actually frost artists who snapped photos of their creations. No different than her snowflake photographs, but they did manipulate nature, while she did not.

This morning her window had been clear and frost free. A bit of a letdown. Was it so weird to want to see more frost on her window? Like a message from a lover, she took giddy joy in seeing the intricate patterns.

A sip of noodles and chicken broth ended lunch. "Yuck. Cold."

Kate set the bowl in the sink, and then poured herself a glass of red wine. It warmed in her mouth and didn't so much sooth her sore throat as make her care less if it did hurt. The sky was overcast today. For some reason she didn't feel like getting all bundled up and hauling her equipment out to snap pictures. If she were getting a cold, a day of rest sounded perfect.

Her camera had not been damaged in the freak avalanche, thanks to the hard case exterior. The tripod and the staging platform she used to collect snowflakes were a little twisted, but with a wrench and some muscle, she figured they could be fixed.

Sucking in the corner of her lip, images of Jal formed in her brain. The touch of him as he'd glided his hands over her body last night. Jal had not only made her climax, he'd pressed her *on* button, and she hadn't come down since.

Gliding her hand between her legs, she squeezed her thighs together, and the tingling scurried throughout her loins. A delicious reminder of his mastery.

"That man really knows how to touch a woman." She sipped the wine. "But how to keep him around for longer than it takes me to orgasm? Not that there's anything wrong with a quickie. What is with that guy?"

Mysterious didn't even come close to describing Jal. Enigmatic. Sexy. Elusive.

If she were smart, she'd bolt her doors and not allow him entrance until she saw a legitimate ID, a work badge and probably a car or practical means of travel. Yet, opening the door to Jal was a thoughtless, automatic act. She couldn't deny him.

Because he was different from any other person. Physically, she thought there were moments when his flesh appeared of ice, vivid with color and luminous. She knew it was impossible. People were not like nature. Perhaps the man had a connection to nature she could not imagine?

"Disturbing," she muttered. "He's not even here, and I can't concentrate enough to work."

She turned on the water to rinse her dishes, and then spied a movement outside her front window. "Oh!"

Kate hurried to the window. Tight, spiraling coils and long feathery plumes formed what looked like… "A bouquet of flowers?"

And then a face appeared in the window, and her heart leapt. "Jal?" She rushed to open the door. "It's you! You scared me."

"Was it a good, heart-racing scare?" Cool fingers slipped inside her terry robe and—she hadn't dressed

since her shower—the shock of his icy touch lasted so
long as it took her to meld against his body and kiss
him.

"You brought me flowers?" she asked.

"You like them?"

"Frost flowers. They're gorgeous. Your job
finished?"

"Huh? Oh, yes. Had a…er, good flight back. I'm
free for the day, actually. And some hot chocolate."

"I could put some on the stove?"

"Actually, I like the hot chocolate running in your
veins, Kate. My sweet, sweet Kate. I want you, Kate."

"Oh, yes, that sounds—yes."

He slipped the robe from her shoulders and it fell to
the floor. As quickly, he shrugged off his silver suit
coat. Beneath he wore a shimmery white shirt, run
through with silver threading. The silky fabric glided
over Kate's bare flesh as he teased her ruched nipples.

"The door isn't completely closed," Kate muttered,
but it didn't matter. Be damned the high heating bills.
Who could care when the sultan of cool had just
stripped her in one masterful move?

"Mmm, touch me, Jal. Set me on fire."

He walked her up the step and toward her bed.
Kneeling on the patchwork quilt, Kate pulled him to
her and unbuttoned his shirt. His flesh was pale, but
hard as the ice coloring his eyes.

The thick vein on the underside of his elbow bulged.
She traced a finger along it, sliding higher to the muscle

on his bicep. He sucked in a breath and unbuttoned his pants. The sound of his restrained desire spurred her on. Licking over his shoulder, she reached his neck, where a sexy vampire nip stirred a satisfying moan from her lover.

"You tease me, Kate."

A shimmy of her hips rubbed her nipples across his chest. "What are you going to do about it?"

The arc of his brow spoke of devious mischief. And his tickling touch along her waist reduced Kate to a delicious shiver. He didn't relent, and quickly found the most ticklish spot on her body. Lifting one of her bare feet, he lashed his tongue across the arch.

"Oh, no," she pleaded. "I'm such a spaz when I'm tickled. I don't want to kick you."

He gripped her foot firmly. A glitter of naughtiness twinkled in his eyes. He licked the underside of her biggest toe. Kate cringed and laughed at the same time.

He struggled to hold her foot but would not cease his torment. Such unabashed playfulness felt a reward after weeks of self-imposed exile. And though she could no longer catch her breath to laugh, Kate gasped and winced as each slow lash of his wintry tongue shivered waves of melting laughter through her bones.

And then she clutched the edge of the bed, gripping the patchwork quilt. The tickle had changed to pleasure and the slow trace of his tongue guided an erotic tingle into her groin. And swirling higher across her abdomen and at her breasts.

"Oh, my God, I can't believe this," she managed. "All these years I've been so ticklish. But if I'd known—oh, Jal, that's so good."

"I'm just getting started." And though her toes waggled at the loss of his attention, the next hot spot started humming as he kissed the rise of her anklebone.

Jal moved slowly, attending to every inch of her body. As if he were learning her, marking her every curve, rise and indent, his mouth took her measure. To the back of her calves, and around to glide his fingers aside her knees. A dash of tongue there at the back of her knee titillated. Kate tucked her head into the goose-down pillow and bit the corner of it.

At once Kate felt as if she were involved in an illicit liaison that would prompt an admonishing finger wave from voyeurs—and then she didn't care. This was her pleasure. To own. Be damned, the vibrator. When had she abandoned real men?

Jal's rigid nipples skimmed her thighs as he bent to kiss her mons. He tickled her there with his tongue, nestling deep within her sex, but much as she desired it, he didn't give a repeat performance of last night. Instead, he continued his journey up, over the small rise on her tummy and along the angles of her ribcage.

Kate clung to the mattress as if it were a ship floating in the ocean. Each wave threatened to suck her down into sweet oblivion. She wanted to drown, to know if Jal's strong arms would catch her. But not too quickly. She preferred a lingering, slow death.

A lash to her nipple strummed a giddy cord that stretched from breasts to between her legs, and Kate cried out. The silky weave of his pants stroked her thighs.

"Your pants," she said tightly. "Off. Quickly."

"As my lady commands." The zip and toss happened in a blur. Jal lay upon her and kissed her mouth. Roughly. Wickedly. He bruised her with his urgency. "My fire, Kate, my death."

"Don't stop. We can drown together."

She reached down and encircled his cock. Heavy and hard like a column of marble. Directing him inside her, she shivered at his bold entrance. The uniqueness of him fascinated her—and rocketed her desire through the roof.

He moved but a few times inside her, sliding his hardness masterfully, claiming her with each thrust. And then she let go, sinking, drowning and loving him for the fatality.

Chapter 9

Jal startled out of sleep and blew strands of copper hair from his face. Cold fire, the silken strands. Everything about Kate Wilson blazed across his being and left him marked, as if scarred by flame.

When he'd plunged inside her body the burn of her had enveloped him in a wondrous lost dream. He'd never imagined heat could feel so incredible. So freeing. So connective. He'd felt a part of Kate. It was not a feeling he'd ever known before.

Love? Truly. It was an amazing feeling.

He'd touched a human and had not melted.

What Snow had said to him returned. *A chosen changeling is born in the mortal realm.*

He'd been born to mortals? That meant he had once been human, like Kate. They had more in common than he'd first thought.

Did that mean he could have love? Ice had fiercely warned against it. Do the deed, but don't let the heart begin to feel.

No, he must not. Jal pushed the warm ache aside. The world needed him. He mustn't allow one gorgeous woman to distract him beyond this brief interlude into pleasure. It had been a foray into happiness, not love. And he must be satisfied with that.

He rolled onto his side. Kate slumbered beside him. Moonlight shivered across her flat belly. He reached to touch her but pulled back. Angling his head level with her stomach he eyed the faint steam brewing up from her flesh. Probably human eyes could not see it.

Though there was no fire in the hearth, the blankets and sheets and—hell, the afterglow of sex, made him feel heavy and a little disoriented.

"Have to cool off. Now."

Grabbing his clothes, because to leave them behind would cause Kate more questions, he slid off the bed. But he didn't bother to dress. Dashing across the wood floor, he paused in the open doorway and turned an eye to the bed. She didn't rouse.

He hated to leave her looking so luscious, smelling so delicious. And oh, her sweet moans as his every touch had imprinted her shape, texture and fire upon him.

"I'll be back," he whispered, and stepped outside into the below zero air.

* * *

It was not disconcerting to wake and find Jal's side of the bed empty. Kate shrugged it off as another of his eccentricities. Besides, her morning perkiness might scare the man. Best he learned that side of her gradually.

She tripped off to the shower, humming a Christmas tune. She giggled to think of her Jack Frost, her cool but sensuous lover, nipping at her toes last night.

"Oh, yeah!" Her enthusiasm echoed in the shower, and she didn't emerge until the entire room was drenched in steam.

Shrugging into undies and yoga pants, she forewent a bra in favor of a neat fur-lined sweater she'd picked up last month after a shopping trip to Minneapolis. The feel of the luxurious, albeit fake, fur against her nipples should be illegal.

"So freakin' good," she muttered as she went to mix up some hot chocolate. "But not nearly so nice as Jal licking my nipples."

A surprise coughing attack bent her over the countertop. She hadn't noticed in the steamy shower, but now, the scratch had returned to her throat. It ached and felt as if sharp ice cubes bumped down her esophagus.

"But I don't feel sick," she muttered. "I hope I'm not coming down with something. I'd hate to give it to Jal."

The microwave dinged. Sipping the cinnamon-laced hot chocolate soothed her throat. Absently, she slid her hand across her sweater. The fur caressed her hard nipple. It was going to be a long day without him around.

Distraction was in order. She'd work on her equipment and check the weather report for snow. Fingers crossed, snow would fall, and she'd have work to do.

Kate strolled to the computer desk—but halfway there, choked on the hot liquid. "Holy…"

The front window glittered with sunlight—and another frost pattern. This one said *Sweet*.

Kate blinked. But she didn't struggle with the bizarre impossibility of the situation. She knew there were no intelligent spiders braving the chill to leave her love notes. No, a sexy frost artist had left behind another of his masterpieces.

"Sweet? Yeah, well you are crazy sexy cool, Mr. Frosti. Heh." She sat down before the computer.

"Frosti. I've my own Jack Frost for the holidays. He's even cool enough to qualify. Bet he could wear snowflakes on his lips and they'd not melt."

Yet, he could melt *her* with but a dash of his masterful tongue.

"Oh, baby." And she shivered one of those good after-sex shivers that tingled in her loins and breasts. A cough quickly chased away the feeling.

Kate stroked her throat. "Have I been kissing too much? Am I getting mono?" Jal's kisses, while amazing, had been met with his wintergreen cool breath. "Maybe I'm allergic to his kisses? Nah."

Clasping the mug of hot chocolate and drawing up a knee to her chest, she checked the printer. No printout waited, which was odd, but only until she recalled she had taken yesterday off. No data to review today.

She had to fix her equipment. She wasn't going to become a millionaire sipping hot drinks and dreaming about sex with Jack Frost.

"I'll go out and snap more pictures this afternoon. After a nice toasty fire and some oatmeal for breakfast."

Decided, she set to retrieving a couple logs from outside and around back of the cabin. After breakfast, she filled a tin bucket with water, which she always kept by the door in case of emergencies—she had a fire extinguisher, too, but one can never be too prepared— she then settled before the crackling fire with her crumpled equipment to assess the damage.

The tripod was easily bent back into shape. The staging table where she caught snowflakes was a loss, but by replacing it with black foam, she could get some photos taken today after all.

There was a knock at her door. Jal poked his head in and called her name. "Did you miss me, Kate?"

"I did!" She looked up from the floor where she sat amongst scattered parts and gestured him over. "Come sit by the fire with me."

"Uh, that's fine. Maybe I'll just..." He eyed the bucket of water near the door. "You plan on creating an ice rink today?"

"No, it's in case of fire."

"Right. Fire. You are the queen of fire."

"You don't want to snuggle with me?" She pouted appropriately. "I missed you."

"Come over here—" he waggled a finger suggestively "—and I'll make you forget I was ever gone."

"Sounds promising." She joined him by the door. A hug fit her body against his hard muscled form. "Are you allergic to heat or something? You don't like to get too hot, do you?"

"It's fire. I…have a thing about it."

"Childhood scare?"

"Something like that."

"Poor guy. We can snuggle on the couch before the window where it's kinda cool."

Kate muffled a cough behind a fist and Jal gently smoothed his fingers over her throat. "What's the cough from?"

"Not sure. I'm not sick. I've been spending too much time in below-zero weather. Though that makes little sense. Weather does not make a person sick. My throat is just scratchy. Maybe I've been kissing you too much."

His reaction wasn't at all teasing, instead Jal's eyes widened, then he quickly looked away. "So what are you up to over there?"

"Assessing the damage to my equipment. The camera survived. I'm heading out for more pictures this afternoon."

"How long before you think you'll find matching snowflakes? Those elusive doubles?"

"Maybe tomorrow. Maybe never. It's a long shot."

"Then why even attempt it? Is it the money?"

"Money is nice but it doesn't buy happiness. I do it because the process is very rewarding."

"How so?"

"Well, I've published a book of my pictures, with another slated for publication next winter, which allows me to live this sheltered lifestyle of the cold and slightly eccentric. I'm pretty much the only snowflakologist in the country, so my advice and knowledge is sought, on occasion, which I enjoy. But you know…"

"What?"

"I just want people to believe. To see nature as I do. No one has ever believed in what I see."

"I do."

"Yes, I think you do. Too bad the rest of the world isn't like you. But Jal, I mean it when I say I see nature as it is. It's three dimensional and breathes with all the colors of the rainbow. A simple rock isn't solid and plain to me. It has depth. Insides. A soul."

"Of course it does. Humans don't usually see nature that way?"

"Humans? Jal, you're the strangest guy sometimes. No, humans only see the outside of things. And you, I see you, Jal. You're a part of nature, aren't you?"

His jaw muscle tensed. He took the fingers she

stroked along his cheek and kissed them. "I am." He looked aside and down.

"What's wrong? You don't seem yourself today. You're not having regrets about last night?"

"Regret making love with you? Never." His kiss renewed the giddy tingles of last night's encounter.

Jal had but to touch her stomach and glide his finger across her flesh. The stir of orgasm snuck upon her.

"Lower," she whispered into his kiss. "Make me yours, Jal. You know exactly how to touch me, to make me come."

"I like playing with your fire. You are like no other woman." His fingers slid between her legs, finding the easy rhythm he'd mastered last night. "You make me feel things I've never experienced before."

"Really? I can't imagine what."

"Things like companionship, playfulness, a desire born of true want and not a simple reflex. Happiness."

"All that from one night of lovemaking? You don't date often, do you, Jal?"

"I don't date at all— Wh-what's that sound?"

Kate listened. Even while orgasm charged upon her, she was able to focus outside her body's surrender to Jal—and she felt the strange disturbance. Something wasn't right. Clinging to Jal's shoulders, she opened her eyes. The front window darkened and an immense thud literally shook her home. The windowpane cracked and glass shattered inside.

Jal lifted Kate from the couch and pushed her back

toward the hearth. Overhead, the ceiling beams
creaked. Wood dust sifted down in buff-colored clouds.

"What is that?" she shouted. "Feels like a train hit
my house."

"I'm not sure. This is not normal?"

"Normal? There's snow packed up against the house
and it blew out my front window. No, that's not a
normal snow storm."

"Snow— She did not!"

Jal rushed to the door and flung it open. A litter of
snowflakes sifted inside, tumbling to loose heaps at his
feet. It had banked halfway up the doorway opening.
He scrambled up the packed wall of white.

"Jal! Stay inside! If it was an avalanche—"

Kate stopped herself before she ran barefoot
through the shattered glass. "Avalanche? What am I
saying? I live on flat land with gentle slopes surrounded by tall pine trees. An avalanche is impossible
in Minnesota."

So what had happened? Snowstorms didn't drop
what looked like four feet of snow in seconds. And she
didn't live at the bottom of a hill or mountain.

This is insane. What is he doing?

Stuffing her feet into her boots, Kate then scrambled
for her gloves.

She heard shouts outside. Jal's voice. And…a woman?

"You will not do this, Snow!"

Jal tromped across the thick, wet snow, his fleshed-out human-formed feet sinking deeply. The heaviest, deadliest snow was dense with water and would suffocate a mortal if buried in the stuff.

Taking frost form, Jal retained human shape.

Snow stood at the top of her disaster, brilliant in her cold beauty. She thrust out a hand and sent a blast of ice crystals at Jal. They were large and deadly, razor-edged ninja snowstars.

One menacing flake pierced Jal's forehead and cut through. Snapping out a curse, he shook off the pain. Ichor dripped onto his nose. He quickly reformed.

"I didn't know you'd be here, Frost. What's up with you and the bitch?"

"She is not— I won't allow you to harm Kate. She had nothing to do with not getting chosen as your replacement. Killing her isn't going to change things."

"It's worth a shot." Snow blew again. This time Jal ducked. A focused blizzard soared over his head. "Come on, Frost. Show me what you're made of."

"Indeed?" Spinning about, he unleashed a fury of sharp hoar frost that cut through Snow's form and embedded deep in her flakes. "You like that?"

"Ouch." Snow shook off his frost, but the hoar clung tenaciously to her flakes.

"How do you do it? Get Winter to do your bidding?"

"I asked nicely."

With a stomp of her foot, Snow set the thick layer of snow beneath Jal's feet to an unsteady wobble. The liquid evaporated and the flakes hardened. He fell through the fine, powdered depths up to his waist.

Feeling the water level increase, Jal quickly transformed to a crystal fog and soared toward Snow, who beat at him with her snow crystal fists, but missed each time.

He landed behind her, assuming human shape, and breathed a command to his folk. The air crackled with legions of frost folk. They chattered and skimmed the frozen air, glinting in the anemic winter sunlight.

With a gesture, Jal sent them toward Snow, but she summoned her own army, and the air hissed with the clash of frost and snow.

What Kate saw on her front yard should have made her scream. Instead, she lost grip on the ice-hard packed snow, slipped down the embankment before her door, and slid into her living room.

"What the hell? He's— And he's battling a—"

She couldn't vocalize what she'd witnessed. It was something that only happened in movies enhanced by expensive CGI effects.

Not real beings. Maybe? Snowflakes and hoarfrost, and they seemed to…battle?

Gripping the edge of the tin water bucket, Kate's scattered thoughts cohered to form a conclusion. Not necessarily a rational one, but a working plan. She had to stop whatever was happening out front. And the only way to settle a snow and frost storm?

Lugging up the water bucket, she fit her boots into the packed snow, taking steps to the surface that leveled with her rooftop. The air was white with snowflakes. But they moved purposefully, not fluttering to ground, as they should. Back and forth and up and down and frenzied.

And the creature composed of frost pummeled the strange feminine-shaped snowman.

"Snowperson," Kate corrected her thoughts. "I'm going to need some serious therapy after this."

Kate swung up the bucket and doused the battle with water.

Flakes melted, some froze, others dispersed to powder, but all ceased whatever it was they were doing.

Eaten in half by the water, the snow creature quickly dissipated. Though Kate couldn't be sure the whiff of snow stirred up by the wind wasn't part of the same creature.

And the frost man—thing, *person?*—froze, one arm lunged out to swing a punch. As quickly, the ice cracked and hoarfrost jutted out from the human-shaped figure, growing at an impossible pace. A figure that wore Jal's face.

"Oh, my God." Stumbling backward, Kate's boot slipped from the snow. She scrambled as she fell, dragging huge clods of snow down with her and into the foyer.

"Kate, no!"

The thing shouted at her. In Jal's voice.

Not a thing. It was…her lover?

She grabbed the door and tried to shove it closed. Kicking at the packed clods of snow, she scraped her boot along the floor to clear it from the threshold.

The frost man appeared above at the rim of the snow bank. "Kate, please."

"No!" She slammed the door and struggled with the chain lock. Her fingers shook horribly, and her breath misted from the cold.

A glance to the side spied the broken window. Packed snow completely blocked entrance to the cabin. She was safe, unless he tried to dig through.

A thudding beat upon the door sent a wicked vibration through her heart.

"Kate? Please open the door."

She shook her head, unable to voice her fear.

That's what happens when you invite strangers into your house. They become frost monsters.

Kate shook her head, but no amount of thrashing would erase what she had just witnessed.

"Let me touch you. Then you will see me as I have been. Kate?"

Stepping away from the door, she stared at the unvarnished wood as if to look hard enough would summon an image of Jal to the fore.

But what image? The handsome Norse warrior her latent snow queen had only dreamed would sweep her away? Or the awful image of a frost creature made entirely of…

Frost?

The pounding at the door stopped. Kate sank to her knees and began to cry.

Chapter 10

Kate sat on the snow-wet living room floor for over an hour. When a chunk of compressed snow fell through the broken window, she sniffed back tears and shook herself out of her stunned state.

"Right. Major disaster in my living room. Must do something about it or I'll freeze to death tonight."

It took her three tries to correctly dial the number for the carpenter in town, she still shook so much. Roger Barnes was one of those hire-a-husband handymen. He said he'd be to Kate's cabin in less than an hour, and not to worry.

"Yeah, right," Kate said as she hung up. "But how to explain the avalanche in my front yard when he gets here?"

A flash of the strange battle she'd witnessed notched up her shivers.

The compulsion to step outside and survey the havoc in the front yard pushed her to crawl up the snow pack before the stoop. The yard was four feet higher than ground level, due to the heavily packed snow.

Her breath hushed out in a cloud as she crept on all fours across the top of the snow. The snow glinted and pulsed and glowed with depth.

"Not a single footprint," she noticed.

Nor was there a depression where the water she'd thrown at the battle should have settled into the snow. Everywhere, ice crystals glittered in the sunlight. Big crystals.

"Like hoarfrost, but…not."

Kate bent low to inspect a thin formation of snow and frost and ice. "I need a closer look."

Retrieving a handheld magnifier she kept in her coat pocket, Kate gasped when the low-magnification revealed very strange snow crystals. The formations were about a quarter of an inch, which was large for a snowflake.

"Almost looks like—no, can't be." She studied one formation, then another. "Little arms and legs and—People?"

Impossible.

"Nothing is impossible," she muttered. "The camera will show me the truth."

* * *

An hour later, Kate had taken dozens of shots of the crystal formations on her front yard. Roger, the carpenter, had called to say he'd had to replace a snow chain on his truck, so give him another hour.

Meanwhile, she loaded the digital pictures onto the computer. While she waited for iPhoto to sort them, she surfed online and Googled *snow battle,* which didn't pan out. *Frost fights* brought up nothing, save a reference to Alan Frost, a lightweight boxer.

The notion to type in *Jack Frost* brought up a few sites that explained the mythological creature.

"Norse myth names him Jakul Frosti?" She tapped her fingers on her lip and tried to remember the original name Jal had given her. "Vij—something or other."

It hadn't been Jakul. But the last name had definitely been Frosti.

Could he be?

"Nah," she muttered. That was myth. Folklore. A creature made of frost? A physical and scientific impossibility. "Thought you believed in the impossible, Kate, you insane woman."

A stream of coughs bent her double. "I still don't feel sick. Is this what happens when you kiss—" No, she wouldn't say it.

Not without proof.

All the sites summarized various versions of Jack Frost. He was either a god or a faery, or both, according to which nation's legend a person chose to believe.

Jack Frost was usually benevolent, creating delicate frost pictures and nipping at caroler's noses around Christmas time—but not always.

Jack Frost, the god, was attributed to assassinating those mortals who caused irrevocable harm to the environment.

"Sort of a hitman for trees, eh?"

Kate dropped her head and shook it. "No, that's just weird."

And yet, he had been very interested in how her work impacted the environment.

Pushing back in her chair, she couldn't remove the image of Jal, in a weird frost form, battling that snow monster. She had seen it with her own eyes. She was not delusional; only slightly eccentric.

"He does like the cold. And he never seems to completely warm up. Oh, God, he can't be. Can he?"

She tapped the mouse over a woodcut of a dancing faery with knees kicking high as it created frost patterns on the window. Another click opened up the pictures she'd taken from the front yard.

The images showed at three hundred percent, filling her twenty-four inch monitor, and clearly revealing what they were.

"No way."

Kate clicked on the next photo. And the next. The outline of the form. The tiny features. The…wings?

"Little snow people?"

But none had moved, which meant they must be…

"I've a front yard filled with dead frost creatures? They have wings." She traced the tiny wings on one of the forms. "And faces, and limbs and…is this what Jal is, too?"

Realizing the truth with a gulp, Kate pushed back in the chair. When the computer screen seemed to shout at her with clear evidence of something so unreal, she moved the mouse to the corner to bring up a screen saver of falling snowflakes.

"Kate, you seriously screwed up, woman. I do believe you've been having sex with the real Jack Frost."

Roger arrived ten minutes after her startling revelation and helped Kate sweep up the glass and shovel away the snow from the front of the cabin. He reported the framework was still intact, and marveled at the weird avalanche that couldn't be possible had he not seen all the snow himself.

Kate boiled some pasta and heated up a jar of Alfredo sauce while Roger pounded away, extra nails jutting from the corner of his mouth. She fed him and sent him off with a check for his services, and when he offered to look back on her tomorrow, she accepted.

Because even if she had nothing to fear from her strange otherworldly lover, there was still the mystery regarding the snow plowing into the cabin and that other snow creature. And the winged snow people.

Was that it? They'd engaged in a literal battle outside her home? Over what? And why was Jal involved?

Did she seriously believe she'd had sex with Jack Frost?

"I can go there."

Much easier, she felt sure, than the average woman who had never dreamed of being a snow queen as a child.

"You're going to accept him, just like that?" she wondered as she washed the dishes and set them aside on a dishtowel to dry. "He's made of freaking frost, for heaven's sake. How can he— How did he—"

Touch her without melting. Kiss her. Put himself inside her and master her as no other man had.

He could do all that if he were a solid, human man. He had felt like a normal man. All his parts had worked the way they should. And those lips really could serve some amazing kisses.

Did gods have special powers to change to human form?

Kate smirked. "I'm dating a god," she singsonged, but couldn't find the appropriate enthusiasm. What *was* the appropriate enthusiasm?

Or was he like those tiny crystal people she'd snapped pictures of? Did Jal have wings? "I'm sleeping with a faery?"

That didn't sound as exciting, or virile, as a god.

Dropping the wet dishrag in the sink and leaning over the dishes to stretch out her arms and close her eyes, Kate sniffed back a surprise tear.

"I find the coolest guy ever, and he turns out to be literally cool. So cool he's frost."

Isn't this what she'd always dreamed of?

"My dream was *I* was the snow queen."

What about the Norse warrior?

"Yes, but I never imagined he'd be—oh, Kate, what are you doing? You can accept this. Maybe. Unless he never comes back. I dumped water on him. I could have turned him to ice. Not that he isn't already sort of ice. Frost is basically ice crystals, as is snow—oh, Kate, who cares! He's Jack Frost!"

He inspected the wood planks hammered over the front of Kate's missing window. Good work. He was glad she'd found someone to do this for her.

Himself, he might have created a window of frost for her, but it wouldn't have kept her nearly so warm as real building materials.

Behind him, the snow the Snow goddess had dropped down in an angry fit had melted by half. Miniscule bodies of snow and frost folk lay scattered across the surface. They had given all for the fight.

A nod of acknowledgement for the fallen, and then he stepped up the stoop and lifted his hand. Dare he knock?

Kate had seen him in his natural state. A human wasn't supposed to see such things. And Jal was seriously worried word would get back to Old Man Winter, and he'd be out of a job. Snow couldn't tell without revealing she'd been seen, too. But if she was so miserable as Snow goddess, then perhaps the secret would be worth spilling?

Jal couldn't stay away from this cabin. Not when he didn't know what Snow's next move might be. The goddess had it in for Kate, and gave no sign of ceasing her angry vengeance.

What was so wrong with waiting it out another thousand years for the next Snow to be born? A god could track years in but a few steps, season to season could be but a nap.

The tin bucket sat on the ice-glossed front stoop. What a shock for Kate to have seen him freeze and then transform into hoar.

Checking his hands for flesh, Jal grimaced. Frost shape. Unacceptable to a frightened human woman.

Before he could knock, the door opened. He reached in quickly and touched Kate's cheek. His form took on human coloring and his body grew solid, shedding frost for flesh. Kate's expression tracked from stunned, to worried, to calm in a matter of blinks.

"Jal. You're looking…whole." She coughed, and her voice was raspy. "When you touch me, you…?"

"Take on mortal flesh and form. Can we talk?"

"I think that's a good idea."

She was acting rather calmly. A good thing. Unless the storm was waiting to rage. Females. They were very unpredictable. And no, he had not even begun to tread the surface of understanding them.

"Do you want me to get my coat so we can stand outside?" she asked.

"No, inside is good. I won't…"

"Melt?"

He wanted to touch her. To burn himself on her flesh. But he must be careful not to frighten her more than she may already be.

"So you saw everything," he said as he closed the door.

At the far wall a fire blazed. Kate paced before the end of the bed. She wore soft pink pants and a tight camisole with no bra. The jut of her nipples through the thin white fabric stirred him. Hell, he got a hard on.

Jal studied the missing window to keep from looking at Kate.

"Yes, I saw, well…" She coughed so roughly Jal felt the ache of her pain. "…a lot of freaky strange stuff."

"Your voice, Kate."

"It's a winter cold, or something. Like I said before, I don't feel sick, but my throat feels like I've been breathing icy air continually."

Like *his* air?

"Did you—" She stroked her throat. "Did *you* cause this?"

"I'm not sure, Kate. I'm sorry if I did. Please know I never told you my truths because, well, how does one go about saying they are the Frost god to a human woman?"

"So you *are* a god?" Her voice grew softer, the raspy affliction almost swallowing the tones. Her actions grew more disjointed, as if she was trying to understand, but her physicality wouldn't allow easy acceptance. "Not a faery?"

"That, too."

"A faery god?"

"I was born a changeling and was recruited into the folk—the lesser faery ranks—for the former Frost. Every thousand years a new Frost is chosen. Same with Ice and Snow."

"I see."

"Do you really?"

"Yes. No." She fisted delicate fingers near her ears and squeezed her eyelids shut. "I don't know. You've got to give me credit for not running from you screaming."

"That I do." He shuffled his feet and thought to walk over to her, but perhaps he should let her come to him. "Kate, I…I'm not a monster."

"I don't believe in monsters."

"But you did once believe in snow queens."

"I did. I…still do."

"I was once mortal," he said softly. "I'm like you, at least my origins are. I…I can touch you without causing frostbite so long as I'm fleshed out."

"But when you're frost? Would a touch—"

"Deadly."

"I see." She grabbed a pink sweater from the end of the bed and put it on, tugging up the collar and rubbing it against her neck as if to sooth the ache. "Speaking of snow queens, what was that snow thing I saw you fighting out on my front yard? It looked…female."

"That was the Snow goddess. She's having a bad year. You shouldn't blame her for her anger. Ice calls it her cycle."

Kate smirked and hid a smile behind the sweater collar. "You're telling me the goddess of snow is having her period?"

"I don't know what that means, but she's been cranky and irritable for some time. She was the cause of the massive snowfall in your yard. And before that, I believe she was responsible for burying us out in the gorge. She's…angry with you, Kate."

"Me? Why?" Her voice cracked awkwardly. "Oh wait. Did I sleep with her boyfriend?"

"Who, me? Oh, no, Kate, I would never—well, we can't, we Winter gods. It's just not done. And besides, she's not my type."

"Your type? Exactly what type does Jack Frost have?"

"My name's Jal, not Jack. And until I met you, the frost folk satisfied my needs."

"Those little things I saw on the front yard?"

"Yes, when thousands get together they can reform into one solid human shape, fitting for, well, you know."

"All righty then. So! I was satisfying a need for you? Like a cup of hot chocolate on a chilly afternoon?"

"No, Kate, our being together was much more than anything I've ever had or wanted. It was… That first day I saw you outside getting your mail, that's when this ache in my heart began to pulse."

"Getting my mail? I thought we met when I was taking pictures?"

"I saw you once before. I was…watching you. You were my mark. You came out that morning with your lacy pink underthings flashing brightly beneath the big parka. When you bent over I thought I'd never seen such a sweet sight."

She sat on the end of the bed and shrugged fingers through her hair. "You were checking out my ass?"

"It's like peaches and lace."

Kate bristled appreciatively. "So what do you mean I was your mark? What does *mark* mean? Is that like in the mafia movies when they talk about a— Oh, my God, Jal, were you…after me for a not-so-nice purpose? What did I read online…"

"I'm an assassin, Kate. I take my orders from Old Man Winter. I touch environmental offenders and kill them with my frost."

A heavy swallow blocked Kate's throat. What he'd revealed, and so casually! "What kind of man are you? You sleep with the person you plan to then kill?"

"It's not like that, Kate."

"Then what is it like?"

"Like nothing I've ever known before. There was a mistake," he said softly. "I knew it the moment I saw you. I knew you couldn't possibly do harm to the world or any portion of it."

"I would never."

"So I had to discover the truth. I couldn't carry out my orders."

"But you've killed other mortals?"

He nodded. "It is what I am."

"I see."

Not only was Jack Frost the winter faery who could delight all ages with his frost designs, but indeed, his touch was deadly.

"But when you've touched me—"

"In this human form my touch does no harm. Only when I am frost."

"Then you look like those tiny bodies on my front yard?"

"My frost folk? You saw them?"

"I took pictures."

"They're faery, certainly. But I am *more*. I was once as they are; now I am a god. Can you accept me, Kate?"

"I, um…whew!" She stood, but then sat on the end of the bed. "Accept you. A killer who delivers death by frostbite, yet can bring me to some kind of crazy wonderful with a mere kiss. I think it is your kisses that have given me this sore throat."

"I like you, Kate. I don't want to stop seeing you. But I'd understand if you wanted nothing to do with me. Maybe. I don't know. Feeling…it's very new to me."

She gestured for him to sit by her, and Jal crossed the room and settled next to her on the bed. She wanted him to kiss her. But if his kisses had made her ill, then what would prolonged exposure do to her?

"I know when I like a person and when I can trust him," she offered. "This sounds weird to say," she said, "but I have always felt something was missing in my life. That snow queen dream, you know? And then— now—a knight made of frost sweeps me off my feet and I'm feeling kind of fulfilled, like maybe some- thing missing has finally been found. I want you in my life, Jal. But how will that work? I don't know if I can do this sore throat for much longer. And you, what effect do I have on you? Can I melt you?"

"We can have sex and touch and hold each other and I won't melt. I just need to go outside and cool off as soon after as I can."

"Is that why you were gone this morning? Because you needed to get cold?"

He nodded.

Okay, freak level should be off the scale, but Kate's strange calm reigned. Was it because the fantasy was too exquisite? That she wanted the impossible to work no matter what the price? Could she have a relationship with a man—*god*—who freely admitted he was an assassin?

"Kate, I have to tell you something. I am a god, and we don't have all the emotions you humans do. I lust, I get angry, but I never hunger, nor do I feel sympathy. That's an alien emotion I've only seen in the tears of children. And love, well, that's never been in my vocabulary. Until now."

He drew her hand over to his knee and held it. "Kate, I need you to know my truth. I love you. And I would die if I could not keep you safe."

"Can gods die?"

"We can all be destroyed. In whatever manner serves our bane." Such as laying his heart before her to melt? "You can't stay here in the northern states, Kate. You should go south where Snow can't get to you."

"You actually think she's going to try to do something to me?"

"She can, and she will."

"You told me you love me," she said. "But you also said you don't know what love is."

"I do now." And he leaned in to kiss her—and she let him.

Bittersweet, this kiss. For Kate sensed she could never enjoy it again, now knowing what she knew. Jal's breath cooled her throat, making her throat itch and she pushed him away.

"Am I too warm for you? Is your heart warm, Jal? Any part of you?"

"My heart is of frost, as I am. But I do feel warmth spread through this human body. A dip in a snow bank is due. Have you family you can stay with? Far from the snow and ice and frost of this Minnesota winter?"

"My parents used to live in Florida."

"That's perfect."

"They've both passed, my mother just last year. Besides, I'm not going to let the abominable snowbitch scare me away."

"Kate, this is not a joke. The danger Snow presents is very real. Just for a few days? Take a vacation, fly south to the beach."

"I wish I did have parents to visit. We were never close." Kate sighed and looked to the side. "I was adopted twenty-four hours after my birth. My search for answers about my birth parents put my mother and I at odds."

"You were adopted? So these parents who recently passed, they were not your blood parents?"

"No, my real parents died in a car crash on the way to the hospital while my mother was in labor with me. I was the only survivor. Told you I have this weird ability to survive catastrophe."

A tiny ping sounded from the center of the living room. Kate stepped down from the bed to check her computer screen. Jal followed, looking over her shoulder at two digital photographs of snowflakes.

"Oh, my God," she said. "I've done it. Two snowflakes. Exactly alike."

Chapter 11

"Are you sure?" Jal asked. Snowflakes could look very similar and yet be minutely different due to small imperfections or rime deposits. "Perhaps that's the same photograph, twice?"

Jal needn't argue. He knew the truth. Snow was bored; it didn't matter to her to create unique snowflakes. Truly, a new Snow goddess was needed.

And the one woman who could step up and take her place stood but a breath away. So unknowing. Yet so eager for the job according to dreams she'd had since childhood.

Kate couldn't be expected to sacrifice her cozy mortal life for that of a goddess. The very reason the

gods were taken as newborns was so they were immediately acclimated, not forced to abandon a life, friends,
family and perhaps a job. It is what made him so emotionless.

What *had* made him emotionless. Things had
changed.

Jal wondered now about Kate being his mark. Had
he taken her out that first day, she would have never
made this discovery. Snow's secret would be safe.

"I've got to call Professor McClean." Kate reached
for the phone. "This is worth a million dollars! Wait.
I have to put together a presentation first. Yes, do this
right, Kate. Don't jump into it until I've checked everything out. I've got to study all the points of delin-
eation and recheck the computer's accuracy. Oh."

As if suddenly remembering Jal's presence, Kate
turned and hesitantly touched his jaw.

"You've mastered what you set out to do," he said.
A dip of his head nuzzled his cheek into her palm. "I
should leave you to work. You're not angry with me for
concealing my truth?"

She kissed him. The morsel touched the corner of
his mouth, warming, threatening. For his heart pulsed
hotly. Could he feel it melt?

"I love you, too," Kate whispered. "Can we make
this work?"

"I'm not sure. This thing called love." He clasped a
hand over his chest. There, it burned. "It is wondrous.
Should a god be allowed such wonder? Is it not my bane

to serve this world without its carnal rewards? I was once an unfeeling thing who did as he was told, to the benefit of your mortal realm. You've changed me, Kate."

She turned in his embrace and he wrapped an arm around under her breasts. "It is a completely different realm where you come from, isn't it?"

"Nordika. And it is."

"Is it a world of snow and ice and frost?"

"As marvelous as Kate the snow queen can imagine."

"Will she come after me again? Now that I've found two matching snowflakes? That's why the snow goddess is angry with me, isn't it?"

"It is. But I will protect you, Kate. I promise. Snow is...not doing her job as it must be done according to the very law of nature. I have to leave you for a bit, but I promise I'll return. If you'll have me?"

"Of course I will. I'll wait for you tonight, outside."

"Will you hold off on reporting your find until after I've spoken to you again?"

She nodded and kissed him again.

"You saw the evidence?" Ice asked as he paced a thick snow-drifted glacier over the Arctic Sea.

Jal stood studying the blue wall of ice not a hundred yards away. The sea lashed up against the immense iceberg. The color of it was incredible. Ice did good work.

"Evidence. Yes, it was on her computer. She used the machine to detect similarities in various points on the snowflake, and it produced an exact match. But as I've told you, Snow has already confessed to making duplicates."

"Man, this cannot happen. She defies nature with her insolence! What is wrong with that goddess?"

"Perhaps..." The image of Snow stroking the red scarf came to him. No. Could she be? "I think she is in love."

"Love? With what? The abominable snowman? That chick is not in love. Nothing could love something so pestiferous in return."

And yet, Jal knew Kate had found it in her heart to love something not even mortal. Where there was a will, one in love would fall. "There's no question, a new Snow goddess is necessary. Kate's the one, Ice, the next Snow goddess."

"Your mortal fling?"

"Yes, and her blood parents died before she was born."

"That doesn't make sense. I thought the Universe tried but failed to kill her parents?"

"Her adopted parents. The real ones were in an accident on the way to the hospital. The adults were killed, and Kate was born through the miracle of medical intervention. The Universe was successful. Kate was orphaned *before* birth, but she was adopted less than twenty-four hours later. For some reason, the gods have always believed those to be her real parents."

"Then she could become Snow," Ice declared.

"Yes. Maybe. Would it not be impossible, mentally debilitating to ask her to shed her life for that of a god?"

"I don't know, man, this *is* a sweet life."

"You've nothing to compare it to. It is unlike the lives of mortals, that's sure. It is immense and powerful, and yet, we don't have things like hot chocolate and pink lace panties here."

"Pink lace? Frost, my man, you've really got it bad for her, don't you?"

"I told her I love her."

"You did not! Frost, you cannot afford emotion. It will be the death of you!"

"Too late, Ice." Jal smiled, and he felt it stretch deep into his heart. "I'd rather die than hide my true feelings from Kate again."

Winter had demanded an audience with Frost. And as the presence of the greatest season of all surrounded Frost, he began to question his actions. He'd done something wrong. He must accept the punishment.

And yet, acceptance did not mean he had to like it.

"Her discovery will devastate the mortal realm. You insolent!" Winter boomed.

"I don't understand how."

"It's...it's..." Never had Frost heard Winter struggle to form his thoughts. "The global warming thing."

"I don't buy that."

"Humans go mad over issues like that."

"Please, if they haven't panicked yet—and well they should be—two identical snowflakes is not going to push them over the edge."

"Yes, that is the pitiful truth. But there is also belief."

"Belief?"

"Yes, Vilhjalmur Frosti, what happens when the humans find out Frost is an assassin, the Snow goddess is a bored artist and Ice is a sex-crazed Lothario? Belief will be shattered. Myth, legend and lore will be altered. Humans rely on those things as staples in their history, why, their very existence! And I will not tolerate their belief being shattered."

Good points, all of them. But worth Kate's death? Never.

"There's more to this. Something you're not telling me."

"You don't need to know the reason. Do you forfeit your position as Frost god?"

"No."

"Then you will complete the task set to you before the night is dead!"

After a day spent leaning before the computer screen, Kate curved her body backward and stretched out her shoulders and spine. Whew, she hadn't realized how knotted up she had become sitting in one position for so long.

Everything checked out. The calculations and data

point checks were all correct. She had found two identical snowflakes.

An amazing discovery she still shook her head over, but the data did not lie. And the pictures, she'd moved them over one another and tracked their points so many times she knew both snowflakes by heart. They were the same.

It was late, well past supper, so she would wait until tomorrow to call Professor McClean. Prolonging the moment would give her time to digest what had occurred.

She'd told Jal she would wait for him tonight, and she'd meant it.

"So you're going to date the Frost god?"

She smiled and nodded in agreement. Yet a fit of coughs sent her rushing for the bathroom. "Need some humidity. Gotta kick this cold in the butt."

If only she weren't fooling herself. This was no cold. This was a result of breathing in Jal's kisses, it had to be.

Kate flicked on the shower to warm the room, then, the sight of the moon glinting on the small window made her shut off the water to stop the condensation.

There on the frost-covered window, he'd written: *I love you.*

And Kate started to cry, because she loved him, too. And what an impossible love.

A knock on the door lured her out to the living room. She wore a robe and underthings, and entirely expected Jal to be on the other side as she swung open the door.

Kate let out a chirp. It was not Jal, but instead, a tall woman with icy eyes and a crown of glittering snow-flakes dancing about her white hair.

Chapter 12

Kate hadn't chance to protest before the woman stepped inside and walked past her. A long white robe—hell, it was made of snow—flowed across the floor, the hem of it melting and staining the wood floorboards dark.

Dread crept up the back of Kate's neck. Would she get far if she ran? The goddess would laugh at the stupid human as she conjured something like a monster snowball to throw after her. Not on Kate's list of favorite ways to bite the big one.

"You must be Snow," Kate tried. Her raspy voice wavered uneasily. *Get it together, girl.* Jal said he'd protect her. Would he arrive soon? Like, now!

"Kate Wilson." The goddess hooked her hands at her hips. She stood in fleshed human form and wore mortal clothing—of snow. Fashion-model bone structure and a sexy white slip of a dress hugged long pale legs. She radiated all colors and exhaled gorgeous silver breath. "Not at all charmed to meet you."

Jal had been right about the PMSing goddess. Crabby for an entire year? Kate could be thankful she was only grumpy once a month.

Well, if she had come to kill her, Kate had no intention of going down without a fight. "What do you want?"

"I like a woman who gets right to it. Points for you, Kate Wilson."

The goddess strolled the length of the sofa and wandered before the computer desk. "What's that?" She pointed to the printouts and photographs of the snowflakes Kate had slaved over all afternoon.

"Field work," Kate offered. "I'm a snowflakologist."

"Uhuh." The goddess leaned over the images. Flakes fell from her hair and dusted the dry paper.

Kate cringed. The melting snowflakes would ruin the printouts. But she had all her work backed up on disk.

"Looks like you've found out my secret." Snow trailed a finger along Kate's work. "I could destroy it all."

"You c-could." A cough was imminent, but she held it back out of fear.

"Or I could give you this boon in exchange for your help."

"My help?"

Not for one moment did Kate believe the goddess had a compassionate flake in her body. And yet, they were both women. She could relate to her frustrations, surely. So she'd become bored with creating snow-flakes? What woman wasn't allowed a little respite every once in a while? Especially with a job so tedious.

No, creating snowflakes could not be boring. It must be the most wondrous job ever.

Snow approached. Kate stepped back, but the sofa behind her stopped her retreat.

"You're lovely," Snow said. "A determined woman, am I correct?"

"I take pride in my work. I love a good challenge." And even while shaking at standing before this goddess who had tried to kill her, she meant that statement as a thrown gauntlet.

The cool touch of the woman's finger traced Kate's jaw. Not so cold as Jal's touches, and softer, as if kissed by winter.

"Winter gods are not meant to love the warm-blooded," Snow said.

She knew? Had Jal told her?

"Frost's heart grows dangerously warm," she continued. "You will kill him if you continue to allow him to love you."

"Don't gods have free will?"

"We do."

"Then I can't be the one to tell Jal how to feel."

"Feelings. Emotion. Love. That is what threatens your lover. Do you want the world to suddenly be without frost?"

"Well, no, but frost isn't everywhere. The tropics—"

"Insolent," the snow goddess hissed. "You're a smart woman, Kate. Think. Frost has never known love until you. First loves are...quite spectacular. One does not think rationally. They do things detrimental to their well-being. They rush blindly toward the unknown. Do you really want to kill him?"

"K-kill him? No," Kate breathed out. Her love could really—

"Then release him from your harmful love. Break his heart. Send him away. Restore balance to the world, Kate Wilson. It is in your hands."

Kate exhaled heavily.

"Do so and I will allow you your silly photographs. No one will believe you anyway. Those fancy machines are designed to replicate lies and the data to back up such falsities. Can I trust you'll do as I ask?"

The cool aura wavering off the goddess tickled a shiver over Kate's arms. If she did not do as asked, she felt very sure the goddess would not only destroy her research, but her, as well.

Her love was killing Jal? His heart, which must be cold, was warming to feel such an emotion. And a warm heart in a man made of frost could not be a good thing.

Kate nodded. "I never thought about Jal's impact on

the world. Or what could happen if he began to love a human. I'll send him away. I'll…stop loving him. I have to. I promise."

"Good girl."

And the goddess swirled into a storm of snow. The front door opened, and the storm whisked through.

The printouts were soggy. Kate lifted them carefully. The ink had smeared from the goddess's touch.

"She's right. You have goals, dreams. You want that million dollars so you can travel the world. Who has time for a boyfriend?" A swallow cut like razors inside her throat. "And what a fool to think I could make a go of it with a man made of frost."

She reached for the phone receiver but didn't lift it from the cradle. The professor's number was on speed dial. Whatever he wanted to do with the results was out of her hands. He could publish it in a science journal or plaster it across the headlines of the *New York Times* for all she cared.

Really?

Her niggling conscience made her release the phone. Kate sucked in the corner of her lower lip. "If the world knows two identical snowflakes exist, then…"

She'd only wanted people to believe in her, and in the world as she saw it. But by publishing her discovery… Could belief be threatened?

It was a weird thing to consider, but the results *could* devastate. Childhood dreams would be crushed. The belief in the magical, that out of all the uncountable number of snowflakes in the world not one was the same—it must be protected. If not, people would become disenchanted with winter.

Kate knew her finding was an anomaly only because the Snow goddess admitted to making copies. Explain that one to the world.

"I can't do this," she whispered. "I can't take money because the Snow goddess is bored. I need to make things right. I need to…"

For starters, she had to break it off with Jal.

How to kill a woman he loved?

He had his orders. They were to be taken seriously. And now he knew Kate's discovery could prove cataclysmic to the world. Should she announce her find, the repercussions would move through the mortal world as if dominos clacking across the divide.

She had to be stopped. And he was the assassin to do it.

"No!" Too late, he had fallen in love. No longer could he dispassionately give death to a mortal. Was he finished as Frost?

Did he care? Because to be with Kate…

There was another option. And for the first time, Jal desperately wanted options. If he could destroy Kate's research then he would not have to destroy her.

"Selfish," Jal muttered as he paced the road before Kate's house. "Do I wish this for my benefit? The current Snow goddess can survive another thousand years."

And yet, his heart pleaded for options. A fighting chance to be with the woman he loved.

"I must at least explain things to Kate. Reveal her destiny. Oh."

He clutched his chest. It did not so much ache now as bleed. Blood did not flow in the gods' veins. Should he take human form, ichor would ooze from his heart. Had she warmed him beyond all hope?

No, it was emotion, an intangible brand of contact that would bring his end. He'd confessed his love. It felt splendid. And it hurt.

But if his chest cracked open and his insides melted upon the ground today, it would have been worth it for the brief time he'd had with Kate.

"What have you done to me, Kate? You've… changed me. Shown me happiness. I don't want to destroy, I simply want to sustain."

Striding up the drive, Jal held up his hand as a breeze whisked a sparkling powder of crystals from the rooftop. Snow folk. They landed on his palm—and he crushed them.

"Snow will not harm Kate. If I must surround this cabin with my own folk and build a fierce wall of rime to keep back Snow's army, I shall."

Kate stood in the doorway, bundled in a dark turtleneck sweater and matching pants. She didn't waver or protest when Jal—formed of frost—reached to kiss her cheek. Human flesh and clothing glamorized his form.

"Going out?" he asked.

"No. You're incredible in your natural frost form, Jal. So beautiful."

"I usually brush against your flesh and change so quickly you don't register it. I didn't want to frighten you before."

"And now?"

Her voice was tiny and sore, bruised by his icy kisses. He felt her pain tangibly. He had harmed her? But love was not supposed to hurt, was it?

"There are many truths you must have, Kate. Might I come inside?"

"Yes, of course. Over by the hearth? I didn't light a fire."

"That's why you're dressed so warmly. I thank you for your consideration."

She kissed him, but quickly, and at only the corner of his mouth.

"Is something wrong, Kate?"

Of course something was wrong. She had just kissed the man who was supposed to kill her.

It was easier to stand and distance herself from Jal than to sit close to him. Close enough to kiss. Close enough to forget she was killing him.

She was *killing* him.

Each time he returned to her his heart grew warmer. Did he not realize that? Or did he, and yet, not care?

She would not be responsible for harming a god who served the world, why, who made it beautiful with his creations, and yes, even warned and sometimes killed with his touch. It was the way of nature. Vilhjalmur Frosti *was* nature. Before she'd known what he was, she had seen him for what he truly was, but simply wasn't willing to believe her eyes.

Now she knew how her parents had felt when they'd tried to understand her odd manner of seeing the world. It's easier to not believe than to accept what might be standing right before you.

"This isn't working," she said abruptly.

Jal stood and reached for her, but she turned to pace before the hearth. Should have lit a fire, a safe zone to flee to from her lover's disappointed stare.

"I've given it a lot of thought. All night, in fact."

Kate crossed her arms over her chest. Most of those thoughts had been sexy images of she and Jal entwined on the bed. They had only made love once. It wasn't enough. She wanted him. Always. But it wasn't meant to be. "I don't want you to come here ever again."

"What are you saying? You don't—"

"I can't love you," she enunciated firmly. *And please don't argue with me, because I can't do this either.* His hurt expression stabbed her. "We're not even the same species. This is so wrong, Jal. Besides, my throat hurts so much." She forced a sniffle.

"Kate?" He moved so quickly, she tried to back away from the imminent embrace, but before she knew it, Jal held her in his arms. "You're shivering."

"I'm upset. And you're—" cruel to say it "—cold!"

Kate pushed him away from the embrace that threatened to change her mind, and crossed to the door. Holding it open, a gush of chilly air brushed her shoulders. Like Jal's kiss. But his kisses had never chilled her so dreadfully as this conversation. He wasn't cold at heart. And that was the problem. Warm heart; death sentence.

"Please leave, Jal. Don't make this harder than it has to be."

He walked slowly across the room, his eyes not meeting hers. His fingertips traced the top of the couch, retracting, then touching the soft yarn on her pink mitten.

"Kate?"

Lowering her head, she looked aside, unable to meet those incredible ice blue eyes and his sad kicked puppydog expression.

"I will always love you," he whispered.

No, please no, she thought. It will kill you.

And when she couldn't stand it any longer, Kate gasped back the tears and turned to embrace her lover.

But he wasn't there.

Fresh snow swirled in from the open doorway. Moonlight shimmered across the packed snow, dancing in the wings and limbs of Frost's fallen folk.

And Kate could no longer hold back the tears.

* * *

He stumbled across the drive, clutching his chest. It bled copiously now. And the ichor was not ice cold but hot, thick and deadly. Tripping forward, Jal caught himself in the snow where his own folk had battled fiercely against the snow goddess.

He clutched the pink mitten, rubbing the warmth of it aside his cheek. One last touch of Kate.

Taking on the crystals of his fallen folk, his body transformed to frost—all, save his weeping heart.

Chapter 13

Kate dropped the pine log in the snow. She kicked it, and then kicked at the snow bank.

She plopped down on the bank and threw back her arms to land on the powdery snow. Moonglow dazzled the midnight landscape. Snowflakes fell noisily, their crystals clicking on the cottonwood branches and skittering across the sparkling surface of snow around her.

The seductive winter illumination boldly toyed with her need to be angry, to want to kick and shout and scream.

She'd made her lover leave—by lying to him.

"To save him," she whispered.

Denying her heart was something she'd never con-

sciously done before. Yet, to think on it, she'd denied
herself relationships for years by moving out here to
the cabin.

And oh, did it hurt. How cruel to send Jal away with
a few brisk words. The look in his eyes had reached in
and crushed her heart. She had been his only experience with love. And look what she'd done with that
fragile, new emotion.

"Oh, Kate, you've done a bad thing."

And yet, it could only be bad for her. The world
needed Vilhjalmur Frosti. She mustn't be selfish.

A kiss of snow dusted her cheeks and nose. The
flakes melted and teared down her flesh.

"Well done," a female voice said.

Kate's heart shuddered, but then she exhaled to
release the apprehension. "He won't die now?" she
asked the Snow goddess who stood just out of sight
behind her. "His heart will grow cold again, and Frost
will live?"

"That's not what I've come to discuss."

"I need to know!"

"Sure." Prickling snow crystals sifted across Kate's
face. "My thanks for not revealing the snowflake
copies to the world. It could have proven catastrophic
in ways mere humans cannot begin to imagine."

"Loss of enchantment," Kate muttered, "loss of
belief, of wonder. I can understand."

Whoopee for her, she'd saved the world. So why did
she feel so miserable?

Kate leaned forward. To her side the goddess, in human form, sat upon the snow bank, her weight not crushing a single flake. Knee-high white boots and a tight-fitted skirt and shirt exposed bare arms glittering with flakes. Long hair spilled past her hips and sifted flakes onto Kate's leg.

"What do you want now?" Kate leaned back against the snow chair formed by her body. "To kill me?"

The goddess flicked her fingers, dispersing flakes through the air. "Not at the moment."

"Great. I've sent away the man I love, and now I have to live with it."

"But you saved the world."

"Joy."

"You humans are difficult to please. Whatever. I am little disturbed by your heartbreak." The goddess leaned an elbow on the snow. She touched a strand of Kate's hair and shivered. "Humans, so warm."

"Can I kill you with my warmth?"

"Do you want to?"

Kate sighed. "Not so much."

This whole experience had worn her ragged. She didn't want to harm anyone, god or faery or whatever the heck they called themselves. Especially not after she'd seen the look in Jal's eyes.

"I've a proposal for you," Snow offered.

"Swell." Kate tugged her hair from the goddess's playful touch.

"I wonder if you're interested in taking my job?"

"Your job? You mean, Snow goddess?" What the hell?

And in her next thought, Kate's mind zoomed to the childhood dream of being snow queen. Yes! She could create snow and blanket the world with her gorgeous white crystals, and—

No. A human become a goddess? The offer was too bizarre.

"Now you're teasing me, and I'm not sure what for."

"It's not a tease." Snow leaned back on her elbows. Lashes resembling fernlike branches on a snowflake blinked over her cold white eyes. "Obviously Frost didn't let you in on your secret."

"My secret? It doesn't work that way, lady. If I have a secret I'd have to let Jal in on it."

"So why didn't you tell him you were the snow goddess changeling?"

"The what?"

"You see? Just close your mouth and listen, human. These are the details. I learned from Ice about your adoption."

"That happened twenty-eight years ago. My real parents died before I was even born."

"Yes, well, none of the gods were aware of that switcheroo. We always believed the adopted pair your blood parents. If we had known your real parents had died—well, I wouldn't be talking to you right now. Or rather I would be, while I was training you."

"You are talking in code."

"You were born into this world a changeling, Kate Wilson. A snow faery."

Kate sat upright and twisted on her snow seat to better eye the goddess. "Like those little bodies I found littered all over my yard yesterday? I'm not—no, that's not right."

Snow blew out a breath of snow crystals that lingered in the air before her. They began to dance about, and Kate knew they were snow folk, tiny beings with wings and designed of ice crystals. It was not even dreadful to admire their magical dance swirling high into the air until they dispersed over the treetops.

"Every thousand years a new changeling is born into the mortal realm," Snow explained. "The parents are immediately disposed of and the child is taken to be trained for their future task as Snow god. Or Frost god. Or Ice, whichever. The gods tried to kill your adopted parents—not knowing the real ones were already dead—three times."

"I—I know that," Kate gasped. "We've always had the family joke we can survive even the craziest of situations. That was the gods? And me, I'm…"

"You should have been my replacement."

"That makes so much sense."

"It does?"

Struck silent, Kate could merely nod, and the tiniest of grins curled her mouth. That certainly explained the way she saw nature. Because…she was a part of it, too?

"Good, then I'm going to cut to the chase. I want you

to take over my job. I'm tired of it. And besides, I have *things* waiting for me. Places to be. So you'll do it?"

"Just like that? Become made of snow and ice crystals and— But how?"

"It's a god thing."

"To be like you…" Composed entirely of snow? To live somewhere only the gods lived? What had Jal call it? Nordika.

It was too overwhelming to fathom. And yet, Kate's heart raced not out of fear, but with excitement. Because if she became a goddess, then she would be the same as—

"Can I be with Jal if I become the Snow goddess?"

"Sure," Snow purred. "Once cold ichor fills your veins, you can share your life with Frost, and make love to him and help him spread winter across the land. It's what you were born to be, Kate."

"I'll do it. If I can be with Jal. And—just yes."

"Splendid."

The snow swirled into a land funnel and Snow glimmered out of sight.

Kate turned and propped her elbows on the snow and followed the tendril of spinning dazzle high into the midnight sky.

"I've always known," she murmured.

Jal landed on Ice's doorstep. Hoar and rime crystals deformed his torso. Ice water dripped down his thighs, freezing the frost and in places melting it into painful ice.

He gathered all his energy to reform and knock on the door.

An ice faery answered. Her clear ice nipples jutted suggestively. Jal stepped inside, uninterested in the naked faery. Flakes of hoar fluttered from his form with each step.

"Ice!" the faery screamed and directed Frost toward the frozen sofa, without touching him. "Hurry up, your friend is in a bad way."

Ice slid across the skating rink floor and landed on the sofa next to Jal's. He reached over and plucked a crumbling chunk of hoar from Jal's knee.

"What in the Arctic Ocean? What's up with you, man?"

"She…" Jal shuddered. A few crystals fell from his jaw. Here in Ice's palace he knew the means to survive would be greater. He sucked in the cool icy air to reform his dwindling shape. "…doesn't love me."

"Oh, hell no, Frost, don't let this happen. Every thought you have about the human is one step closer to your death. You're feeling! Stop it!"

"Can't. Love…h-her."

Ice directed the faery away. He held his crystal clear hands before Jal, unsure or maybe deciding what he could do to help. A touch to Jal's arm hardened his crystals and allowed Jal to sit upright.

"That'll help for a bit," Ice said. "But you're dying, man. Snap out of it. Don't let that human do this to you."

"I will die...h-happily...for having known..."

"Don't say it, just don't. I'm going down there to talk to that woman."

A gust of frigid wind froze Jal to the sofa. It was a good thing—but not for long.

Ice slid along the shores of Greenland, when he sighted Snow and the mortal woman.

"What the hell is *she* doing here?" he shouted at the Snow goddess.

"You must be Ice," the mortal said, far too accepting of a man shaped of ice for his comfort. "You're a friend of Jal's."

"And you broke his heart, you nasty—"

Snow grabbed the mortal's hand, but Ice was not finished. "She's killed him!"

"What?" The mortal tugged out of Snow's grip. Though bundled in snow gear, her cheeks showed signs of frostbite. The red circles at the centers of her cheeks were turning white and waxy. "But she said if I broke Jal's heart, it would grow cold again."

"Oh, did she?" Ice turned to Snow, who delivered a cocky sneer. "You knew he was in love. The man can't turn off the emotion and harden his heart. It's completely melted. He's going down fast."

"Too bad." Snow grabbed Kate's hand and whisked them into a whirl of snow. "If I can't have my lover, Frost won't have his."

* * *

Kate stumbled over hard, iced snow chunks in the goddess's wake. She had no idea where Ice had gone. But what he'd said. Frost's heart was still melting? "But you said Jal and I could be together."

"I lied. I've no power to make you a goddess. That is Old Man Winter's boon. But you remain a deterrence to my next replacement. I must remove that deterrent."

Kate inspected the goddess's pale eyes. There was no determining if she spoke truth or was lying. But what reason had she to lie? If only Jal were here.

You sent him away. You killed him.

"Stupid human." The goddess gripped Kate's arm. "Keep your eyes closed."

"But why—" A gust of ice crystals blew roughly across Kate's face, like sandpaper of ice. She pressed her gloved hands over her eyes.

The twosome lifted into the air, and the world slipped away. Kate's body soared weightlessly forward. Though she wore her good Arctic Cat snow wear, bracing wind curled around Kate's neck and down her spine.

"Keep 'em closed," Snow said. "We're here."

"Where's here?" Kate shouted because the wind whistled loudly. "Is it storming?"

"Not yet. It's a beautiful sunny day here on top of Everest."

Everest? Kate wasn't prepared to stand atop Everest.

That required oxygen and sunglasses and more clothing than she was wearing.

"Thanks for tricks, Kate Wilson."

And the goddess let go of Kate's arm. Kate wobbled, knowing she had to keep her hands over her eyes. To open them would risk burning her corneas, snowblindness would quickly follow.

"She said something about you not having your lover if she couldn't have hers. I didn't know Snow had a thing going on."

"But I told you before—" The pink mitten Jal still held made him consider. "The red scarf."

"What?"

Jal reached out to touch Ice. The chill contact seeped through his melting crystals and hardened them. But each time he refroze the melting crystals, his shape became more distorted. "The mortal object, it was a scarf. Snow was fixated on it when I visited her. It's like this mitten.

"From her lover?"

"Possibly."

"That would explain her urgency to lose the job. Bitch. So she's going to punish you, but then she'll be changed to a mortal and she can go shack up with her human lover."

"I don't think Old Man Winter will let it happen," Jal said. "He's the only one who can make Kate a goddess. Snow's got Kate?"

Ice nodded. "Ran into them off the coast of Greenland, but she's headed northeast, I'm sure."

"I've got to find her. Kate's not safe."

"Take this with you." Ice handed Jal a shard of ice. "It'll keep you cold enough, I hope."

Frost clutched the icicle. It permeated his system, hardening the melting portions and sent out tendrils of fernlike frost all over.

He couldn't stop his heart from melting. There was no going back, no changing his thoughts to what they'd been those few moments before he'd met Kate. She was a part of him now. He carried her smile in his heart. Even though that same smile had straightened, and had denied him love.

If she could stop loving him, wasn't it possible he could do the same?

But he didn't want to. The wondrous emotion was all that he had.

"I'll go talk to Old Man Winter," Ice said. "You go rescue the girl."

"I'm on it."

Frost stood, and his legs shattered, dropping him in a pile of crisp crystals. At that instant a sweep of brisk air coiled about him, reforming his crystals, and bringing him to stand upright. But he wasn't doing this. Jal could but wonder at his sudden return of strength.

"You've a new mark," Old Man Winter's voice vibrated in all of Jal's crystals. "In Iceland. I've the coordinates—"

"No!" No marks now. Nothing mattered but saving Kate. "Kate is in trouble. She needs me."

"The mortal photographer? You defy me, Frost."

"I do not wish to, my liege. But right now a mortal's life is at stake."

"Another mortal's life must be extinguished! If you refuse this task, Frost, then you forfeit your job. You will no longer be a Winter god!"

Winter left in a fierce storm that obliterated the room Jal stood in and left him out in the open air, standing atop a glistening rise of snow crystals. Snow stretched as far as he could see. Gorgeous, glittering. His home, here in Nordika.

No longer a winter god? The thought disturbed him. "But Kate." He clutched his chest where the warming sensation had not ceased.

She doesn't love you. Do not sacrifice your job for a mere mortal.

The memory of her kiss, sweet upon his lips, could never be erased.

Chapter 14

Ice waited a long time for Old Man Winter to show. When he finally did, Ice sensed tension in the god's presence. But, determined to help a friend, he explained Snow's devious plays against Frost and Kate to Old Man Winter. Together, the two of them tracked the human man Snow had been having an affair with, an Alaskan truck driver.

The affair with a mortal did not disturb Old Man Winter so much as that Snow had set out to murder a mortal only for the reason that she would then be released from her job. He was outraged his gods would harbor such foul deeds under his very nose. Juneau experienced a freak snowstorm as a result. No lives were lost, but the city was brought to a silent standstill for three days.

"I'll have to find a new changeling within the day," Old Man Winter growled.

"But there's Kate Wilson," Ice suggested. "She was born to be Snow. Put her on the fast track to becoming a goddess, and she may be able to save Frost."

"Frost will choose his own destiny. And I do not wager in love, underling."

"Of course you do." Ice slid across the rink that formed before him. A twirl and masterful jump displayed the whimsical wintertime activity lovers shared. "Winter is the most romantic time of the year. Couples fall in love in the winter all the time. Ice-skating in Central Park. Snowball fights that result in laughter and snuggling before a cozy fire. Ice storms that strand young lovers in an out-of-the-way hotel. Chilly kisses under pine trees that shower snow crystals over their wool-capped heads."

"Perhaps."

"That's the spirit!" Not really, but Ice was working against the clock, so he had to appeal to the Winter god's ego because there was no compassion in the master god's form.

"Kate is missing. Snow took her somewhere; she may have killed her. Frost is searching for her. What can you do about this?"

"For romance?" Winter grumbled.

Ice nodded eagerly.

Old Man Winter's heavy sigh blasted snow and crystals over Ice's frozen body. Felt great.

The Winter god declared, "Kate Wilson is Snow, as I command."

"Right now?"

Old Man Winter shrugged. "She needs to stand before me for the transformation to occur."

"Great!" Ice turned to skate off, but paused and glanced over a shoulder. "What about the former Snow?"

"She is granted mortality, as is our way."

"And her lover?"

"He—" Old Man Winter said with a glint to his icy voice "—has suddenly developed an interest in tropical climes."

Ice bowed gratefully. "Thanks, my liege."

No job was more important than the life of another.

Jal knew the one spot in the entire mortal world Snow frequented most. He went there often, himself. All the Winter gods convened at Everest; it was the one mortal place fit for them.

But it was not fit for humans. If Snow had taken Kate there—

In a fog of frost, he glided off from Nordika and aimed for the world's highest mountain peak. The sun was cold and cruel, glittering across the deadly mountain with deceptive invitation—a summons Jal admired.

He spied a train of mortals hiking up toward what he knew was called Base Camp 3. One more stop before the hikers would require oxygen. Most would not make it to the peak. Today the four men and their sherpas would be successful, for Frost had not a mark.

But they'd never make it there to see what Jal saw. A small figure heaped over on the top of Everest.

Kate.

Dispersing, Jal fell swiftly to ground, his crystals gathering on the snow pack near Kate's face. But he was yet weak. His heart still bled.

"She said she didn't love me."

Half-formed, Frost clutched at his dripping heart. Hoar crystals clattered as his fingers scraped over them and dropped onto Kate's exposed cheek. A cheek white with frostbite.

"Not from me," he muttered. "I would never, Kate. I love you. I always will."

It mattered not what she thought of him, that she could not love him. Of course she could not. He asked far too much of a human. But he would not allow her to die for having once loved him.

He touched her cheek. No warmth. His frost form did not assume flesh.

A fierce wind razored the air, tearing apart Jal's structure and scattering him across the snow and over Kate's body.

Something moaned. She was alive. Not for long.

Jal focused and called on his folk. The air glittered

with dancing frost folk. He commanded them to him and minute crystal structures bonded with his, forming, shaping, making him whole, until he sat beside Kate, his legs stretched out before him. He held a hand before his face, watching as the last two fingers formed.

Another moan alerted him. Jal twisted and tugged at Kate's coat. He had to work fast, or his melting heart would see him decimated. He plunged a hand inside her coat and up under her shirt.

"So cold."

But there, between her breasts, the tiniest pulse of warmth imbued his crystals. Kate's last remnant of body heat moved through him, giving him solid form and human flesh. Fully formed, Jal gasped at the lacking oxygen and brisk cold.

She moaned as he lifted her into his arms.

"Don't open your eyes, Kate. It's Jal."

Now what to do? He couldn't descend the mountain and deposit her at the base camp. He'd never make it that far. Kate hadn't enough body heat to keep him in human form. He'd change to frost and she would fall through his grasp.

"Jal?"

"Quiet. Save your breath. I love you, Kate, even if you cannot love me."

"But...I..."

He shushed her. "Never forget that. I love you."

He looked about, scanning the vast horizon. The

sun burned his human eyes. Perhaps this is how it would be from now on. He'd defied Old Man Winter by refusing to go after the mark.

So would he die here on Everest as punishment?

Not before he saw Kate safe.

Jal lifted Kate high in his arms and called out to Old Man Winter, "I have her! She is here. The Snow goddess!"

Chapter 15

Ten months later...

Jal finished off a letter to the editor at Stellar Publishing. He'd spent the week looking through the photographic galleys for the book he'd pieced together from Kate's snowflake photographs. It was ready to go to press.

He plunked out the last few letters, cursing his fear of taking one of those online typing classes. Hunt-and-peck worked fine enough for the little typing he did. He was slow to embrace the electronics in this little cabin. It had proved wonder enough just walking through the spring and summer months, learning all the foliage and weather and human foibles.

He'd survive. Had to. This human experience would not defeat him. It was growing on him, actually. But the emotion part was quite a wallop.

Shutting off the computer, he then noticed something wondrous through the front window.

"Snow." He rushed to the door, bare feet tramping the scattered clothes he never could get accustomed to hanging up after use.

Drawing open the door, stirred in a swirl of thick cotton-puff flakes. Winter's kiss gave Jal a chuckle. He stepped out onto the stoop, already thick with snow and gave a whoop at the chill of it. He stepped back inside and made a beeline for the closet where he'd stored winter gear in anticipation of just this moment.

"So cold," he said gleefully as he pulled on winter boots and jacket. "I never imagined it could be like that."

He straightened. The things he caught himself saying. No longer a god, he was completely mortal, and had grown to adore the heat of the sun on his bare shoulders and face. Yet, always, he pined for winter.

And it had arrived. His first winter as a human.

Sweeping a scarf about his neck, Jal tugged on a ski cap as he dashed outside, leaving the front door wide open. It was late, but moonlight sparkled across the thin expanse of snow. Thick flakes landed on the sleeve of his jacket and he brought up his arm to delight at the crystals.

Squinting, he tried to see the shapes of snow folk

mixed within the flakes, but the flakes were simply white, glittery clumps. He could no longer see the depth, the color and various branches and formations his Frost god eyes had seen.

But no matter. Jal licked the thick clump of flakes from his sleeve. Such delight! Snow!

He rushed through the yard, seeking the silvery band that glittered between the spacing of the trees. "It is magnificent!"

He had not felt so carefree for months. Missing winter as he had, missing *her*. Could there be a chance—

But of course—he held up his palm, catching the snowflakes—this must be her work.

A soft wind soughed through the tree branches, moving the falling flakes in a sudden dodge to the left. Jal turned and there, in the center of the yard, where the moon spotlighted the new snow, the crystals began to swirl and rise.

Brilliant cold moonlight danced in the coil. It began to form, to sweep in falling snowflakes, and soon the hands caressed the air, moving up along the figure as if directing snow folk to position.

When completed, Jal could but gasp. Never had he looked upon so gorgeous a sight. Not even in all his centuries as a god. His heart pulsed and speeded. That initial ache he'd first felt when spying her last winter returned. He reached out, but then snapped back his hand to clutch at his chest.

And she approached, every step stirring and swirling the flakes and glinting crystals that designed the gown hugging her legs and torso.

Had he dreamed of this moment? Or had his every waking moment been but steps, moves and pining closer to her presence?

Did she remember him? Could she?

Jal had thought he'd forgotten the scent of winter, of crisp, brisk cold so perfect it made his insides stir. Now it approached and as the Snow goddess stopped before him, he felt the hot touch of a tear slip down his cheek.

"Kate?"

The Snow goddess smiled and reached to touch his cheek, just shy of the tear trail. Jal's warmth permeated her snow crystals, rushing over snow flesh and forming human skin and features and hair. And Kate's spring green eyes.

A spill of frothy white fabric skimmed to her ankles. The Snow goddess had come home.

"I've been waiting for first snow," she said. Grasping the ends of Jal's scarf, she stepped closer, a little tentative. "You sacrificed your life for me."

"I've still a human life. We could have never been together if we were both gods."

"Not cool to mix snow and frost." She smirked. "But snow and mortal flesh?"

"So long as you cool down if you get too warm."

"Oh, lover."

Her lips were cool, and that made Jal smile against her mouth. He pulled her close, shivering as their flesh touched and her body limned to his. "I've hot chocolate," he whispered against her silky hair. "Let me go ahead inside and put out the fire, yes?"

She unzipped his jacket. A cold hand to his abdomen made him jump, yet again, he could only smile. "So that's how it's to be?"

"Right here." She shed the silky dress with a shimmy of her shoulders and hips. "Right now."

"What if I get frostbite?"

"I don't bite, Jal. Unless you want me to."

* * * * *

ICE BOUND

VIVI ANNA

Dear Reader,

I love mythology. Any type from any culture. The way people use stories to make sense of what is happening around them fascinates me.

When asked if I wanted to do this story, I was immediately excited. I knew I could incorporate some interesting mythology into it. I searched different texts for deities or myths, and found one from Japan. The story about Yuki-Onna. I was intrigued by the tale and knew instantly it would work for the story I had in mind.

I hope you enjoy "Ice Bound." It was refreshing to write it.

All my best,

Vivi Anna
Visit me at www.vivianna.net.

Vivi Anna likes to burn up the pages with her unique brand of fantasy fiction. Whether it's in the Amazon jungle, an apocalyptic future or the otherworld city of Necropolis, Vivi always writes fast-paced action-adventure featuring strong, independent women and dark, delicious heroes.

For Kim. My BFF in every sense.

Chapter 1

Beneath the steel hull of the *Aurora* ship, the sound of ice cracking broke the eerie silence of the frozen landscape. Leaning over the side of the boat, Dr. Darien Calder watched as the boat cut a path through the ice. Twenty years ago, the ship would've had difficulty getting through the sea ice shelf, but after years of global warming, it didn't take much to break the frozen topography.

That was why he was here in Hokkaido, Japan, floating in a ship in the middle of an ice shelf—to observe and record the transformation in the environment.

He was also there to learn more about a legend that

had haunted him, had invaded his dreams nightly, from the moment he learned of it—the legend of Koori-Onna. It told of a beautiful, ghostly woman appearing to lost travelers in snowstorms, who with one kiss from her icy lips literally froze the doomed victim from the inside out.

Every culture had a similar myth. The Ice Princess, the Snow Queen. But for some reason this one stood out to him.

Although he was a scientist, there was something about the story that resonated with him, something that moved past his analytical side and captured his imagination. Since arriving in Japan, his dreams had become more vivid, more stirring. He'd awoken twice now in a cold sweat, a tingling sensation lingering on his lips. But for now, he was here to study the ice flow and do the job he was paid to do. Not to fantasize about a legend.

The drifting ice was having a hell of an effect on the climate conditions in the area. Because the freezing process removed salt from the water, when it melted, as it had been doing in record amounts, it changed the water from salt to fresh water. At the rate things were changing, it wouldn't be long before the surrounding wildlife was irrevocably affected. Darien sighed. It was his job to make sure that didn't happen.

"What do you think?"

Darien looked over at Jiro Noda, the local scientist he'd been e-mailing for the past five months, and nodded. Over the months they had formed a friendship. "The ice levels are definitely thinning."

"And it is early yet." Jiro motioned toward the shelf with the sweep of his hand. "It is only December, and the flow is moving already. We usually do not see this until mid-January."

"Climate shifts have taken place all over the world." Darien glanced down into the dark water beneath the boat. "I sense a major shift coming. Maybe the poles are really going to switch."

Jiro simply lifted a dark brow in answer, as if he didn't have the words to equal Darien's statement. "God, I really hope not."

The thought scared Darien, too. He could imagine the disasters that would follow if magnetic north all of a sudden became magnetic south. He wasn't sure if the earth would survive that. Or not so much the earth, as the people living on its surface.

Resigned to their individual thoughts, Darien and Jiro spent another three hours out in the water, checking and measuring the thickness of the ice shelf. By the time the ship docked, the tips of Darien's fingers were beginning to throb from the bitter cold. Frost had formed on the stubble along his jaw. He imagined he looked like a young version of Old Man Winter.

After the crew tied off the boat, Jiro and Darien carried the equipment to shore and stored it in Darien's rented SUV. His plan was to drive back to Kushiro, where he had rented the vehicle, and catch a small plane back to Sapporo, and from there continue to Tokyo. However much he appreciated the icy beauty of the north, he really wanted to get back to the main city and play tourist for a few days before heading back to America.

Glancing up into the hazy sky, he figured he still had about five good hours to make the two-hour trip. As long as it didn't snow, he'd be fine on the usually hazardous roads. Winter driving in Japan was sometimes considered a contact sport—slipping and sliding on the awful roads while trying desperately not to hit an oncoming vehicle.

With the equipment tightly packed, Darien offered his hand to the other man. "It was good working with you, Jiro. I hope to see you again soon."

Jiro took his hand and shook it firmly. "I packed that tent I told you about in the back. I think it will be good for your next trip to the mountains in America."

"Thank you, Jiro. You're a good friend."

"Come have some hot ramen before you go. There is still time yet."

"I don't know. I should get on the roads before the snow comes."

"You must have a drink with me. Sapporo beer is the best in all of Japan." He pulled Darien toward the small building near the dock. "Come. It will warm you up."

"Okay."

Darien followed Jiro to the quaint wooden house that served as a fishing house, restaurant and bar to the villagers who lived along the icy eastern shore. The moment he stepped inside the warmth and bustle of the quaint building, he felt comfortable and at home. Everyone greeted him with warm cheer, and the old woman who obviously ran the place immediately sat him at their "best" table and brought him a bottle of Sapporo beer as if he'd been expected all along.

After an hour, Darien was surrounded by eight men, young and old, laughing and talking, a few trying out their English and failing miserably, although he'd done no better with his Japanese. The ramen noodles filled him and warmed his insides with their spicy flavoring. And the beer, although bitter, went down quite nicely with the noodles.

Draining the last of his drink, Darien announced to the group that he needed to get on the road. After Jiro translated there was a chorus of disappointed remarks. Bowing and shaking hands, Darien finally made his way to the exit. There the oldest of the group bowed to him and spoke. His Japanese rusty, the only thing Darien clearly heard was the name Koori-Onna.

Darien glanced at Jiro. "What did he say?"

"He said to take great care and do not fall to Koori-Onna's charms. It will be the death of you."

Darien smiled. "Tell him there's no worry of that. Women don't find me all that attractive, not even mythical ice maidens."

Jiro translated to the old man who watched Darien

with interest. With a strange smile, he bowed to Darien and opened the exit door for him.

Once Darien was safely buckled into his SUV, the hair stood up on the back of his neck. A shiver raced down his spine. The moment the old man had said her name, a sense of cold dread had crept over Darien.

He knew it was nonsense to be bothered by a myth, a folktale passed down through the generations to give some meaning to tragic events, but he was troubled nonetheless. Maybe it had been the way the old man had looked at him, as if he knew what was to become of Darien, as if he knew some terrible event was in store for him.

Tugging his jacket tighter at the collar, Darien shifted the vehicle in gear and pulled away from the small port, hoping he could beat the snow before it fell.

After an hour on the road, the snow started. But it didn't just fall so much as raged down upon him like a bad omen.

At first big fat flakes floated down, carefree and lazy, but Darien knew that was just the preshow. The dark sky threatened so much more than the pretty flakes of storybook Christmases. After the first fall, the wind picked up and started to howl. At one point it became so fierce, Darien had trouble keeping the SUV on the road.

As visibility reduced close to zero, Darien slowed the vehicle down to ten miles an hour. He prayed silently that there was no one else stupid enough to be out on the roads. Even at this speed, a head-on collision would definitely cause some injuries.

A brutal gust of wind howled against the glass, rattling the vehicle. Darien could feel the cold creeping over his body. Even through the hat, gloves and heavy thermal jacket, the cold still seeped in. He went to turn the dial on the heater but stopped, realizing it was already cranked to the maximum.

He'd been to the coldest places on earth—Antarctica, North Pole, Greenland, but for some reason it felt colder here. Maybe it was the fact that he couldn't get the sense of trepidation out of his system. Something was going to happen.

He shook his head to clear it. "Don't be stupid, man. It's just a silly story."

Even though he said the words, he didn't fully feel the conviction behind them.

When he first heard about the ice maiden myth, he'd done some research on it. Like everything he did, he approached it systematically. But there was no reasoning behind the myth; it was a story and nothing more.

He'd gone on too long without a woman, he thought. He was just lonely. He was pathetic if just the mention of a beautiful woman incited hot dreams. And they'd been extremely hot. He'd woken up a few times, harder than steel.

"Like a damn teenager." He chuckled to himself. He really was pathetic.

No wonder Jessica had left him all those months ago. She had accused him of being too wrapped up in his work, and she'd been right. If he wasn't out in the field researching, he was at home in his office writing about his findings on his laptop, or he was preparing for his next time out in the field.

She hadn't needed him anyway. After a year together, he had realized what a strong independent woman she was. A corporate lawyer, she'd been more interested in getting ahead in her job, owning an amazing wardrobe and hanging with the best people. It still baffled him how they had ever ended up together in the first place. Probably because they had grown up together and their parents had been friends. Other than that, they really hadn't had much in common. Darien certainly hadn't been the right man for her. And she hadn't been the woman for him.

He'd gone too long without a healthy relationship. Maybe when he got to Tokyo he'd go to one of those gentlemen clubs and acquire some female companionship for the night. Something uncomplicated and temporary. Just enough company to break him out of his dry spell.

As he mused over the possibilities, bright lights flashed at him through the windshield. Another vehicle was bearing down at him and at high speed.

Cursing, Darien wrenched the steering wheel. There was no traction on the road. It was pure ice.

He tried to correct the spin he put the vehicle in, but

it was too late. He plowed into a huge snowdrift on the side of the road before he could even think.

From the impact, he knocked his head on the steering wheel. Thankfully, the air bag didn't pop. He didn't really want to deal with trying to shove it back into the wheel.

The SUV was still running. Darien put it in Reverse, but it didn't budge. The sound coming from the rear indicated that the tires were spinning in place. There was too much ice.

Cursing again, he banged his fist on the steering wheel, and then shifted it into Park. He was going to have to get out and put something behind the tires to give them some traction.

Pulling his hat down over his ears, Darien opened the door and jumped out into the blizzard. As he made his way around to the back, he searched the surroundings for the other vehicle. There was no way that it didn't also go off the road. Not in this weather, not on this icy stretch of highway. But he couldn't see anything through the howling, blistering white wall of snow.

Opening the hatch on the SUV, he dug through the equipment and found a short-handled shovel, especially designed to dig out of snow and ice. He slammed the hatch shut and proceeded to dig the back tires out of the snow.

After fifteen minutes of digging, Darien climbed back into the SUV and tried to back out. Still the tires spun in place. He got out again and continued to dig, chipping at the ice underneath the heavy blanket of white.

Once more he tried to move the vehicle, to no avail. He was good and stuck. He wasn't going anywhere any time soon, not until the blizzard stopped and he could either flag down someone, or find something to jam under the tires to garner some traction.

Luckily he was well-equipped with thermal blankets, a hot plate, bottled water, dried food and a full gas tank. He could wait it out for at least twelve hours if he had to. He just hoped it didn't come to that.

Darien jumped out into the snow again to go around the back to the hatch. He'd grab some supplies to hunker down for a few hours. As he opened the back, a sound whispered to him on the wind. Shivers, not just from the cold, raced down his spine.

He turned to survey the area. Was there someone there calling to him? Maybe the driver of the other vehicle.

"Darien." The haunting voice echoed all around him. He stared into the blustering snow, desperate to see something, anything concrete.

Something caught his eye, and he turned toward it. A shape materialized in the blinding white.

"Darien, I've been waiting for you."

Darien wiped at his eyes with the back of his gloved hand. Surely he was seeing things. The combination of the blinding snowscape, the fact that his eyes were watering and the Sapporo beer he had downed had to be playing tricks on his vision. Because there couldn't possibly be a woman dressed in a blue kimono floating to him on a wisp of cold air.

The old man's warning sounded in his head. *It will be the death of you.*

"*Darien,*" she whispered on a breeze. Her voice was seductive. A sudden urge to go to her rushed over him. He clamped his eyes shut and fought against the ridiculous notion.

When he opened his eyes again, she was still there, floating above the snow. He noticed she was barefoot, her toenails painted a sensual crimson. With a demure smile she beckoned him to her.

Oh, Darien wanted to go to her, to lose himself in the exquisite beauty of her. But he fought against the urge, knowing full well it was a hallucination brought on by the stories he'd heard and his dire situation. It was just that she seemed so real and not a figment of his overactive imagination.

"It's an illusion," he chanted to himself, then shook his head trying to shake off the haunting image.

I am no illusion, Darien. I am your destiny.

His foot moved forward. It surprised him. It was as if he wasn't in control of his body. He knew it was a huge mistake to move into the snowstorm away from the safety of his vehicle, but that didn't stop him from taking another step and another until he was six feet from the bumper of the SUV.

He turned and looked back at the vehicle, stunned

that he had moved so far without fully realizing it. He was on autopilot and fueled by the allure of the ice maiden beckoning him to move even farther into the blizzard. Although Darien knew full well that to do so would be his death, he walked even closer toward her.

She smiled at him, and his heart swelled with emotion. She was breathtaking, and he couldn't stop looking at her. Her pale face and perfect painted cupid-bow of a mouth drew him closer and closer until he was so close he knew if he lifted his hand he'd be able to touch the silk of her kimono. But he feared to do just that. Because what if his touch made her disappear? Where would he be then but alone in a violent snowstorm with no hope of survival?

An ache so raw, so violent, pounded in his heart and in his body. He had to touch her; he had to have her, if only for a moment before he died. Because he knew that death was knocking, no, pounding, on his door. And even though he knew that fundamentally, and had no real desire to die, Darien welcomed it.

He reached for her. "Please," he begged. Although he had no idea what he was pleading for. Her touch? Her kiss? Release from this mortal coil? At this point, anything would be a relief to the pain hammering inside him.

Still smiling, she floated down to him. He gasped when at last her hand caressed his cheek. Her touch was like ice, but he didn't shudder from it, not from the cold of it. It felt like heaven on his skin and a shiver of pleasure rushed down his spine.

When she stood next to him, he realized how petite she was. The top of her head came to his chin, and he wanted to envelop her in his arms and hold her until the summer sun came. Instead, he leaned down to her mouth, eager for her kiss.

With her head tilted up, her lips parted in anticipation, it was all Darien could do to stop from putting his mouth to hers, to take her finally. As she met his gaze, she brushed her lips against his and he was done. Nothing now or ever again could feel as good as the cool press of her frozen lips.

Greedily, he drank her in. Wrapping his arms around her, he deepened the kiss. That was when he felt the air being sucked from his lungs. But he didn't care. She was his at long last and that was all that mattered.

With his last breath, he whispered against her lips, *"I'm yours, forever."*

Chapter 2

Although his eyelids were hot, sore and difficult to open, Darien finally forced them apart and looked around. His whole body ached and every move, however small it seemed, caused him blistering agony.

He stared up at the white ceiling and tried to focus on where he was and what had happened. The last thing he could clearly remember was getting stuck in a snowbank on the side of the road to Kushiro. After that, everything was hazy and confusing.

Lifting his head, he gazed down at himself. He was on a platform bed, hard and uncomfortable beneath his back, under a few layers of mocha-colored silk, in a large white room. Except the walls weren't painted, at least with any paint he'd ever seen. They appeared shiny and wet like melting icicles.

There seemed to be no windows in the room, but there was light radiating from somewhere. Not from lamps or any visible light fixtures but almost as if the walls, floor and ceiling glowed from within.

Shifting his position on the bed, Darien lifted up the cover and saw that he was naked. Where were his clothes? Craning his neck, he glanced around the odd room searching for anything familiar, anything to indicate to him that he wasn't going mad. Stacked in one corner appeared to be all the equipment from his SUV. Folded neatly on a chair—also white and glistening like the walls—were his clothes.

He was hoping that it would help to see his things, but it didn't. He was more confused than before. If this was a dream would he really see concrete items like a hot plate and a jerry can of gasoline? Why not dancing naked women with insatiable libidos? That would be way more interesting.

Maybe he wasn't dreaming or hallucinating, but was dead. And this was his purgatory—a pristine white room made out of ice.

Lowering his hands, he ran his fingers over the "mattress" underneath him. The angular lines were smooth and slick to the touch. Curious, he rolled over and looked down the side of his bed. It was completely crafted from ice. The frame, intricately carved with sleek designs, was like crystal and cool to the touch. It seemed impossible, but there it was, and he was lying on top of it. The interesting thing was he wasn't cold. In fact, he didn't feel any chill whatsoever. Not from the air and not from the structure he was on, yet there was no mistaking that he was completely surrounded by a frozen landscape.

He tried to sit up, determined to find out exactly what was going on and where he was, but nausea swept over him, and he had to lay back down to catch his breath. His head ached fiercely, and then he remembered hitting it on the steering wheel when he ran into the snowbank.

As he gathered himself, his thoughts strayed toward the impossible. An image of a breathtaking Japanese woman in a blue kimono filled his mind. He had seen her, hadn't he? She *had* spoken his name.

He pressed his fingers to his lips. They were cool but dry against his skin. The sensation triggered another thought and image. She had kissed him. As sure as he existed, so had she. He could still feel the tingling of ice on his face from her touch.

He wasn't going mad, was he? He'd always been sane and rational. Even as a child he'd analyzed everything, including the possibility of there being a closet monster and if Santa Claus could truly exist. He had always been the levelheaded one, the guy others relied on to explain and reason.

But now, he wasn't too confident. He was completely out of his element, and he hated the lost feeling coming over him.

The sound of a door opening drew his attention to the far corner of the room. Framed in the doorway stood the woman from his dreams, from his vision of a beautiful woman in a sapphire-blue kimono floating to him across the snow. The woman from the myth.

The ice maiden.

Without meeting his gaze, she entered the room and crossed the floor to his bed. She carried a tray in her arms. On it he could see steam rising from a cup and from a plate. The smell of food wafted to his nose and he inhaled deeply, his stomach growling in response.

Avidly, he watched her as she busied herself next to the bed, setting the tray down on a table. She didn't look at him as she worked. She acted as if he wasn't even there.

"Where am I?" he asked, his voice cracking from thirst.

She avoided his question and handed him the cup, making sure he took it with two hands.

"Where am I?" he asked again, this time in Japanese. Still she didn't answer.

Resigned to her silence, he raised his head and took a sip of the hot liquid. It was some sort of tea and it warmed him instantly, soothing his dry mouth and throat.

He handed it back to her and she set it onto the tray. "Who are you?"

Instead of answering, she spooned up what looked like soup and set it against his lips. He opened his mouth and she fed him. Spoonful after spoonful, she ladled the soup into his mouth until the bowl was empty and his stomach was blissfully full.

Fatigue washed over him and he tried to fight back a yawn, but it was no use. His eyelids drooped, and he wanted nothing but to sleep. He fought it, wanting, needing, answers instead.

"Why won't you answer me?" he demanded. "Where am I? I deserve an answer."

She looked at him then. It was brief but he saw something there in her gaze. Sympathy maybe? Regret?

Before he could ponder it further, she gathered the tray in her arms and started for the door.

"Wait! Please tell me something. Anything."

But she didn't. Without a word, or a second glance, she went through the door and closed it firmly behind her. He was alone again.

Another rush of fatigue surged over him, and he struggled to keep his eyes open. Biting down on his tongue he tried to stay awake. But it was no use. The pull of sleep lulled him under. Slowly, slowly he slipped into the black folds and dreamed of dancing snowflakes in blue.

Chapter 3

He was floating on an iceberg in the middle of the ice sea shelf off the coast of Hokkaido. The strange thing about that was his nakedness.

But he wasn't cold.

He actually felt right at home, standing on the floating ice, gazing out across the vast ocean. He'd always been at home in the cold. There was nothing he liked more than to go snowshoeing after a fresh snowfall or go spelunking in British Columbia at the Columbia Icefield. He'd been born in a winter month and had always felt at home in its grasp.

This wasn't home, though. This was odd and strange and definitely not real.

A dream maybe. A wild, strange dream. Like the ones he'd been having lately since coming to Japan.

Before Darien could figure out what was happening, another iceberg floated up next to his. On it stood a beautiful Japanese woman in a blue kimono. She was exquisite, and he couldn't take his eyes off her.

It was her, the ice maiden from the myth. It was Koori-Onna.

She smiled at him, and he felt every bone in his body melt at the sight. She was stunning. Like the first snowflake of the winter season, perfect in its construction and unique. Every snowflake was an original.

Like her.

When she looked upon him, he became very aware of his state of undress. Her gaze was heated, and he reacted like any hot-blooded male would.

He hardened instantly, his heart fluttering and stomach clenching at the possibility of being with her. If only they weren't floating on icebergs in the middle of the frigid ocean. Why couldn't they have been floating on soft, cushiony beds?

Stranger things had happened—especially in his dreams of late.

As she floated toward him, she slowly undid her kimono and let it slide off her body. She was perfect underneath. High small breasts, the tips painted a delicate rose color, flat belly and a soft flare of hips. The light sprinkling of hair between her thighs was as dark as the mass of shiny ebony hair on her head. Her skin was as pale as moonlight and looked as soft as cream-colored silk.

She raised her hand toward him. "Darien. Come to me. I am yours."

He didn't hesitate. With one giant step, he crossed the threshold separating them. The iceberg didn't even wobble as he stepped onto it. Without a word, Darien gathered her into his arms.

She fit perfectly against his chest, the top of her head touching the bottom of his chin. She smelled like rain and cool winter breezes. Burying his face into her hair, he inhaled her scent, reveling in her.

She reached down between them and grasped his cock in the slim, silky palm of her hand. Darien groaned loudly and ground his teeth as she stroked the length of him. It was all he could do to keep on his feet as she caressed him up and down, up and down. He didn't know it was possible, but he hardened even more. It was almost painful.

She continued to stroke him until he thought he'd go insane. Burying his hands in the silk of her hair, he crushed his mouth to hers, sweeping his tongue between her lips to taste her. She was as cool as mint.

He wanted her. He ached for her. Nothing in his life had ever made him feel this wanton, this lusty. It raged inside him like a caged beast. And he desperately wanted to unleash it. Onto her, into her.

Running his hands down her back, he gripped her around her buttocks and picked her up, to brace her against the icy wall of the berg. He couldn't wait any longer. He had to have her. Without ceremony, he parted her legs with his knee and entered her with one swift thrust.

She cried out and dug her nails into his back.

Koori sat up in bed. Sweat actually dotted her upper lip and the back of her neck. She hadn't experienced that sensation in more years than she could count. She swung her legs around the bed and stood.

Her sleep was ruined now. There was no way she could go back. The dream had been powerful, and vivid. She shivered, remembering the feel of his wide, hard hands on her body. Even now, there was a throb between her thighs.

She was surprised to feel it. Desire was not something she felt often. Or at least not in the last millennia.

Standing, she slipped on her kimono and left her bedroom. She walked to the frozen fireplace and poured from the pot of green tea sitting on the mantel as it was every time she woke, likely deposited there by an unseen servant while she slept.

As she sipped from the cup, she gazed across the expanse of her chamber. It would've been beautiful if it hadn't been her prison for so long. Now she didn't see beauty, only shackles.

While she drank, relaxing her body, she thought of the golden-haired man she'd brought to her home.

Maybe it had been a bad idea to do so. She didn't want or need the dreams he'd been inducing. She'd gone on long enough without conflicted emotions that having them now was only a lesson in futility.

Maybe she should go to him now and just end it. She could dispose of him while he slept and he'd never be aware of it. Theoretically he should be dead anyway. That had been her mission when the phantom door had opened to her and she had been compelled to walk to the road. Her goal had been simple. To ferry him from this world to the next. To give him the kiss of death.

But something had stayed her. It might've been the look in his eyes or the words that he had uttered. Words she hadn't ever heard before, and he had whispered them to her as if he had truly meant them.

No. She shook her head. He was more trouble than he was worth. She should end it now before it became worse. Before the magic of this place lashed out at her and punished her even more for what she'd done.

She'd had enough of the punishments. She didn't think she could endure them any longer.

Setting her tea down on the table, she decided she'd go to the room she'd put the sleeping man in and end it. Nothing good could come of it. She'd been a fool to spare his life and bring him here.

What could he possibly do for her? Nothing. He wasn't going to be her savior. There was no such thing. At least not for her.

Chapter 4

Koori watched him sleep from the edge of the bed. Darien, the light-skinned man that had come out of the snow and spoken to her. At first she had come to his room to send him to the next world. But again her hand was stayed. She couldn't do it. Now that he was here in her care, she couldn't ferry him on.

Now she was back in his room watching him. For the last two days and nights, he had slipped in and out of consciousness, babbling on about a snowstorm and a woman in blue.

She assumed he was talking about her.

Groaning, he shifted on the bed, his face grimacing as if in pain. She moved alongside the bed. Hand shaking, she touched his rugged cheek. His skin was hot, slick with sweat. She moved her fingers over him up to his forehead which was also warm and moist. He was definitely fighting a fever.

"Mizu," she called out.

Within seconds, a servant woman made entirely out of ice shuffled into the room carrying a medium-sized crystal bowl full of water. The servant handed it to Koori then shuffled back out of the room from where she had come from.

A cloth floated in the water. Koori wrung it out and set it on Darien's forehead. He moaned as she pressed it against his skin. She watched his mouth as he mumbled. He had sensual lips, full and soft.

When she had kissed him, it had been pleasant. For the first time in so long, she had enjoyed the ceremony of giving the kiss of death.

Why she had spared this particular man's life, she still didn't know. It was a puzzle to her and one she hoped to figure out soon.

I'm yours, forever.

His words still haunted her thoughts. Not one of the plethora of men and women she'd encountered over the years had ever come to her willingly. He had been the first.

By having him here in her home—prison really—she was breaking the laws of the curse that had been laid on her. She just hoped he was worth the risk she was taking.

When he groaned again, she dipped the cloth in the water, wrung it out, then rubbed it over his cheeks and down to his neck. Water dripped down and wet the ends of the tawny-colored hair that curled around his ears. She liked the golden color of his hair, the way it almost glowed in the light. Feeling brave, she ran her fingers through his soft waves, reveling in the feel of it on her skin.

He responded to her touch. The corners of his mouth twitched up. Not only did the reaction surprise her, but it pleased her as well. A warmth she hadn't felt in a thousand years started to swell in her belly. She'd almost forgotten what that feeling was.

Wanting that sensation to grow, she continued to wet the cloth and run it over his face and neck. Each time, he moaned or moved his head with her touch. And soon her hesitant touches turned to gentle caresses, with pleasure in mind more than healing.

As he continued to move and flinch, the silk blanket on top of him shifted. Each time more of his chest showed. Koori couldn't help her gaze from drifting down to his body. He was a tall man with wide shoulders, solidly built and appealing to her eyes.

She couldn't remember the last time a man of his coloring or stature had stumbled into her snowstorm. Maybe never. He intrigued her on so many levels; it was a muddled mess in her mind.

Guilt at admiring him as he lay unconscious pulled her gaze away and back to the business at hand. She was here to heal him, help his fever dissipate. It was just that his reaction to her touches seemed like those of a man in the thrall of pleasure.

Setting the cool, wet cloth on his forehead, Koori found she couldn't control her curiosity any longer. Slowly she slid the blanket down, revealing more of him.

She knew he was naked, as she had been the one to remove his wet clothing, but at the time she had only thoughts of his survival on her mind. But now, rare carnal notions swam unhindered in her head.

Licking her lips, she raked her gaze over him, taking in every angle and slope of his well-defined form. He was a man made for the rugged outdoors. His strong but lean arms and trim waist told her he was athletic, maybe a runner, or a hiker—if she remembered his muscular legs correctly. And she had to admit, she did remember the powerful length of them as she had removed his pants.

As Koori took in his beautiful features, she found she itched to touch him. The tips of her fingers actually tingled in anticipation of the hot smoothness of his flesh. Uncertain of how her body would react, she drew a finger down his body, tracing the line between his chest muscles.

The warmth at her center grew, swirling lower to between her legs. The sensation surprised her as she hadn't experienced that kind of pleasure in more years than she wanted to think about. It had been torture to be alone for so long. Once she was a very sensual being, a woman who enjoyed the sexual arts, who excelled at them. It had been so long, she'd forgotten who that woman truly was.

But now, touching this man, the ice solidifying her insides started to melt. Maybe with him she'd finally have a chance to be free of her cold constraints.

Closing her eyes, she settled her hand over his chest. Under her palm she felt the thump of his heart and the heat of his blood rushing through his veins. It'd been so long since she heard that sound, so long since she experienced the rush of life-giving essence that the power of the sensation surprised her.

She moved her hand over him, feeling his flesh, his heat, reveling in his mortal qualities. Oh, what she'd give to be like that again. To have the sensation of touch, and pleasure at her beck and call. To be a real woman again with a man at her side. A man eager to please her, eager to do whatever she wanted him to. Oh, how she longed to have that delight.

Her guilt long gone, Koori let her hand travel lower still. Eyes open wide, she watched as her fingers traced a circle around his navel. She played one tip through the light sprinkling of tawny hair that dipped even lower under the blanket. She knew where it led and for the first time in a millennia, she hungered for it. To feel the hard length of a man in her hand would be her greatest pleasure.

Darien let out a sensual moan as if he was privy to

her erotic thoughts. The sound lifted her gaze and she brought it back to his face.

His eyes were open and watching her.

Startled, she snatched her hand back. She dropped her gaze and busied herself with the bowl of water. Embarrassment surged over her, and she wanted to dig a hole in the ice and climb in. Instead, she took up the bowl and started for the door.

Darien reached for her, grasping her wrist. "Wait," he croaked, his voice barely audible. "Don't go."

"You must rest." She pulled from his grip. He was too weak to offer any resistance. Head down, she continued toward the door.

"Please."

His plea nearly stopped her, but she knew she had to go. She'd been a fool to do what she did. And she'd been caught at it.

When she reached the threshold and turned to close the door, she noticed that he had fallen back asleep. It was for the best, because if she had turned and he'd been watching her, with his vivid blue eyes beckoning her, she was uncertain she'd have been able to leave.

Chapter 5

A stiffness in his neck brought Darien out of a restless sleep. He'd been dreaming of pale eyes in a blinding snow. He'd been dreaming of her, the ice maiden, again.

In one feverish dream, he swore she'd touched him. And not a slight brushing of fingers but a sensual caress full of passion. The image had been so real in his mind that even now he ached in remembrance.

Lifting his arms over his head, he stretched. His body felt better, not as sore and stiff. He wondered how long he'd been in and out of consciousness. A day? Two? A week?

He ran his hand over his chin. His usual five o'clock

shadow was now a good half-inch scruff. By the feel of it, he imagined he looked like a crazed mountain man, with his longish scraggly hair and full unkempt beard. He'd just about kill for a shave right now.

After stretching again, Darien sat up. Nausea didn't plague him this time, and he was able to swing his legs over the mattress, and his feet to the floor. Surprisingly, the ice floor wasn't cold.

He stood up and surveyed the room, keeping his eye on the closed door. He really didn't want to be in the buff if he suddenly received company. Although if the ice maiden chose to return at that moment, he wasn't too sure he'd be too put out by it. There was no denying that she was unearthly beautiful and his groin twitched when he thought about her.

An image of them locked in an embrace, her lips traveling his chin and down his neck made his groin twitch even more. Had he dreamed that?

He ambled to the corner where his stuff had been placed. His right leg was still a little achy and he massaged the thigh as he moved. He dressed quickly, and then took stock of the equipment piled high. Everything was there, intact, no obvious damage to any of it.

After he surveyed his items, he put his attention to the walls around him. He placed his hand on the sparkling crystal and rubbed it up and down. It was definitely crafted from ice. It amazed him that something like this could exist. A room, possibly a whole house, constructed from frozen water. Although, there were a few ice bars in Hokkaido; Japan's northernmost island was famous for them. As were other countries including Norway and Sweden, even Canada. So, Darien assumed it was possible. But it just seemed so surreal. Especially since everything in the room had been created from it: the chairs, the bed, the gorgeous four-tier chandelier hanging from the high ceiling that shed no light. All seemingly impossible but all as real as he was.

Or maybe that was the issue. Maybe he wasn't real anymore. He still hadn't resigned himself to actually being awake and aware. There was still the remote possibility that he was in a coma and dreaming all of it.

Curious to see more, he ventured toward the door, opened it and peered out into another large area, also made of ice. This room seemed like a lofty sitting room or parlor, and images of old English castles came to his mind. That's what it all seemed like to him as he turned, eyeing the surroundings—a huge elegant palace made of ice. So instead of the ice maiden, maybe she was the ice princess.

And was he to be the prince charming coming to rescue her? He laughed at that. If Darien was a prince then he was surely dreaming. Besides that, he realized that he had been the one in need of rescuing. If that was indeed what she had done—saved him from freezing to death in the blizzard.

But then all the stories told about her would be

untrue, the myth of Koori-Onna a false one. Or this was something else altogether. Maybe he was here for a completely different reason.

Darien continued his search of the palace, becoming more and more intrigued with every ice furnishing he came across. Chairs, tables, the mantel over an unlit fireplace, everything crystalline and glowing pale blue from the inside. It was breathtaking but eerie. And a whisper of dread crept over him. It was too pristine and perfect as if it was constructed all in the hopes of being torn down. As if a well-placed hammer could shatter it into a million tiny crystal shards.

Darien marveled at everything as he walked through rooms and down halls. One thing he did notice was that none of the rooms had windows or doors that led to anywhere but more rooms. The three doors he'd come upon he had opened in hopes of finding a way out, only to find another room to explore.

He didn't know how long he'd moved through the palace. It seemed like hours, because when he happened upon the last room his legs were shaky, but it might've been because of what he found.

This room was different.

It wasn't as large as the others and had lower ceilings. In the middle of the room was a pool of water, a hot springs. Steam rose from the water, filling the area.

Then he saw the ice princess soaking in the water, naked. The steam wasn't so thick that he couldn't fully see her beautiful curves and perfect pale skin.

Her eyes widened when she saw him, and her arms instinctively wrapped around her body, covering her naked breasts.

Hand out toward her, he approached the pool, cautiously. "Don't be afraid."

She watched him curiously but said nothing. By the look in her eyes, he didn't think she was all that indifferent to him coming across her.

"Do you understand English?"

She nodded.

"I want to thank you for saving me." He rubbed a hand over his chin. "At least that's what I think you did," he mumbled as an afterthought. He looked at her, waiting for a response to anything he'd said. She just watched him with those impossibly pale eyes.

He gestured to the pool, hoping to find common ground with her. He was completely out of his element here. How did a man talk to an ice princess supposedly from a thousand-year-old myth? "The water looks inviting. May I join you?"

She didn't answer him, but he thought he saw something change on her face. She didn't look so cold, so unapproachable. Was there an invitation in the slight twitch of her lips?

Slowly, he slipped his boots off and stuffed his socks inside the opening. Hooking his thumbs into the hem of his long-sleeved henley, he pulled it up and over his head. He set it next to his boots, and then proceeded to remove his khaki pants. He shed them quickly, to not frighten her or, he had to admit, embarrass himself. He left his shorts on.

There was something unsettling about having a woman just watching as he undressed, without a word or movement. As if she was studying him objectively and not looking at him as a seminaked man.

As swiftly as he could without slipping and cracking his head open on the icy floor, Darien lowered himself into the scalding hot water. Instantly he relaxed. The heat from the pool massaged and caressed his sore, tired muscles. When he entered he made sure he was on the opposite end as she was. He didn't want to scare her away. Now that they were here together, he wanted to talk to her, wanted to hear her voice. He wanted to know what was going on.

He wasn't usually one to crave human interaction. He could go months out in the bush with no company but nature itself and the few critters that usually found their way into his tent. But he craved it now.

As he sank down into the healing liquid, he found a ledge to sit on. He kept his gaze on her. Only when he was fully submerged did she seem to relax, unfurling her arms and sinking back into the water. She kept his gaze the entire time.

He felt both unnerved and aroused as she watched him. Her actions dictated that he stay away, but at the same time, he got the strong sensation that she wanted him to breech the space between them. She was definitely the most confusing woman he'd ever been around. He supposed considering the circumstances of his situation that probably wasn't saying too much.

"You know, this is all very strange. I'm in a palace made of ice with a woman who I believe is named Koori-Onna."

She flinched a little at her name. He wondered how long it'd been since she heard it spoken out loud by someone. He had a feeling that she didn't have too many visitors in her frozen home.

"You are Koori-Onna, aren't you?"

She nodded.

"Am I dead? Did you freeze my insides like the stories say?"

"Do you feel frozen?"

The sultry sound of her accented voice startled him. Despite the heat from the water, gooseflesh rose on his skin. The sensation tightened all the muscles in his thighs and other lower regions.

"No," he finally answered after the shock of hearing her speak wore off.

"Then you are not."

He took the start of their conversation as an opening to move closer to her. He could've been completely off base, but he knew if she truly didn't want to be around him, she would've gotten out of the water the moment he entered the pool.

"Why am I here? Why didn't you kill me as the legend says?"

She stared at him for a few seconds, under the hood

of her long black eyelashes, then shook her head. "I don't know."

She looked sad as she spoke and Darien had the sudden urge to cross the pool in one swift motion and gather her in his arms. For the first time since he'd seen her, vulnerability shone through her stoic exterior. He imagined it was something she usually didn't reveal to anyone.

Why him? What was the reason he was here and not lying dead in some snowstorm?

He shook his head, the truth or nontruth of the situation was making his head spin. "I just can't believe this. How can this be real? How can you be real?"

"You are a scientist, yes?"

He nodded.

"Then can you not see and touch what is around you?"

"Yes."

"Do you doubt your own observations?"

She was right. He did doubt. "Yes."

"Why?"

"Because this can't possibly be real. It's a myth. You are a myth, a story passed down from generation to generation over a thousand years."

"I am real, Darien. As real as you are."

"How do you know who I am?"

Her lips curled up then, in a shy smile. "I don't know exactly. Just as you have heard stories of me, maybe I have heard stories of you."

He smiled in return, his gaze not leaving her face.

She was spectacular to watch. So dainty and elegant, like a porcelain doll.

"Your English is very good."

"I've had a long time to learn."

He wondered what her skin would feel like if he touched her. Would she be cold to the touch? Or would he feel the warmth inside her?

Her smile faded as if she were privy to his thoughts. Maybe she could read his mind. Maybe that was how she knew who he was. He really hoped that wasn't the case, especially with the way he'd been imaging her. Naked, wrapped around his body, kissing his face and other parts of him.

She shifted in the water and Darien knew she was getting ready to escape.

Before she could get out of the water, Darien crossed the pool. "Please don't go." He reached out and grasped her arm. Despite the heat from the water, her flesh was still icy cold, but he didn't let go.

She looked down at his hand on her arm then back up to his face. He saw confusion there, but also longing. God, she was desirable. He'd never wanted a woman as much as he wanted her right now. Every part of his body ached for her.

When her lips parted, Darien leaned into her, eager to have her mouth. Her eyes widened as he moved in, but she made no attempt to pull away. She stayed very still, stiff under his touch, as his lips brushed hers.

It was then that the room shook.

Chapter 6

The whole room moved as if something had picked it up and rattled it. Panicked, Koori tried to scramble out of the pool, but the motion of the ground slapped her firmly into Darien's lap. He wrapped his arms around her as the walls in the room started to crack.

The breaking sound filled the room. It was so loud she wanted to put her hands over her ears and squeeze her eyes shut. She'd never heard such a noise before, especially not in her home.

She didn't know what was happening, but it almost felt like an earthquake. It was improbable, but not impossible. She remembered the last two powerful quakes to hit Japan. One in 1923 and the last in 1995, but both had occurred on the main island and hadn't affected Hokkaido all that much. Maybe it was just the northern island's turn to be blasted.

Koori clutched Darien as pieces of ice fell from the walls, shattering into tiny shards on the hard floor. She couldn't believe the walls were breaking. She didn't think it would ever be possible.

She should know; she'd tried breaking them apart herself on many occasions.

During her first year imprisoned in the ice palace, she'd lifted every piece of furniture she could and beat against the walls. All that ever came of it was broken furniture, which was magically reconstructed the next day. Every five years or so after that, she tried again, but to no avail. Everything she had tried to use to break the ice had failed.

Until now. But this was not of her making.

Then she glanced at Darien who was hugging her close and eyeing the shaking room, and she wondered. Could this be the reason she was compelled to bring him here? Could he be the catalyst to the changes happening right now?

Finally the room stopped vibrating. One last piece of ice dropped from the far wall onto the ground and slid across the floor to fall into the hot pool. Steam hissed the second it hit the water. Slowly it dissolved into nothing.

They both watched it in silence.

Suddenly conscious of Darien's arms around her

and the heat from his body, Koori pushed out of his embrace and scrambled out of the pool.

"Wait!" he called.

She couldn't. It was all too much for her to handle. She grabbed her kimono from the floor, slid it on and raced from the room before Darien could get out of the water and touch her again.

She sprinted down the hallway toward the east wing and her private chambers. She passed two of her servants standing to attention along the way, but they paid her no mind. Their only purpose was to see to her physical needs. Her mental needs were her own.

When she reached the double doors to her rooms, she pushed them open without pause and shut them firmly behind her. In her mind she summoned two guards to stand at her doors. She didn't want Darien to stumble upon her if he haphazardly searched the castle for her. She needed time alone to gather her thoughts, which seemed ironic to her since she'd been alone for so long. She'd wished countless times for someone to talk to, someone that she could touch and be touched by, and all her wishing had brought Darien to her.

Yet here she was squirreled away in her room, knees trembling, too afraid to let him get close to her. Or was it the fear of what might happen if she did that made her shudder?

Koori walked into her sitting room and poured herself a cup of warm sake that was waiting for her on the small table. She drank it quickly, and then poured another. She sat, then, pretending there was a roaring fire in the frozen hearth.

For a thousand years she'd been cursed to live in this ice palace. The only times she'd been allowed out were to bring death to those stranded in snowstorms. It was her penance for a crime she committed over a hundred lifetimes ago.

During the first decade, Koori spent it grieving for the man who she had lost—her lover, Shiro Tagawa, and for the man whom she'd wronged—her husband, Kyoshi Iwasaki. Her affair had doomed them all and had sent her to this hell to spend an eternity.

Her husband had died in a snowstorm after discovering her and Shiro together. In his anger and dismay, he ventured into a blizzard no man could survive. She often wondered if he had done it deliberately to kill himself. She hadn't ever thought that Kyoshi loved her enough to do such a thing. Love had never been part of their marriage.

Arranged when she was just fourteen, Koori had married the powerful daimyo of the land she was born to. He had not been a kind or gentle man. She lost her virginity violently the night of her wedding and every coupling with Kyoshi after that night had been steeped in brutality.

It wasn't until she'd met a young foolhardy artist named Shiro did she finally understand the meaning of making love. She knew it was wrong, but she'd gone on so long without kindness and gentleness that Shiro's alluring face and laugh couldn't sway her from her desires.

They both had paid for it with their lives.

After Kyoshi's body was found frozen a mere mile from the house, his brother, Junzo, a man rumored to possess powerful magic, came to find Koori and Shiro. Shiro was brutally executed in front of her. Even after so long, she could still see the macabre scene in her dreams. With Koori, he wanted her to suffer. He had called her an ice-hearted whore and murderess. Instead of killing her outright, he put a curse on her.

To ferry those stranded in the snow to their icy death until she found someone that could love her for who she truly was. Only then would she be free of her icy prison. How could anyone love their murderer?

She tossed back the rest of her sake and stared into the empty cup. Maybe Darien was her one and only chance at redemption.

But she was scared. Hope could be such a damaging thing.

Chapter 7

After getting out of the pool and meagerly drying off, Darien searched the castle for her. He had to know what was going on. She couldn't leave him without answers. The earthquake was just the final straw in an already heavy load on his mind.

He assumed she probably had a private wing of her own. Or it could be that he'd read too many fairy tales as a child and thought that all princesses had rooms of their own in the castle. But he had nothing else to go on, so that was the best he could come up with.

After an hour of blindly walking down hallway after hallway, he finally came across a new area that looked different. Two huge guards made of ice were standing in front of a set of double doors.

When he approached, the guards came alive. Both had been sculpted wearing matching uniforms and with long pointy spears in their massive ham-sized hands. They both aimed the spears at him as he took another step forward.

"Koori!" he shouted.

No answer.

He tried again. "Koori! We need to talk. I have to know what's going on."

Several seconds ticked by before, finally, the guards stood down, lowered their spears and stepped off to the side of the doors. Cautiously, Darien moved forward and gripped the handle to one door. Eyeing both guards, looking for any sign that they would attack, he slowly opened the door and slid through.

Koori sat on a golden silk-covered chaise waiting for him, her back straight and her hands resting demurely in her lap.

"Okay, what the hell was that?"

"You mean my guards?"

"No—" he shook his head "—well, yes, they're definitely strange, but I mean the earthquake in the hot springs."

"I don't know."

"Does it happen often?"

"That was the first time."

Darien ran a hand through his hair as he paced the room. "Why did it happen?"

She shook her head but didn't meet his gaze.

He stopped in front of her. "You're not telling me the truth."

She looked at him then, and he saw a commanding spark in her eye. "I'm not a liar. I just don't know what is going on."

"Start from the beginning then." He sat down beside her. "How did you get here?"

She smoothed a hand down her kimono as she spoke. Was it nerves or guilt he saw in her face?

"Many years ago, I committed a terrible act and betrayed my vow and this is my penance. I am forced to live in this place like a prisoner. The only time I am allowed to leave is to ferry those lost in the snow to their deaths." She wouldn't look at him as she told her story. He couldn't blame her; it wasn't pleasant to hear.

"But you saved me and brought me here."

She nodded. "There was something different about you. Some quality that even now I can't name. You were the first person who ever willingly came to me." She licked her lips nervously. "And you looked at me. Really looked." She raised her head and met his gaze.

Her eyes should've startled him. They were so pale, so luminous, and completely unnatural, but they drew him in like a moth to a flame. Her gaze enchanted him in a single moment and he was lost to her.

Had it been magic that compelled him to her in that snowstorm? Did she cast some spell over him? If she did, she seemed utterly ignorant of it. He couldn't say why he had been drawn to her. There wasn't just one certain thing, not one quality that mesmerized him. It was everything about her. Her cold beauty stunned him, but she had an inner warmth he sensed deep inside her that made him want to touch her, to be with her.

If it was magic then he was bewitched and there was nothing he could do about it. Or *wanted* to do about it.

Hesitantly, he caressed her cheek. Her skin was soft like creamed silk. He once touched a petal of a dewy flower during the early days of spring and thought it the softest thing he'd ever touched, but it didn't compare to the reality of her.

"You're the most beautiful woman I've ever seen."

She gave him a small smile and leaned into his touch. He stroked her cheek and ran the pad of his thumb over her plump, pink mouth. Her lips parted on a sigh. He took that as an invitation for more.

Leaning in, he tilted her head up and lightly brushed his lips against hers. He was hesitant at first, testing the waters. When she didn't draw back, Darien deepened the kiss, the tip of his tongue dipping inside her mouth.

She tasted of icy cold mint. Happy memories of all the times he'd spent skiing in the mountains flooded back to him. He loved the winter and everything it brought. The first snowfall, icicles hanging from the eaves of his family home, brisk breezes, the sense of belonging especially during the holidays. It all came to him in that single moment of kissing her.

She tasted of his home back in Montana where the

winters lasted for five months of the year. And the summers were unusually sultry and pleasant.

He kissed her until he thought the room was shaking beneath him again. But when he broke away and stared into her eyes, he realized it was just him. He was vibrating with desire like an overeager teenage boy on his first date with the girl of his dreams.

Except she *was* the girl of his dreams. At least from the dreams he'd been having for the past five or six nights since arriving in Japan. They were linked somehow. He knew it as fundamentally as he knew the Earth was round and spun on its axis.

Although he was a scientist and everything about this situation screamed that it was impossible, he believed in it. He believed in her.

"I don't know why I'm here, but I'm glad that I am." He brushed a stray dark hair from her brow and leaned in to kiss her again.

This time as he took her mouth, she wrapped her arms around him, burying her hands in his hair. Each small moan that escaped her lips he swallowed down, eager to hear more, willing to give her more to get that sound. He wanted to please her.

His hands at her back, he gathered her closer, while he nibbled on her bottom lip and moved on to her chin. At first she was stiff and her skin cool even through the silk of her kimono, but he could feel the rise in temperature with each gasp from her lips. It was as if she was heating up from his embrace.

While he continued to feast on her neck and the curve of her shoulder, she ran her hands down his back. He could feel the press of her nails, and that sent sparks of pleasure zinging over him. Instantly he was hard, his erection straining against the increasingly tight fit of his pants.

An image from one of his dreams flashed behind his eyes. Koori naked, with her hand wrapped around the hard length of him. He groaned remembering the feel of her cool skin on his hot searing flesh. He bit down lightly on her shoulder urging a moan from her lips.

The sound of the doors slamming open brought both their heads up. Koori screamed when one of the guards marched into the room with his spear pointed at Darien.

Darien jumped to his feet. He really had no intention of getting shish-kebabbed by an eight-foot iceman with an anger problem. He put his hands up to ward off the attack.

"Whoa, man, point that thing somewhere else." To his chagrin the guard kept coming.

Koori stood and marched toward the guard, her hands fisted at her sides. *"Shuushi!"*

The guard slowed but still advanced on them. By this time, Darien was behind the chaise hoping the thick ice would protect him. Except the point on the spear looked like it could pierce ten times the thickness of the sofa.

Koori stood right in front of the advancing iceman

with no evidence that she was going to move. *"Shuushi!"* she shouted again.

This time it stopped. It lowered its sword and almost appeared to look sheepishly at her.

"Darien, go back to your room."

"What?"

"Please, return to your room. It won't hurt you if you just leave."

He hesitated. He didn't want to leave her, especially when he didn't quite know what was going on. Was the ice guard going to hurt her when he was gone?

Koori turned and looked at him. "I will be fine," she said, as if reading his mind again. "It won't hurt me. But you must leave. It will most definitely hurt you."

Seeing the serious look in her eyes, Darien nodded and then went to exit the room.

"I will come to you later. Please don't come looking for me again."

As he passed her and the guard he noticed a few pieces of ice lying on the ground, as if something had just melted. But he couldn't tell if it had come from the guard or from Koori.

Chapter 8

By the time Darien decided to take a break from pacing his room, he swore there was a groove in the floor. But he didn't know what else he could do. It wasn't as if there was a television to watch or a gym he could work out in to pass the time.

For the past day or more, he really couldn't tell, he'd been alone. Koori hadn't come to see him like she said she would. Worry for her made him a bundle of nerves and energy with no outlet.

Between doing sit-ups, push-ups and running the halls, he was going mad with just his paranoia and dread-filled thoughts to keep him company. He'd gone to the hot springs twice, but she hadn't been there. He'd gotten into the water hoping she'd show up. She hadn't.

Despite the guards at her door, he'd gone there twice as well, yelling for her to open the doors. But there was no response. The guards hadn't even moved, except when he got too close to the doors, and then the spears came down. He got pricked in the arm at that point.

When he returned to his room, food and drink had been deposited onto the table. So, at least he wouldn't starve to death. But he felt as if he was starving, and it didn't have anything to do with food.

He ran a hand through his hair and sighed. He had to be losing his mind. There was no other explanation for everything that had happened, everything that he'd seen so far. It was like an episode of *The Twilight Zone* and he was the guest star. He really hoped he didn't get killed off as so many guest stars had in the past.

Darien startled when the door opened.

Koori came in, carrying another tray. This time, there were two plates of steaming hot food. Head down, she walked to the small table, set the tray upon it, and then nervously turned toward him and lifted her gaze.

"Are you hungry?"

Standing, Darien nodded, then came toward her. She sat in one of the chairs and swept her hand toward the other gesturing for him to sit. He did.

"Are you okay? I thought maybe the guards had hurt you."

She gave him a small smile. "I'm perfectly fine as you can see. Please do not worry. The guards would never harm me." She poured the sake into small cups and handed one to him. Then she set a plate of noodles and vegetables in front of him. The scent of the hot food tickled his nose. His stomach growled reminding Darien that he hadn't eaten in a while.

"Please eat," she said.

Darien dug into the noodles with gusto. The second the spicy pasta hit his tongue he forgot that he had so many questions to ask her. Instead, he shoveled the food in, only taking long enough breaks to drink sake.

When he was finished, he set his fork down on the plate and leaned back in his chair, contented. He sighed and rubbed at his chin. "I'm sorry. I didn't realize how hungry I was."

She shook her head. "No, I'm sorry. I should have brought food to you sooner."

"It's all right."

He stared at her across the table. It was the strangest thing sitting in this room of ice, having something as mundane as dinner. An act so simple took on new meaning in this unusual environment. So many questions swirled in his head.

"Where does the food come from? Every time I left the room and came back there was a tray of something on the table."

"All my physical needs are taken care of. I only have to ask for it and one of the servants brings it to me."

"So if you wanted a bottle of beer, you would get it?"

She nodded. "Do you want a beer? I can get it for you."

"No." He shook his head. "I was just using that as an example. How does it work?"

"I don't know exactly. It's like magic, I suppose. The man that imprisoned me here was very powerful."

"Like magic," he murmured while he played his fingers through the scruff on his chin. "It's funny. I was the last person ever to believe in it. But since arriving here—" he chuckled "—I might have to amend my beliefs."

She looked down into her lap as she spoke. "Yes, but unfortunately it isn't all for fun."

"No, I suppose it isn't." He ran a hand over his chin again. "Have you ever tried to leave?"

She glanced at him and he saw a spark of something in her eyes. Anger maybe. "Many times. It is pointless. The only time there is a door to the outside is when I must go to the road. A few times I have tried to veer off the path only to be right back where I started." Her face tightened as she spoke as if just telling the story made her angrier and angrier. "I have tried to break down these walls with everything I could think of, only to have it reform again."

He could see a multitude of emotions cross her face—hope, loss, anger, regret and despair.

"There's no hope that I can leave?"

"If you can find a way out, you may take it."

"So, I'm stuck here then, like you." He hadn't meant for it to sound final, but the reality of his situation just hit him in full force like a sledgehammer to the face. He was never going home again.

"Yes, like me." She stood, tossing her cloth napkin onto the table. "I'm truly sorry for that. But I could not…" Tears welled in her eyes. "I could not kill you like the rest." She turned on her heel and marched for the door.

Darien was up out of his chair in her wake. He reached for her arm and spun her back around. The tears were now falling freely down her pale cheeks to dot her silk kimono.

She tried to pull from his grasp, but he held firm. "I'm sorry. I didn't mean to sound angry or ungrateful. I guess in the back of my mind, I'm still holding on to the hope that this is all a dream and that I'll wake up soon."

"This is no dream, Darien." Her voice quivered. "I know this because I have been trying to wake for over a thousand years."

Darien pulled her close and wrapped his arms around her. At first she resisted him, but he wouldn't relinquish his tight hold on her. He wanted her to know how much he felt for her, how much her situation affected him. Finally, she stopped fighting him. Sighing, she fisted her hands in his shirt and laid her head against his chest.

He ran a hand down her back, and buried his face

into her hair. He loved the smell of her. He inhaled deeply. She was so petite in his arms. He had a sudden urge to sweep her up and cradle her in his lap, to keep her safe from everything that would see her harm. She brought out the protector in him. No other woman had ever done that to him.

"I'll find a way out, Koori. I'll find a way for the both of us to leave."

Pulling back, she looked up at him, brow furrowed. "You would want to help me escape?"

He smoothed a hand down her hair. "Yes. I want you to come with me. We can escape together."

"Why? Why would you do this for me? When I have brought you to this place for an eternity?"

He kept her gaze, drowning in the pale pools of her eyes. "Because you don't deserve to stay here any longer. You deserve to have a life outside of these walls. No matter what you did, I think you've paid for it a long time ago."

Another tear rolled down her cheek and Darien caught it on his fingertip. As he brought his finger to his mouth, her lips parted on a gasp. He licked the salty liquid off his tip.

Cupping her cheek with his hand, he tilted her mouth up to meet his. He leaned down and brushed his lips against hers, once, twice until she gasped from it. Swallowing down her whimper, Darien covered her mouth with his and kissed her hard.

She moaned as he took her mouth, sweeping his

tongue between her lips. This time she was flavored by spices and sake. Warm and inviting. And he couldn't get enough of the taste of her.

Wrapping a hand behind her neck, Darien bent her back and deepened the kiss. Although he'd just eaten, he felt ravenous for her, as if he'd not eaten or drank in more days than he could count. She was his sustenance, his drink, and only kissing her, having her body next to his, could sate his hunger.

Nibbling on her bottom lip, Darien broke the kiss and proceeded to press his mouth to her chin and neck. Her skin was cool under his touch, but he could feel a slight rise in temperature with each stroke of his lips. Her flesh was warming from his eager touch. And that just incited him further.

Moving his hands down, he swept her into his arms. She gasped at his actions, but as he walked with her to the bed, she wrapped her arms around his neck and held on.

When they neared the bed, Koori reached up and slid the pins out that were holding her hair up. Her mass of ebony hair tumbled down around her, sweeping over her shoulders like a dark curtain of silk. She smiled at him as he set her down onto the bed.

He watched her face as he kneeled down beside her. In her eyes, he saw both trepidation and need. He understood both with equal measure. Being locked up in a prison without human contact for a thousand years had made her freeze up inside, but he hoped that he could help thaw her. He wanted to feel her flesh warm with every caress of his hands, with every touch of his lips.

"I want to look at you, Koori. You are so beautiful."

Licking his lips, Darien untied her kimono and slowly pulled the two halves apart revealing her perfect pale flesh. He had to bite down on his lip to stop himself from pressing his mouth to her taut nipples on her gorgeous breasts. He'd never seen a woman with such flawless skin. He wondered if she'd feel like silk under his fingers.

He trailed his gaze over her, as if his eyes could touch and caress. From the tips of her breasts to the light sprinkling of dark hair at the V of her legs, everything was exquisite.

Darien felt the shivers radiate over her body as he leaned down and trailed his tongue over her nipples, sucking one between his lips. The moans he pulled from her with each suck of her breasts made him quiver with pent-up desire. It was all he could do not to devour her in one greedy gulp.

He knew he had to go slowly, to show her with each touch, each kiss, just how desirable she was to him, but to do so would take every ounce of restraint he'd ever possessed.

Chapter 9

With each deliberate flick of his tongue, Koori thought she'd go mad with desire. Electrifying blows zigzagged down her torso and gathered deep within her sex. She'd not felt something so powerful, so pleasurable for so long the sensation nearly staggered her. It was as if she were a virgin all over again. But this time, her lover was a gentleman, not a barbarian.

She bowed her back as Darien trailed his tongue to the valley of her breasts and down the line of her torso. He stopped at her navel and nipped playfully at her skin. The whiskers on his chin added a delicious contradiction to the soft press of his lips. She flinched at the tingling sensation between her legs. She knew if he touched her there, she'd be ready for him.

As he brushed his fingertips lightly across her inner thighs, she gasped. He was so close to her, so close she could feel his hot breath on her flesh. Jolts of bliss fired through her. She fisted her hands in the silk cover on the bed in preparation for the orgasm she could already feel building deep inside her. It was going to be hard and explosive.

"You are so damn beautiful, Koori."

"But my skin…it is so cold. How can you stand to touch me?"

He smiled at her then, his eyes wide and dark with desire. "I can feel the heat inside." With one finger, he traced the outline of her navel, and then dipped lower over her pubic mound. In one deft stroke, he separated her slick folds.

Gasping, she arched her back. She'd never been so near orgasm before in such a short time. It was because she'd gone too long without it, without pleasure and passion. During her first years imprisoned, she had only her memories of her past lover, Shiro, to keep her warm.

But now here was this man eager to give her as much as he could.

"You're so hot and wet for me. You're driving me crazy."

Tears brimmed in her eyes. She brought a hand up to wipe them away before Darien could see them there.

She didn't need or want his sympathy. Not now. Not ever. She just wanted him.

After pressing an openmouthed kiss to just above her sex, Darien made his way up her body and settled in beside her. She could feel the hard length of him pressing against her leg. He smiled down into her face and lightly traced his finger over her mouth.

"Are you ready for me?"

Too overcome with emotion to form any words, she just nodded. She was more than ready for him. For a thousand years, she'd been waiting for him.

Standing, Darien quickly pulled his shirt off, and then his pants and shorts. He lay back down beside her. Bringing his hand up, he cupped her cheek, then leaned down and kissed her. It was a beautiful, beguiling kiss. A fairy-tale kiss.

Koori moaned into his mouth and trailed her hand down his body. She needed to feel him in her hand. He was hot and heavy against her palm, like silk and steel meshed together. She stroked him once, then twice, until he broke the kiss and gasped.

"I want you bad, Koori," he groaned, "I have to be inside you now."

"Yes," she breathed, "yes, I want that, too. I want you."

Crazy with the need to have him, she rolled him onto his back and lay on top of him. Purring low in her throat, she pressed kisses to his chin and neck. She trailed her tongue over his pulse points and up to the lobe of his ear to suck it into her mouth. All the while she continued to stroke him. "I'm hungry for you, Darien. It's you who I have been waiting for, for so long."

Still gripping him, Koori moved down his body until she was straddling his thighs. Leaning forward, she flicked her tongue over the tip of his hard length. Darien clamped his eyes shut and moaned as she took him into her mouth. She licked and sucked him until she could feel his legs quivering. He was close to climax. To prevent him from coming too soon, she gripped him at the base of his erection and squeezed.

"Koori, I can't hold on," he panted.

She held him still until he softened a little and retained his control. Then she licked down the length of him wanting him to lose it all over again. "Yes, you can."

His eyes were dark and hooded. The muscles ticked along the rugged line of his jaw. She loved that look about him. Dark, fierce, barely holding on. She'd remember that look for the rest of her days.

After one final stroke of her tongue, she moved up his body to straddle his hips. The wait was destroying her. She'd waited long enough to find bliss. She held him firmly in her hand as she lowered herself. Inch by exquisite inch, he filled her. He was a big man, but still the perfect size for her. When she was fully seated, she held herself still and looked at him.

She dreamed of finally being set free. And he'd been sent to her. Darien was her ultimate salvation.

She rubbed her hands up and down his chest, enjoying the way his hard muscles felt under her palms. Watching his face, she contracted the muscles of her sex, squeezing him tight inside her. Every flicker and grimace of emotion that flashed over his handsome face gifted her some of the power she'd lost over the years. She didn't feel so helpless or hopeless any longer. Even if she never escaped these icy walls, Darien had at least given her that back.

As she started to rock her hips, Darien reached up and molded her breasts in his hands. He squeezed and flicked his thumbs over her nipples. Waves of pleasure swept over her and she arched her back to catch them cresting. Up and down, back and forth, she moved on him, finding a rhythm, squeezing her muscles with every stroke.

She watched his beautiful face contort with strain as she quickened her pace. She knew he struggled for control and that he was quickly losing it as she took him up and over. There was a sense of power in that, and she reveled in it.

"I can feel you burning up," he panted. "So damn hot." Darien moved one hand down to where they joined. He circled his fingers into her slick core, finding her pleasure point with expert ease.

He stroked her, as she stroked him. Firmly, pushing her toward climax. Biting down on her lip, she tried to stop from screaming out his name.

Grabbing hold of his shoulders, she picked up her

pace, moving faster, harder, taking them to the edge. As the first crest of orgasm mounted inside, she dug her nails into his flesh. With a loud drawn-out moan, she pushed down on him, filling herself completely with his hot male flesh.

He pressed down on her sensitive bundle of nerves one more time and flipped her over that edge. She collapsed forward onto his chest as she spiraled toward her climax. He wrapped his arms around her, burying himself deep, soaring over into ecstasy with her.

He found her mouth and kissed her hard as the delirious passion drowned them. Everything went white behind her eyes and she thought she'd pass out. Everything was clearer, everything brighter in her mind's eye. And she knew deep down inside that everything she'd ever wished for would come true.

Chapter 10

Darien didn't know how long they had lain there on the bed; arms and legs tangled together, the scent of sex still heavy in the air. It could've been a few minutes or two hours, he couldn't tell. Time failed to mean anything anymore. He wasn't even sure how long he'd been in the ice palace.

He thought about what it would mean if he was stuck here in this strange reality for an eternity. Rubbing a lazy thumb down the soft skin of Koori's arm, he considered that it may not be a hardship after all. He wouldn't lack for anything—he had clothing, a bed to sleep in, food would be provided, and he had her. He could think of worse fates to stumble into.

But still he clung to the hope that there was a way out. There was something different about the icy walls in the past couple of days. They'd changed somehow. He didn't think they were as solid as they once had been. And he knew it had something to do with him.

When Koori stirred beside him, he pulled her up onto his chest. A sigh of contentment escaped his lips.

She nuzzled into him and smiled. "You seem very satisfied."

"Yeah, I guess I am." He rubbed her arm, reveling in the fact that her skin was not nearly as cool as it had been before.

"Good. Because I am, as well. You're very good at sex."

He laughed. "Well, thank you very much. I've been practicing."

That made her laugh.

Darien loved the sound of her throaty chuckle. It provoked a surge of desire to rush over him. Wrapping both hands around her waist, he pulled her up to his mouth. She was still giggling when he covered her lips with his. The laugh was quickly replaced by a long satisfied moan as they kissed.

He nipped and nibbled at her bottom lip, enjoying the little mewls she made each time he did it. Trailing just the tip of his tongue over her lips then into her mouth, he stroked her jawline with the tips of his fingers. He loved kissing her.

And that's when the room started to shake.

Like before, the floor and walls trembled. A sound like thunder echoed through the room. Cracks started to show in the ice.

Koori clutched Darien as the bed rocked back and forth, and not in a good way. The quake seemed to be a hell of a lot more violent than before. Furniture upended and crashed to the floor. Some pieces shattered on impact.

"What's happening?" Koori asked, her voice quivering with fear.

"I don't know. I was just going to ask you that."

Darien didn't quite know, but he was starting to suspect how Koori was attached to the palace, her prison. Each time she touched him or he touched her, the world around them seemed to protest. And now that they'd made love, it was having a temper tantrum. Maybe afraid that its hold on Koori was slowly slipping away.

He couldn't really explain it or understand it in any other way.

"I think the walls are coming down."

She looked at him then, her eyes wide, hope and questions in them. She understood what he was insinuating. Maybe he really was on to something and not wishful thinking.

As the room moved, vibrating and shaking violently, pieces of ice fell from the walls and ceiling. At first they were small pieces, the size of oranges and baseballs, breaking apart and sliding around the floor where they hit.

One small bit cracked Darien in the shoulder. It smarted where it hit. He imagined if it were any bigger it would've definitely left some damage. That was when he saw the enormous crack in the ceiling near the four-tier chandelier.

In seconds, he was off the bed, pulling Koori with him. She looked around the room in panic, as the walls and ceiling continued to crack and break apart. The noise was deafening, and Darien had to yell over the clamor.

"We need to get somewhere safe. If that ceiling comes down it'll crush us."

He felt odd dashing around the room stark naked, but there really wasn't any time to consider it. If they didn't get out of the room, one or both of them were going to get hurt.

Hand in hand, they ran to the door, dodging the rain of ice chunks. Darien twisted the doorknob and went to yank the door open, but it wouldn't come.

"It's locked."

Koori shook her head. "Impossible. This door has no lock."

He tried it again, turning and pulling on it as hard as he could. Still it wouldn't open. Maybe the shifting walls had inadvertently crushed down on the door. They were stuck in the room without another exit.

Darien turned and examined the room, looking for something they could hide under or near that wouldn't shatter and break. He had visions of the air being filled by flying ice shrapnel as things inside continued to shatter.

A thunderous cracking resonated through the room. He could actually feel the sound waves rolling over his skin. It was difficult to discern where it originated from, but Darien raised his head and looked at the ceiling.

Without a doubt, it was coming down.

Crouching, he pulled Koori to the floor and covered her with his body. He hoped they were close enough to the wall that the ceiling would miss crushing them. He didn't really want to go out this way.

This whole thing was a cruel joke, and he wasn't laughing.

After another thunderous warning, the roof collapsed. A slab twelve feet long and wide fell and crushed the king-sized mattress that they'd been lying on. The bed's frame shattered under the weight of the ice. Shards burst out to the sides like that shrapnel Darien feared and peppered him across his back and legs. Thankfully none pierced his skin, just nicked him like tiny razor blades. Pain seared him from toe to head and he winced to stop from crying out.

And just like that, the room ceased to shake. Sucked into a silent vacuum, it was as if the event had never happened.

Koori blinked up at him. "Is it over?" Her voice was so small and full of fear. He wrapped his arms around her and hugged her close, running a soothing hand over her hair.

"I think so."

Still linked together, they stood and surveyed the damage. Every piece of furniture had been smashed into small pieces. There were small holes in the walls. In one instance, Darien could peer through one and see the next room. The most telling evidence of the quake was the giant gaping hole in the ceiling.

Taking Koori's hand in his, they walked to the center of the room and looked up. Through the jagged hole, they could clearly see something gray and swirling. *Storm clouds,* Darien thought. Bitter cold air rushed through the room and Koori nuzzled closer to him. Gooseflesh popped up all over his skin.

Darien had no doubt that it was the sky above him. The palace had been breached. There was a way out.

"This is it, Koori, our way out."

"What?"

He nodded toward the gaping hole. "We can climb up and go through that to the outside."

"How?"

"I have rope, grappling hooks, everything we need." He glanced toward the corner where Koori had stacked all of his equipment from the ditched SUV. It was lucky that she had possessed the presence of mind to bring his things with him. Or maybe it was fate.

He was never one to believe in such things, more confident to rely only on what he could see, touch and measure. But with the way events were turning out, he couldn't rely on stone-cold logic anymore—because everything that had happened since waking on the bed of ice just didn't exist within that logical realm.

She shook her head. "It won't let us leave."

He held her by the shoulders and looked into her eyes. "We have to try, Koori. It's our only opportunity."

When she met his gaze, he saw a kaleidoscope of emotions in the pale depths. He could imagine what she was feeling—fear and hope. He felt it, too. Hope that they could be free of the ice prison and fear that it was completely and utterly pointless.

"Do you trust me?" he asked.

She hesitated for a brief second before nodding. "Yes, I trust you, Darien."

Cupping her cheeks, he leaned in and kissed her. Not a quick peck of lips but a long, thorough tasting of her. He needed her to know that he cared for her, that he would do whatever he could to free her from this curse.

He hugged her close and buried his face into the silk of her hair. "I'll get us out of here. I promise you."

Chapter 11

Twenty minutes later, Darien was outfitted for the blistering cold outdoors. He had the grappling hook and rope wrapped around his shoulder, ready to go. In the large hiking pack he put on his back, he shoved the rest of his stuff—a hot plate, thermal blanket and the small pup tent designed for extreme temperatures that Jiro had given to him.

Beside him, Koori stood only dressed in her kimono staring up at the ceiling. She told him she was impervious to the cold temperature and didn't need the extra clothing and equipment. She didn't even want or need shoes. He definitely would need everything he could carry, once they reached the outdoors.

As she surveyed the roof, he could see in her face that she was just waiting for it to disappear. She'd shared with him the different ways she'd tried to escape and all of them had failed miserably with the palace reconstructing itself.

He glanced at the gaping hole and hoped it was too much damage for the castle to heal itself. He guessed they'd soon find out.

Holding the hook in one hand, he swung his arm up toward the break. The hook soared through the air, the rope trailing behind it like a kite's tail. Darien held his breath, praying as the hook disappeared through the gap. In seconds he was pulling on the rope. He could feel the hook move until finally, thankfully, it found purchase and stuck. He yanked on the rope again. It held firm.

"I'm going to go first and make sure it's safe up top."

Koori nodded and watched as he grabbed the rope in both hands and started to climb. The ceilings were high in the palace, so it took him a bit to make it to the top. Once there, he swung his leg up and onto the jagged ledge and pulled himself up. The ice didn't break. It held under his weight.

Leaning over the edge, he called down to Koori. "It's your turn. Grab the rope, and climb up to my hand." He held it out to show her she didn't have to climb that far to reach him.

Without hesitation, she gripped the rope and made her way up. She was strong, showing great power in both her arms and legs as she climbed hand over hand, bare feet clutching at the rope.

Six inches from reaching his outstretched hand, the ice started to reform.

By the way Koori's eyes widened in alarm she noticed it about the same time he did. "Darien!" she called, fear making her voice shrill.

"Keep coming! You can make it."

With every inch she advanced up the rope, the ice made the same progress. Darien watched in horror as it knitted back together faster than he could see. The sound was deafening, like a knife being sharpened faster and faster on a flint.

Wrapping his hand in the rope near the hook, Darien leaned farther into the hole stretching his fingers out to her. A long, agonizing minute later, she reached him.

Once they hooked fingers, he started to pull her up. Thankfully she weighed next to nothing, and progress was quick. But not as quick as the sheet of ice forming over the hole. It was going to be tight.

"Oh, God, Darien!"

He had her hand now firmly in his, now her arm, her head. Her shoulders came through, and he wrapped his hands around her waist to yank her body the rest of the way out. But the ice was forming too quickly. He wasn't strong or fast enough to save her. Her legs were going to be stuck in between. What would happen then? Would she be half in and half out of the palace for an eternity? He couldn't let that happen. He wouldn't.

With all his power, he yanked her up. Falling backward, he pulled her with him until finally she was through, the ice skimming her toes. The hole sealed shut with a final earsplitting shrill.

Darien lay on his back, breathing hard, Koori clutched to his chest. His arms were cramping, but he was afraid to let her go. Adrenaline still shot through his system, but it was starting to slow. He could hear her ragged breathing and knew she was struggling, too. It had been close. Too close for his heart to take.

Finally, she stirred against him. "You can let go now, Darien. I'm safe." He released his hold on her and she rolled off him onto the roof. Rising to her knees, she looked down at him and caressed his cheek. "Are you hurt?"

Sitting up, he shook his head. "No. But that was much too close for my liking."

She smiled. "Mine, as well."

Darien took in their surroundings. The wind howled around them, swirling snow and bits of ice into their faces. He didn't know how Koori could be unaffected as he was already starting to feel the bite of the cold. But she was. She wasn't even shivering. Long strands of black hair swirled around her head like a dark cloud of silk, but other than that there was no indication that the weather bothered her at all.

Luckily they were on a flat part of the roof, but the rest of it was constructed with turrets and points. They would definitely need the grappling hook and rope to get to the ground. He hoped he brought enough rope or else this might all be just an exercise in futility and they wouldn't be going anywhere.

He stood to get a better picture of their situation.

The view didn't do much for his confidence in getting them out. All he could see was gray. Above them, below them. All around. The blowing snow didn't help, either. It was as if he were standing in the middle of a gray tornado, directly in the center with no sense of direction. Despair washed over him, draining him of all the hope he'd mustered before attempting this crazy escape. He was going to fail her.

Movement at his side startled him from his reverie. Koori stood beside him, her hand curled around his.

"You have done more for me than I could possibly imagine. More than I have been able to do for myself." She squeezed his hand tight. "We can make it out of here together. I can feel it. For the first time in a thousand years I have hope. It is because of you."

He met her gaze and saw there the strength he needed to move on. She believed in him. Koori made him feel invincible, as if he could take on the world and win.

"Okay. The first thing we need to do is get off this roof."

He twisted around looking for the best and safest way to make their descent. Gathering the hook and rope, Darien walked to the edge of the flat surface and looked down. There was another level below this one. It was flat like this one and appeared to be stable.

"How many levels are there in this place?"

Koori shook her head. "I don't know. I've only ever been on one level."

Darien looked down again. He couldn't remember ever seeing any staircases in the castle, especially during his search for Koori's room. He guessed there could've been stairs possibly tucked into obscure corners, but he wondered why he never ran across one. The castle was huge, but as far as he could tell it was all on one level. Obviously, the palace had a mind of its own and decided to grow a few floors to make it more difficult for them to leave.

"It's more trickery and magic. Junzo was always very good at punishing people." Her voice was filled with hopelessness. He hated to hear it. It tore at him.

Digging the hook into the ice until he thought it was secure, he tossed the twenty feet of rope over the edge. Thankfully it reached the next tier so they wouldn't have to jump too far.

Once Darien was sure the grapple was safe, he motioned for Koori to come ahead. "You go down first. I'll make sure the rope holds. When you reach the bottom give me a sign that everything's okay."

Koori made her way down without any problem. When she reached the end, she gave Darien the thumbs-up. He smiled at that.

After pulling the rope up, he tied his pack onto the end. But before he let it down the side of the wall, he took out a set of boot picks and handheld ice picks used for mountain climbing. After securing the rope again, he tossed it over the side and let out slack slowly to prevent dumping the pack onto the next level. He didn't want anything inside it to break apart unnecessarily.

When it reached the bottom, Koori untied it and gave him another thumbs-up. He pulled the rope up but this time he pulled the hook out of the ground and tossed the whole thing over the edge. He couldn't use it to go down. He had to climb down another way.

Sitting down near the edge, Darien strapped the ice picks to the toes of his boots. Once secure, he swung his legs over the edge of the roof and stuck two ice picks into the roof to hold on to. So far so good. Slowly and steadily he made his way down.

It wasn't the first time he'd climbed down ice cliffs. He'd done some spelunking at the Columbia Icefield in Alberta, Canada, and in Iceland. But the slick walls on the castle weren't exactly like the cliffs he'd climbed. Instead of a gradual descent and small mounds and bumps to find purchase and footholds on, it was a straight slide down to the bottom. And he didn't have an anchor rope. Falling and breaking his legs wasn't exactly the way he wanted to get to the next tier.

About halfway down the wind picked up. At first it didn't bother him, but eventually it became a problem. Violent gusts pushed and prodded him. It was as if it were a separate entity trying to yank him off the wall. Whipping at his coat and pants, Darien felt the cold taking hold. It wouldn't be long before his legs went numb from the constant battering of the bitter wind. His only chance at making it was to keep moving.

Foot, foot, hand, hand. Darien concentrated on every motion he made. One small slip and he'd fall. He glanced down to see Koori waiting anxiously for him at the bottom. He was far enough down that even if he did fall, he wouldn't break anything vital. At least he didn't think he would.

Another violent flurry blew up and whipped at him. Squeezing his eyes shut against the barrage, Darien stilled and flattened his body against the icy wall. He could feel the wind racing over him as if trying to find a way to tear him away from the wall. Over and over it swirled around him until he could hear nothing but the strident cry of it.

He couldn't let it stop him. He had to make it down. He had to save Koori. That's all that mattered to him now. Gathering his strength, Darien started to move again, putting one foot down after another, using one handhold he made with the pick to the next. Methodical. Determined. Another few steps, and he finally set his foot down on the level roof.

Koori rushed to him, wrapping her arms around him. "I thought you were going to fall."

He hugged her close. "For a second there, so did I."

"What now?"

"Now, we go to the next level." Holding Koori's hand, Darien walked to the edge of the roof and looked down. He still couldn't see the ground. But he did see the next flat rooftop. It was another twenty feet down.

Glancing up into the sky, he wondered when night was going to fall. Doing this was dangerous enough in the murky gray light of the day; he couldn't imagine what it would be like in the absolute dark. He had a flashlight in his pack, but it wouldn't cast enough light to be helpful. One small slip and either of them could fall and get injured or worse. He hadn't come this far with Koori to fail. He just wouldn't.

"We need to hurry. Night is coming." And with that, he hooked the grapple into the ice and tossed the rope over. It was going to be a long day.

Chapter 12

Another three hours and they finally reached the ground. Koori sent up a silent prayer that they had made it right before full dark. The last leg of the descent had been treacherous at best in the waning light. Darien had slipped once, nearly falling the last ten feet and she had, too. The palms of her hands still ached from the rope burn.

Because they had no idea where they were, Darien didn't want to wander in the dark, so he had pitched a small tent at the base of the palace out of the worst of the wind. Inside the nylon hut it was surprisingly cozy and warm, but cramped. They had to lie down side by side. There wasn't much room to sit up. They drank water and ate the freeze-dried food Darien had in his pack.

They weren't ideal conditions but at least Koori felt like they had a fighting chance to escape. Hope warmed her heart. And that was something she hadn't allowed herself in so long she could hardly remember what it actually felt like.

Darien handed her the canteen of water so she could wash down the barely edible food bar that she'd been chewing for the past ten minutes. She took a long drink and handed it back to him.

He glanced at his own bar and shrugged. "Hey, it's vitamins and energy that we'll need." He bit off another piece and chewed. After he swallowed, he said, "Once we're out of here I'll take you to the best restaurant in Tokyo."

She smiled, touched that he made the offer. "I've never been to Tokyo."

"Really? Well, let me tell you, it is something to see." He smiled. "Mind you, it's changed some in the past millennium."

"Yes, I imagine it has." Her smile faded.

She hadn't considered what it would be like for her if she ever got free. She couldn't even picture what the world would look like. Over the years, she had glimpses of some changes with every stranded stranger she came across. She could discern some things by the way they dressed or what vehicle they had driven. But she never let herself wonder for too long. It was too painful to think about. But now because of Darien, it was a possibility.

"What is your home like?" she asked.

He took another swig of water then capped the canteen and set it to the side. "It's a small town in Montana. A place where everybody knows everybody whether you want them to or not." He smiled. "There're lots of trees and a small stream that runs just on the edge of my family farm. I'd go swimming in that stream every summer as a kid."

"I wish I could remember summer. I can't even remember the sun."

Darien set his hand over hers, linking their fingers together. "When we get out of here, I'll take you to that stream, and we'll go swimming in the hot summer sun."

"You would take me to your family home?"

"Yes." He squeezed her hand tight. "I'll take you wherever you want to go for however long you want to."

She didn't know what to say to that. She was overwhelmed with emotion. Emotions she hadn't experienced in so long that her heart throbbed with the intensity of everything. Here was this man, a man she had plucked out of his world and into hers, risking himself for her, to free her from this curse and offering more of his life and his time to her.

A tear slipped from her eye and she hurried to wipe it away before he saw it. But he beat her to it and brushed her cheek with his thumb. That was the second time he'd wiped her tears away. She didn't deserve such a sweet and caring man like Darien. There was so much about him that reminded her of Shiro, her lost lover, but there was a lot that was different. Where Shiro was feckless and unmotivated, Darien was strong and determined and spirited. She felt safe and protected with him. And the way he looked at her made her stomach clench and her thighs tingle with pleasure.

Exactly in the way he was looking at her now.

She lowered her gaze, aware that the temperature in the tent was rising. But she lifted her eyes again when he brushed the stray hairs from her face with the tips of his fingers. The touch sent shivers from the top of her head to the bottom of her feet.

"I don't know what it is about you," he sighed. "But every time I look at you my heart aches just a little bit more."

Smiling, she nuzzled against his palm as he cupped her cheek. Slowly, he stroked his thumb over her mouth. On a sigh, she parted her lips and pressed her tongue against his skin.

His eyes darkened to flint and she found she could hardly breathe as he leaned toward her mouth. It was torture waiting for his lips to touch hers, but when they did she felt a surge of fire between her legs.

The kiss was slow and liquid like melted honey in her mouth. Koori thought she would never taste anything as delectable as Darien's kiss. Not even the sweet taste of sugar could compare.

She moved her hands into the suppleness of his hair and deepened the kiss, pressing her tongue against his. As he moved his hands over the bodice of her kimono, she quivered under his touch. Her breasts ached for his caresses; her nipples peaked and throbbed in desperate need.

Darien slowly untied the ribbon at the side of her garment. She groaned against his mouth, begging him to hurry. Soon it was undone and the fabric loosened, affording ample room for him to maneuver.

Koori moaned and arched her back as he captured her breast in the palm of his hand. The heat of his skin against hers sent waves of rapture over her body. She needed more, wanted his flesh pressed to her, to feel his hunger.

"Oh, please hurry, Darien."

He licked her earlobe and whispered into her ear. "I have thought of this moment too many times today to rush it away."

He watched her face as he pulled the top of her kimono down over her breasts, exposing them to the cool night air. With just one finger, he traced the slope of her breasts, circling her nipple with every stroke. Bending down, he brushed his tongue over her flesh, flicking her nipples with the tip.

"Beautiful," he moaned before pulling a nipple into his mouth and rolling it between his teeth.

Koori cried out as bolts of pleasure surged over her and nestled deep in her sex. She instinctively spread her legs to quiet the aching, but the movement only made it grow more intense.

As he sucked at her breast, Darien moved his hand down her body to her leg. He gathered her skirt and pushed it up, revealing her long legs. Slowly, he trailed his fingers up the smooth line of her skin and circled them over the soft, sensitive flesh of her inner thigh.

Shivering with desire, she pushed her hips up, inviting him in, to touch, to feel how she ached for him. He didn't need any more encouragement as his fingers found her wet and open for his touch. He growled low in his throat and she felt his jaw clench at her breast as he continued to lick her creamy flesh.

"You feel like heaven in my hand."

As he gently stroked her, Koori could feel her desire building deep within her belly. No man had excited her as Darien had. There was something about his quiet manner that drove her mad. She moaned as his fingers pressed into her.

"Darien!" she cried. "Take me now. I need you inside me."

He let his hand slide out from between her legs, and quickly shed his thermal shirt and pants. With one mighty yank, he pulled her kimono down her body and tossed it to their feet. He leaned over her, gazing at her, as if drinking in his fill of her naked form.

"You are the most enchanting woman I have ever known, Koori, my ice maiden."

She smiled up at him and let her gaze travel over his

body. She took in his tousled golden hair, the dark of his eyes, the hard rippling muscles of his chest, down to the full length of his cock. He was perfect in every way to her.

Wrapping her hands around his neck, she rolled him over her, wrapping her legs around his waist, inviting him in.

He nestled between her legs and kissed her hard. As he moved his mouth over hers, Koori could feel the rigidness of his sex pressing against her. She pushed toward him as he inched himself into her slowly. She felt every glorious inch of him as he went deep within her, filling her up. They fit perfectly, she thought, like two pieces of the same sculpture.

Pushed up on his elbows, Darien stared down into her face while he cradled her head in his hands. She could feel him pulsing inside her like a second heart-beat. She moved against him, but he stilled her. She felt the thud of his heart against her chest. It was hard and fast and strong, and made her feel more alive than anything before.

His intensity scared her as well as filled her with passion. When he looked at her, it was as if he were staring through her and into her soul. She wondered what he saw there. Was it as black as Junzo had told her it was? Or was it as wholesome and pure as she hoped it to be?

Whatever he saw must've pleased him because he pressed his lips to hers and started to move inside her.

With each thrust of his hard length, Koori held on to him. She wrapped her arms around him and whimpered as he drove her up a massive rise then cried out with her as they tumbled down the other side in an explosion of need and pleasure. Koori felt it deep within the place inside her that had solidified into ice so long ago.

Sweat trickled down his forehead as he moved inside her with a relentless rhythm. He took her up, and then back down again and again, until all she could do was feel. Every nerve ending in her body fired at once, and she was bombarded with a kaleidoscope of sensory overload. She could no longer discern where she started and Darien ended. It was as if they had fused into one entity from the heat burning up both of them.

Wrapping his hands around her head, he buried his face in her neck and drove himself deep into her. She dug her nails into his back and held on as she spiraled out of control. A deep violent vibration exploded inside her belly and radiated out to every part of her body. She even felt it in the tips of her fingers and toes.

With one final moan, Darien came, crying out in his pleasure. "Koori."

When their bodies quieted, Darien rolled off her and snuggled her into his body from behind, curling around her. He kissed the back of her neck with a sigh. His whiskers tickled her skin, and she squirmed against him, finding a perfect groove to snuggle into.

Koori felt sore, tired and completely blissful as Darien wrapped his arms around her and pressed his lips to the back of her neck again. His heat warmed her, drugging her like too much sake. Soon, her eyes felt heavy, and she started to drift on the edge of sleep.

Darien stroked his thumbs over the hollow of her belly and whispered into her ear. "I think I'm falling in love with you."

But Koori pretended not to hear. She wasn't sure if she was ready to hope for that. It had been so long she wasn't sure she even knew how to love or how to accept it. For now, it was enough to know that Darien really cared and that she did, too.

To expect any more was a fool's journey.

Chapter 13

It was the shrieking howl of the wind that woke Darien from his idyllic dreamsleep. Blinking to adjust to the gloom in the tent, he finally focused on where he was. Face-to-face, legs tangled, with a still-sleeping Koori, he smiled to himself. At first he'd thought he'd been dreaming of her, but now he realized that she was by his side, she was a reality.

He watched her sleep, the gentle rise and fall of her chest, the way her lips pursed together in a perfect cupid bow. She was extraordinary in every way.

A sudden blast of wind startled him from his reverie. He rolled onto his back and stared up at the flapping roof of the tent. The gravity of the situation smothered him in a sudden rush. They had escaped the palace but were now outside in a blizzard with no idea at all where to go. He had a compass, but he had a distinct feeling it wasn't going to help him in the least. He didn't think knowing north from south was going to aid him here in this place. Because it was quite possible that this place wasn't even real.

The thought had crossed his mind on several occasions as they made their way down impossible walls of ice of an impossibly structured castle that had no business being four stories high. Again, the notion that he was dreaming crossed his mind.

I could very well be going nuts.

Koori stirred beside him. With a small satisfied sigh, she ran her hand over his chest. He glanced down and realized that he was still naked. Surprisingly he wasn't in the least bit cold.

She nuzzled along his side, the feel of her body stirring more than just his mind. She stretched and yawned. "Is it morning?"

"I think so."

Yawning again, she laid her head on him and pressed a kiss to his chest. "I've not slept so well in more years than I care to consider."

"Me, either." He wrapped an arm around her and held her close, nuzzling his face into her hair. She smelled like fresh clean rain. It was one of his favorite scents.

"Do you think it wrong if we just stayed here, like this forever?"

He smiled. He had just been thinking the same thing, except in his version they were doing more than just lying there. "No, but I think eventually we'd run out of food. I only have enough food bars to last a week."

He had said it in jest, but the seriousness of the situation hung in the air like a rancid odor. They had to get moving, or one or both of them would die. And his big money was definitely on his own demise. Koori was immune to the cold, but he wasn't. Already he could feel the bitter wind beginning to seep in through the zipper and flaps of the tent tainting the air with ice.

"We should get moving."

"Yes." She rolled off him and reached for her kimono that he had earlier tore off her and thrown into the corner.

While she dressed, he, too, busied himself with clothing. He pulled on his thermals, then his sweatshirt and khaki pants. Next came his wool socks and boots, then his jacket.

Before he slipped on his gloves and wool hat, he rolled up the sleeping bags and thin insulated mat and shoved them into his pack. He handed Koori the canteen of water and an energy bar.

She took it without comment. He hated that the business of getting to safety ruined the magic brimming between them. But if he didn't get them out of here, they'd never have another magical moment together again.

"I'm going to go check things outside." He unzipped

the tent and crawled out. He also had a bursting bladder to take care of.

The harsh wind hit him full-on in the face before he had a chance to put up the fur hood on his jacket. It stung his cheeks instantly. Gazing around at the surroundings, Darien could make out a few things in the gray haze of blowing snow. There did seem to be a path, or what should've been a path, between some barren trees running alongside the palace. Maybe it led to the road. Or maybe it led to absolutely nowhere. Regardless, they had to find out. They couldn't stay where they were and survive.

After finishing his business, he crawled back into the tent. Koori was busy chewing on the food bar.

"I think I see a path through some trees. It goes to the east. Does that sound familiar?"

She shook her head. "I take a different path just about every time I'm required to return to the road. At least it never seems like the same way." She shrugged. "I'm sorry that I'm of no help."

"That's okay." He smiled at her, but the defeated look on her face compelled him to lean into her and brush his lips against hers. He cupped her face with his hands and kissed her again. "We will get out."

She gave him a small smile, and a nod, but he didn't think she was too convinced of his declaration. Truth be told, he wasn't much, either.

After about an hour of walking through the barren craggy trees, it became evident to Darien that it wasn't leading them to a road. In fact, he felt like they'd somehow been going in circles. His compass wasn't working worth a damn.

What he wouldn't give for a gas station nearby so he could ask directions.

Stopping, he glanced over at Koori. "Does any of this look familiar?"

"Maybe," she said looking around at the surroundings. "But it all looks the same. Everywhere there are trees and snow and gray sky. That's all there ever is."

Darien could hear the panic in her voice. He wrapped an arm around her and squeezed her close. She shivered under his embrace.

He stared down at her. "Are you cold?"

"Yes, a little." Her teeth were starting to chatter. Her eyes widened in surprise by the action. She clutched at him. "Why am I cold?"

"I don't know." He dug into his pack and came away with another thermal shirt, a pair of long thermal underwear, wool socks and a pair of runners that he had stashed. He handed them to her to put them on. "Maybe it means we're getting closer. Maybe you're starting to become mortal again."

As she slid the clothes on under her kimono she seemed cheered by the idea. But Darien wasn't so quick to applaud. This could just be another trick, another layer to Junzo's cruel punishment.

Once Koori was outfitted, he took her in from head to toe. His thermal wear swam on her, but she managed to roll the pant legs up a bit. The sleeves also hung over her hands but at least they would provide warmth and protection to her hands. He smiled; she looked like a little girl playing dress-up.

"Why do you laugh?"

"You look—" he chuckled "—interesting."

She looked down at herself and started to laugh. Darien hugged her to him, and pressed his cold lips to the top of her head. He held her as she laughed, never wanting to let go. It felt too damn good having her pressed against him, sharing a light moment. He imagined they could have more of these times when they finally escaped this nightmare.

Just as they broke apart and were going to continue on, the wind picked up. It had already been blowing; a mild gust at best, but now it swirled around them like an angry tornado. Snow and ice pelted them from all sides.

Darien gathered Koori close again, trying to block the worst of it with his body. But it didn't matter where they turned, the wind whipped at them. It was as if they had done some terrible deed and the wind was inflicting its bitter retribution down on them. In any case, it came at them like hell's fury and made no sign of ever letting up.

Darien dug the rolled up nylon tent out of his pack and prepared to set it up, so they could at least have some reprieve from the howling, brutal wind. But just as soon as he had it unraveled, silence enveloped them and the wind died instantaneously as if it never had existed to begin with.

Stunned, Darien looked around them eyeing the surroundings, preparing for anything. Something had changed, something that he wasn't too sure he was going to like much.

And then Koori pointed to the north through the thin spattering of trees. "Look."

He followed her line of motion and saw a huge white wall of ice. It had to have been at least twenty-five feet tall, maybe even more. It was hard to tell from his line of sight. Was it the palace? Did they get turned around and walk right back to where they'd started?

Koori moved toward it and, after stuffing the tent back into the pack and hefting the bag onto his back, Darien followed her lead. As they approached, he reconsidered his first notion. It definitely wasn't the palace wall. It was too high and too long. He looked down the length of it both ways. It appeared to have no end.

"What is it, do you think?" Koori asked as she placed her hand on the wall, sliding it back and forth.

"Your guess is as good as mine. But it's a roadblock, that's for sure."

But it was as if Koori hadn't heard him. Looking up at the wall with glassy eyes, she ran her hand along the slick surface. Mesmerized, she moved down the wall caressing its surface. Darien wondered why it had enthralled her. More magic?

"Darien," she called, stopping along the wall only about four feet away from him. "There's an entrance."

He moved down to where she stood. Indeed there was an entrance, a wide opening with an arch over top. Looking down the wall, a person would've easily missed it, as it was cleverly camouflaged against the generic white of the surroundings.

Clasping hands, Darien and Koori stepped through the opening and into what appeared to be some sort of labyrinth that stretched out like a giant octopus with unending arms. He'd seen one or two in his lifetime but nothing of this magnitude. The first path in front of them was a straight lane into what appeared to be the center. There he saw a huge structure that looked like a sculpture of a woman. Who the woman was he couldn't be sure, but he had a strong suspicion she was standing right beside him.

"It's beautiful."

Darien nodded. It was stunning, but it was also eerie. He didn't like the dread creeping over him, as if they'd stepped into a trap that was going to snap on them at any moment.

"We should keep moving." He glanced behind him at the entrance they had just passed through. "I don't like the feel of this place."

Dropping his hand, Koori took a few steps forward. "I feel like we're almost there. I don't know why, but I almost feel free." She glanced over her shoulder at him and smiled.

And that was the last he saw of her before the walls moved.

Chapter 14

"Darien!" Koori rushed forward, but it was too late. The thick wall of ice slid in front of her, effectively blocking her from him. Again she shouted, "Darien!"

She received no reply.

Turning, she decided to proceed to the center of the maze and wait for him. That was the most logical course of action. But after taking only two steps another wall moved, sliding in front of her and preventing her from reaching the center.

Now there was only one way to proceed and that was to her left. Just as, she assumed, the labyrinth wanted her to go.

She walked along the path, fingers trailing along the

icy wall. Maybe she could sense the next time the walls were about to move again. Maybe she could outsmart it or outrun it. Or maybe she was just thoroughly trapped without a hope of ever escaping.

Despair nearly ripped her in half. Tears threatened to spill from her eyes. She wanted to crouch down on the ground and succumb to it. But instead she wiped at her eyes and continued putting one foot in front of the other. She wouldn't quit. Not now. Not after all she'd been through, and all that Darien had done for her. To quit would be to quit on him. And she couldn't do that. She still believed that he would be her savior.

She followed the path through the maze, turning right, and then left. Then she came to a T and didn't know which way to turn. If she turned left, maybe she could backtrack and find Darien, but if she turned right, maybe she could find the center and stay there until Darien found her, which she knew he would. She turned right, hope making her stride quicken.

As she walked each path, she tried to keep her thoughts positive. But it was difficult. Especially when she made a wrong turn at another T and ended up at a dead end. She had to retrace her steps back to the T and turn the other way. By the eleventh corner she thought that she'd gone in a complete circle.

Dismissing the defeatist thought, Koori continued on. Sooner or later she'd either come across the center or Darien. The maze couldn't possibly be that enormous.

After another series of turns and dead ends, she had to retrace her steps again. Her feet were starting to throb. Not only from the cold but from the continual walking back and forth. Darien's runners weren't the most comfortable footwear, and the wool socks kept rubbing. She predicted she probably had at least three blisters on each foot.

But she pressed on, walking down pathway after pathway, every single one looking exactly like the last. The only way she could tell if she'd already walked down it was by the footprints in the snow. Hours passed without a break in the complicated maze.

Stopping to rest, Koori pressed her hands against the frozen barrier. If only she could feel through it to the other side. Maybe right this second Darien was on the opposite side thinking about her, wondering when he'd see her again and how to get to her.

"Darien!" she called, desperation starting to take a grip on her. There was no call in return, only the sounds of her own ragged breathing echoed back to her ears.

Defeat weighed down on her. Fighting the tears, Koori leaned against the wall and took in some deep breaths. She had to stop and think if she was going to get out of this. She couldn't let her emotions run rampant. Usually a levelheaded woman, she still couldn't stop the rush of anger and hopelessness surging through her. What if she never got out again? By the way her body shivered, it wouldn't be long before she succumbed to the cold and died. She never thought it would ever happen. Her death. She'd been alive for over a thousand years without ever a hope of ending her torment. Over the years she had certainly thought about ending it herself, but she'd always considered suicide a coward's way out.

But maybe now the day had finally come. Maybe the whole time when she hoped that Darien would free her, this was truly the only outcome that could happen. Actually leaving this world and being with Darien could have never been a possibility. Maybe it would only be a fleeting thought, a wishful dream and nothing more.

With that final thought, she let the tears fall. Her back braced against the wall, she slid to the ground. Wrapping her arms around her knees, she let the anguish take over, and she wept. For the first time in a thousand years, she let Junzo's curse overpower her will.

Darien didn't know how long he'd been running along the various pathways, but he figured at least two hours had passed. Every turn he took that didn't lead him to the center of the maze just propelled him on faster and harder. He had to find Koori.

He had the pack with all the food, the water and the tent for warmth. She had nothing but the few clothes on her back. If she was changing like he suspected she was, she wouldn't last very long exposed to the cold. The only grateful thing was that they were inside the walls of the maze and not out in the brutal wind.

Using his compass, Darien tried to keep to the north. That was the direction in which he'd seen the sculpture. It was the center of the maze and he knew he needed to get there. Koori would've thought the same. She might already be there waiting for him.

That thought spurred him on. Turn after turn he maneuvered through the labyrinth, his heart racing with anxiety. He couldn't believe they'd come this far to be thwarted by a maze made out of ice. Yes, it moved with a seeming life of its own, but it wasn't going to stop him from finding her.

Determined, Darien started to jog down the next path, taking one turn, then another. With his last turn, he stumbled out into an open clearing. He'd made it to the center.

"Koori," he called as he moved toward the middle, his gaze searching every crevice and entrance into and out of the maze. He didn't see her anywhere.

He kept walking until he was standing in the middle looking up at the twelve-foot sculpture crafted from blue ice on a crystal pedestal. It was indeed a woman, and there was no mistaking her dainty features and fierce gaze. The resemblance was uncanny. It was Koori larger than life, dressed in her kimono with her beautiful hair up in a complicated knot on top of her head, pinned there with the traditional Japanese hairpins.

Her frozen gaze peered over the tops of the maze toward the east. Darien wondered if she looked toward the way out, searching for her freedom. Or back toward the palace that had held her prisoner for so long.

As he looked up at the sculpture of Koori, he realized just how tied to the ice and to this place she truly was. Her cold skin, the rumblings in the palace, the breaking of the walls and ceiling right after they had made love. It all made sense to him now, in a strange, mystic way.

Every time he had touched her, the palace had shaken in response. When they had made love and he felt the heat of her body within, so the ice that made up the walls and ceiling had broken apart. As if she *was* the palace. Slowly, Darien had been thawing her out with every caress, every kind thought and every emotion.

Koori had been cursed with a heart of ice. And Darien had been the first man ever to find his way through the frozen layers.

Reaching out, he laid his hand on top of her frozen foot aching to be able to touch the real thing.

"Darien!"

He turned toward her voice. Smiling, she was running down one of the last paths heading toward the center, her hair an ebony cloud, his clothes hanging off her small frame. Setting his pack down, he rushed to meet her, anxious to have her safe in his arms again.

But as he walked he heard a soft rumbling that reminded him of the noise a mountain makes before an avalanche.

The walls were going to move again, effectively shutting them off from each other. He could feel it in his bones.

"Run faster!" he yelled as he charged ahead.

Eyes widening in alarm, Koori sprinted toward him. He was at the maze entrance when he saw the wall to her right begin to move. She was still five feet away from him. If either of them got in the way of the wall, it would crush them to death; he had no doubt in his mind.

With a loud whoosh, the wall slid forward, aiming right at them. It was going to be close.

He reached for her. She reached for him. Their fingers brushed, and finally Darien was able to grab her hand and pull her forward.

Taking in a deep breath, Darien yanked Koori to his chest, wrapped her in his arms and swiveled to the right. They fell to the ground in a heap, barely out of harm's way. The wall smashed shut mere inches from Darien's feet. He could feel the sonic impact even through the hard rubber soles of his insulated boots.

He ran a gloved hand over her head, trying to find her face. "Are you okay?"

Clutching at him, she turned her head and found his mouth. She pressed her lips to his chin and cheeks in a smattering of kisses. "Oh, God, I thought I'd never see you again."

Smiling, he held her face still in his hands. "I didn't find you only to lose you. I'll always come for you." He covered her mouth with his, angling her head to deepen the kiss.

As they hugged and kissed, Darien felt the ground move beneath him. And this time he didn't think it was his nerves shaking his body.

Chapter 15

Darien scrambled to his feet, pulling Koori with him. He kept his arm around her to keep her from falling. The ground moved again, and they stumbled to the side, still holding on to each other.

"I don't think this place is very happy that we're back together."

Holding hands, they ran to the pack. Darien scooped it up and they went to stand in the middle of the eye of the labyrinth, away from anything that could break apart and fall on them.

A riotous rumbling sounded from underground. Darien had never heard anything like it. It sounded like a groaning giant awakening from a long sleep. Again the ground shook, a little faster and little harder than before.

All around them, pieces of the maze's walls began to crack and crumble to the ground. Large chunks came sliding across the slick ground toward them. They had to skate out of the way several times or be hit in the ankles by pounds of ice.

"I'm scared, Darien."

He hugged Koori tighter. Fear gripped him, too, but he couldn't let her see it. He had to be strong for her. "We'll be okay. We just need to hang on a little longer."

As if trying to contradict his statement, a loud resonating crack rang out in the air, echoing off the icy walls. The sound made Darien's ears and jaw ache. From the corner of his eye, he saw the ice maiden statue rock back and forth on its pedestal as if someone were actually pushing it.

Koori turned then, nudging Darien's arm from her view and watched in horror as the sculpture with her face started to crack. At first, small crystalline pieces fell off. They tinkled like bells as they hit the ground one by one. The sound became louder, harsher, as they fell in larger chunks and in mass quantities.

She struggled in his arms, as if she wanted to rush to her icy self's aid. But Darien kept her still. "Let it happen, Koori. When it's over we'll be free."

"Are you sure?"

He hesitated, and then said, "No, but I don't want you to get hurt."

She glanced at him, maybe searching his face for the truth or reassurance. He wasn't sure what she found when she looked but she finally settled back into his arms and didn't make another attempt to rush toward the crumbling statue.

Darien didn't know how long the ground kept shaking. It could've been a good half hour while the walls around them broke apart and the ice sculpture collapsed. They had fallen a couple of times because of the intensity of the tremors in the ground. But they had gotten back up, arms around each other and watched as everything around them fall apart.

Then it became quiet, and every single wall of the maze had been knocked down. For as far as he could see, there were jagged white pieces of ice sticking up haphazardly here and there. In some places, the wall had been completely obliterated. It appeared to go on for miles.

The ice sculpture of Koori was unrecognizable as ten thousand shards, chunks and pieces littered the area. Some had slid across the ground in an explosive array.

"Is it over?" Koori asked as she eyed the destruction around them.

Darien moved toward the ruined statue, kicking chunks of ice with the toes of his boots. "I think so."

"Do you think we'll be able to get out of here now?"

He heard the hesitancy in her voice. She wasn't convinced that it was over. To be honest, he wasn't sure, either. The wind had died down, the snow had stopped blowing. It even seemed a bit brighter out. All signs pointed to an end to something, but he couldn't be sure what that end meant.

"Well, the maze is destroyed so it should be straight walking to the road from here." *I hope.* He kept that last little bit to himself as he continued to circle the destroyed statue and pedestal.

"Darien?"

When he glanced at her, his chest tightened. Something was wrong. He could see it on her face.

"I feel different."

"How?"

She put a hand to her chest and frowned. "I don't know. Something inside me feels...strange. Warm, like the sensation I remember from the sun." She rubbed at her chest with the heel of her hand. Tears trickled down her cheeks.

Darien moved toward her, his hand outstretched. "It's okay, Koori. I think you're finally free of this place. I think you were actually part of this place and your heart was the last thing that needed to thaw."

She smiled through the tears and lifted her hand toward him. Before he could touch her fingers, the ground trembled again. But this time it sounded different.

The ground cracked open between them. Like a strike of lightning it zigzagged the length of the courtyard, pieces of the walls falling into the crevice.

Wobbling, Darien fell to his knees, unable to keep

his footing. He watched in horror as Koori also fell to the ground, but she was also sliding toward the ever-expanding crater between them.

"Koori!" he yelled as he scrambled toward the gap in the ground.

Flailing her arms and legs, she couldn't stop from slipping on the ice toward the crack. She was heading feetfirst without the hint of slowing down.

Darien dove across the ground, sliding on his stomach with his arms outstretched as far as they could go. He had to catch her. He couldn't let her go. Not this way.

Screaming, she tumbled into the expanding fracture. Digging her fingers into the ice edge, she tried to stop her fall, but it was useless. Her nails broke off as she continued to slide down. Both runners on her feet slid off and tumbled into the dark gap.

Darien kept reaching for her.

Reaching.

Straining.

Darien caught her by the fingertips with one hand. Legs dangling in midair, Koori tried to keep still so she could get a better hold on him.

"Reach up, and grab my arm," he grunted, as he teetered on the edge of the crevice on his stomach. Luckily he had kept one of the ice picks in his jacket pocket and it was now jabbed into the ice and he was holding on to it with his other hand. It kept him anchored.

Koori stretched up with her other hand and gripped his forearm. Darien started to shuffle backward, drawing her with him.

"I'm slipping," she cried.

"I got you, darling. I got you." But the truth was he could feel his glove starting to slide off his hand. He just needed to get a little bit closer to the edge, so he could use his other hand to grab her. "Just a little bit farther. Hold on to me."

"Don't let go, Darien."

"I won't."

He kept her gaze as he continued to shimmy backward, pulling her with him. He saw the fear in the breathtaking pale depths but also something else, something that surprised him. He saw love. For him.

His heart throbbed, and his chest tightened even more. He could hardly breathe. He had to save her. He'd fallen in love with her, and now she was going to be taken from him.

"We're almost there, Koori. I won't let you fall."

He glanced over his shoulder to see how far he was. Just another few inches, and he'd be stable enough to use his other hand without the threat of falling in face-first.

"Darien?"

When he looked back at her, she slipped a bit from his hold. Tears streaked her pale cheeks, but gone was the fear in her eyes. Resignation had replaced it. She was barely gripping his gloved hand.

Fear made him readjust his grip. But when he turned his arm, there was a sickening, aching popping sound as his shoulder joint popped out of its socket.

Pain tore through him like wildfire. Tears welled in his eyes and he had to swallow down the bile that rose in his throat. Blinking back the tears, he bit down on his lip to push back the pain. He'd been through worse. He tried to remember the time he'd broken his arm skiing. The pain had been worse. He managed to get through that.

"Don't forget me," she whispered.

"You're not going anywhere." Just one more inch. Just one more. *Hang on.*

"It's okay. You can let go."

He shook his head. He was almost there. "I won't."

She smiled up at him. "I've fallen in love with you. You thawed this ice maiden out. My heart belongs to you forever."

"Koori!" he cried. "No!"

But it was too late. His glove gave, and she fell.

Unable to breathe, Darien reached for her. Letting himself slide down the ice, he tried to grab her. His fingers brushed hers, but that was it. He couldn't get a grip on her hand.

He released his hold on the ice pick and dove in after her.

Chapter 16

He was falling.

Darkness swallowed him. He couldn't see anything or feel anything around him. It was as if he were floating in the air. Although he felt no wind on his face or in his hair. And the air always had a certain smell.

He couldn't smell anything now.

His stomach flipped over and over. Doing somersaults in his gut. He had dove into the crevice to save Koori. So he had to be falling.

Wasn't he?

Reaching out with his arms, Darien grasped for something, anything to stop his fall. But his hands came up empty. There was nothing there to grasp. The crater hadn't been that deep, had it?

The pain was even gone. He couldn't feel the ripping agony searing him from his dislocated shoulder. He still should be in pain. It should be tearing through him like an angry grizzly bear with his next meal.

A sense of extreme loss surged through him. Something was deathly wrong.

"Koori!" he shouted.

No response. Even his voice didn't echo back to him.

It felt like he was in a vacuum. No air, no sound, no smell, no sight. When he thought about it, he couldn't really feel himself, either.

He thought he was moving his hand, wanted it to touch his shoulder. But he had no sensation of actually moving and no feeling of touch. What was happening?

"Koori!" he shouted again. But did his mouth actually move? Or was he just thinking of her name?

Tears welled in his eyes, but he didn't feel them on his face. He couldn't feel anything, not physically anyway.

But mentally, he was in agony.

Was he dead? Was this what death felt like? An empty sensation-free vacuum? Where was the bright light? Where were the singing angels welcoming him to the heavenly gates?

There was no heaven, he thought. There couldn't be without Koori.

Sinking into himself, Darien tried to shut it all down. Tried to turn off the emotions raging through him. He wanted to wrap his arms around himself, but knew he'd never feel it, anyway. So he tried to do that inside his mind.

But that was when he saw the light.

At first it was only a white pinprick, hardly anything to discern. Regardless, he felt his mind rushing toward it in desperation. If this was the way to end his torment, then he'd do it. He'd run to the light.

The light grew in scope and in hue. Sound hummed in his ears. A strong stringent odor erupted in his nostrils. Physical sensations began to prickle across his arms and hands. Like pins and needles they tingled across his body.

It was too much. It was sensory overload and it felt like his brain was going to explode. Pain pounded at his temples, and he cried out.

"Mr. Calder?"

The voice nearly burst his eardrums. He shook his head from side to side to dislodge the painful ringing in his ears.

There was pressure against his temples and his forehead.

"Mr. Calder? Can you hear me?"

The light was too bright. It was going to blind him. He tried to close his eyelids, but something pried them open. Panicked, he tried to lift his hands to cover his face. But he found he couldn't move them.

"Someone help me!" he shouted. His voice pinged in his ears.

"I am here to help, Mr. Calder." More pressure on his head. "You have to calm down."

There was something in the man's accented voice that gave Darien pause. He'd heard that kind of tone before. It was the voice of someone used to being in charge, used to being listened to.

Calming his breathing, he tried to relax. He stopped fighting the pressure on his eyes and his head. When he did that, some of the discomfort abated. Blinking several times, his vision cleared, and he could see someone leaning into his line of sight.

It was a Japanese man with glasses. He was holding a thin penlight in one hand; his other hand was on Darien's forehead.

"Can you see me, Mr. Calder?" the man asked.

Darien nodded.

"I am Dr. Iwasaki."

Realization flooded Darien like a tsunami. Turning his head, he looked around. He was in a small area with a faded green curtain cutting him off from the rest of the white-walled room. Machines beeped beside him. An IV was stuck in his hand, the pole next to his bed, the water bag hanging from a cord.

He was in a hospital.

Darien licked his lips. They were cracked and sore. "Where—" his throat hurt bad; he tried again "—where am I?"

"You are in Sapporo City Hospital."

He licked his lips again. The doctor brought a plastic cup with a straw sticking out of it to his mouth.

"Drink."

Darien took a couple of sips of water. His throat had

felt like it'd been torn into by large sharp claws. The cool liquid instantly soothed the ache.

The doctor set the cup on the swinging tray attached to his bed. "Take it slowly."

"How…"

"You were flown here from Kushiro three days ago."

Panic started to take root. Reality was closing in on him, and he didn't want to face it. He struggled to sit up, but the doctor held him still.

"You must rest. You do not suffer from any life-threatening injuries now, but you must stay still and rest. You came in with a dislocated shoulder and severe frostbite in some of your extremities. You were in the early stages of hypothermia. If you'd been found any later, I do not think you would have made it." He shook his head. "I am surprised because according to Jiro, your scientist friend, you have been missing for over a week. Seven days out in that cold and snow without shelter, food and water, you should technically be dead."

Darien didn't want to hear it. The doctor had to be wrong.

Craning his neck, he looked over to his right hand where the IV had been deposited. The tips of two of his fingers were black like he'd dipped them in ink. He tried to wriggle his feet and imagined the same type of effects on his toes.

The doctor patted him on his good shoulder. "You rest. I will be back to see you later. The nurse will be in to take your vitals and give you some food." He turned to leave, then said, "Oh, and someone from your embassy will also be by to see you." With that, he disappeared behind the flimsy green curtain, leaving Darien with only his despair for comfort.

He could feel it welling up inside him, drowning his heart in the agony. Clamping his eyes shut, he tried to keep it back, tried to ignore the reality of his situation. He shook his head. He didn't want to believe it. He couldn't and survive. The pain would be too much.

Behind his eyes, an image of Koori took root. She was smiling, her eyes swimming with love for him. She was real. He could still smell her; still feel her on the tips of his fingers. She'd been real. As real as the bed beneath his body was real or the IV sticking in his veins.

He had not dreamed the past few days. It hadn't been a hallucination while he'd been in and out of consciousness, nearly frozen on the side of the road to Kushiro.

His heart panged, and he had to gasp to get a breath. Pain ripped through him, clawing at his insides, ripping at his soul. He brought a hand up to his chest and rubbed at his sternum. He'd never felt agony like that before. Not after falls off mountains or a plethora of broken limbs.

This was pain he didn't think he could ever heal.

Tears slipped from his eyes and rolled down his temples to drip onto the pillow. The agony of what he'd lost couldn't compare to any of his physical injuries. Those would eventually heal in time. This pain, this suffering, how could it ever be fixed?

The curtain fluttered open, and the nurse came in.

She was an older woman, petite and quiet, unassuming in her manner as she set a tray of food on the swivel tray.

Darien ignored her as she took his temperature and blood pressure. She then listened to his heartbeat. He didn't care whether that organ ever beat again. It was broken, anyway. What good was it now? The doctor might as well cut it out of him. It was frostbitten just like his fingers and toes.

When she was checking him out, she pushed the tray forward. "You eat."

Darien ignored her, his face turned away from her. He didn't want her to see his pain. She couldn't help him with it.

Before she left, she patted him on the leg. "Girlfriend is here. She help you eat." She then disappeared through the curtain.

Darien turned toward the still-fluttering curtain. Girlfriend? He didn't have one, unless Jessica decided that she still cared for him and flew all the way to Japan to see him. Highly unlikely.

The curtain swished aside. All his breath left him in one powerful whoosh. How could it be?

"Hello, Darien." She smiled that little smile of hers and he felt as if he was falling all over again.

Koori. She was real.

As she moved into the cubicle, he noticed she was wearing jeans and a deep-green V-neck sweater that hugged her curves. Her hair was unbound, cascading over her shoulders and around her pale neck like ebony waves. He'd never seen anyone more beautiful than her.

She slid a hip up onto his bed and touched his arm.
The heat from her fingertips warmed every part of his
body. Especially his heart. It began to beat again, as if
waking from a deep sleep.

"How are you feeling?"

He opened and closed his mouth unable to form
any coherent words. He shook his head.

"You're going to be okay. The doctor says you won't
lose any of your fingers or toes." She caressed each of
his blackened digits. "They just look bad."

He turned his hand over and caught her fingers in
his. The weight and heat of her touch made him ache.
"Are you real?"

She smiled. "Yes, Darien. I'm real. I'm here, sitting
at your side."

"I'm not going to wake up from a dream and you'll
be gone forever?"

She shook her head and squeezed his hand tightly
to show him how very real she was. "I'm not going
anywhere. I'm staying right here with you."

"I saw you fall."

"We both fell."

"I don't understand. How are we not both dead?"

"The crack in the ground was the way out, Darien.
It was the slip between our worlds. When we fell
through, we both landed not far from the main road."

"Why don't I remember it?"

She lifted his hand up to her mouth and pressed her
lips to the back. Her touch was warm, not the cold press
he remembered.

"You hit your head during the fall. When we arrived at the road, you were unconscious. The storm had stopped, so I was able to pitch the tent around you for heat, and I ran to the road and flagged down help."

"We're out."

She nodded, her lovely mouth lifting at the corners. "You're free?"

"Yes, Darien, I'm free, all because of you." She shuffled closer to him and leaned down to his face. She pressed a soft kiss to his cheek and murmured against his skin, "You lifted the curse from me. You saved my life."

"And you saved mine," he whispered back.

She sat back up and ran her fingers over his cheek, jaw and finally down to his chest. She placed her palm over his heart. "Do you hurt anywhere?"

He shook his head and covered her hand with his. "Not anymore."

A single tear rolled down her cheek and dripped onto their covered hands. It was warm and real and the most perfect thing he'd ever felt.

"Come here." He motioned with his chin for her to bend down.

She did, moving slowly, a small smile on her lips. And when she was the barest of breaths away from his mouth, he whispered, "I'm yours forever."

And then he kissed her.

* * * * *

A COLLECTION OF THREE POWERFUL PARANORMAL ROMANCES

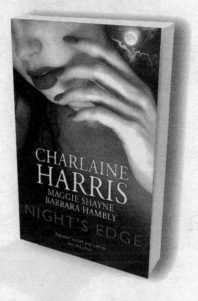

Dancers in the Dark by Charlaine Harris

Her Best Enemy by Maggie Shayne

Someone Else's Shadow by Barbara Hambly

www.mirabooks.co.uk